NEIGHBOURING EYES

A TALE OF 1951

Where perhaps some beauty lies
The cynosure of neighbouring eyes
~Milton

by

JOHN OFFORD

Feuilleton

2001

To order additional copies of this book, contact:
Xlibris Corporation
1-888-795-4274
www.Xlibris.com
Orders@Xlibris.com
23396

For Anne Gentry

sine qua non

Contents

PART ONE

FROM LONDON NOT FAR

Where perhaps some beauty lies
The cynosure of neighbouring eyes

~Milton

Chapter One

A Chapel Parlous

i

But let my due feet never fail
To walk the studious cloister's pale

~Milton

He found it full of silence: fragrant, a little musty, tense. There was wood, not stone, everywhere—polished, carved, embossed, crossbeamed, paneled, even lettered. What sunlight there was spilled in from a tiny rose red window up at the holy end. The signs were that, though empty now, it was still in service as a house of God: Saint Luke's Within The Hospital, 1695. "More than likely designed by Wren," said Pevsner, not yet in print.

He came in, as one would, at the west, only upstairs from the main entrance, stepping awkwardly down through a narrow door from the landing into a steep little gallery or choir loft. Suddenly the roof and all its timber were much nearer to his head than his feet were to the aisle floor far below. In front of him a deep nave fell shadowily away like the hold of some Dutch merchantman of the late seventeenth lying in dock. Silence encouragingly endured, so he let the door thud shut behind him and, putting down his brown paper parcel tied with string, seated himself on the highest tier, waiting for his eyes to adapt to the gloom. It was a bit like being a child again, teetering for the first time in the gods at Lewisham Hippodrome before a Christmas show—but much less frightening. "No head for heights," his mother had said severely, shaking her head.

He had been meaning for the longest while to look in at the old redbrick hospital and its William and Mary chapel, "domestic as against representational" (Pevsner again), having lived all his life within walking distance of it. There had been no urgency, especially when it survived the Blitz; but now that it was being taken over by the Ministry of Works and he was coming to the end of his last long vacation as an undergraduate—where would he be next October?—now seemed to be the moment, at the height of a Saint Luke's summer, to bring out his letter of permission from the trustees and go and make his visit. ". . . [W]ill be pleased to accede to your request on any Friday inst., between 2 and 4 pm, no further notice to the chaplain or the maniple being requisite . . . ." The letter was so clearly the good work of some long articled clerk without much of a clue. The afternoon was yet again glorious and cloud-capped, bucolic, so he had decided to walk, not directly through Angerstein Lane and along Saint German's Place—the curtain of prefabs put up there in the war for the bombed out of Greenwich had not improved the view—but in a very roundabout way from Vanbrugh East where he lived, across the heath to the village where he had shoes to pick up from the cobbler's, and back by Montpelier Row, the Prince of Wales' Pond and the Paragon to the hospital itself, hardly visible to passers by at the end of a long drive through crowding shade trees ("handsomely landscaped in C 18") and grassy knolls lapped in rhododendron.

He had made his way on to the estate, not by the

ornamental gateway and matching redbrick lodge just over the southern lip of the heath, but well along the perimeter railings to the east, where he knew from experience a not always locked side gate gave almost immediately on to the north wing. Once through the gate, he had soon come upon the chaplain, absentmindedly keeping his bees in an overgrown fruit garden, who had waved him benignly on without more than a word or two in passing. "Whatever you do, young man, don't miss the cloister on either side of the chapel." He had seen a cleric in his vest without a collar before but never one gardening in carpet slippers. The whole hospital was E-shaped, with the chapel forming the central cross piece and the almsmen's apartments tenemented around the two inner courtyards. This afternoon it all felt deserted, derelict, as if the successors of those "decayed Turkey merchants" for whom it was founded had also departed—as well they might have, faced with an impending Ministry of Works. They were gone—not "each in his narrow cell forever laid" but scattered heaven knew where— and he would never so much as lay eyes on one of them.

Inside the chapel, up in the gallery, nothing looked to him much less obscure than it had some minutes earlier. Saint Luke was keeping his summer with all its sunlight and zephyrs very much on the outside—which was where anyone of sound mind would be, out on the heath, with its springy turf and whispering grasses being mown here and there by a heathkeeper on a huge machine and then rolled into pitches for late season cricket on the weekend. West Kent Wanderers *versus* whom, he wondered. His father would know. Now he could decipher the nearest of the black letter inscriptions on the paneling below where he sat: "His mercy is on them that fear him from generation to generation." Not bad, he mused with the complaisance of one to whom confession had never come easily. But not nearly so good as the all but indecipherable one on the Victorian drinking altar and horse trough by the pond which he had paused at, not for the first time in his life, on the way here: "Fear of the Lord is a fountain of life." Now that, he said silently, as if in confrontation, *that* has the true proverbial ring. He thought of Graham Greene, the early entertainments. How long he might have crouched there, idling, he never knew.

The first sound that came to him, unignorably, was a painful, laborious breathing which spoke of desperation. The next was a murmurous scuffle, as of several pursuers scrambling to catch up with a quarry. Something stealthy in the tone of this made the skin under his hair begin to bristle. Then the door down below thudded shut, ending the sounds of pursuit; and he watched a heavy, silver-haired man of about sixty in a splendid gray uniform but all disheveled move cagily down the aisle, peering about for an exit. Obviously disoriented, the fugitive steadied himself against a pew, and in the split second of looking upwards and behind him he became recognizable from the gallery as the front page figure and newsreel image that he unmistakably was.

Then the door broke open and his pursuers swept in over the pews and down towards the sanctuary, driving him before them. They sounded foreign—perhaps Russian—in their snarls of warning and command which now filled the nave, but they looked more like a gang of ex-service building workers from the provinces or Ireland, taken by surprise in some street skirmish. One of them carried a familiar service rifle, Lee Enfield .303. The others—there were four in all—cornered the fugitive in front of the organ, which for him led nowhere; and, while he stood there in that rosy light defying them to take him, the fourth came at him from behind, holding the rifle by its barrel, jabbing with the butt, and knocked him senseless into the first row of pews.

It was all over in an instant. The one with the rifle wore an army haversack, and out of this he took a hypodermic and serum which he administered with the ease of a medic, once the others had pulled the prisoner's trousers down. Then they all lugged him out of the chapel like stretcherbearers without a stretcher, never once looking up at the dim gallery in which a frightened witness skulked secure.

He caught himself with one foot across the doorsill and his mouth open to shout. In his panic he wondered if he already had shouted. Whether he had or not seemed to make no difference. All sound of the explosion he had been in had died away, and he relaxed trembling against the doorcase, blood shaking his heart, the last fragments of debris pattering in his head. Once again he was in endless sunlight from the cupola and high windows of the landing and west corridor. He glanced back down at the silent nave, half expecting the scene to reenact itself. But nothing more than his own image of the big man's face stared dazedly up at him. Tievas—his memory began to tick out the name that till now had meant no more to him than a thousand others in the news—Jurgis Tievas—Marshal Jurgis Tievas—President of the Baltic States—the People's Republic of Baltija—capital city, Gdainys—population, a few millions . . . . He pulled himself together. All he had to do was quietly close the gallery door, go downstairs and get out of here as quickly and easily as he had got in.

Started on the lefthand stairway, like the one on the right curving gracefully down to the main entrance hall, he was at once stopped short. Across the landing one of the double doors was opening and a young woman was coming out into the corridor, meeting him eye to eye. In her hand she held, not a gun, but a book.

ii

Tell me not now, it needs not saying,
What tune the enchantress plays

~Housman

"Michael Brenan," she said deliberately, as if answering a question in court. Her voice was low, clear, and—allowing for the circumstances—not discomfiting, in spite of the foreign accent. She recognized him from college, where they were students together, and came forward a step or two in welcome, smiling with her eyes. She could do this, smile with her eyes, disarmingly well, as he remembered from their first meeting. It had been at one of Marianne's get-togethers in Highfield last term: a little room full of smoking, drinking, chattering students, and only slightly less crowded than the ship's cabin in *A Night At The Opera*.

When he did not at once respond, she raised her tone inquiringly, affecting a new formality: "Mr. Brenan, what in the world brings you here?" She prided herself on a very easy command of idiomatic English, which was in fact her subject of choice as a student. Foreign students at the college tended to be graduates doing research. The Baltic accent, with its sliding rhythms and affinity to fricatives (whether present in the English or not), had in her low-pitched voice an effect that was strangely calming. It even made his name sound more Irish than usual. But the set of her eyes in the delicate oval face now struck him, as it had once before, as trouble. She appeared always to be looking, with eyebrow raised, right into one's eyes and even a little behind them.

He fell with relief into the fellow student repartee that she seemed to be looking for: "Hello, Valija. How nice to see you again. I live here—I mean, not in this noble pile, but just across the heath." He nodded vaguely to the north, his hand steadied on the balustrade. "But what in the world are *you* doing here?"

"I meant, 'What brings you here to the Hospital?' I am here for the seminar my uncle Dr. Didelis has been giving on Ben Jonson's tragedies." So serious, as usual; so matter of fact. She made no gesture with the sizeable green book she was holding, nor took her eyes off his. He came from the stairhead and stood before her, where he could see through the open door into the sunlit room beyond, a delightful stanza of ordered bookcases, bookstrewn tabletops, a desk, and long windows overlooking the front terrace and drive. And, best of all, empty of everyone. The sunlight was tempered by faded green curtains.

"I had no idea this was a college, as well as an almshouse for old men who were once well off. Another redbrick college. Ever since I was a schoolboy I've meant to make a tour of this place. My old school across the heath, neo-Georgian 1928, is modeled on this building—architecturally, if you see what I mean—the school itself goes back to the 1640s. This room, I knew, would have to be the library." He reached into the inside breast pocket of his jacket and took out his letter of permission from the trustees, but she seemed not to be interested in it. He was explaining too much. Establishing innocence is always awkward.

"So you were once one of those boys in green coats and caps I see roaring about on their bicycles at four in the afternoon? No, this isn't a college. I think it is going to be opened to the public as a national monument like Chiswick House. Dr. Didelis is the first to be allowed to use it for a student conference during the transition."

"How many of you are there, then? Is it a Northfleet affair?"

"No. He has nothing to do with Northfleet. We are all from the Baltic States. There are five of us. The seminar is sponsored by our embassy. Dr. Didelis is a cultural attaché. But since you are here sightseeing, won't you come and sit down for a few minutes."

"Thank you, but I ought to be going. You were on your way somewhere, too." Putting his life in his hand, he followed her into the delightful room and they sat at the first of the tables, across the corner from one another. There were four more chairs at their table, variously displaced, and the books it was strewn with were volumes of the Herford and Simpson edition, as if there had indeed been a Jonson seminar recently in session. He realized he sat with his back to the door.

She put down the book she had been carrying. "I was going to my room to read. It's in the chaplain's wing. Do you know where that is?"

"Yes, I do, but I've got it tagged as Chemistry and Physics. I didn't spend much time there. You say Dr. Didelis is your uncle? Is he here now?"

"No, he was called away this morning on embassy business, and we are left to finish up without him. Why? Do you know him?" Her discontent with the way things had gone was at once very clear. Uncle Jurgis fails to deliver on Friday.

"No, I'm afraid I'd never heard of him till you said just now he is your uncle. Should I have? Heard of him, I mean."

The discontent vanished into one of her slow, searching smiles and she shook her head indulgently. "You were not likely to have heard of him. He is not even well-known in Gdainys outside the English faculty. But his translations of Ben Jonson's plays into Lithuanian are very good, and his productions in the *Baroktheater* were even better—though they are not for everyone, of course. His looks? Oh, I suppose you would say, 'Rather like Joseph Conrad's around the time of *The Secret Agent* or *Under Western Eyes*—only blond, and somewhat bigger, of course.'"

Brenan realized that he had touched a nerve with his timid probing, but not the one he had expected to touch. Valija's bearded uncle was evidently dear to her, and probably even to her less amiable fellow students, the gang of four. But, guilty or not, she was a good deal better prepared to slip confidentially into his lingo than he was into hers. That night at Marianne's he must have spilt much more of his life and opinions than he meant to. When she wanted, she could talk to him as if she were a confidante. He let the reference to Conrad go unremarked. "You are close to your uncle."

"He is my only surviving relative."

There was more than a moment of silence, in which he wondered where to begin on the middle European holocaust. Then she began for him, only somewhere else. "So here is where you live—from London not far. With your parents? Spending the summer on your set books for finals next June?"

"Yes, 'straet waes stanfah' and all that. Beowulf on the

beach. You'd think they'd have adopted the Cambridge curriculum at Northfleet by now, wouldn't you?" Then he realized that, as a graduate student of language, she would probably not, as he did, prefer literature, any literature, to linguistics. But once again her manners came to the rescue.

"And did you get to Carinthia, as you and your friend Offord were proposing last term? I hope so. There in the mountains, there one feels that life might after all have a purpose."

"No, I'm afraid not. Offord finally went to the Pyrenees to tutor in a French family, and I stayed at home."

"And your poetry? You were at least able to give yourself to that. As well as see plenty of films, I suppose."

It was painful how much she seemed to know about him. "My poetry. How do you know about that?"

Again the look, the gaze of confidence, yet of mildness, too. "It was Dr. Anstruther who broke the code of your initials in the college magazine for me. Your poem was very good. I especially liked the lines that go:

The cloth, immaculate, sustains
A drop of wine and words.

The choice of verb works so well, after the adjective."

He was, of course, undone by such attention. He felt blood infusing his cheeks; as when the man in the chapel had been struck down, the skin on the back of his neck crawled. They sat for a moment saying nothing, the level afternoon sunlight no longer sufficiently tempered by the faded green curtains to be comfortable. "Yes, there was time for poetry. I also had time to read the new American crime novels that have been coming out as Penguin books—the ones with the green cover, you know. Raymond Chandler is the writer's name. Quite extraordinary. Like nothing we've seen before in this line. A nice change from Edgar Wallace."

"I haven't read any of them yet, though I noticed that they were praised very highly by Elizabeth Bowen when they first came out over here. There have been films, too, haven't there? I might have seen one of those. I suppose there hasn't been anything remotely like Chandler in English since Wilkie Collins." She rose tentatively from her chair, prompting him to rise from his and move first to the door.

"Yes. I really must be getting along."

"Let me see you off the premises. This has been a most pleasant surprise." There still seemed to be a friendly smile behind everything she said.

"When shall I see you again?"

"Aren't you going back to college this weekend?"

"On Sunday. I'm taking the 7:35 in the evening from King's Cross."

"I too. You might see me on the train; and if not, then at college next week. Will you be living in Somersby again? I shall be in Highfield."

They moved together across the empty upper landing, past the closed gallery door, and on to the same lefthand staircase where he had first been caught sight of by her. Unable, as his mother would say, to leave well enough alone, he asked, with his heart racing, "What's behind that door?" And as if he were still sightseeing, Valija answered, absently, "Oh, a founders' gallery, I think. But the chapel is best seen from down here. The west door will be open."

Down in the dim, silent chapel they lingered hardly at all. For him the ambiance was now grotesque. "I did look in here on my way upstairs," he said, descrying yet one more of the quaint black letter inscriptions from Luke that glossed the walls of the nave: "Lord, are there few that be saved?" She was already poised in the wood-carved doorway as if for flight. It was curious: neither of them had yet, in all they had said, even mentioned the name of Tievas.

He was seized by the impulse to ask her an all-important question. But which? He heard himself saying fatuously as they crossed the foyer to the great front doors of the hospital, "Are you a Christian, Valija?"

Again the smile from the eyes, not unkind, waiting for him to open one of the doors and follow her out on to the terrace: "Why, of course. What do you think?"

She meant to see him all the way to the main gates it appeared. They crossed the terrace and started down the long, winding drive between elms and chestnuts and rhododendrons and plats of lawn. There still seemed to be nobody about except the two of them. Over at the south end of the facade, by the manciple's door, a small, blackish, greenish van, an Austin like those used in government service, stood parked in the shade, the one sign of invisible life.

"Before the war," she said, "my brothers and sisters and I lived with our parents in a town house in Vilnius, where my father had an import/export business with Britain and the United States. We were a Roman Catholic family. We spent summers in the country at the farm where my mother grew up before the first war. The 1930s, when I was a child too young to appreciate everything, now seem to me a magic time. School, sports, choir, dancing, plays, concerts, parties, Christmas, Easter, first loves—Christianity was simply part of it all. Now we have the world as it really is."

"I know what you are saying," he said. "For my brother and me and our friends, the 1930s became a magic time when we looked back from the war in the 1940s. Family holidays at the seaside, the BBC Children's Hour, dance music, spy and detective serials; no news so frightful that football matches and tennis tournaments and horse races couldn't come first. In the '30s my father and mother seemed to be in love; in the '40s they became a wartime husband and wife who were anxious middle aged parents. During the Blitz they kept us here in London; the city was going to pieces around us, so Patrick and I and our friend John, whom you know, made a sort of cult of the '30s just because they were pre-war. We always looked first for pre-war films to go to, pre-war books to read, the printings of West End plays for preference, no matter how trivial. The Greenwich public library had been wonderfully well-stocked before the war. We would make a fetish of some old newspaper or magazine—*Flight, Argosy, Picturegoer*—that could tell us in small print and with photos how much happiness we had missed by being too young in an age of gold—or, perhaps, an age of gilt. I can't quite say what Christianity had to do with all this, but my father and mother were always believers and trying to make a believer of me."

She had let him maunder on, and now was looking again as if they shared some secret. "Havened in the past," she said gently, seeming to quote, though he knew not what. Their secret, if they had a secret, was not a guilty one. At first he had been suspicious of her, even fearful, but at no time had they actually been watching one another out of fear of betrayal or discovery. Between them, they seemed rather to have been looking for something to share, and now for a moment they had found it.

"Where is your brother now?" she asked.

"Doing his National Service. He's a couple of years younger than me. In Germany. A sergeant in the Education Corps."

They had come at last to the end of the drive, and were standing beneath the windows of the gabled red brick lodge, just inside the huge wrought iron gates. Still nobody else seemed to be interested in his coming and going. No tinkle of glass, no glint of gun barrels. Outside and up the road to the left, a postman on his bicycle appeared, making for the mail box in the wall by the Paragon. They said their polite goodbyes, touching hands briefly. She turned away towards the hospital, not looking back; and he let himself out through the wicket on to the empty unyielding pavement.

At this lowlying point, across the metalled street the heath rises suddenly in a bank to the north and west before leveling out; little of its square mile of well kept grasses can be clearly overlooked. Moving up the sweet short turf, he felt at every step a widening scope of action and desire. The smell of fresh cut hay called him forward. Once up that steep green shore, with his back to the hospital gates, he could take a first deep breath of the afternoon. All before him the heath opened out like a great, shining leaf. The sun, unobscured by a few high clouds, would be hours and hours going down. Along the main road from the village a solitary red doubledecker bus trundled north and east. The evening traffic, pressing homeward, had yet to start. That night, he remembered, he had a visit to a pub planned with one of his old friends from school, Gordon McGill, whom he had not seen for almost a year.

Without thinking, he began to run across the open heath towards Vanbrugh East, faster and faster, as if he were once again practicing the quarter mile. A little flock of gulls, standing and picking among the grasses, rose up startled by his running; with a great flutter of wings, they wheeled above him before sweeping away southwestwards to the pond.

When his heart was pounding and the sweat trickled under his shirt, he stopped at a public bench by the first main road he came to. The only people in sight were a woman and child frolicking with a dog, and, more distant, a heath keeper patroling with a spiked stick and a sack for picking up litter. In every direction that he looked the horizon was the old familiar one of terraces and tree tops. The big four-storied balconied grey brick Victorian villa that his father so much admired, Heath House, stood boldly out on the corner of Shooter's Hill Road and Vanbrugh Terrace; and half a mile beyond it to the west, the high walls and great old trees of Greenwich Park as usual waited. An occasional car or lorry chugged along one or other of the roads edging or intersecting the heath. To his right, at Cooper's Corner, a singledecker Green Line bus stood at the traffic lights.

He collapsed on to the bench where he had stopped running, and hung his head in his hands, shutting out the world, waiting for his breath. At his feet, saved from the mowers by the bench's underpinning, clumps of blue chicory, another of October's bonuses, flowered above the grasses.

"God damn," he whispered exultantly.

iii

Must we turn soldier then?

~Webster

What had he done so far to find out if he were dreaming? The question was McGill's, who had called for him at home after dinner and was now trying, on their way to the pub, to keep him honest in his tale telling. "Trust you to begin with two or three coincidences!" McGill and Brenan were an unlikely combination of Scottish right wing and Irish right half that went back to the second year of the war at the emergency school in Lewisham, where the difference in their ages had been overlooked and Brenan had, for once, found himself in the part of younger brother. When McGill had taken the first opportunity to leave school and join the merchant marine in wartime, he and Brenan had remained fast, if mostly absent, friends. With the evening sun behind them across the heath and park, and the distant woods of Shooter's Hill all laid out ahead above the chimneys, McGill was setting the pace and relishing his part of world traveler, played out to streets at this hour more than half deserted. He and Brenan had strolled along Vanbrugh Park to the Royal Standard—never their pub of choice for some reason—past the Roxy, where Sunday's old film would be *Crossfire*, and up the Old Dover Road without once meeting a face they were used to meeting, or one that Brenan would, in the circumstances, rather not meet again.

What did he suppose these Baltic thugs were waiting for, in not coming after him—and his family—at once? McGill had seen their like, too many times, breaking down doors in the docklands of Gdainys or Klaipeda. It was as well he had to be back to his ship by Sunday morning—being caught in Brenan's company could prove fatal.

Brenan tried to argue that nobody knew what he had or hadn't seen in the chapel that afternoon, not even his "new pusher," as McGill called her. How could she be at all sure? At worst he had been nervous, diffident, in the presence of a pretty young woman. She must be used to that in a young man by now. "I'm not even sure," he said, "that she knows about Tievas being there." McGill looked at him pityingly. Of his several friends from boyhood, McGill had always been the special favourite of Brenan's mother. A few hours earlier, when seated on the roadside bench in the middle of the heath, catching his breath, Brenan had thought of two things he could do besides be home in time for dinner. Tell his parents about the scene in the chapel was not one of them: to do that would only cause them pointless distress. Like the air raids all over again, it would make them desperate to help and helpless to do any good, his mother nervous and exclamatory, his father broody. To McGill's later surmise that over dinner they must at least have asked about his afternoon visit to the chapel, he would be able to retort truthfully that they knew nothing at all about it. His mother's only concern at dinner had been whether or not he remembered to pick up his mended shoes at the cobbler's in the village, to which he had answered, less than truthfully, they would not be ready until the next day. "You're running it close, my boy," she had said, predictably, "if you want to wear them back to college on Sunday."

He thought he knew perfectly well what his father would do in this situation. Go and see Gilbert Vaughan, the 'tec rumored to be in the Special Branch, who had taken the house Dr. Thomas used to live in round the corner on Westcombe Edge. Mr. Vaughan was rather a gent for his father to be calling on socially, but together they went a long way back, as far as the 3rd West Kents in the first war. But Brenan had decided to save going to Vaughan for help as a very last resort. So he said nothing about him to his father or, now, to McGill. Besides, he had not relished trying to get past Mrs. Vaughan to speak with her husband at five on a Friday evening, even with his father's help. For the time being, the only thing to do had been to go by the public library on his way home and see what the newspapers had to say about Marshal Tievas.

It turned out that McGill already knew more about Tievas' visit to England than Brenan had discovered by leafing through the dailies and weeklies in the quiet little branch behind the church in St. John's Road. Ever since its postwar conversion from rectory to local reading room he had haunted it whenever staying with his parents, but never before in sudden need of a particular item of the day's news rather than some wellworn volume of clubland heroes fiction. Newspapers do not make it their business to print all one needs to know about something in particular when one needs to know it, as novels always do. McGill knew, not only that Tievas had been expected in London, but also that his flotilla, the frigate *Dolphynas* plus the Royal Naval escort that had met him somewhere in the Skagerrak, had been due to berth at Greenwich buoys that very morning, prior to his landing from his launch at the Naval College steps and taking up weekend residence in one of the state apartments. Ceremony, according to McGill, would be at a minimum, as might be expected of Labour government spokesmen conferring with a Cominform politico, whereas security would probably be at a maximum. As a Cold War icon in the Stalin mould, Tievas would never be setting foot in England, the 1945 election notwithstanding, were it not for the Tory Winston's wartime fascination with him as a redoubtable guerilla general in the forests of Lithuania and highlands of Estonia. But whoever would be the top brass lending an ear at the banquet in his honor that night in the Painted Hall, neither Winston nor Prince Philip, the new naval consort, would be one of them—let alone that self-appointed pundit of Iron Curtain protocol Evelyn Waugh, who seemed to think that small nations were best kept in their appointed sphere of influence, seen but not heard. And calendaring a state occasion in early October was hardly the done thing anyway. It was a pity about Winston and Philip, because the postwar Tievas now fancied himself a bit of an admiral in the Edwardian manner, with Gdainys firmly occupied as his maritime capital and a splendid little motor yacht, refitted as a frigate, all to himself for presidential seafaring in the Baltic and beyond.

Brenan was impressed by how well McGill kept up with world news while on watch as radar and communications officer in an oil tanker at sea, and he said so. "I thought when you were alone on duty it was all music by one of the four B's or nothing." They had cut through Delacourt into Shooter's Hill Road and were passing the well-lighted rowdy Sun in the Sands, which had everything McGill looked for in a pub, beginning with a Scottish brewer, except sawdust on the floor. Out on the street dusk was already gathering in the corners of the evening. He said, breaking their stroll, "What about the Sun, then?"

"What do you say we go as far as the Fox? There's a television set in the saloon now, and tonight, I see, the BBC is supposed to do a broadcast from the Naval College." The Fox Under the Hill was wrong for McGill, wrong brewer, wrong concrete forecourt with geraniums in tuns, wrong atmosphere all round. But he knew when to go along.

The Friday night saloon bar crowd at the Fox was gathering fast along the counter where the stools were and in the lamplit booths and at tables about the polished floor. There were as many women as men, their arms bare in summer dresses, the men in short-sleeved shirts, as if it were still early September. In this most sociable of the three bars there was no dart board and no billiards table. Given the least encouragement, ballroom dancing could have broken out. Mercifully, there was no music, recorded or live. If there had been any, the chance of its being a pub tenor like Tom Makem singing "Johnny, I hardly knew ye" was nil. Polite conversation was audible; laughter now and then rang out; a waiter or two loitered purposefully; few if any of the patrons appeared interested in the console television which was flickering and murmuring away in a farther bay of curtained french windows. Brenan and McGill took their pints over to it and found empty chairs waiting. Their nearest neighbouring viewer was an elderly gent in well-cared for black walking boots, wearing a spectacular gold watch chain across his ample waistcoat and dozing peacefully, an empty brandy glass on the table at his elbow. It was as if the landlord's latest notion of entertainment were no more novel or in demand than a magic lantern show would be. On a milky gray handkerchief of screen the leonine head of Marshal Tievas was talking English with his usual difficulty, but not stumbling because he had a script.

They were only in time to hear the last few pronouncements before the polite burst of applause, which left them wondering what the explicit point of the speech, if any, might have been. Tievas had evidently begun by saying whatever he had to say of immediate concern to his hosts, because he ended by animadverting on Russia and America. The world's debt to Russia, he said, to the people of Russia and to the Red Army, for breaking Hitler's *Wehrmacht* even before the Second Front was opened, was never to be denied and always to be taken seriously into account. Europe was also much indebted to America, especially for a victory of peace in implementing the Marshall Plan for economic assistance. But, as to the formation of NATO and its intimidation of Communist peoples, he, Tievas was of the same opinion as Mr. George F. Kennan, former American *chargé d'affaires* in Moscow and old hand on embassies to the Baltic States, to Tallinn and Riga in the years after Versailles—a man who had learned to understand the northern Slavic peoples—this aggressive policy of containment was shortsighted, unstatesmanlike, and against history, and so would prove to be its own undoing. Of the atomic bomb, Russian or American, and of Truman's recent provision for a hydrogen bomb, no mention was made.

Whatever Tievas might have meant by all this was not pursued by the BBC television commentary, which turned at once in its invisible and unaccountable way to the more aesthetic aspects of the occasion: Wren's dramatic division of the great hall into three ascending and competing stages, vestibule, main, and upper, by means first of huge pilasters and columns and then of a narrowed, lowered, and arched proscenium for the high table—Wren's or Hawksmoor's, or was it even Vanbrugh's, this unEnglish infusion of the continental baroque, the cultured voice wondered. And Thornhill's spectacular ceiling, an encyclopedia of allegory, showing King William III's offer of the cap of Liberty to Europe, while at his feet Tyranny cowers—what should be said of this . . . ? To McGill, if not to Brenan, the meaning of it all was painfully obvious. Far from being the prisoner of Ruritanian subversives at the Merchant Hospital as reported, Tievas was patently enjoying himself at the high table in the Naval College, passing the bottle among attendant lords of Admiralty and Foreign Office.

"Same again?" Brenan picked up their empty pint glasses but avoided McGill's eye. He made his way through the now crowded saloon to the bar and returned in due time with a tin tray on which no fewer than four brimming glasses stood. "I thought in the circumstances a shot of Jameson's might be indicated as well."

McGill was not to be mollified. "Looks to me as if your Tievas business is nothing but a load of guff." Brenan felt an incomprehensible urge to punch him in the mouth, one foolishness he had never before contemplated. Instead he sat down and began drinking his boilermaker in silence. On screen, the long white banqueting tables and serried diners dressed in black were being discreetly stared at, while the commentary continued to reflect unctuously on the collective artistic genius of the Office of Works around the year 1700. A crescendo of chatter in the saloon at the Fox was beginning to drown the voice of the BBC. The elderly gent seated near Brenan and McGill woke up without fuss, consulted his pocket watch, got to his feet, nodded to them amiably, and without once looking at the television set, toddled off.

"I'll tell you what," said McGill at last, "we'll go by the house, get the lizzie, and take a drive up to the Hospital to see what there is to be seen."

"Have you got her going again?"

They finished their drinks and left the pub with alacrity. Outside, a soft October night had fallen. "If the old lady took the old man for a spin," said McGill, "they'll have her back by now." An antiquated MG Midget, one of the four-gear models, much neglected in its middle years, had been passed down to McGill by a late uncle. It was McGill's only conspicuous vanity, and a frequent cause of chagrin to him. His mother, whose brother had been its first owner in the early 1930s, had driven an ambulance for the local Auxiliary Service throughout the war, yet even now she still had no car of her own.

"What was wrong this time?"

"Electrical."

By the time they had marched to where the McGills had a flat in Kidbrooke Grove and coaxed the testy MG into raucous life, it was well after closing time and there was nowhere more enticing to go than the now legendary Hospital. Throatily, they swerved into a dusky deserted Shooter's Hill Road and accelerated towards the heath. McGill twiddled the knobs of a radio which he had fitted under the dashboard, finding at last among the atmospherics and snatches of foreign language a rush of orchestral sound, led by violin and viola in thrilling *discordia concors*. He grunted his satisfaction.

"You talk about the four B's—they don't come any better than this. It's the viola that makes the difference."

"Where is this from—Hilversum?"

Now they swerved into St. German's Place and swept along the open heath as far as the prefabs and down to the huge Hospital gates, gleaming in the moonlight. Brenan hopped out and found that he could release one of them and swing it groaningly open. The lodge, dark and silent as it had been seven hours before, stared back at him. He hopped back into the bucket seat beside McGill, and they cruised up the shadowy drive between clumps of rhododendron with the radio still sending out the sounds of danger by Brahms, but now muted. Brenan was awash with feelings of fear and desire. Live only in this moment, he told himself; try not to think what will become of you—or of poor old Mackie. If only this were an October night in 1937, and I were behind the wheel and alone, calling for Valija at the outset of a romantic weekend at some village inn below the downs in Kent . . . . McGill, for the first time that evening, seemed to be enjoying himself. He had become gaily purposeful, focused, intent. When the long west front with its imposing pediment and cupola began to come into full view through the trees, he said, "Sort of place you'd expect to hear a bell tolling." He swung the car round on the gravel drive at the south end of the terrace, in front of the manciple's wing, and put on the hand brake with the engine in neutral, ready for a getaway. "I've always wanted to see a manciple on the hoof. Didn't become extinct with the Canterbury pilgrims after all, eh?" They crossed the terrace to the hooded porch in which the south door was set and he leaned long but intermittently on the bell push beside the polished brass nameplate. "No answer was the stern reply," he intoned bitterly.

The only lighted windows in the whole facade were in the north, or Chaplain's, wing. McGill backed the car parallel with the terrace as far as the other hooded porch, and again stopped with the engine still running, but this time he sat and watched Brenan try his luck. Lights came on in the ground floor windows, the front door opened, and there was Valija, in an ankle length blue dressing gown, asking him with a certain amused surprise what had he come to see of the Hospital at this hour.

"Forgive me if this is impossibly late, but I was passing by, out for a drive with a friend, and your lights were on. When I was here this afternoon I put down a parcel I was carrying—in the library or the chapel, somewhere—and went off without it. I don't want to lose it." He affected a look of helplessness.

She eyed him a little dubiously and stepped out of the porch to look at the idling MG with McGill behind the wheel. When he saw them, he turned off the ignition and climbed out to come and speak to them. The sound of music persisted. She was saying, "I have no memory at all of your carrying anything."

"Let me introduce an old friend of mine, from the same green coat school that we were talking about. This is Gordon McGuffin and that is his old jalopy, a genuine MG Midget from 1930. He likes Brahms. Mackie, this is Valija Didel—." He broke off, having forgotten how she had been introduced to him.

"'Didelis' will do. With my uncle as my sponsor here in England, I have given up the feminine patronymic. I use his surname." She held out her hand, smiling with her eyes.

"You mustn't mind my young friend, the Irish outlaw, Miss Didelis. He's a little light headed tonight. He promised to introduce me to a real live manciple, as well as someone from Klaipeda, or is it Gdainys?"

"I'm afraid the manciple has already taken his leave for good, Mr. McGuffin. I never actually met him. So have my fellow Baltic students. The south wing is quite unoccupied now. I suppose I couldn't interest you in a C. of E. Chaplain? All that is left of the ministry of faith." She gestured with head and hand at the fine fabric of brick and stone all around them. "Klaipeda is where I was born and first went to school, but you know in March 1939 it was seized by the Germans under Hitler. Have you been there lately?" Her charm began to make itself felt on McGill.

Brenan said, "If you two will excuse me for a moment, I'll run in and find my parcel," and was gone through the door into the north wing before she could respond. He found his way without difficulty around to the central foyer and climbed the lefthand staircase under the moonlit cupola. At the door to the gallery he paused but, deciding that it was pointless to look about for an assailant, he opened the creaking door and stepped boldly down into the eerie chapel. First he smelled what he was looking for, the pungent smell of edge ink redolent

of the cobbler's shop in the village; then his hands closed on
the brown paper parcel tied with string, just where he had left
it. He slammed the gallery door shut and raced back to the
terrace the way he had come.

Valija had seen McGill back to his driver's seat, said her
goodnight, and was reentering the well-lighted porch of the
north door. The MG was growling again; Brahms was still on
the air. Meeting Brenan, she said coyly, "Am I never to know
what is wrapped in your brown paper and string?"

When he told her, wishing it something more heroic, she
nodded soberly and moved around him into the hallway,
preparing to close the door. He took her hand.

"Look, Valija, I'd love to see you tomorrow. There must be
some local sight you could let me show you. Let's meet in the
village at Christy's and have tea. Do you know it, in Royal
Parade? At three o'clock. There must be some last-minute
shopping you have to do."

Her expression seemed to presage refusal, but she said
evenly, "Yes, I know Christy's. All right. At three o'clock,
tomorrow—no, today, isn't it? Thank you. But on one
condition: you wear those newly cobbled shoes. I still do not
see where you can have put them down this afternoon without
my noticing. Good night, Michael." She closed the door and
the porch light went out.

McGill was still in high spirits as he drove Brenan home.
The concerto ended and he switched off the radio.

"You can do a lot worse than one of those Baltic bints, my
boy-o. *Eine schöne mädchen von Memel. O welt, muss Ich dich lassen.*
This calls for a toast."

He reached under the dashboard for a whisky flask, which
he offered Brenan, who took a pull of it; then he drank from it
deeply himself. Putting on the stagiest of Irish brogues, so
different from his own usually clipped speech, he began with
unduly maudlin emphasis to sing against the engine's roar and
the rush of night air:

Now, Brennan made an outlaw,
Upon the mountainside
And infantry and cavalry
To take him there they tried.

At Cooper's Corner the light was with them and, warming to the stint, he tried for some of the true Tommy Makem swagger:

He laughed them all to scorn
Until at last 'tis said,
By a false hearted woman
He was cruelly betrayed.

At the speed at which McGill was driving and given the dragging tempo in which he chose to sing, there was time between the Merchant Hospital and Vanbrugh East where Brenan lived for only two lugubrious verses, and these without refrain.

Chapter Two

Offord Epiloguizes

i

Forty years back, when much had place
That since has perished out of mind

~Hardy

Michael Brenan moved to America after taking his degree; he did not take a First. Much had been expected of him by his mentors and friends here in Northfleet, but when the moment came he proved to be answering different questions from the ones asked. "Being expected much of," he once said, "is the beginning of the end." Why a promising contender fails to distinguish himself is often a mystery, but not more so than why distinction should be wished upon him in the first place. What never ceases to surprise me about college life, where good talk seems to count for so much, is how little need be said when some particular hope dies, or is born, least of all by the ones most concerned—though lately manners may have begun to change among undergraduates.

In those days men students seldom used a four letter word, and women never. Most knew well enough what life—and language—could be like but, having been in the services or only just managed to keep out of them, the men as well as the women acted as if college ought to be a different story—as indeed it was—and were more inclined to shrug or joke than to say anything obscene or protest when they were nonplussed. And Brenan was no exception. Like others of our generation, which had been still a little too young for war service proper when peace came in 1945, he simply looked abroad later for the opening he could no longer see at home.

Once he went, I heard nothing from him, although at any moment up to the present, if the occasion arose, I know that we would pick up our conversation without missing a beat. After all these years he may, of course, be dead—like so many of those I still wish I had seen more of. Yet the thought of him, looking up unguardedly from his chair by the window, with that peculiar black Irish set of the eyes and cheekbones, has never for me been very far from mind. As late middle age sets in, one turns ever more curiously to what little remains from a time when all was less painfully clear than now. For me Brenan will always embody those lean, urgent years after the war which now seem stranger and more remote than any I can remember—or any I have read a good deal about, such as the 1920s and the years of the first war. He was never much of a talker, rather a sharer of silences. Some afterthought would come between him and the end of a sentence, making him impatient with what he was saying—a rare impediment among those I have since associated with in the academic life. Where they tend to slide, seamlessly, into some new sentence, he would come to a stop. "Time . . . must have a stop" was his favourite saying—from *King Henry IV* surprisingly enough, which he read with care (as well as the shock of recognition) in the fifth form at school because it was a set text for the General Schools Certificate in London that year. On second thought, it may have been Aldous Huxley's not so good novel of the same title that, a year or two later, confirmed his admiration of it as a sentiment. Time must have a stop. But when, if ever? Meantime, we have politics and endless talk.

All the more remarkable that not long before leaving for the United States he should tell me something—a rambling anecdote, full of ellipses and fresh starts—which for forty years has remained vivid in my mind, has taken root there. It is one of those strangely treasurable little things, to be thought of, to be turned to, if infrequently, on nights when sleep will not come without being lured. At the time it totally upset my familiar sense of him as one of us, the happy few to whom nothing happens. For days I could think of little else—it was during the lapse between examinations and results, finals for him, second year sessionals for me—and I would go about the college and the town looking for him to answer some new query or hear my latest explanation. I was always the historian; he the poet. He would listen, and respond pleasantly, but without much interest now that he had said what he wanted me to know. Then his degree result came through, unofficially at first as is the custom. We were watching a cricket game in the tree-lined grounds across from Somersby (now built over), sitting on the verandah of the pavilion where we could also keep an eye on the tennis, when someone in the outfield nearby, a serious-minded engineer who must have seen the list newly posted, turned and pointed at Brenan and shouted "upper second." Just then everyone still in residence had the examination results on the brain. I do not know to this day whether the newsbearer, a neighbour of Brenan's in D block— his name was Cook and he had done his National Service as a lieutenant in the Ordnance Corps—was modest enough in his own expectations to be unmalicious in his glee or not. I suspect he was at least a little gratified that a student as cavalier as Brenan was not to be rewarded without due reservation. In any case, the reluctant subject of this untoward notice now got up from his deck chair, looked at me as if we shared a confidence, and left. The next day he was gone for good. I went over to France to the Vermeulens for the summer, as usual, and when I arrived home in September his mother told me that his travel grant and student visa had soon come through and he was already somewhere in the Deep South—Alabama, Mississippi, I believe.

I shall never forget the night when he first gave me his version of the Tievas affair. These outlying halls of residence were much less suburban then than they are today. Noises from the level crossing along by the village pub now reach here only as part of an endless rumble of road traffic. The little river still races at the back of Somersby, taking that sharp turn between steep overgrown banks before going underground and out to the estuary, but a city housing estate with all the attendant amenities has since gone up in the meadows less than a mile away. How I have come to be one of the History men at Northfleet, now a university in its own right, is a story for another time. From my study window on the ninth floor of the new student housing block behind Louth Hall I can look down over slate roofs, the church tower, lawn and trees—still mostly elm and cedar—right into the quad of Somersby, still much as it was then, and (if I use field glasses) into the very room on the second floor where Brenan and I sat. We were talking idly about the man in hall with us that year, one in about a hundred—I forget his name—who committed suicide. What was it that made all the difference between one who found the world intolerable and the others who found it more or less a delight? Brenan, who rarely knew the details of whatever was going on around him, wondered aloud how the dead one actually did it; and I was saying by hanging himself, I shouldn't wonder, this being the usual way. The authorities had been unforthcoming about the case. There is nothing like an after-dinner storm in early summer for unsettling the mind with thoughts of wrongs hushed up and the like. Ordinarily, we would have been studying apart or, if it were not pouring with rain, walking down to the Dragon for a drink. Brenan's girl had never come back to Northfleet after the Christmas vacation but had transferred to a London college, Bedford, to work on her thesis; so he was rather more at loose ends socially just then than ever before. Outside his open window, in the treetops, the rain was hissing; down among the rhododendron and laurel leaves it was splattering; and in the gutters and drains it sang. No traffic sounded from the road, and silent movements of damp air were carrying whiffs of woodsmoke and midden from across the fields into the room. Vivid yet invisible, a night train to the north went through the level crossing half a mile away.

"I have never told you, have I," Brenan said, "why I was in trouble with the college high ups last October, and might never have taken a degree here at all?" He settled down and forward in one of those Morris chairs we all had in our rooms and put his feet up comfortably on the bookstrewn desk top against the wall. For a moment he considered me, his lazy eyes searching for mine in the half light. "Huby in particular had it in for me for a while. He became very upset over that phone box death, you remember. Thought he was on the right track and leading the local police by the nose. When he realized how wrong he was and that I had known all along what was going on, he turned really nasty. For a moment I thought I was going to have to threaten him with a counter charge of—well, buggery or whatever. If someone higher up, in the Special Branch, hadn't intervened I'd have been kicked out at the beginning of the year. 'Employed in matters touching the benefit of his country' and all that. You know, people don't realize it but the police keep a sharp eye on the universities: it's a standard part of their surveillance of left wingers and terrorists." Brenan and I had been sharing confidences of one sort and another for most of our young lives, beginning back at home and at school in Greenwich, but he had never before been so tellingly confidential or, thanks to my relentless debriefing, so long suffering as this time. It was well after midnight, the storm having finally passed over, that I let him put me out of doors to find my way back to the one of those much sought after third floor rooms in E block which was mine.

If, without being asked, I now undertake to tell his story over, "with advantages," it is in the belief that he will never again have bothered with it—not on paper, at least. No matter how or where he settled, I do not see him doing any more History, certainly not his own. He lacked the gall to be a writer, especially of autobiography. It was part of his charm that he did not impose, was not provident, and had no mental economy, easily though words and understanding came to him. He liked that saying of the poet Cocteau that one should write but without being a writer. In his view, nothing that made too much sense seemed to matter. He had no time for the work of finding the context, only for knowing the anecdote, whatever it might be. Indeed, to my knowledge he went blithely through twenty and more years without ever admitting that the context might be lost. By looking back at who he was and what he meant to me, I shall see if I can say, before it is too late, how it once felt to be young and alive in the world—and how very different English life was in those far off days.

The first I ever saw of him was in that long late summer of '38 when the war was still a twelvemonth away but the Munich crisis had made the old world of peacetime already a thing of the past. Precautions against air attack began to be taken all over London; public and private shelters were dug in parks and gardens, and public ones also put up in quiet streets; and the evacuation of school children from the cities to the countryside was sternly rehearsed. Gas masks began to be considered a necessary of life. Everywhere in London there were "To Let" signs. Many families—those who could—moved house for reason of safety, mine among them, but not for reason of safety. My father, who was too old and wise to consider volunteering for active service again, though more than a few Young Contemptibles tried to do so, was offered a new job in the burgeoning Ministry of Food, which he accepted because it seemed to be a step up economically as well as war work of significance. It took us only marginally closer to Westminster and the City to live, and soon proved to be yet another serious disappointment for him and my mother. But for me personally, at the impressionable age of eight, it happened to carry with it the very considerable perk of going to live in Greenwich near the heath under the same roof as the Brenans, and more especially Michael, who was then well into his tenth year and tall enough to be twelve.

My earliest impression of him is a glimpse through the windscreen from our newly arrived pantechnicon—from the driver's seat no less, which I had been allowed to share on the road from Sydenham that sullen Saturday morning in October. The three movers in their green baize aprons were struggling manfully to get my mother's piano undamaged through the not so narrow gates, across the gravel, up the front steps, and into the hall, where they could rest it for a moment; and watching them patiently from the left wing of the drive at the side of the house where steps down to the basement door begin, stands a bright-faced boy on a bicycle almost too big for him, both feet on the pedals, precariously balancing by means of many tiny thrusts, accompanied by well-judged twists of the handlebar, waiting, suspended, dancing until he can swoop out of the garden on to the pavement and then, at the first up-and-down, outside the garage house next door, into the roadway, pedalling as fast as he can towards the heath. As he passes I note that strapped to the crossbar of his wellworn Hercules, the roadster model with twenty-six inch wheels, is an air rifle, probably a Diana.

The house Michael and I both lived in for the next ten years and more, with two additional families other than our own, was the first from the corner on the west side of Vanbrugh East, a tall doublefronted grey brick villa with stucco facings, four storeys high in its own walled gardens front and back, built in the 1870s or '80s for one of the permanent staff at the nearby Royal Military Academy in Woolwich. Mature, climbable trees, a sycamore, several chestnuts, a lilac, as well as shrubs and ivy, framed and softened a severe facade. In the years after 1918 there was probably nothing my parents would have liked more than to move into Heathdene, as it was hopefully named (there never can have been an actual view of the heath from it) and to make their family life there, perhaps with a servant or two and a motor car instead of the horse and carriage for which the garage next door with upstairs rooms had once been designed. But even if, by then, the house had not been bought by a landlord and converted into three flats and the garage separately leased, my parents would never have been able to live there in the semi-genteel manner of their respective families back in well-set Edwardian Hereford. Legacies had not materialized as hoped; and neither my father, Charles, nor my mother, Vivien, had been brought up to earn money in the world as it was after the first war. My mother was schooled, unrealistically, as a lady of some means; and my father, though a gent and an officer, had not had a good war.

At the age of eighteen he had sailed round the world before the mast in a merchant schooner that, on the homeward voyage, inexplicably found itself in the battle zone of the British and German navies off the Falkland and Coromandel Islands. Thus was the first war brought to his youthful attention. After an early start in Kitchener's army, achieving a captaincy in the Royal Engineers, and commanding a transport column of men, horses, and wagons on the western front between Béthune and La Bassée, he was stopped short in May 1916 by shrapnel in the chest, and spent the rest of the war languishing in hospitals and training camps. His lungs had been punctured and his breathing was never to be the same. He and my mother had met and fallen in love in their teens, a little before his voyage and the outbreak of war: they married in 1915, when my father was home on leave from the front; and my sister Babs was born the next year while my father was in a military hospital at Étaples and likely to die.

When I was born, well over ten years later—"quite improbably," as my mother liked to say—they were all three rather grimly making the best of it in Sydenham on the Kentish edge of London, a few suburban miles from the heath. My father had eventually found a position, after being released from the army, as manager of one of the many depots from which in those days milk was delivered daily by horse and van and roundsman to the doorsteps of rich and poor alike. Managing the Home Farm Dairy was not an employment either he or my mother thought suitable for him, but it did give her a small neat house and garden next to the stables to make her own, and him a yardful of men, horses, and vans to care for, as well as the milk supply from the bottling factory and the never-satisfied demands of some important customers to worry about. So they busied themselves for the better part of twenty years and endured. It was only the faintest echo of the ideal *Daily Telegraph* reader's life to which they aspired, yet my sister went to a good day school for girls, where she won prizes and prepared to take a degree at Birkbeck in Social Studies; and my mother had a piano to play when she felt up to it, and a shady lawn and herbaceous border to watch over, as well as a vegetable garden. I was the one who, as virtually an only child, felt most keenly (without quite realizing why) that there ought to be more to life in a family than I was enjoying at the dairy.

Heathdene proved to be a step up in the world for none of us except me, the Brenans being, as my luck would have it, available as an extended family only to a boy of more or less their own boys' ages. Sometimes I inclined towards Patrick as a friend, more often toward Michael, whom I was bound to look up to so long as he was a year ahead of me on the way to the adult world. I became, as Mr. Brenan liked to say, the second musketeer, not Athos, not Aramis, but Porthos. My sister Babs was now mostly out of the picture, or rather in some other picture, having found her first salaried appointment with the London County Council and her own bedsitter, way out in a northwestern suburb. My father became even more moody and precoccupied than before, naturally enough perhaps, given the new, more bureaucratic line of work he had to master at the awkward age of forty-seven. However, it did not take him and Michael's father more than a moment, when they first met, to recognize each other as former British Expeditionary Force types, initiates of the old trench war on the western front and, consequently, for him to approve of my joining in at cricket or any other game on the heath with the Brenan family.

"Don't be afraid to listen to what Mr. Brenan has to say," he would tell me, after removing his pipe from his mouth and refolding his *Standard* in the front parlour of an evening, "he knows what he's talking about." My homework done, I would have yet once more proposed joining the Brenans on one of their outings, whatever it might be for and however fiercely my mother might be frowning over her *Telegraph* crossword. I soon discovered that, like Michael and Patrick, Bill Brenan was not much for "talking for the sake of talking," as he would put it, but very good company for me at that stage of my life, whether for supervising ball games in the park, swimming at the Greenwich public baths, sailing model ships on the ponds about the heath, or staying indoors when it rained for board games, sketching, carpentry, or toy soldiers—all of which made a welcome relief and recreation after a day in the preparatory class of the local grammar school where I had been duly enrolled as a fee payer.

Like my own father, he was then about fifty, but still youthful and athletic in manner, especially when in uniform. His work as a postman had kept him fit, active, out of doors in all weathers, and tanned like a country labourer. At the age of fourteen he had been signed on by his father, a respectable Roman Catholic cricket ball maker of very modest means, with the General Post Office, still in 1906 at the height of its Victorian prestige as a paramilitary service of the state—chiefly for the sake of tenure (no dole for him during the Slump) and a government pension upon retirement at sixty. As a messenger boy in blue with red piping and a pill box cap, boots highly polished, he had delivered telegrams by bicycle at high speed about Greenwich and, in the evenings twice a week, drilled with rifle and bayonet as an infantryman to be. When the first war came he was already a fully fledged postman, collecting and delivering letters and parcels around the heath, based at the foursquare librarylike office opposite the railway station in the village. He joined one of the territorial battalions, but not the Post Office Rifles, rather the London Irish, and saw the fighting on the Somme in front of High Wood as a brigadier's runner in the 47th division. Invalided home with trench fever before the third battle of Ypres—a lucky escape, as he would be the first to say—he found himself tapped for an Aldershot course and a different military career with the Royal West Kents as a physical training instructor, finishing the war at the enviable rank of warrant officer, "with some of the leverage of a commission at field rank but none of the agony." Staff Sergeant Brenan had paid for his good fortune easily by the loss of the top joint of his fifth finger in a bayonet fighting exhibition on his twenty fourth birthday in October, 1917. It was not a wound he lamented, except when he needed to make a catch with his left hand; trying to crook the decapitated little finger round the ball he would sometimes let it slip.

As my mother could have pointed out, and occasionally would, though never emphatically, the Brenans were a family I ought to have looked down on, "keeping myself to myself" as much as possible. Their humble origins, their brief schooling, their wage earning as compared with our salaried poverty, their unambitiousness, their less than Englishness in being an Irish Catholic Londoner, a Baptist country girl from deepest Suffolk, and their issue, two near-Cockney boys—all should have put me off. When Bill and Bessie Brenan married, they had perforce given up churchgoing for reading the Bible at home and a quiet bond with a few local Jehovah's Witnesses. But in my eyes they took on a certain natural grace: they were so good looking, so self-possessed, so interesting in their differentness from our social conformity and correctness. My parents, who had also given up churchgoing after the first war, were, of course, secular C. of E. The Brenans were not "common," as my mother might have said but did not; they were uncommon. Their joy in life seemed to be, simply, in being the family, the parents and their children, that they so eminently were. Mr. Brenan was the sort of father who, against the law, would give his younger son a quick ride to school on the crossbar of his big all-weather Raleigh bicycle, so that the boy would be in time for a game of rounders before the bell rang; or who would make time between delivery and collection to watch his older boy through the playground fence taking part in a physical training class. Above all, they were very kind to me for some reason, taking me for granted, letting me take them for granted, and always being there, my first and most benign experience of "other folk," except for Jonathan, the stable hand and jobbing gardener at the dairy, and his wife Bella, whom I had left behind forever. "Come you in and sit you down," Bessie Brenan would say from in front of the stove or the sink or the pastry board or the ironing table in her blunt Mickfield brogue, unabated by twenty years of listening to whining Londoners. "Them hooligans'll be home in no time. They've gone to get their hair cut at Mr. Williamson's. Their father and I can't bear to see them so *bushy*." She had a way of emphasizing her more exotic choices of word. "Will you have a cup of tea while you're waiting, John? Or how about an apple? They're Coxes, you know, from my mother's own tree down home." In early summer it would be a handful of cherries from the bowl on the well-scrubbed table top. She seemed always to have a kettle on the boil, some housework in hand, but not too much to be ready to smile, say something funny, and make me feel at home in her kitchen. She was the fifth of a family of nine boys and girls, all still alive except the boy who had been killed with the Suffolks at Gallipoli, and most of them married with children of their own: hearing her tell their histories to Michael and Patrick, keeping up with their misadventures, was one of my many pleasures in her company. Service in the Women's Army Corps towards the end of the war was what had brought her to London, where afterwards she had worked as a housemaid in one of the grander houses in Vanbrugh Terrace. It was there that she had met her husband-to-be when he delivered a battered box of Cox's orange pippins to her at the kitchen door, and he and she got talking and she offered him one.

My mother found it very hard to enjoy what Heathdene had to offer me in the way of society, especially the new experience of living at close quarters between one family she could only look down on and another, the Fordhams in the top flat, who were inclined to look down on her. She approved of the high ceilings and distinctive plasterwork in our new home, which set off the finer pieces of her furniture well enough but, because the Brenans lived in what had formerly been the servants' quarters, her kitchen and scullery had to be a conversion of the former conservatory—"a great pity," she would say sadly. Complete with refrigerator, electric oven, water heater, and full view of the back garden—the landlord and my father had tried to indulge her—the kitchen might have been all well and good if a Bessie Brenan could have been found, and afforded, to do all the cooking instead of Mother. Wisely enough, Mrs. Brenan decided that she was not available as a charwoman, or even for occasional housekeeping, not to my mother at least. It transpired that she had been known, upon occasion, to help out the impossible Mrs. Gilbert Vaughan with spring cleaning at that preposterous villa of hers in the Bauhaus style along Westcombe Edge; and if only she had been willing, she could have cooked for us in her own big kitchen, the original, downstairs, and mother could have used the former conservatory for her plants and flowers, "as was proper." Then there were the two bedrooms and one bathroom—none for guests or for Babs when she visited—narrowly apportioned in what had once been a spacious dining room and study, overlooking the back garden. This, at least, should have pleased her, a generous lawn, shaded by beech, apple, and walnut, and margined by delphinium and chrysanthemum beds. But by fiat of the landlord, a kindly man with a sharp eye for detail and for what is only fair, the upper reach of this unpartitioned garden was for the use of the tenants in the top flat, not of my mother, green thumb and landscaper's eye though she had. In the front garden, used by all tenants and visible to every passer by, it was Mrs. Brenan, whose taste ran to wall flowers and frequent weeding, who had the care of the beds bordering the gravel walk. At Heathdene everyone was expected to do her or his bit and know her or his place, but not everyone was happy.

Only the outbreak of war in September '39 could have made my parents and Michael's into allies, if not comrades, and could make me now, after all these years, into his Boswell. It was the Fordhams in the top flat, two storeys that had once been all bedroom, bathroom, and attic, who first managed to bring my parents and his together. Fordham—I do not remember his Christian name, Percival perhaps—was a lieutenant colonel in the Royal Catering Corps who had spent most of the time between the two wars in India, a small dyspeptic man in his fifties with a ginger moustache, given to wearing service dress and Sam Browne instead of battledress whenever possible. He had been returned to the UK and sent on a course at Woolwich a little before my father moved to the Ministry of Food; so he and his wife, a large toothy woman with a penetrating voice, had taken the top flat only a few months before we took the one below them. They probably had no intention of perching there for long, but the landlord, with his usual concern, tried to gratify them, and us, by having a handsome flight of brick and concrete steps built to the third floor, and a side door and hallway constructed at the top of them. Previous tenants, to reach the top flat, had used the front door—now our front door exclusively—and our part of the staircase which coiled through the house like a spine but was now closed off; the Fordhams, however, seemed to merit a new means of ascent and ingress, steep but substantial, and all their own.

When we moved in, unrest and skirmishing between them and the Brenans had already broken out over Mrs. Fordham's daily routine of walking her two poodles in the tidy front garden which Mrs. Brenan had the care of. The Fordhams were the sort of people who never look behind them; and, said she, leave their messes to be cleaned up by others. Mrs. Fordham thus earned from Mr. Brenan the nickname of "Lady Pouf de la rue, the dog fancier," an appellation which caught on with one or two other less than respectful tenants of the house. Mr. Brenan had had no opinion of the French and their hygiene since the first war when, as he liked to pretend, they charged rent for even the filthiest of trenches. This skirmishing lasted most of the year between the Munich crisis and the invasion of Poland, during which I was becoming friends with Michael and Patrick. It was ended, even after a personal representation by Mr. Brenan to the landlord, only by the posting of the Fordhams at the outbreak of war to an army installation somewhere off the coast of Inverness.

How could I not cleave to Michael and Patrick when they were willing to let me join in their toy defence of Verdun, carefully modeled in the little rockery that sloped steeply up to the back lawn, outside our respective bedroom windows? My collection of toy soldiers made a welcome reinforcement of theirs and, despite my mother's warnings, I spent many a damp evening hour standing to with them in that trenchlike area of mossy drains and downpipes. We took our bearings in the game from a photographic fortnightly about the first war called *I Was There* which Mr. Brenan subscribed to until the new war got going and made it an anachronism on Fetter Lane. Of course, we had silently to reread the defenders of Verdun as mostly British tommies, not French *poilus*.

And how could my parents not begin to be moved to a certain compassion for the adult Brenans when, that first balmy Sunday evening of the new war, they heard through open windows on to the front garden the egregious Mrs. Fordham shrilly enjoin a stoic Mr. Brenan to "be sure that the Colonel's and my steamer trunks—all our gear—get to Westcombe Park station by noon tomorrow"—as if she were still a memsahib and he a swaddy in longlost British India? "This is part of the *war* effort you understand, Mr. Brenan." Hardly able to believe their ears, my parents were still more impressed by the quiet competence with which the former Staff Sergeant, borrowing a light handcart from the local dealer in fine luggage, the next day managed singlehanded the timely dispatch of the Fordhams' effects from Heathdene once and for all. The top flat, predictably, stood vacant until the Blitz, then not yet upon us, had become a thing of the past and the whole war was on the wane.

It was the Blitz the following year that finally brought my mother round to recognizing the Brenans for the neighbours they were; but it took only the first weeks of war, when schools were closed for evacuation and the Germans did nothing dangerous against London, to confirm the Brenan boys and me finally as friends. Everything on our margin of the heath became an adventure ground. Michael and Patrick and I were three of an undisclosed number of boys and girls not evacuated to the country with our schools immediately that war was declared. Why my parents so uncharacteristically exempted me from the done thing, I do not remember; Michael and Patrick, I learned, were kept at home by their parents to "take their chances" in a stubborn, though selective, spirit of resistance to any official interference which had extended, incredibly enough, even to vaccination. When Michael reported for National Service at eighteen, just after the end of the war, his examiners were astonished to find that he had somehow missed being vaccinated as an infant. We boys found ourselves attending school with a dozen other stragglers, girls as well as boys, a few afternoons a week in the old drill hall in Charlton village, where the antique rector of Saint Luke's (the parish church, not the Hospital chapel) read to us from, unpredictably, a children's version of the *Iliad*—presumably in deference to the then popular spirit of "Don't you know there's a war on?"

We did know; and so far we found it fascinating. Everywhere in our shady suburb troops had been billeted in vacant houses and sandbag defences against blast thrown up. Pavements rang three times a day under the hobnail boots of Pioneers as they slouched back from the mess hall with tin and knife, fork, and spoon; snatches of their strange talk and laughter carried over the garden walls to us. They were there to deal, when the time came, with unexploded bombs, blocked roads, flaring gas mains, tottering facades and, perhaps, civilian panic. Down Vanbrugh East at the junction with Hardy Road there was a much admired pair of highly hedged tennis courts, belonging to the great house there that overlooked the river, where now a squad of Royal Air Force men and women tended one of the many enormous barrage balloons tethered restively about the city and suburbs. Out on the heath, beyond the denes of gravel and gorse which had yet to be made plain with rubble from the bombing, all open spaces of level turf sufficient to let aircraft touch down were deeply trenched and duned; and in the middle, behind barbed wire, a searchlight and two anti-aircraft guns were emplaced, their long barrels camouflaged during daylight by green and brown netting. They were not fired during that first year, but at night in the warm weather we would be wakened by the whine of motor lorries in low gear delivering supplies. I can still see Mrs. Brenan, a diminutive figure, toiling across the heath between the grassy dunes and trenches in the sunshine, her shopping bags full of lunch for her boys and me, who are tenting for the day at a predetermined spot where Mr. Brenan on his midday dinner hour can find us all, and we can be together, all five, playing cricket and picnicking on cucumber sandwiches and barley water.

Before France fell and the battle of Britain began, my parents did get round to evacuating me to where my schoolmates already were in Sussex, just in time, as it turned out, for a much more unsettling removal of the whole school to the Amman Valley in Wales. Michael and Patrick, meanwhile, settled into the local emergency school that had been opened by the Council in response to a quorum of returned evacuees. And so for months we were out of touch. By the time I had prevailed upon my parents to rescue me, at whatever risk, from durance vile in a mining village, Michael was in his twelfth year and had taken the statutory Council examination in Maths and English and passed—which made him, with his parents' dubious approval, a scholarship boy at the very school which my parents were paying fees for me to attend. Entering the emergency grammar school in Lewisham together that first winter of the Blitz and thereafter till our own school reopened locally in '43, he and I sealed our friendship. It was at this stage of life that we began to adopt the mores of the classroom and call one another by surname and I, joining in with our classmates, began on occasion to call him teasingly by the nickname of Bresnahan, especially when he went into his outlaw mode. "There goes that boy-o Bresnahan again," someone in the fourth form would say in mock disgust. "Top o' the classroom to you, Mick." At home, my mother also began addressing him in that we're-all-grown-ups-here tone of hers, not as Michael, but as Brenan. His mother, however, never addressed me otherwise than as John, or John boy.

My parents had by then fallen into the habit of spending the long nights of *Luftwaffe* attack downstairs in the Brenans' reinforced back hall. "The best dugout on this bit of the front," my father said with finality. Indoors from where his new side steps had formed an invaluable blast wall, the landlord had had the staircase between downstairs and upstairs removed. Much frequented in former times by busy servants, and in the past two years by us boys, its polished treads curved rakishly between wall and bannister all the way down from a yellowish wooden wicket and pooplike landing at the top to broad flat stairs at the bottom, an all-purpose proving ground for boys of a certain age, not quite up and not quite down, as the poet says. When I got home from Ammanford, I was heartsick to see it gone, and the Brenans, as it were, battened down below hatches; but in its stead they had an indoor air raid shelter to share with us (no Anderson in the garden or Morrison in the parlour), with massive minelike trusses from floor to ceiling which, in case of a direct hit, would tip the upper storeys to the other side of the site like a seesaw and leave us all sleeping safely in our bunks and bags, dreaming of mail trains. All except my mother, that is, who took the nightly bombing and general emergency very much to heart and by doing so shortened her life.

Heathdene never did sustain a direct hit from a high explosive bomb, though more than once my father and Mr. Brenan had to deal with incendiaries in the attic by means of stirrup pump and sandbag. The nearest a high explosive came to the house was at the bottom of the garden, beyond the copper beech tree and the wartime vegetable patch where my mother and Mrs. Brenan both dug for victory (with a little help from the men and boys). The bomb was not a big one, but it took out every window and brought down most of the ceiling plaster. This explosion, for the long moment of inflation and splitting noise and suffocating dust, unforgettably terrified those of us, like Michael and me, who had only been told and read what it really means to be caught in a bombardment.

When I ask why I think I am able to tell Michael's Tievas story for him, the answer is not only an accident of place and time, Heathdene and the war—"we were young then, we were together." It is also a matter of crazes, as Mrs. Brenan would call them, one after another, over the many months of growing up, of shared crazes of all descriptions: cigarette cards, boys' weeklies, whips and tops, Zenda, Meccano, Biggles, public school stories, model aircraft, Robin Hood, metalwork, William books, aircraft recognition, badminton, Tarzan films, water colour painting, jazz, Westerns, shove ha'penny, maps, detectives, photography, darts, war books, geology, billiards, films as films, the poems of Robert Browning, who lived with his parents not far from the heath in New Cross and saw his last duchess in a painting at Dulwich . . . ; the list is *in toto* irretrievable. *Parce que c'était lui; parce que c'était moi.*

To the extent that it is mine, this book about Brenan must be one of well-tried commonplaces, familiar genres of fact and fiction, autobiography and mystery. For seven or eight years he was always there before me. Then he finished school and went to do his National Service in the Royal West Kents, an infantry regiment in which, after failing to pass the War Office Selection Board as an officer cadet, he found himself shelved as an orderly room clerk (and invaluable wicket keeper for the battalion cricket team). A year behind him, I did my two years as a translator in the Intelligence Corps. There was a tendency for colleges and universities in those immediately postwar years to give precedence to ex-service entrants over eighteen-year olds. When I was demobbed in 1950, Michael had done his first year in English here at Northfleet, then a college preparing students to take the University of London degree externally. As fate would have it, I found myself turned down by both King's and U.C., but accepted at Northfleet, and the rest is history.

I like to think that Michael would have told me at once about Tievas that Friday in October '51 if I had been at home, as McGill was. But I was on my way back from Pau, lingering in Paris, and would not see him until the first Monday of term in Northfleet. When I passed through London, my parents were taking a late summer holiday in Torquay, and I stayed the night with my sister Babs in Finchley, bypassing Greenwich altogether. I rather doubt if, after the Tievas affair was over, Michael ever told anyone else but me who would care enough about it or, more importantly, about Michael Brenan and his obscure Baltic contacts, to be able to write it up for general reading as a novel. It is, after all, like any other little tragedy, the story of a failure. And even after he had told it me, I had as many questions about it to be answered as he had—and still do have a few, such as how much did the woman in the case actually know?

ii

Who is Sylvia? What is she
That all our swains commend her?
~Shakespeare

Valija Didelis was living in a University of London student residence off the Edgware Road, behind Marble Arch, when I traced her through Bedford College department of English in late November 1952. Over the telephone she sounded as pleasantly neutral as ever, recognized my voice at once and asked how I was. I said I had not heard from Michael Brenan since before he went away, and I was wondering if she had. And, anyway, how was she herself getting along these days? It occurred to me as I said this that, for all I knew, she was lucky not to be in custody, if not dead.

She said she was still very busy winding up her thesis work on verbic extension, but would like very much to see me again. The University Senate in Gdainys wanted her back for the new year to carry on Dr. Didelis' work in the school of English. Would I come for high tea in hall on Saturday evening and perhaps a film at the Classic afterwards? For me it was midterm in the next to last term before finals, but I was taking a short break from study to visit my sister Babs in her latest flat. I did not say to Valija that I could hardly wait to put some long mulled questions to her about things Brenan had told me five months before, questions that perhaps I should not have the right to ask, let alone have answered.

When I arrived, she was waiting for me in the tiled front hall, looking as neatly tailored and continental as I remembered, but not nearly so youthful. She was still, in her slightly diminished way, what we from Greenwich would call an eyeful

(Gilbert Vaughan liked to refer to her unofficially as Veronica Lake), yet I realized for the first time that she was no Juliet, but probably older than Brenan and me by five or six years, not one of our lustrum after all. It was her expression, especially as given by the eyes, that was beautiful. We shook hands and went up to her room on the third floor to wait for the bell to ring us in to high tea. Hers was a large ugly institutional room, heavily distempered in yellow and rose but made intimate by the smoky dusk and by her studied arrangement of several Slavic odds and ends of decor. We settled at opposite ends of an overstuffed brocade sofa, across from the fireplace with its indispensable but unlighted gas fire. She helped herself to a cigarette from the end table, after offering me one, a Du Maurier, which I declined. She sighed.

"Like Michael, a nonsmoker. How ever have you two managed to avoid the pleasure of tobacco for so long? It is one of the first things friends learn to do together." I forebore breaking to her that it was Michael's father, Bill Brenan, who had with great difficulty given up for all of us when he was forty. "No, I have heard nothing from him since he moved to America. No doubt he has found himself in every way preoccupied over there. You and he were both already half in love with your ideas of the United States when we first met. It was Marianne who introduced us all, wasn't it?"

Again I did not respond, this time because she must have known very well that for me, if not for Brenan, France and things French, would always come first. Even if only one person of two smokes, smoking does make for comfortable silences in the conversation. After the pause, she said, "I imagine Michael is seeing Marianne again, there in Montgomery and Sylacauga. They were very close the year before last when she was at Northfleet. I remember being shocked to see in her room in Highfield a photo of Michael which he must have given her, looking very dark and romantically sullen." She smiled wryly and glanced about her own busy room as if there ought somewhere to be such a photo, lurking among the bric à brac.

"I know the one you mean. Flattering in a Hollywood studio sort of way. He had that taken when he came out of the army and went to college. The first thing he did was fall in love with a French girl from Oran, and she talked him into having himself photographed for posterity, like an actor."

Now was my chance to ask her about absent Baltic pin ups of her own, the distinguished bearded Didelis, and young Baltrušaitis, the pretty one with a marksman's eye, but I was careful not to do so. For her to know that before he left Brenan had taken me into his confidence about the Tievas business could still prove fatal for me, if not for him. Instead I said, "When did you last see Michael? I had gone abroad for the summer long before his visa came through."

"He and I had dinner here in town a few days before he sailed from Southampton. He was very subdued. By that time I am afraid we hadn't much left to say to one another. You know how departures can be; and you know how he was—withdrawn into himself, though still pleasant enough to be with. People have always taken to him easily—I certainly did—but I suspect that deep down he is an unreachable solitary."

"Perhaps so. It may be a matter of having comrades rather than making friends. College life confirms some people in a certain solitariness previously learned. But how many of his friends did you ever see him with, other than Marianne and me? Arthur Bresnahan, for instance. Michael was once close to Arthur . . . ." And, if so, I asked myself, why had he not been outraged at Arthur's fate when he told me about it? Perhaps he had, in his way.

Precipitating a *crise de nerfs* in a woman, without seeming to do so, is harder than the poets would have us believe. Valija showed no sign except evasiveness—if that is what it was—that this particular ground was dangerous.

"It is true that Michael and I kept to ourselves much of the time. He did once introduce me to an old friend from school whom you, John, must know, a Scot he called Mackie. He liked Brahms." My little flutter on Man Found Murdered was going nowhere. I let it ride. But if I had my way, we were still going to have our evening of reminiscence as proposed. "When was it you first came to Northfleet to study, Valija? And why?"

She gave me a misty smile. "'Why' is such a long, long story. It all has to do with my mother's younger brother, Dr. Didelis, who, as you know, was at Gdainys after the war and later a cultural attaché at our embassy here in London. A brilliant, eccentric man, quite the most interesting person I have ever known, a fine teacher and a serious scholar in his own right. He revered Ben Jonson in the way that so many English dons revere Samuel Johnson. I came to depend on him totally in 1945, a very difficult time for me because everyone else in my family had died or disappeared during the invasions of '40, '41, '44, and after. He taught me to let my imagination do the work that actual experience often fails to do. I believe that you and Michael both know how important this lesson can be to one's survival in the world as it is.

"When Marshal Tievas finally came to power in Baltija, I took the name of Didelis, which was, of course, my mother's family name. He had not been one of the partisans with Tievas but a staff officer in the Baltic division which the Germans, for their own purposes, kept intact. This continued to liaise secretly with the partisans and, when the Red Army returned, attacked the *Wehrmacht* openly. As a student of European History you know, I expect, that it took five German divisions to keep the Balts occupied, while the Red Army advancing on Germany more or less bypassed Baltija. We were not an ex-Nazi satellite to be liberated like Poland or Czecho-Slovakia; we were a people's revolution in progress. Support from Britain and America—recognition by the Allies—of course helped."

I nodded assent. I could tell from the way she spoke in paragraphs that she was all set to become an academic or a politician. She had that trick of listening carefully to what she was saying and never giving away as much as one might wish.

"At the time Nazi Germany collapsed, I was in Rügen Island working as a translator; and as soon as things settled down somewhat, Dr. Didelis claimed me from the Allied Military Government as next of kin, and I was repatriated. From then on he sponsored me as a student of English at the university— I have always been fascinated by your language (even if it is not as ancient as Lithuanian) and your literature—so eventually I came to England with him in the spring of '50. There happened to be a vacancy at Northfleet that year, and I began my London M.A. in the autumn. In the following spring I met Michael and you."

"But the following winter you transferred here, leaving him . . . vulnerable in the frozen northeast."

She forgave me this facetiousness with another misty smile. "By then my research was coming together, and relations with Dr. Anstruther were becoming . . . complicated. For my topic, the better tutor was turning out to be Natasha Tempel here at Bedford. But let's not talk about Michael anymore. Tell me your Northfleet news. Are you going to be ready in June to . . . prevail? Everyone seems to think that you will, with distinction, and go on in History."

"Michael and I always thought the very best of Anstruther. He was in Intelligence in Germany at the end of the war, you know. He took a serious interest in Michael as a poet; and I like his notion of European Studies as a department and a subject."

"Please don't misunderstand. I shall always be most grateful for all he did for me. It was just that Linguistics is not his specialty, and we came to a parting of the ways."

The room seemed to have grown darker. I asked myself what I was doing here.

"When you spoke of your uncle just now, it was as if he might be dead."

A look of utter bereavement came over her face and she
u know? He died last year quite suddenly at a
olk—castle actually—Merewell Castle it is
onounced it correctly, of course, with three
police sent for me to identify his body. It wa

terribly distended and disfigured, a horror in red and yellow. Apparently he suffered from porphyria, among other things such as cirrhosis, and these had been exacerbated by his taking a barbiturate which caused renal and hepatic failure. He was quite alone at the end. It was shockingly sudden, a *cauchemar*!"

And whose name was on his lips, I wanted to ask. Or should I have the right to smile? What I said was, "What a terrible loss for you, Valija. Where did you bury him?"

"He was cremated. It was all over in a day or two: Michael and I were scattering his ashes in the Thames, one handful at Westminster for Ben Jonson and the other near Wapping New Stairs where Baltic Wharf used to be, before the bombing. He got his first taste for things English at the University of Tallinn in the '20s, when Anglo-Baltic trade and cultural exchange was at its most promising. His first visit to England was in the *SS Baltallinn*, which used to dock at Hay's Wharf; it was torpedoed early in the war."

This scattering of ashes in the Thames with Brenan was news to me; and I was still wondering how much else he might have omitted to mention about those latter days at Merewell and Westminster when an urgent bell sounded and I had to follow Valija downstairs with the rest of her floormates.

The dining hall where we took high tea together, two at a table for four, was nothing like the refectory at Somersby that I was used to in those days. In furnishing and layout it was more like a Lyon's Corner House, though much less frequented this particular Saturday evening. There was kippered herring and toast with a cup of tea and Peek Frean biscuits; and we waited on ourselves cafeteria style. Seated and looking as sincerely as I could into Valija's eyes, I said, "Those must have been stirring times postwar in Gdainys, when Tievas first took control of all the Baltic States and began his five year plan for a people's democracy."

"They were. Brief as it may turn out to be, peace after war is a euphoria like no other. There were different positions with· the Party and among the people but, for the time being, Ma

Tievas enjoyed everyone's respect. Everyone wanted to trust him after the patriotic war against the Germans and the concessions he was able to wring out of Stalin and the West."

"The Cult of Personality being then a thing of the future?"

"In those days, and even recently, he spent less time than you might think lording it in Gdainys, especially given the trouble he had had taking it from under the noses of the Poles. He traveled all over the new Baltija and abroad trying to consolidate the advantages he had gained in the war. He is part Byelo-Russian, you know, under his Baltic ethnicity, and he had serious prejudices to overcome. During the war there had been crimes and offences against most of the people, inevitably, in so ruthless a drive for independence. The sacrifices exacted were frightful. For example, during the Russian occupation of '41, the pro-British liberal intellectuals in Tallinn were purged, deported to the Gulag, friends of Dr. Didelis among them. My own family was decimated for various reasons. Postwar in Gdainys, at the university, my uncle's cadre of ex-service students, of which I was one, put out a newspaper called *Atradimai (Discoveries)*, trying to keep up with all that was going on."

"How interesting. How many of you were there?"

"Only a handful, but of all sorts and conditions, as was the spirit of the age in Baltija just then. My uncle's admirers on the faculty referred to us teasingly in German as his department, *der Fachbereich*, but his enemies called us *die Zwergen*, the dwarves, after Wagner."

"He did have enemies, then? And the Department came to England with him in '50? Or should I call them the Dwarves?"

"A few enemies. They never forgot that he had not been a partisan proper but a soldier, a mercenary, in the war. Yes, in the end all the Department came here to work with him. There was no one else with his imagination, his energy, and his devotion— not in English studies, certainly—no one else like him at all. But I was never very close to the Department, perhaps because of being a woman, though I knew them all and, for a while, enjoyed the . . . provocation of their company. They were a knot of vipers." She said it derisively. "Always reeling and writhing. The one I knew best is Antanas Baltrušaitis, from Vilnius. He visited Northfleet last year. You may have run into him."

"I'm afraid not. And is he still in England?"

"My sense is that he has gone back to Baltija since the death of Dr. Didelis, but I am not sure. For myself, I shall be sorry in one way to leave England now. These are historic times, what with the Festival last year and a Coronation in the offing."

"And the eclipse of postwar Labour government by the Tories who are always with us, like the poor . . . . Speaking of death, isn't it curious that, as the rumours have increased lately about Stalin's failing health, Tievas has seemed to take on a new lease of life? His visit to England last year has turned out to be beneficial after all."

She was not to be drawn. Looking at her watch, which she wore pinned on her left lapel, she began gathering our meagre crocks on her tray. "We have twenty minutes or so before we leave for the Classic. Let's go back to my room for schnapps."

Upstairs in her room, I went back to my seat on the end of the sofa. Someone in a neighbouring room had begun to play Chopin quite well on the violin, one of the Preludes. Valija carefully poured me a glass of kirsch. When she had poured herself one, she brought it over and stood before me with a little smile from the eyes that was, for her, unusually coy. I found myself touching glasses with her, and she said, "John, you do not know how much it means to me that you should have thought to look me up after all these months."

It was true, I had not seen her since the autumn of '51, when so much had gone on that I was unaware of at the time, both during the week of Tievas' visit and for weeks afterwards. Brenan and I rarely talked with or about one of his girl friends, whether she was on hand or not. Even at the end of the year, when he had taken it into his head to tell me about the Tievas business, he had talked more about all the other suspects than about Valija. I saw her now with new eyes as she said "look me up after all these months" and did something that astonished me. It always comes to mind first whenever I rethink this awkward evening. With her glass in her right hand, she walked over to the fireplace in her sensible half-heeled shoes and stepped up on to the raised hearth, resting her left arm along the mantel. It made her taller and more statuesque than she was by at least six inches. For the first time ever I wondered how it would be to stand breast to breast, thigh to thigh, and kiss her. She smiled down at me and said nothing.

As a gesture of will or desire, a velleity, it touched me to the quick, yet how true or false it was and what it meant I had no idea. Looking up at her in the candlelight and its reflection in the glass over the mantel, I could say or do nothing. Should I stand up, put down my schnapps, step forward and embrace her? It was the only moment of sexual latency during a long uneventful visit. Until this moment I had been too suspicious, too anxious, to feel anything but danger, coverture, and betrayal. She, from her pedestal under the chimney, said and did nothing more than smile. From that other room the sound of Chopin wound down deliberately and at last stopped.

We drank up, slipped into topcoats and gloves, and left for the cinema.

Coming out of the Classic, two and a half hours later, I said, "Let me walk you back. I'll take the tube from Marble Arch." What is more melancholy than having sat and watched a film that other people once delighted in, but which one has found insipid? Yet, with the darkness pouring down above the busy lighted thoroughfare, and the rain still holding off, we started chattering together like fans of Michael Brenan. The film we had suffered through was *The Women*, a silly bedroom opera in technicolour with no male voices, done in MGM's notion of the high New York salon style of 1939. Its divas were Shearer, Crawford, Russell, and Goddard, none of whom mattered a damn to me except maybe Crawford later in *Mildred*

Pierce. Valija said by way of excuse, "I knew you and Michael had a thing about the films of the '30s, so I gambled on this one. But it can't have pleased you any more than it did me. So pretentious, so artificial."

"As Michael used to say 'If only Graham Greene had had time to libel Louis B. Mayer, as well as Darryl F. Zanuck, before running away to Mexico.'"

"But he would also say, 'Much as we may detest MGM sometimes, we must never forget that they once gave Fritz Lang his first chance in Hollywood.'"

"Do you know *Fury*? After seeing that shot of the woman at the lynching, whirling a lighted kerosene rag round her head and letting it fly on to the woodpile, Michael and I at ages thirteen and twelve could not sleep for a week."

"In Vilnius at that age, I was in love with Zarah Leander, the singer in *La Habañera*, who never to my knowledge set a man on fire in any of her films."

"Did you ever see that lovely film of Sirk's called *Schlussakkord*? It was not a musical. There was no dancing. It was orchestral. The most velvety black and white you ever saw."

"Detlef Sierck, the Dane? Yes . . . of course."

And so on, back to the front door of whatever that hall of residence was called. I had given up hoping to learn anything politically sensitive from her about the Tievas affair. She had the advantage, when being questioned about anything like that, of having been sadly disabled as a child by some ruthless wartime "need to know" policy. Brilliant as she could be, there was always too much going on around her that somebody else had decided she did not need to know. Didelis, the Department, Brenan— perhaps even her father and mother and brothers and sisters. Saying goodbye to her in the porch, where she stood for a moment like Lili Marlene,

Unter die Laterne
Vor dem grossen Tor,

I thought furiously of poor Arthur Bresnahan, who may never have been known to her personally, but whom somebody must later have tackled her about.

"Perhaps you can write to me," she said; but I never did, though there may have been a picture post card of Gdainys from her six months later, which I have not kept.

It was a relief that night to be returning home, not to Heathdene, unfortunately—life there was never again to be as it once had been—but to Babs, now in Islington, who, as I opened the door, would look up from the *Economist* and say in her dry, matter of fact way, "Well, Johnny, and what *has* become of Waring?"

iii

So swift a pace hath thought, that even now
You may imagine him upon Blackheath
~Shakespeare

Marshal Jurgis Tievas, together with Brenan's anecdote about him, came to mind again tonight when I chanced upon a television news program in which the three current presidents of the Baltic States, Lennart Meri of Estonia, Guntis Ulmanis of Latvia, and Algirdas Brazauskas of Lithuania, were all representing themselves and their peoples *seriatim* to the United Nations in New York City. Much more was said about the IMF than about NATO, of course; and relations with the former Soviet Union were smoothly referred to as "largely border disputes ended by Russian superiority in manpower," in other words "rectification of frontiers." Orwell must be spinning in his grave. But at one point, one of the three—Meri, I believe—referred complacently to Stalin's "historic" readiness at the end of the second war to compromise with the West on control of Eastern Europe and especially of the Baltic States. The notorious fifty-fifty policy on spheres of influence, worked out on the spur of the moment by Stalin and Churchill at their

Moscow meeting in November 1944, applied only to the Baltic States and to Jugo-Slavia, in return for ninety-ten in Rumania, eighty-twenty in Bulgaria, seventy five-twenty five in Hungary, while Stalin acknowledged ten-ninety Western influence in Greece and one hundred per cent in Italy. Poland does not appear to have been up for grabs at all. Or Czecho-Slovakia, reflecting perhaps the immediate presence in strength of the advancing Red Army. As to the Baltic States, where the megarivals were then supposed to be equal in influence, the implication now seems to be that economic providence operating from the West would in any case always have prevailed over the military force of the Red Army, if not over mere immigration from Russia. Not a word about the Tievas factor, which Stalin once thought he could count on in a crunch, and which for more than a decade provided for a virtually autonomous union of the Baltic peoples that disintegrated only upon his death. His name may as well have gone down a memory hole.

It is not easy to know now what a charismatic figure for the left-leaning young, what a mysterious, largely invisible, lord of a cult, Tievas still was in 1951. He had yet to be eclipsed in the socialist firmament by Fidel Castro of Cuba. He was European at a time when Europe—especially England, and the right-leaning English newspaper reader—was still nostalgic for world hegemony; so he was taken as seriously in his weight as Stalin was taken in his. How he managed to defend, unify, and satisfy the mutually hostile Baltic peoples in the face of, successively, Hitler, Stalin, Churchill, Roosevelt, Truman, remains, even to this day, a *Heldenlied* worthy at least of Machiavelli.

In 1951 Brenan did know who Tievas was, or thought he did; and when I pursued him with questions in the days after he told me his anecdote, one of the things he gave me was a clipping from the London *Observer* profiling the great man a week or so before his visit to Greenwich. That Saturday after the epiphany in the chapel, Brenan had rummaged at home in his bedroom, behind cushions on the sofa and armchairs in the front room, under the kitchen dresser, and out in the first and second places (which was what the family inexplicably called their two stone-floored storage rooms at the back) until he found it. An *Observer* profile was in those days a novelty of access comparable, I suppose, to a website on the Internet. It appeared anonymously each Sunday and featured a man or woman in the news: Clement Attlee, Molotov, Jawaharlal Nehru, Aneurin Bevan, Edith Summerskill, Eva Peron, Lord Beveridge, T.S. Eliot, John L. Lewis, Jean-Paul Sartre, Benjamin Britten—as imagined by some journalist or other scribbler in about a thousand words. I can still lay my hand on the webby piece of newsprint Brenan gave me in Somersby that June of 1952. Now yellowed, it is in weight of paper and quality of typography and layout like no newsprint we handle today. It lies folded into the first pages of an old Jonathan Cape edition of Marcus Templeton's memoir entitled *Eastern Inclinings*, which originally laid down the Tievas legend for all readers of English war books. As I unfold it now on my desk blotter, careful not to tear it at the creases, I am taken with the notion of simply transcribing it, sitting pen in hand here in my ninth floor eyrie with darkness coming down above the rooftops of Louth and Somersby Halls:

Profile

Those who have seen the Baltic leader lately say that he looks unagingly bland in the face of an ever mounting political crisis. His benign mask of middle aged aplomb, rarely visible to the public except in mechanical reproduction, and always splendidly offset by uniform, shows little sign of the many years of hard campaigning, Cold War, and intermittent Slavic high living through which he has come. He gives the impression of some Antony who has yet to meet his Cleopatra, some petty Napoleon who may never find his way to Waterloo.

The life of Jurgis Tievas is a twentieth century epyllion in which the hero at every stage remains, incongruously, a man of mystery and rumour.

How many observers of his exploits can claim actually to have met him for more than a mere moment of recognition, let alone to have known him personally? Very few. Not Josef Stalin, certainly, who laid the foundation of Tievas' career as a military leader by making him Secretary-General of the Communist Party of Lithuania in 1926, a position in which his genius for organizing an underground army in all three Baltic States could slowly take effect without his ever becoming a public figure and so vulnerable. Not Marcus Templeton, who was Mr. Churchill's personal emissary to the Baltic partisans in 1943 and who, in his war memoir, did more than anyone else to make Tievas known— unforgettably, if only in profile—to a world audience. Never has Tievas set foot in the New World. But can there be any denying that this shadow of a great man, this ghost of Hamlet's father, is one of the heroes of our time?

Just as the English common reader was getting used to the idea that Carlyle and Emerson were no longer quite to be believed, and collective forces rather than Great Men the cause of what happens among nations, along comes the next modern war and, sure enough, its events prove inexplicable at times, except as the initiative of some great, if not good, man. Hitler, Stalin, Churchill, Roosevelt, Truman—how does one account for at least some recent world events without acknowledging that these wilful individuals have been at work? The case that comes to mind is Hitler's crucial decision ten years ago to launch the overwhelming powers of his Luftwaffe *and his* Wehrmacht, *not against England, but against Stalin's Russia. And so, on the less than continental scale of things in the Baltic States, what has happened there since Hitler invaded is hardly to be explained except as the personal history of one very exceptional man.*

All the big questions about Baltija since 1940 can be answered only by reference to his individuality. For example, how on earth did Baltic partisans prevail, first against Nazi, then against Soviet aggression, and emerge from the war as a self-defending democratic republic? The occupying Germans were at first surprised by a congeries of peasant risings in the former neighbouring states of Lithuania, Latvia, and Estonia. These risings the Germans put down, once they had recovered from their surprise, but already an unquenchable spirit of independence and resistance had taken hold. While the towns and villages of the plain were being reoccupied and thousands of hostages shot, a guerilla army regrouped in the forests and highlands, recruiting widely, women as well as men, from an angry peasantry and a disaffected middle class. Like any guerilla army, the Baltic partisans survived against a numerically and materially superior enemy by means of loose paramilitary organization, surprise attack, and fading back into difficult terrain once an action had been fought. But their success was owing, not only to a fierce refusal to submit peaceably to occupation and allow the enemy's over-extended lines of communication among isolated garrisons to function efficiently—especially after Hitler ordered the invasion of Soviet Russia—it was owing also and more so to an inspiring military leadership in the person of Tievas himself, and to the savage sense of purpose which he conveyed, even to those partisans who were as yet unconverted, by his luminous version of international communism.

Pride in the patriotic resistance ran very high, especially with those who dedicated their lives to the cause, submitting themselves to a rigid discipline. No drinking, no looting, no love-making; this was the rule, according to Templeton: selfish desire and private feelings counted for nothing compared to service in the cause. Nothing less than complete dedication, living in the spirit, would have enabled the partisans to prevail. Only those who were ready to lose their lives would save them and enjoy freedom. And the head and heart of this austere warrior movement was Tievas, elected Marshal by his comrades in the field in 1943—in those days a leader as elusive as the Scarlet Pimpernel, and even rumoured by some to be a woman.

Prevailing over Hitler's Wehrmacht was only the first of the ordeals through which Tievas has led his people. As Thucydides warns in his reflections on the savagery of war, after the end of actual fighting a mentality of unrest, of revolution, continues to exist. Here in England this manifested itself most clearly in the postwar election of a Labour government; there in the Baltic States it did so in perilous shifts and strategems occasioned by the Cold War. The new marshal, Uncle Jurgis to the children of Baltija, now found himself the restive creature of a

*megarivalry between East and West. The will to be free became, in
practice, a Protean readiness to temporize.*

*The Iron Curtain and the Cominform, NATO and the Marshall
Plan, Stalinism* versus *the ever-increasing belligerency of President
Truman's nuclear and economic policies—all cruelly compounded the
dangers to be passed by Tievas and his emergent people's republic. Through
successive crises in Rumania, Greece, and Poland, through Jugo-Slavia's
expulsion from the Cominform, and the siege and relief of West Berlin,
the Yalta notion of accepted spheres of relative influence has proven
volatile in the extreme, a constant threat to Tievas, also, of being torn
in two by implacable forces of eastern and western imperialisms, an
ongoing war of nerves in which Baltija was subjected by the Kremlin to
nearly one thousand border incidents in 1950 alone. Is it any wonder
that Stalin's seventieth birthday the previous year was not officially
celebrated in Gdainys after all?*

*In recent years Tievas has found himself, internationally, with a very
difficult and diminishing hand to play. One suit he has had to rely on
too much is mollifying Stalin by means of humility, promises, and material
sacrifice—for example, the continued purchase of desperately needed
heavy armaments (unavailable under the Marshall Plan) in the form of
obsolete German material captured by the Red Army in the war. It will
be remembered that the very integrity of the three Baltic States under
Tievas, a military* fait accompli *in 1945, had yet to be purchased
from Stalin by Churchill and Roosevelt with thirty million pounds worth
of German property in Lithuania Minor.*

*Courtship of Truman through the United Nations Organization
and through the British Labour Government (if not Mr. Churchill) has
been hardly more rewarding for Tievas than his deference to Stalin.
Truman, who began his presidency by regarding Baltija as a self-
determining democracy, seems to have veered round, perhaps in response
to McCarthyism at home, to a policy of letting any small nation that is
communist collapse in the interest of international capitalism. When
Tievas applied for Baltic membership of the security council of the U.N.,
the Kremlin had just appointed Marshal Rokossovski Minister of
Defence in Poland where border incidents with Baltija were at once*

stepped up, and had just announced the detonation of the first Soviet atomic bomb. Meantime, another legendary Russian hero of the Eastern Front, Marshal Voroshilov, was going from country to country behind the Iron Curtain, denouncing Tievas and his Baltija to the members of the Cominform. Poland too, sponsored by Vishinski himself at the U.N., applied for membership of the security council. Our Labour government representative, while praising Tievas for his independence of the Cominform, voted for the Soviet candidate. And so Tievas was denied once again—the price perhaps of having reminded Mr. Truman that Baltija seeks freedom from western as well as eastern hegemony.

Currently he faces his latest East-West dilemma: how to respond to an urgent invitation to join the Atlantic Pact, while Cominform witnesses at treason trials in Poland already accuse him of soliciting American capital investment, and his people suffer crippling shortages under a Soviet economic blockade. As usual since the Cold War began, his chief comfort has to be that neither beneficiary of the famous fifty-fifty sphere of influence agreement, Stalin nor Truman, would dare precipitate the other's reaction to an actual invasion of Baltija. Indeed, keeping Tievas alive and kicking against the pricks sometimes seems to be their covert common agenda.

So much for the insight into things Baltic of our devoted fourth estate at the time. Whoever he was, our man in Gdainys seems to have been subject to some rather severe editing. Things from long ago usually are remembered as larger than they once were—gardens, houses, rooms, even books and newspaper articles. Till now I remembered this *Observer* profile as being twice its actual length. Since I have come to consider myself, professionally, as an improver on the genre, let me amplify the great man's epiphany a little here.

The third and worst of Tievas' ordeals had been domestic. At home, where religion among Protestants, Catholics, and Jews caused little dissension, politically the Marshal had been eaten up—divided between Party and people, peasant virtue and collectivity, agrarian economics and the pressure to industrialize. Stalin was not the only one to identify Socialism with heavy industry: Baltic adherents to the Cominform line scornfully answered resolutions of timber and construction workers defending Tievas with the question, how many steelworking communists had he purged since 1945? More than a few intellectuals and academics certainly found themselves cutting coal. Any honeymoon between the wartime Marshal and a majority of Balts had long been over. Newspapers and radio bulletins from abroad taught them to suspect him more and more of living reclusively in "kingly splendour," enjoying a life of luxury in power, of being debauched, of being drunk when he should be ministering to their needs. His response had been: "I do not think the press of great importance."

His loneliness and remoteness from his own people became greater than ever. He had no disciples left. The inner circle of his trusted wartime captains dwindled, as time and chance carried them off, the sick to hospital and the disaffected to prison, leaving him a pyramid of government with himself alone at the top. Younger Party officials and army commanders did whatever he said. He had no heir apparent. Residing on country estates and at island resorts, breeding and racing horses from his own stable, fancying wolfhounds, he lived like a king. He even refurbished a former Ruritanian royal train for his own use. Everywhere he went, trigger happy security guards accompanied him. One of these, an ex-partisan thirty-three years his junior, had become his wife—morganatically, one is tempted to say. Yet he never failed to be wrily humorous about his own powers or foibles. Whenever his favourite film, Chaplin's *The Great Dictator*, was shown in the presidential apartments of an evening, he is said to have laughed sadly but appreciatively.

And so, at an extreme point of crisis, he came by sea on a sudden visit to England, which he had not seen since the 1920s, when he was briefly a student of navigation at Northfleet. A night and a day in Greenwich for a televised speech and conferences, two nights in Northfleet, where Sir Marcus Templeton was Vice Chancellor, for auld lang syne, and then what? No involvement with parliament or the London public at first hand. It was the least auspicious state visit in history, a cruising holiday in the genre of Erskine Childers. To what end, one may ask, leaving his wife, his dogs, most of his guards, his army, his kingdom. Why to England?

Of all the paradoxes deriving from the original paradox of a Cold War, this one of Tievas English'd must be the most paradoxical. Could it be that, as the Gravedigger says, "he shall recover his wits here; or, if he do not, it's no great matter . . . the men are as mad as he"? In England, it is true, he could pose to a certain constituency (though not to Evelyn Waugh) as an old comrade and a great man. Not every hero of our time could claim to have been supposed by the author of *A Handful of Dust* to be a woman. Here he had well-wishers in the Labour government, at the Foreign Office, and on the Board of Trade. And here, his beleaguered supporters in Baltija expected him to find, at last resort, desperately needed military and economic aid.

Only a few days previously, Stalin had spoken of his imperium as no longer Socialism in one country but reaching "from the Pacific to the Oder and the Adriatic." Hearing this, Tievas, ever the oracle, remarked, "We have never given reason to hope that we would join the western bloc, or any other bloc, for that matter." Yet there did seem to be something piously and repentantly democratic about his modest return to these shores in 1951, looking back to humble beginnings, as if in him—to quote Burke on Cromwell—'ambition had not suppressed, but only suspended "the *sentiment* of—in his case— Socialism.

Now I am tired. In the morning, when I next take up Brenan on Tievas, my words will be on the wing, not of History, but the merely imagined.

iv

What Englishman will give his mind to politics
as long as he can afford to keep a motor car?
~Shaw

The Deputy Assistant Commissioner broke in before
Vaughan could say two words about security at the Naval
College. "Ours is not to reason why," he said, not for the first
time in his life, as if he already knew all there might be to
know about what the Tievas visit involved. "Ours is not to
die or even to do anything we don't absolutely have to do.
Whatever you may think, this is not really our affair. Fleet
Street may have its knickers in a twist about last night, but
there's no need for us to do so. It is just one more Baltic
fiasco"—his glance flicked at the Saturday morning headlines
screaming from his in tray—"courtesy of MI5 and the Cousins,
with Winston's blessing, no doubt, and the FO washing its
hands, as usual. Still in shock from the Burgess and MacLean
stunt, needless to say.

"This is why I called you in, Vaughan. We are not going to
become invested in this particular visit any more than we have
to"—he gave one of his intolerable twinkles—"even if it does
happen to be taking place in your very own back yard." He
prided himself on a personal acquaintance with most of his
staff.

Vaughan stood in a pool of sunlight and waited. When the
DAC said "we," he meant the Special Branch and more
especially himself. He was not one to grant that any other point
of view than his could conceivably be of importance. There
was more than a touch of the headmaster about him, especially
on a Saturday morning, though Vaughan could not have been
more than a few years younger. "I am just one of your ever
busy, ever youthful Welshmen," he thought. The DAC only
looked and played the elder—as well as, of course, the superior.

Tall, tailored, and craggy of feature, with a heavy iron gray haircut that tended to fall over one eye, he filled any room he was in and did most of the talking if he could. On this occasion he certainly could, and so was at his most benign, which was not very benign at all.

"There is, as you know, a conference waiting to resume in Paris at which the UN are being talked into protecting Baltic minorities abroad, Baltic students and children who are being detained, even the suppressed Baltic languages, against Uncle Joe and the Cominform. Meantime, here in London we have Uncle Jurgis, whom you think isn't adequately protected, telling us he wouldn't be caught dead having anything to do with NATO."

"Is this really so surprising, sir?" Vaughan said, innocently, wondering if he could get a rise out of the Old Man—who was already, as usual, at some altitude of his own finding.

He walked over from behind his desk to where the windows of his office, casements rather, gave generously upon Thameside at Westminster, garish in the October sunshine, and studied the Festival grounds below the new concert hall on the South Bank. His expression seemed to say that earth had any number of things to show more fair, which was probably true. A certain aura of village fête and temporary bandstand arose from the site.

"Let's not try to guess the weight of the cake, shall we," he said sagely, in his great, clear, oratorical bass.

"All you have to do," he went on, when Vaughan said nothing, "is keep an eye on everything without being noticed, and report to me personally, morning and evening at this number, whether you have anything to report or not. This time I want you to indulge me, you understand."

He fished a sheet or two of typescript off his desk and waved it at Vaughan where he stood attentively. "You are not known around here for the fullness of detail of your written reports, are you? I approve of that. Keep them to a minimum.

Save the time to spend on fortifying that glassy German bunker of yours, what? Didn't make it into Pevsner, I see. But this morning, between you and me, I am going to ask for all the details that you left out of this"—he let the sheets flutter to the desk top—"because you thought I wouldn't be interested, or you didn't know what to make of them yourself. Come on, Vaughan; you are going to surprise me. What is it that you haven't put into your report that I should know?"

"You wouldn't believe, sir, how many different interests are on the ground all at once. And no chain of command. The local police are doing what they can to keep order but they are the poor relations at this garden party. It's a staff college in session, as you know, and the Dreadnought Hospital is within the same enclosure between the riverside and Nelson Street, so controlling access is hardly feasible. Anybody and everybody comes and goes."

The DAC was about to break in again, so Vaughan shifted into a higher gear. "Nothing surprising about that, perhaps. All our competitors are there, including the Balts, of course: the reporters, the newsreel, the BBC television people, the public, the Communist Party regulars—though fewer of the public than you might think—all mixing it up and getting nowhere. The Marshal seems to think he's a happy tourist in the land of individual liberty . . . ."

"He is. This way you have all the suspects under your eye."

"But would you believe that at noon yesterday I caught up with him alone, in civvies, looking at the meridian by the Observatory in Greenwich Park, when he should have been lunching with the College command?"

"Waiting for the Time Ball to drop at one o'clock, and the gun to go off at Woolwich Arsenal, I presume. A long wait these days."

"This charade has brought out a face or two among the Balts that I never thought to see again, not only the *Čičilikai*, as you might expect, but the *Tautininkai*, too. Damned if I didn't spot old Garas—from the Courland drop in '41, you remember—sunning himself on Greenwich pier yesterday morning, waiting for the Marshal to come ashore."

It was the DAC's turn to be silent.

"And speaking of faces, there's one name I can't yet put a face to or spell out in full. All I have is the initial D. It showed up in an embassy memo I came across while doing my prep at Holland Park last week. If it wasn't in reference to the Tievas visit, it wouldn't make much sense; but, unfortunately, there are at least a dozen D's connected with the business that we know about, and none of these seems to be the one."

Now he had the DAC's attention, for some reason, though still nothing was said to let him know why. Vaughan found himself the object of a long owlish look of appraisal.

"Well done, though I am not going to award you the prize in this instance. The name you are looking for may be Didelis. See what you make of it. Off you go now. You have Lloyd with you there, I believe, and a car. You will need one when the scene shifts to Northfleet."

Vaughan asked if, since time was of the essence and there were so many possible leads, he could have another man assigned to him. But the DAC shook his head. "That cock won't fight!"

"I have other uses for Morgan," he said upon further reflection. "Besides, you aren't the best of examples for him, are you—a brougham to his wagon? And if I said yes, you'd be asking me for another official car as well.

"You can go now. Just remember what I've been telling you. In our work, one of the golden rules is to avoid finality, as Masterman used to drill into us during the war. 'Refrain from the irrevocable act,' he would say, 'especially at a doubtful moment, and almost invariably you will be right.'"

He moved to the window again, where a fly buzzed, and this time he looked upriver. "Those bloody Balts," he said, shaking his head. "Do you know what Toynbee called them during the first war, when an Englishman could still get away with telling the truth? 'The most backward race in Europe.'"

"Only time Toynbee ever sounded Polish," said Vaughan evenly, as he took his leave.

"My respects to Connie," boomed the DAC.

Vaughan made his way back to Greenwich as if in a dream. He went by train from Charing Cross to Maze Hill, after buying himself a *Listener* at W.H. Smith's, showing his pass at the ticket barrier, and settling down in a warm, dusty compartment, which he had all to himself. It was one of the quiet times of the day at which the string of green coaches, drawn by an electric current, rattled along largely empty, awaiting the onslaught of rush hour crowds from the city. He was still careful not to choose a compartment for nonsmokers. Taking out his pipe and Nosegay tobacco and Swan Vesta matches, he made himself a comforting smoke before opening the *Listener*.

By the time he was being drawn out of London Bridge Station he had enjoyed a brief memoir of the late André Gide but had foraged through the rest of the week's offering without much satisfaction. On his left hand, the factory chimneys and rooftops of Bermondsey and Rotherhithe were falling away behind. Once the train was snaking out on to the viaduct he could take the long view north and east, downriver to Greenwich Reach, where it dwindled into haze and high cloud. He would be home in less than half an hour. What could it be that the Old Man wanted him to know, or not to know, about Tievas? He imagined himself a fly on the wall, all ears, at some awkward briefing of the Old Man by one of his higher ups. Watching the pale dry sunshine pass through the window on to the dull red cushion of the empty seat before him, he lapsed unresisting into a fugue which lasted through three stations, New Cross, Deptford, and Greenwich, and as far as Maze Hill.

Coming out of the station yard, he forced himself to stride, so that when the steep hill suddenly rose under him he could really feel it in his calves and thighs. At the top, under the brick battlements and bastion towers of Vanbrugh's gothick castle, he turned along Westcombe Edge, leaving the ever-inviting walks of Greenwich Park behind him, and began dwelling on his own little folly, number 57A, inaptly named St. Mary's by the previous owner, a Welsh MD, not long deceased. Would Connie be home or not when he got there, he wondered. His sudden swerve uphill from the station nearest the Naval College would be all in vain if she were not. Even allowing for an occasional site emptied by the bombing, 57A still stood out like a sore thumb among the gabled tree-crowded Victoriana of the Edge, he told himself, like the one sound tooth in a ruined smile, like the sport that it was. It was stuccoed, white, and uncompromisingly suburban, a two-storey oblong box with rounded corner windows in that 1937 neo-Bauhaus style which always seemed to want a villa to look like the superstructure of an ocean liner, displaced and grounded. The Old Man was right; it should be of reinforced concrete, not stuccoed brick. Connie was having her way naturalizing it, he noted, as he closed the iron gate behind him and started down the well-planted path to the simple front door. He let himself quietly in.

She was sitting at the kitchen table, smoking a Craven A and reading the *Ladies' Home Journal.* She wore a satiny three-quarter length quilted dressing gown in coral with mules to match. He went in and kissed the back of her neck, under the heavy dark hair, and she smiled, taking his hand fondly in her free one.

"Hello, Gil, what brings you home so early? Who was it you had to see at Scotland Yard today?"

"The DAC, no less."

"Old Gussie? What a puss!"

"He seems to want us to start being secret agents instead of policemen."

"How lovely. I can just see you in one of those gorgeous Gestapo uniforms, looking like Robert Donat or Rex Harrison."

Vaughan reflected silently on the fact that, if he looked like anybody on the silver screen, it was Emlyn Williams. He said, "Be careful what you wish for, love. I might turn out to look like John Gielgud." She gave him her throaty little gurgle of laughter. Hitchcock's 1936 muck up of the Ashenden stories was one of their favourite mutual *bêtes noires*.

"Look, I'd love to linger, Connie, but the great man is still in danger on our very doorstep. I've got to keep moving. With any luck I'll be back tonight. But tomorrow I shall have to go north for a few days."

She looked out of the observation size kitchen window to where, behind a cluster of beeches, the Edge fell away to the river and to the north. "I didn't think we still had a doorstep in this up-to-date type of house, darling." She got up from the table and folded her magazine away in a drawer.

"At least have some lunch before you go. There's some of that nice brisket left over. I have tomatoes and lettuce, and rolls. You can have a glass of beer with it. I'll join you."

Now this was why he had slipped home instead of going straight back on duty with Lloyd—to see her and to be made much of. He said, "You would have had to agree with the Old Man this morning, Connie. He alluded to St. Mary's as 'that glassy German bunker' of mine, and advised me jovially to keep on fortifying it. He sent you his respects."

"The nerve," she said sourly, opening the refrigerator. "Just like his vinegary wife telling me at the garden party that I looked like Norma Shearer only my legs were much prettier than hers. Norma bloody Shearer, mind you!" She had transferred what she needed from the fridge to the counter and now slapped the little white door shut. "By the way, I thought we'd have a dinner party on Friday, and perhaps play bridge. Can you be back from up north by then?"

He reflected for a split second. "Yes, probably," he said. "I'll let you know as soon as I can if anything comes up to interfere." What is it that keeps us going, love, he wondered, but knew enough not to ask.

v

Love mixed with fear is sweetest

~Webster

As to Michael Brenan, for him the interval between midnight and midafternoon that Saturday unfolded like a flash and like a lifetime. He was suddenly in love; he had nothing to do; he could not wait to set eyes on Valija again; he had so much else to worry about; he slept until nine. Awaking with the hint of a headache from the previous night's libations, he dozed until his head cleared. When his mother bustled in, he was watching the play of sunlight on the counterpane and thinking over his dream.

The dream was unusual in that he could recall it in every detail, even to the key words spoken, though as usual it was not in colour. He had been invited to dinner with the family of a girl he was very interested in, if not in love with, named Marjorie, an English girl. She lived across the heath on the Lewisham edge in one of the big old houses on Belmont Hill where E. Nesbit had once lived. The family was all present, but only very shadowily, except for Marjorie's father, a forbidding presence, known as the Professor, who seemed to have some sinister influence over Brenan's working future as well as his love life. Before dinner he went out into the walled, tree-shaded back garden to play catch with Patrick—or was it John?—who just happened to be with him. They were throwing hard, trying to make it difficult for one another to get a hand round the cricket ball—their best, one that their father had been given by the old groundsman at the Phillips' club—when it flew right out of sight, over the wall into the nextdoor garden. It was then that the disaster in the dream occurred. Brenan ran at the nine foot brick wall, reached up, and jumped, meaning to hoist himself on top of it. As he went up, the whole fabric turned out to be nothing but a perilous balancing trick, done without benefit of mortar; and it collapsed under him in one great grinding dustraising heap, leaving him splayed on top like some beached, weatherblown porpoise. At dinner afterwards, the first thing Marjorie's father the Professor said, fixing him in his dishevelment with a beady eye, was, "Now, Mr. Brenan, what precisely is your subject?"

He was thinking this dream question over and at the same time worrying about the man in the chapel—Tievas, as he persisted in believing him to be. What might the President of the Baltic States be doing right at this moment, if not conferring with ministers and secretaries of state just down the hill in Greenwich? He had a vision of the inert, friendless body, heaped into the swaying back of the blackish greenish Austin van with two of the four guardians and all their clobber, while the other two sat up front, the one with the pretty face stonily driving as fast as he dared through the outskirts of the city. ". . . Show thy pity, Lord, upon all prisoners and captives."

His long narrow bedroom, known to the family as the slip room, had always pleased him, narrow as it was—sliced from his parents' much larger bedroom by a solid partitioning wall, and so approachable from the kitchen only after a long turn through the back hall and the rear of the big front room. Cornered in the northwesternmost low point of the whole house, it was decorated in cream and green and well-lighted by a large window which could, in emergency, be a Jacob's Ladder to the back area, the rock garden, steps to the lawn, and a tall wooden side gate to the drive at the front.

"Time you were moving, my boy," said his mother. She handed him a cup of hot tea. "It'll soon be afternoon. I'm going to bring you in your breakfast now, if you feel up to it. I want to get away to do some shopping at the Co-op for tomorrow's dinner; and your father needs new socks, so I shall have to traipse all the way down to the lower road for the in-and-out shop." She scrutinized his face from the foot of the bed where she was standing. "I shall have to speak to that Gordon if he's going to get you into bad habits when he's home on leave."

He noticed, looking back at her, that she was less and less the plump, apple cheeked, dark haired young woman with brown eyes that she had been until well into her forties. Her colour, if not yet her vigour, had gone with the years of war. Rationing, bombing, housework, the shortage of everything including money had told upon her physically in a way that it had not upon his father. What had happened to his father was different, and nothing to do with the war. He gave her the best smile he could, and said, "Thanks, mum. Would you bring me in the *Express*, too, when you can?"

"You'd be far better off getting up and getting out on a fine day like this than lying in kip reading that old squit. I wonder when in the world you're going to *do* anything. Don't forget you still have shoes to collect from the cobbler." They were in fact safely hidden, still in their brown paper and string, far under his bed. But he only smiled at her. She had learned from his father to say "kip" like a soldier, but "squit" was one of her own Mickfield words.

"I won't forget to go across to the village this afternoon," he promised. "This morning there are things I want to do at home."

He would never tell her or his father anything concerning a girlfriend or even a date with one, and they never asked him to. Once, when out of the army and first at college, he had fallen hopelessly in love with a French girl who was soon due to return to her family in North Africa. Desperate not to lose her, he had told his mother and father about his love and talked them into inviting her for the weekend. Highly strung, sickly, striking in looks and intelligence, but hardly fluent in English, she had been like a beautiful fish out of water in austere, wintry, war-scarred London. She had horrified his mother, who was disinclined to entertain potential daughters-in-law anyway; and she had simply failed to get his father's attention at all. They, in turn, usually the kindest of parents, had made her feel unwelcome, unwanted. For everyone the weekend had been a catastrophe, never to be repeated with Justine or with any other girl he met.

His mother reappeared, dressed for the street in her brown raincoat and beret, and bearing his breakfast on a tray—boiled egg, toast, and marmalade—together with the day's *Express*. Why his apolitical, near anabaptist parents persisted in having Beaverbrook's Tory rag delivered daily, including Sunday, he would never fathom. Could it be, inertially, for the Rupert serial, which his mother had long since stopped reading aloud to Patrick, let alone to him? Could it be for the Osbert Lancaster cartoon which all the family still smiled at together on occasion? Or the rare advance publication in installments of a Ngaio Marsh detective novel, which he and his mother especially enjoyed following. It was certainly not for the intelligence and candour of any political commentary, domestic or foreign, that it made space for. And his mother was always complaining about the crassness of the crossword.

"I'm off," she said, by way of valediction.

"Aren't you going to be too warm," he said, noticing again how pale she looked, "in that coat and hat on a day like this?"

"Don't you worry your head about me, my boy," she said crossly. "You'd far better get started on packing for college, if you're going off gallivanting later on." There were freshly washed shirts and underthings, socks and pyjamas, piled on his chest of drawers. When the front door slammed behind her, he had already cracked his three minute egg, salted it, and settled down to read while he ate.

"Tievas Says Thank You But No Thank You," the banner headline snarled. "Red Leader Reneges." There was not a word on the front page about the previous night's speech, or in the brief editorial on it, that made any sense of what he had seen in the chapel. Whatever was actually going on was evidently nothing that newspapers could have anything serious to say about. All they had to hawk, other than unvarnished incident, of which there was hardly enough observable to fill one column, was pre-conceived Cold War attitude. Of this the *Express* had more than enough.

Predictably, the foreigner was mocked for his deplorable

manners, barbarian values, and lack even of political savvy. "Time was," grumbled the editorial, "when we looked to Tievas to set the East dancing, but no longer." The obvious inference from what had been said and done in the Painted Hall before lords of Admiralty and gentlemen of the Foreign Office was all too easily made. A client of the Kremlin first and last, he was as usual making fools of the British Labour government, especially Messrs. Bevin, McNeil, and Bevan if not of wiser heads in far off Washington, by feigning cooperation and then denying it. What conceivable profit there might be in such perversity for him, as leader of a distressed and disaffected Baltija, remained unasked. International politics, like domestic, was to be understood as a team sport in a pro league, spectacular, tactically dangerous, but very simple once you knew, or thought you knew, which side someone was on. Very simple, but very difficult, as Clausewitz says of war.

Brenan sighed, and settled for some of the turns of phrase, reported on the front page, from the opening paragraphs of the speech which he and Mackie had missed on television. "The people of the Baltic States, by their indomitable will and fearful sacrifices, have won the right to say 'No' to any and every neighbouring power in the world . . . . Free, independent, democratic, socialist Baltija is the achievement of no other nation but our own. In a world divided between titanic power blocs, the blackmail of small nations must be ended by their courage to say 'No' and, if need be, to die saying it—as our brothers, the South Slavs, our comrades in Algeria, in Indo China, and in Korea have said, and are saying." Who wrote Tievas' speeches in English for him, Brenan wondered. And what might the well-tempered *Observer* find to say about him on Sunday morning? He tossed aside the *Express*, put his empty breakfast crocks on the nightstand, and went to take a bath. With his mother out shopping and the place to himself, he could run a bumper, foaming bath from the expensive, noisy, gas-fired geyser in the big old bathroom out back, and lie in it for twenty minutes, luxuriant, easing into the day, thinking of Valija, her gentle eyes, her low voice.

"Are you finding anything, Michael?" She came up to him smiling, that afternoon at three. He had been standing outside the village bookshop next door to Christy's—like one of these young men in *The Arabian Nights* who open a market stall in order to capture someone long-lost or much desired—turning over slowly and longingly a furrow of secondhand sixpenny editions of Richard Jefferies and Edward Thomas. "How lovely to see you, Valija. Let me just pay for this one."

It was, she noted, *The Open Air,* collected pieces by Jefferies about wayside London and beyond. "You probably know the books of George Bourne about Surrey, too. I love the ones about Mr. Bettesworth and his wife." His purchase made, they came out of one shop and turned immediately into the next. Christy's was double-fronted, with bow windows; in them old china and fresh cake were tastefully displayed.

"*Change In The Village,* that's the one of Bourne's I know best. At Cambridge, I hear, they like to call him by his proper name, Sturt. No nonsense there. At Northfleet his name is not mentioned in any shape or form. The Oxford example."

"Those are not the newly cobbled shoes you promised to wear for me, are they?" He was wearing his usual tan lace ups with thick crepe soles, which he thought looked best with gaberdine and dark corduroy. She had led the way to a vacant table in the left hand window, looking out across the heath to Talbot Houses and All Saints' Church, and he was holding the back of her chair while she seated herself. Her shoulder length hair looked very blonde against the dark grey tweed dress she was wearing. Several other tables about the floor of the shop were already occupied by customers taking tea and making quiet conversation; and among them one of the waitresses in white cap and apron over a black dress was carefully making her way from behind the glazed counter at the rear in order to say with great formality, "Good afternoon, sir. Good afternoon, madame. May I take your order?" Christy's was very conscious of being old, pre-war Blackheath, and not for everybody.

When they were settled and had ordered, they sat silent, looking at one another across the crisp snowy table linen as if they were listening for something. Her face had the faintest of smiles which, though he had no idea what she might be thinking, reminded him of how agreeable they had seemed to find one another the previous afternoon at the Hospital. This is not some kind of surveillance, he told himself; this is a rendezvous. A red doubledecker bus, either a 54 or a 75, not a 108, trundled round the corner of Royal Parade and stopped opposite their window for a passenger or two to alight or board. On the piece of heath beyond, parents and children were flying kites in the autumn breeze. Farther over, out of sight around the point of Talbot Houses to the west, afternoon cricket was being played, while round to the east beyond All Saints', soccer games had started up despite the persistence of summer. Cricket and soccer both in the the same season, he reflected, a suburban English land of Cockaigne.

"You know, this whole stretch of green in front of us used to be a great pit of gravel before the war. Like the others about the heath, it has been levelled with debris from the Blitz and then turfed. Washerwoman's Hole it was called. I don't know why, because it was dry as dust with none of the gorse that grew in the other denes. Each year on Guy Fawkes' Night a huge bonfire would be lighted in it, and crowds would gather around the rim to watch and let off fireworks. My parents used to bring Patrick and me over here in the dark when we were nippers."

"You were fortunate to grow up in so pleasant and safe a part of the world as this."

"Yes, we owe it to my father. He wouldn't settle anywhere else, even if all he could afford was the bottom flat of a big old Victorian house. He grew up down in Greenwich, near the river, which he also loves. My mother was of two minds. She's a Suffolk woman, and I'm not sure that to her one London

suburb is so much better than another. I suspect that she used
to envy her youngest sister, who also came from the village to
the city, but stayed single and lived on Hill St. in Mayfair as
lady's maid to the Viscountess Chaplin—and died young in
the war or soon after. But you're right; I am lucky to have
grown up in a place that still means more to me than anywhere
in the world." The bus had pulled out of sight up the lip of the
heath, but now another one had pulled into its place opposite
their window with a flurry of Saturday afternoon passengers.
"You realize, the internal combustion engine, if not
overpopulation, is going to ruin it all anyway?"

"But you will be riding with your friend Mackie, or some
other friend, part of the problem, into the twilight, won't you?"

He looked at her with new respect. "This time tomorrow
Mackie will be riding the flood in the Estuary on course for
the port of Aden. But let's talk about you. Tell me about Baltija.
Tell me about Marshal Tievas and Dr. Didelis. He's all over
the papers today, you know—Tievas?"

"My country and its future are no better understood here
than in Moscow. Rationing, arrests, rumours of invasion, what
do they matter? Last Sunday one of your better papers made a
joke about keeping the Marshal alive to avoid a Third World
War between the USA and the USSR—'alive and kicking against
the pricks,'" she repeated sourly. "What can I tell you about
Baltija that will make any difference to such an attitude
towards small nations?"

Hearing in her voice a utopian faith in a people's democracy
under Tievas, he was struck once again by the difference
between her sense of herself as a Balt and his of his own
Britishness. In spite of all the social advantages he had enjoyed,
his sense of indebtedness, of engagement in a cause—to
whom? whose?—was almost nil. "Have you ever considered
asking for asylum and getting a British passport?"

"Of course," she said soberly.

"It's a necessary first step in any getting to America," he

said, teasing. "What about your uncle? Is he taking part in Tievas' doings over here this weekend?"

She hesitated. "I have no reason to think so. We have an arrangement to meet at a house in Norfolk next week; he will be there on Ben Jonson business with one of the Cambridge editors whereas Marshal Tievas, I believe, will be in Northfleet until he leaves for Gdainys on Wednesday or Thursday."

"Quite a coincidence."

"For you and me, perhaps, but not for the Vice Chancellor. He is the obvious one for the Marshal to make a social call on while over here. Have you met the Vice Chancellor? He has that quiet, informal English sort of brilliance that one doesn't seem to find anywhere else in Europe."

"Not to mention a certain saturnine, raised eyebrow effect. He tutors in the English department, you know, and I have had one of his essay questions to answer this summer, on *Antony and Cleopatra* of all things. My last effort for him was on *Tamburlaine,* and as he ran his eyes over it he said, kindly of course, 'You don't exactly *flow* when you write, do you, Mr. Brenan?' I felt like saying, 'And when will your next *Poems* be gushing from the presses, Sir Marcus?' But, of course, I didn't. It occurred to me when you were fuming just now about that *Observer* profile of Tievas, wouldn't the VC be the most likely suspect to have written it? He's our man in Gdainys, isn't he? How many others can there be?"

She was looking at him as if he needed comfort. "Let me pour you another cup of tea," she said, emptying hot water from the jug into the pot and stirring briskly. They had finished up the scones already. "These petits fours are just right." He held out his cup and saucer and, as she finished filling his cup three quarters full, a drop fell from the spout of the pot, leaving a little brown stain on the table linen between them. "Oh!" she sighed in annoyance. "Look at that!" Then she smiled at him, knowingly. "'The cloth immaculate' . . . now maculate as giraffe."

"You do like to dwell on that poem of mine, don't you?"

"Say it for me. I know how it begins—

> *Dusk discovers the Place Dauphine*
> *Calm after the evening's embrace—*

but I can't remember how to get to the lines I like best, about the table cloth."

He had never before said one of his poems aloud to anyone except himself. He finished the sentence she had left unfinished, his voice quavering—

> *Conspiracy! Of careless children, of*
> *Old men deliberate over their wine.*

Then she could join in, whispering so as not to attract the attention of anyone else in the shop—

> *Only the cloth on a cafe table*
> *Murmurs among the listening shadows,*
> 'Que j'ai voulu mourir pour une femme
> Qui ne me plaisait pas, qui n'était pas mon genre.'

He watched her lips. Something about the way they moved together and apart and her mouth shaped itself tended to make more than one sound out of any one syllable. Slavic sound, he told himself. She was a contralto, and always enunciated *largo*, as if speaking a barcarole. This had little to do with whatever she might actually be saying. He kept in time with her—

> *In an evening's quiet course*
> *The cloth, immaculate, sustains*
> *A drop of wine and words,*
> '*No, not again in the afternoon, I'm going out to tea.*'

She was laughing and suppressing her laughter like a school

girl. When they reached the lines she liked, he had broken off, but she went on. "Don't stop," she said. "Finish it." And he did—

> *And leaves of lime trees,*
> *Lately planted before the palace,*
> *Are paling into undertones,*
> 'Est-ce que tu as lu Stendhal? L'Amour . . .
> De l'Amour.'

"That's the trouble," he said. "I don't believe it *can* be finished. Just like in church."

"*Vespérale.* She must have stolen your heart," she said without sarcasm. "I have been in Paris in the summer, when most Parisians are out of the city. The Place Dauphine on the *île de la cité,* across the river from the Samaritain, can be very quiet at times."

"She didn't like my saying in a love poem that she wasn't my type and didn't please me. I'm not sure that she appreciated that those are Swann's words and not mine. She did please me, of course—just not quite as much as I would have liked."

Valija smiled again, as if she understood that even a man who has lost his heart still likes to be made much of. "Proust was not for her. And you were for someone else. And where is she now?"

"In Paris, I suppose. She married a man at the Sorbonne."

She took a packet of De Reszke Minors out of her purse and held them up. "Do you mind if I smoke? Would you like one?" He shook his head apologetically and passed her the ash tray from his side of the table. She had no lighter, and lit her cigarette with a match. "I think I saw the film you echo at the end of your poem. Was it *La Ronde* or *Edouard et Caroline?*"

He looked out at the heath. From where they were each seated, she could see the spired gothic pile of All Saints', anchored in the grassy fairway, while what he saw in the distance was the Hare and Billet corner, the pub with its willow-planted pond and horse rail. "You know, I've been going off French films lately. You'll probably give me a VC smile when I tell you, but the film I couldn't forget all this summer was American. It's four or five years old, a tragic love story, and it has an unforgettable moment between Mitchum and the lovely brunette, whatever her name is, when he kisses her and says, 'Baby, I don't *care*!'"

"Ah, Michael, you will always be ahead of me in film studies. If only there are questions in film instead of philology on your finals next year, you will be in clover. But I did see that American thriller, I think. It has a quite improbable title, *Build My Gallows High*. However, the director, isn't he a Frenchman?"

It was his turn to laugh. "Yes, so he is. But the man who wrote the book is still a Californian." It was her turn to look quizzically out at the heath. "In this creeping Americanism of yours, do I detect the influence of our charming Marianne?"

"Hardly. I came by it all by myself, reading Faulkner and Fitzgerald."

She went on looking out of the window, smoking her cigarette. "There's no cinema here in the village, is there? This must be the largest district in the whole of greater London without one—though, I am forgetting; isn't there one over near the Royal Standard? That would be within the district."

"But you're right about the heath and the village. They are protected by the Society, I expect. Just as well, since there are cinemas in Lee Green, Lewisham, Deptford, Greenwich, Woolwich, all round. I wish we had time to go to the cinema this evening. Cocteau's *Orphée* is on at the Everyman. Wouldn't you love to see it again?"

"The Everyman, in Hampstead!" she exclaimed, ruefully for his sake. "How ever many times have you seen *Orphée* already?" Christy's was fast emptying of its afternoon tea takers. "I think we should start now if we are going to walk back to the Merchant Hospital. Thank you so much for this." They had emptied the teapot and eaten all the scones and cakes. "It has been like being back in Linz for the afternoon. Will you let me pay my share?"

He shook his head. The waitress was at hand with a bill, which he paid; and they left. "It is good of you to offer to share. But the government gives me a generous grant to go to college because I did National Service in the army. It is my treat to have your company."

She said nothing about her own source of income.

He said, "About the village having no cinema, I think the joke is that it once had a film studio of historic importance— in Bennett Park, just opposite the Railway Tavern. Do you know, those wonderful documentaries that the GPO film unit made in the middle '30s—*Night Mail* and so on—were actually worked on there? My father, who is in the P.O., tells of being tapped to appear on the sound stage some morning to act out a scene of a letter box being cleared for the 6:30 collection."

She said nothing about his father in reply. The cinema ceased to be a topic of their conversation, and nothing took its place. They walked in an easy silence up on to the heath and along a much frequented Montpelier Row to the point by the pub where the road divides around the Prince of Wales' Pond. A few children and their parents lingered on its banks, sailing toy boats in the breeze, the children with Wellington boots splashing in the shallows when they could. The Merchant Hospital was now almost in sight along South Row. He was taking the longer way round the pond, to the north and east, when she asked, "Why are we going this way?"

"I want to show you my favourite inscription, on the drinking fountain over there," he indicated the far margin of the pond through the willows. "We can cut across the grass directly to the Hospital gates from there, if this is all right with you." He glanced at her sensible black shoes.

She went along with him, graciously enough, but was not impressed by the inscription; and as they strode on, ankle deep in grasses, she said lightly, "Let me confess something to you, Michael. Your William and Mary chapel doesn't please me very much either, inscribed or not. I can't believe that Sir Christopher Wren had much to do with that wagon roof. The whole room is neither medieval nor classical, not my idea of a chapel at all—a sacred kitchen, rather—no arches, no aisles, no banners 'blown by the night wind of heaven.'"

He hardly knew what to say. "At least the founder and the foundress sleep below."

Now they were in full view of an elegant Regency terrace that curved to its perigee just above the gates of the Hospital. "I should think, if you want me to admire anything, it would be the Paragon," she said in mock reproach. "What else for a crescent is there to compare between Regent's Park and Bath?" Her English syntax seemed for once to have become mixed up with her German.

He could only slip his left hand under her elbow and squeeze gently, while in eloquent silence gesturing with his right. And she inclined her head as if the cross were passing them in church.

"I am not sorry to be moving on north tomorrow." For some reason when she said this, it made him wonder about the Chaplain. But it was the gang of four that he wanted to hear about.

"I've been meaning to ask you about your Ben Jonson seminar. We never have come round to your interest in him and his tragedies. Your fellow students have already moved on, I gather. Pity. I should have liked to meet them. Where are they based?" He tried to sound calm and pleasantly indifferent, but his voice must have betrayed some of the feeling swirling within him—about the grotesquerie of the scene in the chapel, the violence to the helpless man, the threat to himself if he were noticed, and now his own undeniable desire for this unforgettable girl.

"My fellow students? Why do you need to know about my fellow students? Take care how you deal with them, if ever you get involved." She gave her most rueful smile. "They are a very"—she searched for the idiom, found it and, like the pedant she meant to become, put it into quotation marks—"'mixed bag,' a handful. All I have in common with them is that we owe Dr. Didelis everything. Antsoras, Baltrušaitis, Čiabuvis, Draugiski: I wouldn't know where to begin sorting them out. Dispositions that make for a lively seminar on Jonson's tragedies can turn out to be intolerable in any other context. I may never set eyes on any of them again—or, of course, I may."

They came down to the Hospital gates underneath the gabled windows of the porter's lodge and stopped and turned to look each other in the eyes.

"I wish I had known you were here before it was time to move on. There is so much I should like to share with you." He put his arms around her waist and they kissed fondly on the lips. Under the hint of tobacco he tasted a moist and maternal warmth.

"I should like to invite you in, but you know that wouldn't do." She slipped her arms lightly around him and patted him consolingly, "Be brave, now. You are going to find me on the train to Northfleet tomorrow night, aren't you?"

She went through the wicket, and at the first turn in the drive looked back and waved. He waved too, and went on his own way up and across the heath.

Walking home through the mews-like avenue of Angerstein Lane, over shifting pebbles and wanwood, with more leaf fluttering down, he told himself, "I don't want to lose her, now that I've found her"; and the response came, "Only time will tell."

Chapter Three

Gatherings on the Sabbath

i

How I have ever loved the life removed
~Shakespeare

S unday was like no other day of the week for Michael Brenan that summer because his father was free of work and could rest with the family at home. His mother made a special breakfast for the three of them at the scrubbed table in the kitchen, and they sat down together and shared some of what was uppermost in their thoughts over bacon and eggs and toast and tea. Sunday was Sunday, after all, a day of rest, if not for her. There was no delivery of mail, but she'd have thought, she said, that a letter from that boy Patrick in Germany would have come by this time: it was three weeks and more since she had posted him a parcel of necessaries and good things to eat. The tone in which she said "in Germany" made it sound as if her younger son were off in the high Himalayas or Arctic Circle. His father allowed glumly that, for all the flying that was going on nowadays, the mail seemed to be slower and slower in transit.

They sat on three sides of the table, which stood against an inner wall of the kitchen under a counter and shelves where the pots and pans hung from hooks or stood ready for use, their handles to hand. His father sat between Brenan and his mother, at the head of the table as it were, though his well-worn Windsor chair was, as usual, set at an angle facing his wife rather than the wall and her utensils. Brenan, from his chair, could thus look at him in half profile, backlighted from the front window: not precisely handsome, but with a very pleasant turn of features—fine, in fact, with clear blue eyes and a graying head of close-cropped hair, chin freshly shaven, shirt washed and ironed, tie ironed, tie neatly tied, suit pressed, brown shoes polished—all smartened up for walking out on a Sunday morning after church parade—except that there was no longer a church listed in his pay book—and no pay book in his pocket. It was thirty-three years since he had been in the army, yet certain quirks of a soldier's habit of life had never left him. Now, within sight of sixty and retirement from the Post Office on a pension, he had felt his working life crumble beneath him when, immediately after the war, the whole service had been reorganized and redefined on some new mid-century model unacceptably different from the Victorian paramilitary one which he had signed on for as a boy at his father's bidding. "The service has gone to pot," he would say, shaking his head sadly.

Brenan had never been able to grasp just how the Great Reform of the G.P.O. had managed to ruin his father's hitherto happy working life, but it manifestly had. Promotion and wage increases, as bargained for by the Union—of which his father was a reluctant member—did not seem to be lacking. Under the Labour government's new regulation of postal work, grandfathering had provided him—already content though he was—with both. He now went daily by bus to a minor supervisory position at the Rotherhithe office, no longer cycling in uniform about the open heath in all weathers as he loved to do. His new work only rarely treated him to an escape from his desk in the Cage (as it was called by postmen in the field) to answer a call that meant going aboard one of the merchant ships tied up along the Surrey Commercial wharves and dealing with the deck officer on duty. As a boy messenger in Greenwich before the first war, he had once gone so far as to take a boat out to a merchantman anchored in the river and beg the captain to let him sign on for the voyage, only to be kindly but firmly refused—an odd story for his sons to have enjoyed listening to.

His recent trouble, when he spoke of it, seemed to be rather a case of time's revenges than of the new regime at work, something to do with the end of discipline (one of his key words), of respect for seniority, of comradeship, even of being a sort of soldier of the old Queen—this in spite of her being dead before he was ten. Some generational sense of loss, of love as well as of duty, at home as well as at work, had left him with little more faith in life at age fifty-nine than a longing for sunny days between the wars, at his favourite office, in his favourite haunts, when he and his wife were still, not just a young couple, albeit with children, but sweethearts. "You can go off people, you know," he had been heard to say moodily over a Sunday glass of Whitbread's brown at the Anti-Gallican not far from the river.

"I went for a walk round the terrace before breakfast," he now said to his elder son, "and picked up an *Observer* for you when I paid for the week's papers. It's on the front room table. Did you see it?"

Brenan nodded, thanking him with a smile. There had been next to nothing about Tievas in the *Observer* this time. History—newspaper history, at least—was marching on.

They had finished their meal and stacked the plates in the sink for washing by hand with water from the kettle. His father took off his jacket and rolled up his sleeves in order to do the necessary, while his mother began shelling a mound of green peas on the table. Brenan helped her. She said, "These aren't anything to write home about, but we're lucky to have peas at all at this time of the year, *and* I didn't have to pay the earth for them."

His father, watching the suds rehearse down the drain, the breakfast dishes and cutlery drying, said, "If you're not going to church"—for the past year or two Brenan had been openly entertaining the idea of being a Roman Catholic—"what do you say to a walk along the river while the good weather lasts? It'll be high tide around eleven and there should be plenty of shipping on the move. I believe that presidential yacht from the Baltic will be leaving Greenwich buoys this morning."

While Brenan was nodding assent and wondering at the smallness of the world, his mother broke in with, "Now, you together, don't be forgetting that dinner is at one-thirty sharp today. A nice leg of lamb roasted, and no keeping me on tenterhooks, you hear." The riverside, and the beer and billiards in its several pubs were what her husband tended to share with their boys, while her treat for them was always a walk through the park with a picnic tea in its flower garden to follow. "I hope to goodness you've done your packing," she added darkly for Brenan's benefit, "*if* you're still catching a train this evening, that is." He reassured her with a wry grimace, and kissed her sallow cheek. The war had ended long since, but not the anxiety it had caused her.

"I expect our Mick would rather stow away on that little motor yacht of old Tievas' and arrive in Northfleet by sea," said his father, teasing.

"I should smile," his mother said crossly. "That'd be the long way round, and no mistake." She shelled the last of the peas into the colander and swept the empty pods off the table top into a brown paper bag, while Brenan and his father collected themselves quickly and took to the street, "making themselves scarce," as she would put it. "One-thirty sharp," she called after them.

Turning left out of Heathdene's now ungated front garden

into the broad avenue of Vanbrugh East with its plane trees and grey brick villas aloof behind walls, his father took the lead, saying, "This way to the pier always makes me think of those early Saturday morning starts of ours in the middle '30s, going for a fortnight's summer holiday at dear old Herne Bay. You boys would have been only six and four then, at the most. For a few years I was able to talk your mother into going by paddle steamer down river instead of taking the Southern Railway. We had to march through the park to the pier, lugging our suitcases, because there was no bus from here to there unless we went miles roundabout. Young Patrick I had to carry on my back part of the way, you remember. Your mother has always hated to go anywhere by water. But once we'd arrived safely she was fine."

Brenan noted with satisfaction that this morning his father's mood was unreservedly reminiscent. "Yes, they were glorious June days down in Kent, bathing on the sands towards Whitstable, picnicking in Bishopstone Glen at Reculver, sightseeing in Canterbury, riding through the dusky lanes on the open top of the local bus, singing 'Show me the way to go home.'"

Father and son smiled fondly together, their eyes misting. "A sight better than Margate sands, anyway, mobbed as they always were," said his father, seeming to mimic his severe, long suffering Suffolk wife in one of her many judicious findings.

Turning left again along Westcombe Edge towards the park, they began looking mostly to the north where now familiar but nonetheless melancholy bomb sites were fewer than on the south side. Soon it was the flagrant white villa of the Vaughans that they were passing, as softly lapped in Sunday morning calm as any of its more traditional looking neighbours, and enigmatically inscribed on its gate pillars with the name of St. Mary. Prompted perhaps by the coincidence that the village church where Michael sometimes went was also St. Mary's, his father said, "I'm glad you didn't feel you had to go to mass on your last morning at home—last morning for a while, at least."

Brenan knew that the first time his father had refused communion had been on the eve of September 15, 1916, in front of High Wood before going over with the 1st London Irish against the Germans who were well dug in beyond the shattered tree line. "It's not as if it were the first time," Brenan said. He waited a few paces on the much mended pavement— not square paving stones but rough convex tarmac brimming the kerb—and then he tried to make a detour in their talk. "It's a long while since Patrick and John and I last listened to one of your war stories, like losing your good rifle in the mud and fishing out some other poor blighter's dud one instead that took all night to clean for inspection. On that run from B.H.Q. to Bazentin-le-petit, was it?"

His father said nothing, but nodded grimly in reminiscence of the occasion itself.

"I was wondering last night about the story in which you were once guarding those prisoners and they escaped and you first came to know Mr. Vaughan. You must have told us that one when he and Mrs. Vaughan first came to live here, early in the war."

"Yes, Dr. Thomas would probably never have parted with 57A if it hadn't been for the threat of bombing and his being near retirement. He wanted to move away from the Edge, and Mr. Vaughan was somehow on hand, another Welshman, and ready to invest. I don't know where he and Mrs. Vaughan lived before the war, but they obviously didn't mind moving into a Jerry-style house. Can't say I'd care for it myself, would you?" In passing they pondered the finer and worse points of 57A.

"Dr. Thomas was our G.P. up to the war, you remember," his father went on. "He kept surgery hours in the old house next door, 57, where he first lived. He was the doctor that took care of young Patrick's rupture back in '35, when he was in the Miller Hospital for three weeks. As luck would have it, neither 57 nor 57A caught a packet during the Blitz, so the

Vaughans' gamble paid off. You can bet they were able to beat old Thomas down in price a few hundred in the autumn of '39." He shook his head ruefully. "Seems more like a century ago now, doesn't it—that 'phony war' of ours, as the Yanks liked to call it?"

It was not the late doctor's, but his father's own dealing with Vaughan that Brenan wanted to hear about. He was still in two minds—for Valija's sake as much as his own—whether or not to tell his Tievas story to someone in authority. Tired of turning round in his head the possible meanings of what he had seen, he longed for some action, some closure. What he knew about Tievas was now "nearer than the eye." But who that had a stake in the situation—whatever it was—would be grateful to him for confiding and not turn on him, if he told what little he had to tell? He said, "You hadn't set eyes on Vaughan till he came to live here, then, not since you and he had been in the 3rd Battalion together?"

"No, and I can't say I saw much of him then. He was a first lieutenant and I was a sergeant, working for my crown on the P.T. staff at the depot in Rugeley. A training camp, deep in Cannock Chase—coal and iron country—a pretty harsh spot. Acres of huts in the middle of nowhere, nasty atmosphere, what with the constant threat of being posted back to the front, and the Adjutant and the R.S.M., who were both bastards. The R.S.M. had it in for me because I wasn't a regular and was moving up too fast in the sergeants' mess.

"One night I was sergeant of the guard when very early in the morning I realized that four Jerry prisoners had escaped from the cells." He paused at this point, not for effect but because they were crossing the intersection of Vanbrugh West and Coleraine Road. "It was my responsibility. They had been there when I took over the guard room. They must have opened up their tunnel at the very dead of night and all scarpered across the moors. At the moment, I probably had my head down on the guard room table, kipping; and the lads in my detail, those that weren't out at their posts, all had their feet up too. At about 3 a.m. when I saw the cells were empty, talk about panic! But, thank goodness, the best thing to do came to me right away.

"Instead of sounding the alarm, I sent my smartest lad over to the officers' mess at the double to rouse the Orderly Officer—and *only* the Orderly Officer—telling him to come to the guard room, by himself, because there was a five hundred point flap in the making. The lad found him and he came at once: it was Lt. Vaughan of D Company. Needless to say, he hadn't shown his face all night since guard mounting.

"I shall never forget how he took it when I showed him the tunnel under one of the bunks in the cell—an object lesson in using your loaf under pressure, even after a night on the bottle and playing euchre for high stakes. He didn't turn on me at all as he might have. He said, 'Look you, sergeant, this way out wasn't engineered on our watch, yours or mine. So all we have to do is keep our stories straight. Let me sign your book to the effect that all has seemed to be in order till now—as I should have done earlier if I hadn't been blotto. Then I'll get over to the Adjutant and sound the alarm, and you can wake up the R.S.M. Just keep your head. Those Jerries won't get far in this weather.'

"And so we got away with it: no court martial. He ended the war a captain and I got my crown. The Adjutant and the R.S.M. tried to be difficult of course, but the inquiry couldn't get round our individual statements and the evidence of the orderly room book that routine checks had been made. We weren't the only ones responsible by a long chalk. Once the tunnel had been dug, getting away down it immediately after a check had been made could have been done at any time. Of course, prisoners would wait for dark. I was supposed to be out of the guard house changing the guard every two hours anyway."

"Sounds to me," said Brenan thoughtfully, "as if Mr. Vaughan still owes you."

"It was mutual," said his father.

They had now traced Westcombe Edge to its end at Maze Hill and entered Greenwich Park at the narrow iron gate arched in a high brick wall opposite Vanbrugh Castle. Before them the parkland fell steeply away, letting the town, the Queen's house, the National Maritime Museum colonnades, the twin domes of the Naval College, and the great river curving away up to the city in the west, all be seen to advantage over treetops. On the well-planted terrace path below the Observatory, Brenan said, "Talking of panic, I had a queer experience myself a week or two ago, right in here. Quite early one morning—you remember I had a regular tennis game with Des Innes until he went off on his field trip—I was on my way to meet him at the Ranger's House courts, going along that shady footpath outside the flower garden under the chestnuts. The park gates had only just been opened and everywhere was fresh and green and quiet, except for the birds. There was no one about—or so I thought—none of the clash of those thin iron railings all round the garden when someone goes in and out.

"You know how high and heavy the rhododendron is just there, right inside the railing. As I moved along, my tennis shoes making very little noise, the glimpses I got of the flower garden— the dahlia beds and those great old cedars Mum loves—were few and far between. But gradually the sound of voices, two men disagreeing about something, altercating, was carried over to me. I thought at first they would be a couple of the gardeners getting an early start, but it soon dawned on me that the sound was all wrong for labouring men. And when I at last got a good look at them through the shrubbery, they weren't gardeners at all but government men from Whitehall or the City—black coats, pinstripe trousers, bowler hats. One of them was propped on his umbrella, as if it were a shooting stick, and the other looked as if he might be Mr. Vartan, our landlord, on his way to the station— only he wasn't—same *pince nez* but much more dangerous looking."

"I don't think I ever saw Mr. Vartan in a bowler hat," said his father unhelpfully.

"I was amazed, for some reason—astonished, astounded. Before I knew what I was doing, I had come to a full stop, gone into a crouch, and was eavesdropping at a little gap in the leaves where I couldn't be seen. They were arguing angrily, ferociously, but I couldn't make out a single word they said— except, at one moment, the name 'Mary' something.

"I don't know what came over me. I was trembling like a leaf, confident that something very wrong was taking place. Then I came to my senses, caught sight of myself, so to speak, a preposterous figure in whites, clutching his racquet, loitering at 7 a.m. in a royal park in southeast London with intent to overhear . . . but what? . . . who? Who knows who? Ludicrous.

"So I took off like a squirrel, before some park keeper in uniform could haul me off to the Superintendent's office on suspicion. I arrived at the grass courts ahead of Des, but he still beat me handily in straight sets . . . that time."

His father was now contemplating the somewhat drab spectacle of the northeast corner of the park at which they had arrived, the lower end of Croom's Hill overlooked by the church of Our Lady Star of the Sea. Somewhere in West Greenwich or Deptford, over the hum of town, a faint bell was tolling believers to one or another of several churches. "Yes, you can get into trouble that way. There's no telling what may be going on in times like these," he said morosely. "You can only use your loaf and hope for the best, as I was telling you just now."

The road they were taking to the pier led out through a huge ornamental gateway, past the statue of a king outside the National Maritime Museum, and down a sadly battered stretch called King William Walk. The king was William IV, not the founder of the Naval College buildings and husband of Mary. Brenan's father picked up the pace, breathing in with relish the faint riverine smell of oil and tar that floated on the breeze. Occasionally, sounds of a ship's siren or hooter came to them, holiday noise complimenting the Marshal on his departure by sea, none of the thunder and rattle of a working day on the industrial Thames.

They came out on the riverscape right at the entrance to Greenwich Pier, to be greeted by the cry of swooping gulls. The air above Deptford was light with a faint shivering of the currents, and on the wharves of Silvertown only a slight haze rested. Quite a crowd of sightseers had gathered, many more than would ordinarily turn out on a fine Sunday to watch shipping come down on the tide. All the seats on the pier itself ("Admission 1d.") had been taken. An overflow was filling up the nearby bankside where, until the Blitz cleared it, the Ship Hotel had stood looking on to the buoys. Off the end of the pier, in the shadow of pilings, a manned police launch waited, churning the brown swell but neither making way nor drifting.

"One day they'll bring the *Cutty Sark* up here into dry dock," said his father, prompting Brenan to chant facetiously, "'Fairest clipper ever built.'"

Out in the fairway a little upstream, the *Dolphynas* could be seen, still at anchor, swanlike stem plunging and rising on the flood. She was showy in the old-fashioned, Edwardian way, high in superstructure, narrow of beam, one-funnelled, gleaming with white paint, polished wood, brass. Her stern curved under like the stern of a tea clipper, yet fore and aft a twin and a single battery of light guns had been emplaced. Gangway raised, launch inboard, she already had a pair of Royal Naval torpedo boats dancing attendance, raring to go.

All Greenwich Reach seemed to be flattered by her presence this far from Gdainys. Working day or not for bargebuilders, crane drivers, and stevedores, both shores were busy with movement and noise. A string of commerce on its way from London Pool and the Surrey Docks rounded the bend at Deptford Creek and passed the pier and Naval College before rounding the other bend at Blackwall and disappearing down towards Woolwich: a transatlantic freighter under the Panamanian flag; a General Steam Navigation Company coaster; a Union Castle liner from the West India Docks at

Limehouse; and one of the last of the Thames spritsail barges, its ochre red sails full-bellied in the breeze, its strake daringly low in the water. As they passed by the *Dolphynas* on the other side, most of them would sound off; and all along the Isle of Dogs tug boat captains and lightermen would join in the salute.

Unslinging a small leather case from his left shoulder, his father said, "I remembered to bring your Uncle Horace's binoculars. Wish I'd remembered to bring our old Kodak, too. We could have bought film at the shop on the pier."

"See if you can spot what that low-lying black ship with the buff funnel is, astern of the sailing barge. It has no name on the bow, but it looks to be flying the blue ensign."

His father tried to oblige, but the crowd they were now part of surged and jostled unrelentingly around them, hampering focus. Italian ice cream and peanut vendors, crying out in demotic English, urged their barrows through the throng.

"I'll tell you what, Mick. Let's go along to the point by the Trafalgar and watch. It won't be so crowded and we'll have a better view down river."

As they started on the two or three hundred yards to a new vantage point, his father said, "That one with the buff funnel must be a War Department coaster for delivering guns and munitions from Woolwich Arsenal. Her name'll be on the stern like a Navy ship's, you'll see—if we're in time for another glimpse." But they were not. They had to pass viewless through the unpaved, tree-shadowed alley between the backs of the pier buildings and the College perimeter, down below the Dreadnought Hospital.

Coming out on the riverscape again, looking east and north, they were far from any crowd, almost solitary and suddenly dwarfed where they stood by the most spectacular onset of riparian buildings this side of Venice, heroic stone monuments to the imagination of Wren, Vanbrugh, Hawksmoor, and their royal patrons—though for the first hundred and fifty years used as a draughty hospital for old and wounded seamen: the King Charles block ("Carolus II Rex / A.Reg.XVI," said the pediment) and the Queen Anne block with the domed blocks of King William and Queen Mary behind; and between their long colonnades an endless vista from the River Gates where Tievas had landed on Friday up to the Queen's House in the park with Wolfe's statue and the Royal Observatory on the green heights beyond. It was enough to make the skin prickle, the hair start up and stand on end, as well as to render the twin towers of the generating station and the Boord Street gasometer further east virtually invisible.

"To think that Nelson lay in there, dead, and Collingwood, too," said his father. "And Admiral Byng," said Brenan, "alive, after losing Minorca, but about to be shot *pour encourager les autres.*"

To get to the point they were making for, they had to go right across the facade of the College on a narrow footpath, close under tall black railings. It was little more than a ledge where two could hardly walk side by side in comfort. A fathom and more immediately below lay the drowned foreshore where, on days like this at a time other than the height of the tide, children and parents could pretend they were beachcombing at the seaside.

Brenan thought he had never seen the now ebbing tide slap so fiercely at the worn paving of this footpath. With the next wave or two it could plunge through the handrail and sweep them off their feet into the fairway. He was wearing his newly mended, well-polished walking shoes, which Valija still had her doubts about, or pretended to. In his head the whole swirling, centrifugal scene was for once more Turner than Canaletto; nothing reconciled, nothing serene. But his father only remarked, jauntily, that at least they weren't getting their feet wet. When by water, whatever its mood, he was always at his most carefree. "There is a river whose streams make glad the city . . . ."

Gilded river gates and submerged water stairs well behind them, they came to where the tall railings of the College take a sharp corner around a lawn's end and chestnut trees into

Park Row before the Trafalgar Hotel. At this point, a crescendo
of siren and hooter told them that the Tievas flotilla was at
last putting out from the buoys. They turned and stood
watching it approach, pass, and then recede on the flood,
Brenan with the family binoculars. He wondered whirlingly if
what he bent his eye on was, for the third time in two days,
mere vacancy. "Tievas on the brain!" would have been his
mother's remark if she had known what he was experiencing.
But what did it matter, he tried to tell himself, whether the
Ghost was actually present or not, so long as the play went on.

On the bridge of the *Dolphynas* and along her decks and
companion ways, there were occasional uniformed figures to
be made out, indistinctly. He gave his father the binoculars.
"There's a pilot aboard, I suppose."

"As far as Tilbury, I should think."

"How many crew, would you say?"

"Not above ten, I seem to remember reading."

"What would her tonnage be?"

"A thousand or so. Less than two hundred feet long, don't
you think?"

"Hardly a frigate at all, not even a corvette. Why call her
that because of a couple of guns?"

"Honorary. Just a lovely little diesel yacht for cruising at
sea, not for crossing the ocean."

Down Blackwall Reach the flotilla dwindled and
disappeared, leaving them both with a moment of loss. Twenty
miles and more downstream, the sea-reach of the Thames
would open out to the east under a shining blue sky that was
welded to the North Sea waves. Staring silently at a P. & O.
freighter and a little Dutch trader in line astern, they were
surprised to hear an amused Welsh voice saying quietly behind
them, "Brenans, good morning. Lovely morning for a
constitutional. Keeping an eye on things, I see."

It was Inspector Vaughan—in the company of another
man, presumably a plainclothes colleague, up on the grass verge
in the shadow of the chestnut trees—vigilant behind the

College railings. Both Brenans felt awkward, caught off guard, as if redhanded; but there was no avoiding him, so they turned to greet him with suspicious smiles He said to Brenan, "I'm not used to seeing you about, young man. Have you finished your time with the Royal West Kents, like father, like son?"

Brenan nodded. "That was a year or two back. I was demobbed in '49," and his father added, "Now he's doing a college degree, at Northfleet."

"Is he indeed?" Vaughan looked at Brenan with new interest, before looking away down river to where the *Dolphynas* had disappeared. Now might have been the moment for Brenan to confide in Vaughan, if only they had been by themselves; but Brenan's father would never see why his son was turning first to a virtual stranger for help—'tec or not—instead of to him. He would be deeply hurt. And even if Vaughan and his Special Branch colleague were to act at once on information received, rushing over to the Merchant Hospital in flying squad fashion, the suspect they would come up with would be Valija whereas it was the fugitive gang of four that Brenan wanted to see rousted.

"We ought to be moving on," his father said, also looking down river. "We want to make it as far as the Sea Witch before stopping for a pint and still be home in time for Sunday dinner."

Out of earshot of the two watchers, a step or two lag in entering the dismal confines of Crane Street, his heart under his feet, Brenan heard his father whisper, conspiratorially, "On duty, you realize. Why he didn't introduce the other wallah."

ii

Est aliquid prodisse tenus
It is a trap to have produced anything

~Seneca

Whenever the four Balts met in their Committee of Safety mode, Dr. Jurgis Didelis, even if absent as now, was a real presence at the table. Department meetings, he had long since impressed on them, were the very stuff of his social life—by which he meant Jonson seminars and scene rehearsals, as well as mission briefings and committees, any skirmish for several voices that pitted people of intelligence one against another. "Jurgis' adversarial mode" Juozas Draugiski liked to call it with his hint of a smile, as if that somehow disposed of the matter once and for all.

Each of the Dwarves, including Valija, was a perverse mimicry of Didelis in one or other of his finer aspects. Where he was learned, Valija was pedantic; and as for the others, it was the iron of his wilfulness—not his wit, heart, or reason—that had entered their souls and determined their tone and manners when meeting together. But nothing they could do or say, either at home or, as now, in the field, ever seemed to please him. Lover of old plays, soldier, actor, secret agent, he had in his inimitable way once and for all been very generous to each of them after the war, had favoured them as wandering ex-service students of English with his mentorship. Now they were his forever, his punishment, his scourge, the revenge for his love.

Meeting this Sunday under his absent supervision at Merewell Castle in northeast Norfolk, they were a credit to the harsh truth that everyone, in spite of comradeship, ultimately pleases himself and keeps his own secret to the end. But having undergone initiation into the cult, in which speaking English was mandatory, and remained followers for five years and more, they outwardly betrayed only one other collective mark, a stringent, combative intelligence, the ambition to be right. If only this could have overcome in them the self-flattering will simply to have one's own way in everything.

His chosen deputy, intensely serious Jaan Antsoras from Tallinn—known to familiars as the Stork for some wartime fiasco with a captured German Fiesler—had called the meeting for 2 p.m. in the centre of the flagstoned basement of the castle. On this occasion there was for once no table to sit around. Each found a folding, slatted, wood and iron garden chair in green and set it up for himself at one of the four points of the compass. From here, at ground level and regardless of poor light, one or another of them could keep an eye out at all times, not only on the barred door to the prisoner's windowless cell but also, through an open door at every side, on any approach from a distance, north, south, east or west.

For these remaining days of summery October Merewell made a well-chosen hiding place. There was no neighbouring house, no nearby village; any former outbuilding had long since decayed, fallen, and been cleared away, even the little lodge down by the front gate on to the sunken lane. Isolated in high, sheltered ground, inland from bluffs between Sheringham and Wells, little known because privately owned until the war and now vacant and unattended during a transfer from War Department to Ministry of Works control, it was an eighteenth century, not a mediaeval castle. Like Vanbrugh's much bigger one at Greenwich, a folly rather than a fortress, this one was a little hunting lodge *cum* trysting place designed in the 1720s by Colin Campbell on the distant model of Palladio's Villa Capra near Vicenza.

A domed, slightly squat, splendidly porticoed rotunda of two storeys, all plaster and glass within but sadly dilapidated, rests upon a solid foursquare rusticated base, set in a grassy mound, the circle firmly squared, the balloon tethered. The whole *jeu d'esprit* fits neatly into a space of thirty feet cubed. On each side at ground level a twin staircase stands akimbo, rising to the first and only glamorous storey with its somewhat sullen little dome; and in between each of these a great single door, on the model of Inigo Jones's for the Queen's House at Greenwich, opens into a grotto-like garden court, ringed by little rooms serviceable for the barer necessities of country living. It was to this level of the castle, connected by narrow spiral steps in every corner with the pantheon above, that the

Department more or less confined itself, as well as its now inert prisoner.

"You can't say that Jurgis doesn't look out for us when it comes to finding a billet," Draugiski had remarked the Friday night before, chiefly for the benefit of Antsoras as he pulled the Austin out of the lane, through the gate to which he had a key, and—the van whining in low gear—into the upland clearing where the castle lay, virtually unespied except from seaward. The van was foetid after carrying the four with their clobber and prisoner all the way from London, and through its windshield Merewell at first sight had the melancholy aspect of some benighted mausoleum raised by a maniac.

Antsoras and Draugiski were indulging in that serial exchange of theirs concerning the supposed virtue or foible of whatever their mentor had seen fit to bring about this time. "One friend in a high place at the Ministry," Antsoras had replied, "and what whim need be denied? They say Byron himself once slept here."

"Alive? Or Undead?" said Draugiski sourly, having been the one to get out and open the rusty gate and then close it behind them. On the damp night air of the wood there was a briny North Sea smell. But once the van had been stabled in the basement, the prisoner incarcerated, water turned on, and candles and primus stoves lighted, the castle began to seem more than a mere whim of all-providing Jurgis.

By the time the four had got to know their new quarters and settled into them, Saturday's dawn was reddening the sky above the trees. "Not the worst bivouac we've ever made," said Baltrušaitis cheerily, as he handed the .303 rifle and the care of the closely mewed prisoner over to Čiabuvis.

"Not by any means," Čiabuvis had agreed in his expansive, self-satisfied way. "Burlington was already Lord Lieutenant of the East and West Ridings of Yorkshire and Lord Treasurer of Ireland when he dreamed this little beauty up." He looked about the well-appointed base court for Antsoras and Draugiski, not wanting them to miss a better first footnote than either of theirs.

"Upon a summer's day," writes one of the Sitwells about Merewell Castle during the second war, "you may look right through, in at one portico and out through the pillars of the other, while the smaller rooms in the angles seem contrived for shade and cool." Contrived for shade and cool . . . not to mention conspiracy. In the unlikely event of other unexpected intruders' arriving, they might climb the staircases, tour the terraces, try the locks and look through the shutters all in vain, never seeing who lay below, silent, vigilant, behind the massive garden doors.

Except for standing guard two hours out of every eight, the gang had spent the daylight of their first day resting in sleep or solitude, and Saturday night and Sunday morning settling into a mutual routine. Now, in committee, with the doors wide to rustlings and zephyrs from the upland meadow in sunshine, they each sat staring past one another at a distant wood-end, waiting for Antsoras to begin. Having only recently finished eating and drinking their field rations, they nursed no distracting mug of coffee or mess tin of tea. Nobody, not even Draugiski, smoked. Jurgis, who had his puritan side too where meetings were concerned, would certainly have approved.

Antsoras looked west, with the .303 lying on the floor beside him and the prisoner's cell door directly in view. It was on his spell of guard duty that the gang was meeting. Routinely, the one on guard would walk the margin of the court, giving a careful eye to every door, grille, and window. He was the eldest and least athletic of the four, a stringy, brooding caustic person from the Estonian marches of Baltija. A driving worker, a fussbudget, always divided in mind between received scruples of human feeling and some abstruse ideology in process of definition, he was at once horrified by any violence and fascinated by it. Slow of speech, dour, pawky in humour, he had made the others respect but not love him. When necessary he could make them obey him in spite of themselves, but what they did not love was a strain of lofty, self-important, envious contempt which showed itself at odd moments in some careless, sneering remark. Even Draugiski, who came much the closest to him, knew that to Ants the Stork he sometimes was nothing better than *šalte lešiu koše,* cold porridge.

Antsoras opened in his usual roundabout way with a calculated detour. He liked to come at a problem dialectically by indirection. For him everything had to be a production. "Before we hear from you, Baltrus, about the urgent matter that calls for our immediate decision, let's hear from Drauga about the prisoner's state of health. First things first."

Draugiski, youngest and slightest of build, was their Sawbones. Most amiable but not in the least straightforward, he could be an unnervingly persuasive speaker in meetings, a great sounder of alarms actual or imagined. While the others were on occasion journalists, accustomed to putting their thoughts briefly into articles, he was known to be working on an extended work of political theory concerning Marxism and the Cold War. Back in Kaunas, where he had been born of mixed Polish Lithuanian stock, there was, so rumour said, a wife and a child whom he never referred to. Where Antsoras was the mantlewearer, Draugiski was the mischief maker of the the four, the Machiavel. Where the one was caustic, the other could be reassuring, even soothing. He sought, and to a degree found, recognition among them as a still youthful *eminence grise,* the power behind the leader behind the leader. He would sometimes address Antsoras amiably as "my dear dean" in a mock-Trollopian manner.

This afternoon he came in for immediate interference, not from Baltrušaitis, whose time to speak he had been given, but from Šiauliu Čiabuvis, who most envied his growing influence in the Department. "Yes, Drauga, by all means let's hear how the prisoner came to be taking a stroll round the Hospital on your watch, only an hour or two after you had sedated him. I thought that never letting him see our faces was the *sine qua non* of this particular operation." The four had been careful even to dress indistinguishably for this mission in rough workmanlike clothing, bits of secondhand army uniform.

As usual Draugiski made them wait a few beats before he began, small dark head bobbing slightly in deliberation, as if some Handel accompaniment heard only by him had first to come to its close. "You have to understand, the drug we are using depends for its efficacy upon the given patient's dosage being carefully *titrated*—that is . . . calibrated." His gaze rested for a second on Baltrušaitis directly across from him to the north, crisp blond head back lighted from the open door, left leg insolently cocked across right knee, ankle in hand. "No one can ever know to begin with," Draugiski went on quietly, "how much pentobarbitol it will take to do the job without overdoing it."

Čiabuvis was not one to be fobbed off with a technical term or two. "So where are you, Drauga, in your *titration* of the prisoner's dose? That clout you gave him in the chapel must have seriously compromised his whole condition. *Is he going to recover?*" There was always something unctuous about Čiabuvis' humane concerns: it was not for nothing that his nickname was the Saint. If there was one role the Sawbones hated anybody else to play, it was that of inquisitor, but this was one of several that the Saint believed he above all was fitted for. Only Baltrušaitis the Sniper was by temperament disinclined to play the inquisitor whenever an opportunity arose, perhaps because he was of the four the only natural blackguard.

Draugiski said disarmingly, "Šiauliu, you don't want me to go into the logistics of it now. But let me remind you that we are using pentobarbitol because it has the fastest onset of any sodium barbiturate, inducing deep coma and, given the right dose, a half life of up to two days. To sedate Tievas for a few hours only it takes perhaps a thousand milligrams but, to keep him under, the dose has to be increased continually. If he suffers from any pre-existing pathology of the nervous or respiratory system, or of the liver or kidneys, we could lose him to an overdose. So you do see why we had at least to begin with a light hand. This is a sixty-year-old man, with a chequered clinical past, that we are repeatedly drugging."

But Čiabuvis had only begun. He was, in spite of his name, Latvian from Riga, the only son of an old Protestant family, though since the rise of Tievas much of his Lettishness had become assimilated to the dominant Lithuanian culture. He saw himself, if not as the mantlewearer—this was Antsoras who now sat directly across from him to the east—then certainly as the mouthpiece. "We appreciate your expertise, Juozas, of course we do," he said mellowly. "But what assurance can you give us that your patient will be able to walk, or even be carried alive and kicking, aboard the *Dolphynas* on Thursday night? Why was he so terribly shaky, yet still not unconscious, on Friday in the van? Even after being knocked out and given your second injection?"

Draugiski was having to say more than he wanted to be heard saying about his medical responsibilities. "When pentobarbitol is administered to anyone in pain," he said grudgingly, looking from Antsoras to Baltrušaitis but not at his questioner, "there is always a risk of inducing what is called 'paradoxical excitement.'"

"I never have understood why we couldn't have done perfectly well with morphine," said Čiabuvis huffily.

Into the ensuing pause Baltrušaitis now plunged. "On my watch last night I had to empty the urine bag, and I swear his colour is already more red than yellow."

Antsoras had heard enough. "Drauga, do we understand rightly that the prisoner is under sedation as planned and still showing vital signs? All right. That'll do for now. Let's hear from you, Baltrus, about the more urgent matter."

"So long as his beard is growing, you won't hear me pronouncing him dead," Draugiski murmured, more to Baltrušaitis than to Antsoras or Čiabuvis.

Baltrušaitis uncocked his left ankle from his right hand

and leaned forward with both feet planted squarely on the floor in front of him. What a pain these fucking people are, he said to himself, not for the first time ever. He was the Hentzau of the group. As a boy, beautiful and sensitive, growing up anxious not to be taken for a girl, he had cultivated a certain arrogance and cruelty of manner, classic in the case of the handsome criminal according to Adler.

"Look," he said briskly, "I've got bad news, but don't forget I'm only the messenger—and so is Valija. She has opened my eyes to something that happened at the Hospital without herself fully realizing what." He saw by the set of their faces that for once he had their unreserved attention, Ants's included even though he had been given more than an inkling of what was coming.

"This morning, after I had traced the local phone line as usual and hooked us into it, I tried it out by dialing the Hospital number. Valija answered and we chatted for a minute or two." Catching the glance that Drauga gave Ants, he added pointedly, "Just as well I did. She let drop that Friday afternoon there was someone at the Hospital 'sightseeing,' a man she knows from Northfleet, a fellow student."

He paused for effect and was gratified to have all three of his listeners blurt out a different question in unison. Shall a trumpet be blown in the city, and the people not be afraid? Suddenly the all but silent base court, no more than murmurous till now, brimmed over with a shout of anxious query.

"Was he there while the prisoner was loose?"

"What does Valija say he saw, if anything?"

"Who is he, and where will he be today?"

Now would have been the time to sit in derisive silence while they sorted themselves out, but he patiently answered at once, first Ants, then Šiauli, and last of all Drauga. "It's not clear how early he came in. He was with Valija in the library between three and four. He seems to have given her no sign of having seen Tievas, but then he wouldn't, would he, even if

he had? What did Valija know? His name is Brenan, Michael
Brenan—I don't know how it's spelt—and he'll be on the
Northfleet train with her tonight."

Again the other three chimed in all together, defying reason,
as Jurgis would have contemptuously said.

"How much did you *tell* Valija to learn this?"

"Is he a British or United States agent?"

"The question is, how do we silence him?"

This time Baltrušaitis did make them wait for answers,
eying each superciliously from Draugiski to Čiabuvis to
Antsoras. Now was one of those moments of dire emergency
when, of all four, he, Baltrušaitis, was at his coolest and best.
They might have ambition, which is said to be the soldier's
virtue, but he had courage, which is quite rare, and they and
he knew it. The deputy was moved to say a little shamefacedly,
"Let's take this up one question at a time, shall we?" The others
waited, so he went on. "Baltrus doesn't have the answer any
more than we do. But I hope my record is good enough for you
to take my word—the only immediate question is, need we do
anything at all for the time being?" This was not a rhetorical
question expecting the answer no. All of them could see that
their safety had been perilously compromised. Their secrecy
had been breached. Security had failed. The threat of discovery,
now or later, could not be ignored. The challenge was to agree
on some counterstroke that would restore confidence in Jurgis
and his plan.

As so often, Čiabuvis was the first to start thinking aloud.
On rare occasions he could contain himself for most of a
meeting, holding his tongue while the others deliberated until
the psychological moment of climax when his superior clarity
and eloquence would carry the question. But not today. The
question, he fancied, would very soon be answered by Antsoras
to everyone's satisfaction. "What a pity we can't consult Jurgis,"
he began piously. "My own sense of the situation is that the
less we do for the moment the better.

"Think, what is the worst that can come of this Brenan's

having recognized Tievas and seen us dealing with him? He didn't intervene at the time, so he probably isn't a pro. If he alerted the police, Jurgis would have been well in place so they might not have been impressed. If they were, what could he show them? An invisible scene in the chapel. An empty Hospital. Apparently they haven't been there yet. For them the clue runs out before he can point to it—no victim, no crime, no idea where we might be now, no reason to look for us . . . ."

He would have gone on if Draugiski had not broken in. "Šiauliu, you are forgetting Valija. She *is* the clue. A very reliable one, the cynosure"—he smirked for the benefit of Baltrušaitis—"who will eventually lead them all the way to Jurgis himself, even if they only wait and see."

Antsoras could not let the implication of this, although it came from Draugiski, pass without comment. "It goes without saying," he said solemnly, "that Valija herself is above suspicion."

"Caesar's wife," whispered Draugiski in a tone high enough to be self-derisive.

Baltrušaitis said smoothly, "Valija would certainly have told me if the police had come to the Hospital. If they have her under surveillance, she will never lead them here. What can she know, anyway?" He could have denied truthfully that he had given her their exact whereabouts, but he was too insolent ever to make an excuse for himself; and Valija had seemed to know where they were in Norfolk without his telling her. He found himself wondering just how well-informed Uncle Jurgis kept his precious Valija. "Caesar's daughter, let's rather say . . . ."

"But now she does know we are here, doesn't she, thanks to you, Baltrus?" As usual, Drauga was coming at him catlike, purring. "And since this Brenan has access to her, he could come to know it, too. Evidently, they have struck up some sort of liaison. He may be no more than a freelance, a Peeping Tom, but he could still easily use what he learns from Valija to uncover us and expose Jurgis. It is one of the several anomalies of our situation that Caesar has a wife so innocent that she could betray us, and Caesar too, without even knowing that she is doing so." Draugiski had his deep dark gaze turned upon Baltrušaitis, who glared back at him in silence. "To save her from herself, to save us and Jurgis, Brenan has to be removed. The only question is how."

The spirit of Jurgis continued to move them. Neither Antsoras nor Čiabuvis could forbear saying something on his behalf. Eldad and Medad in the camp, thought Baltrus.

"Too much violence has been done already."

"Jurgis would never approve a killing."

Then the deputy fixed his gaze on the distant wood-end, out through the west door in front of him, and began to prophesy, while the others impatiently waited.

"Let me recall for each of us the special sense of purpose, the kind of initiative, that brings us together here. Jurgis conceived of it as a new departure in the history of radical politics. Nobody dies. For our purpose to be realized nobody needs to die. As in *The Alchemist,* everything can be trotted out, translated, and restored without anyone paying the capital price.

"Revolution, the *coup d'état,* should be more of a balloon going up and then coming down than an outbreak of war. Or perhaps, as Jurgis would say, rather a Jonsonian fart or passage of wind than an act of violence. The world is not much changed, yet much the better for it. Nothing could be more important to Jurgis, or to us, than the fitness of the Marshal to resume his new role in life after it has been . . . rectified. And nothing could be less in the spirit of Jurgis' whole conception than the killing of a mere passer by, a spectator, a nobody.

"What Jurgis would have us rely on when carrying out this mission of ours is the power of imagination, not tragic force. He has put it to us many a time in his own words and actions better than ever I can. Remember how he once said to us early on in Gdainys: 'You're not going to be another Baltic death gang, not just one more of the damned *giltininkai.*' Let's not forget that, now he is busy in the midst of things, making his kind of difference to the way they go."

The thought of Jurgis in the person of the Marshal, alone among enemies, out at sea aboard the *Dolphynas* ought to have given them all pause. But Čiabuvis could not wait to demur, could not wait to overween. "All very well and good, Ants. Jurgis will always be our messiah, and you his evangelist. We do acknowledge all this. *But it is not just what you say.* What shall we tell the men from Special Branch when they pull us over on Wednesday outside Northfleet and find the Marshal semi-comatose, if not dead, in the back of the van? Shall we tell them that Jurgis says whatever happens, nobody dies?" Now the love of being the one listened to took hold of him.

"For myself, at that moment I trust Baltrus will pick up the Sten and blow them away, this Brenan with them, if he is there. *Then* we can make our delivery with confidence, collect Jurgis, and fade away with him into the groves of academe, leaving the police and the politicos over here to pick up the pieces of a *fait accompli*." Antsoras seemed taken aback, as well he might, after making his plangent call and having it denied with such animosity—and by the Saint no less.

It was then that Draugiski saw his chance and seized the moment. "You will be expecting a demurrer, Šiauliu, but nothing could be more welcome to me in the present emergency than the call to act decisively and not to delay. I think you are exactly right to ask that Brenan be silenced as soon as feasible. His access to Valija must be ended. The success of Jurgis' initiative and the safety of us all now depend upon it. Things do not always move as fast as we may fear, but let me propose that a sniper be sent out, with support, at once, to do the job and report back by dawn Wednesday at the latest." He always spoke as if his wish were somehow the others' command. He looked, not at Baltrušaitis, but Antsoras, putting on his most responsible expression.

Baltrušaitis glanced around helplessly for support. As usual there was only Ants the Stork, with whom his credit was never so great as the Sawbones' was, and Šiauli, who was of course careering about on his own pathetic hobby horse and this time happened to be galloping against him.

Antsoras seemed about to respond to Draugiski when Baltrušaitis burst out with an exasperated concession of defeat. "God damn you, Drauga, for a sly, manipulative little sod. When I get back on Wednesday and we're striking this camp, you may find I have a round left up the spout for you, too. To *be silenced as soon as feasible.* Thanks a million." He and Draugiski sat and hated one another with their eyes, but for the time being, it was the end of something.

So the Committee of Safety came to its latest meeting of minds. Now that a decision had been collectively reached and their very sighs might be scored against them, most of their wretchedness consisted in watching and being watched. The blanched faces of the other three were in deadly contrast to the scowling blush behind which Draugiski sheltered. As in many a case of *odium philologicum*, it was so great because what was in theory at stake was finally so small, however much personal loss might in practice result for other people, such as the eponymous Brenan.

"Napoleon he say, 'Unity of command is the first necessity of war,'" said Antsoras in a new effort at gaiety. "He also say, 'All the ills and curses which can afflict mankind come from London.'"

"Napoleon he also say," said Baltrušaitis grimly, "'In war cleverness is not wanted. What is wanted is accuracy, character, and simplicity.'"

"I wish Jurgis were here," said Čiabuvis sanctimoniously, "to sort out some of this 'paradoxical excitement' for us." His urge was now to side openly with Baltrus against Drauga, accusing him to his face of always working secretly to undo whatever Jurgis might put together. But having already spoken on both sides of the question to discomfit Ants, Čiabuvis feared that enough had been said for the present, at least by him.

"The situation," said Draugiski solemnly, shaking his head, "is sadly overdetermined." There was silence.

"On that note," said Antsoras, "let me detail you, Šiauli, as driver and support for Baltrus." In front of him and behind Čiabuvis, a brilliant level light had crept into the basement from the meadow, where the westering sun had stretched out all the hillocks of the slope. "Drauga and I will see you both back here on Wednesday at the latest, assuming all goes well." It was as if he had known all along how the meeting would come out.

He rose from his chair, lifting the .303 from the floor beside him, and turned away from the brilliance, screwing up his eyes. "It's after four," he said, checking his wrist watch. "You're on guard, Drauga." He hefted the .303 through the air to be caught with both hands.

Baltrušaitis said, "I shall need that in Northfleet."

"It's yours," said Draugiski, opening the bolt and checking that the rifle was loaded, "whenever you're ready to leave. I'll break out the Webley for Ants and me while you're away." Then, on an afterthought, he added maliciously, "Did you ever locate the magazine for that Sten we have?"

iii

Let me kiss my father and my mother,
and then I will follow you.

~I Kings

The darkness was increasing; the whole sky had clouded; thunder threatened. It was winter, and he was yet once more working for the Post Office during the vac, this time on letters not parcels. He was making— of all things—the midnight collection which for some strange reason had not been abolished in 1939 after all. He was riding his big all-weather Raleigh with the upright handlebars and green gearcase, his canvas postman's bag still half empty over his shoulder. He was in uniform— was it postal blue serge with red piping or army khaki? His hat he had lost—blue peaked cap or steel helmet or wool beret, whichever it had been—on a wild freewheel ride down Pond Road curving past the drenched willows and beaten rushes at the bottom. His cape, too, he seemed to have lost; but perhaps not. He was soaked, but not yet to the skin. Out on the heath the rain was teeming, the wind gusting like the devil from the northeast, rushing through the grasses with a hiss of rustling wings. The last box he had to collect from before returning to the office in the village and signing off stood on the open corner of Montpelier Row, its letter mouth facing the squall from Cooper's Corner. Somehow he knew this one was going to be a sod.

He turned into South Row under bleary street lamps, with the Paragon and the Merchant Hospital well behind him, and tried punching his way past the Prince of Wales' pond. The wind, unbroken by the few madly tossing trees around the troubled water, hit him broadside like the blast from a bomb and almost had him on his back in the streaming roadway. Dismounted, he wheeled his dripping bike the remaining fifty yards to the box. The pub on the corner had long since closed and gone dark; buses had stopped running; not another soul was to be seen, only street lamps strung out across the heath towards home and soon vanishing into total darkness. He propped his bike carefully against the nearest wall—if he had stood it against the kerb as usual, it would have blown over at once. As it was, the wind began to bully it the moment he turned to the box. He could hear the enameled frame shudder and grind against the rough brick wall.

He was just opening the curved iron door in the gleaming scarlet pillar, using his body to block the worst of the wind, when it happened. The front wheel of his bike began to slip away backwards under the handlebars. Slowly the whole machine toppled to the pavement with a sickening jangle and lay there in the downpour, wheels and pedals spinning. Seeing it topple, he started towards it. Then the iron tongue in the wire cage lining the pillar box dropped through the open door like a drawbridge, as it was made to do, and a stream of letters and cards began spilling out before he could get his postman's bag underneath to catch them. None ever reached the pavement where the rain spattered and bounced. The wind from the heath swept under and blew them up and away like angry gulls, their papery wings beating in vain against the blast. There were so many, a great flock of Christmas mail, and all went on being whirled away over the rooftops of the Row until the pillar box was empty, the rain pattering inside it now, and he standing by helpless like Alice at the end when the cards fly up.

Michael Brenan's going away to America after the Tievas affair must have hurt his parents terribly—although they could only encourage him, as always, to make the most of his opportunities in life, and he would never deliberately cause them unhappiness. None of them knew then that he would not eventually return to England to live. "I don't think we can ever repay our parents for their kindness," he once said, "unless perhaps we one day have children." I remember going to see Billy and Bessie not long after my mother died and my father moved back to Stokesay in Shropshire. Heathdene appeared unbearably diminished by all the absences. Billy, like my father retired by then on his Civil Service pension, was about to go into hospital for surgeoning of the colon cancer which would kill him before long. Bessie, busy as ever, was wearing away fast while she nursed him round the clock.

"Well, I never, John boy," she said, fluttering her hands in welcome, "it's an ill wind that blows nobody any good. What a treat to see you looking so fit. Come in and let me make you a cup of tea." In return for Michael's weekly air letter from wherever he then was in the Deep South or Midwest, she was still sending him the *Listener* and the *Picturegoer*, hand wrapped by Billy, with annotated snippets from the *Radio Times*, the *Kentish Mercury*, and the *Local Guide and District Advertiser* tucked between the pages—hopeful little reminders of all that he was missing at home. Patrick, demobbed and then graduated, was newly married to a young German woman, and teaching French at the training college in nearby Avery Hill; they were already expecting a child. By that time in the history of Heathdene we were all well on our way to knowing how brief the stay could be of anything good, let alone gold.

On this particular Sunday in October '51, waking from an after dinner sleep in the sweat of his dream, Brenan put this latest spell down to the novel he had been reading when he dozed off. It was for him the favourite of the moment, *Her Privates We*—his favourite perhaps of all the novels he ever in his life picked up—in a battered copy of the reset printing of '43. He had been sent back once again to its unforgettable third chapter by having listened that morning to his father's reminiscence of the army training camp where he had first met Mr. Vaughan. *"You know, Bourne, ol' chap," said the Sergeant ... . "That wash a lie you tol' that offisher." "I'm afraid it was, Sergeant. It touches my conscience sometimes ... ."*

Brenan extricated himself from the sun-filled slip room, where his books and papers lined every shelf, including the washstand with its flowery china basin and jug, and went along to the bathroom to splash his face with cold water and comb his hair. His father had been napping, too, in one of the Morris chairs by the fireplace in the big front room with his feet comfortably up on a cushioned stool. Brenan's mother had snatched forty winks in the bedroom and now had a kettle singing "on the hob" as she persisted in calling the kitchen gas stove. The season was much too temperate as yet for daily coal fires. In the "best room," where he joined his father to wait for her to bring in the tea tray, the grate was still screened as for the summer with a round brass table top from India or Burma, presented by one of the Suffolk uncles or aunts who had been there in service. Their name—his mother's maiden name—was Aspall. On the hearth in front of this brass screen she had set a tall vase of branching catkins and pussy willows, gathered in early summer but still glowing with gold and silver tints. "Osiers, purple osiers," she would say. "Many's the time as a child I've sat through a thunderstorm with your grandfather while he wove them into a basket. How he did love the purple osier, your grandfather." John Aspall had been dead these thirty years.

Brenan's father, sitting up in his chair now, said pawkily, "I see your paper has got all old Tievas' troubles packed up for him."

"Oh? Did I miss something good when I glanced through it this morning?"

"Well, you know how handy they can be at sorting out somebody else's headache." His father handed over a folded page in which there was indeed a short case analysis that Brenan had failed to spot. In a breathless sprint, someone anonymous had gone through seven possible consequences of the Marshal's speech on Friday evening—and, presumably, of his conferencing at the Naval College the following day.

I vaguely remember noticing the article myself, over breakfast in Finchley, in Babs's copy of the *Observer*. Certainly I would have had time to read it on the train back to Northfleet, an earlier one than Brenan and Valija took in the evening. Years later, with his anecdote still teasing me, I looked up the details in the newspaper library at Colindale. The seven deadly consequences were: one, discrediting himself with his own people; two, becoming yet more enmeshed in the Cominform net; three, disabling Baltija—as opposed to, say, Jugo-Slavia— in the struggle for national autonomy; four, antagonizing President Truman; five, giving Stalin a new pretext for swallowing the Baltic states; six, embarrassing the British Labour government; and seven, inviting his own forcible replacement by some puppet of either East or West.

It was hard to imagine why anyone—least of all the Hero of Gdainys—should do what Tievas ostensibly had done to himself over the past forty-eight hours. Brenan shook his head unhopefully at his father and thought of Valija, at tea in Christy's the day before, saying bitterly, "My country and its future are no better understood here than in Moscow."

Bustling in with a crowded tray, his mother said, "I can't get over this beautiful weather. As soon as you're up on that North Sea coast, my boy, it'll pour fit to drown us, you mark my words." She kept cups and things on a trolley by her fireside chair, and now she began setting them out on the central dining table. It was draped with a heavy fawn velveteen which matched a brief mantle of the same cloth around the high chimney shelf. On this there perched the tall wooden clock in a busy Bavarian style that chimed the hours throughout the flat, flanked by statuettes of Caesar and Vercingetorix cast in some brown substance that hinted at bronze. Decking all these were two tasteful souvenirs from Frinton-on-Sea and several vivid postcards sent by young Patrick from the Rhineland. While his mother clinked crockery and spoons and stirred a fragrant pot of Typhoo tea and poured milk from a little jug into their cups, Brenan found himself taking inventory of this all-too-familiar room of his childhood as if he might never again see it—which of course he would, even though his packed bags and trenchcoat already stood waiting in the narrow front hall.

At this time of day it was well lighted, the former servants' kitchen of Heathdene—searchingly from the west through the brilliant back window and wide open door of his bedroom, and softly from the east where a bay of three windows gave on to the tree-filtered greys and greens of the front area and garden. It was in this quarter, the east northeast, that the windows had from the first been fitted with painted vertical iron bars. Even when the bombing had blown the glass out, as it did more than once during the war, no looter could ever have crept in that way.

Within the bay of windows, which were draped with fawn cloth and half curtained with net, stood the sofa—the "couch"—and twin armchairs, in imitation leather, all set about with embroidered cushions, and a pair of aspidistras in brass bowls on walnut stands. Of antimacassars there was no need. Here in winter the brass table top which now screened the fireplace would find its proper place on folding carved wooden legs as a *point d'appui* for newspaper and magazine reading or card playing and board games. For special occasions—whist or hearts with visiting relatives—there was a green baize table folded away somewhere in a cupboard.

From floor to ceiling, the northwest wall to one side and the other of the fireplace was lined with white paneled cupboards full of useful things; but games, books and other treasures most often in use were kept more readily to hand behind the sloping leaf and in the brass-handled drawers of the much polished writing desk, or "bureau": playing cards, cribbage board, jigsaw puzzles, snakes and ladders, lotto, chess pieces, draughts, her Chambers' dictionary for crosswords, his father's unbound supplements of *I Was There*, a world atlas, an encyclopaedia, the *Wonder Book of Ships*.

All along its narrow top, absent members of the family were gathered in framed photos, the late Grandfather Brenan prominently among them, not everyone smiling or even sanguine for the "faithful and disappointing" camera. Books held in common—not his and Patrick's own school collections— went easily into one of the cupboards, being but few: *Mother Goose, Pilgrim's Progress, Margaret Catchpole, Alice in Wonderland* and *Through the Looking Glass, Our Mutual Friend, Children of the New Forest, Mutiny on the 'Bounty.'* The least readerly of the four, his father had little patience for what he called "fiction," which included all poetry that was not set to music. He had a good singing voice, and in his youth had taught himself to play the dulcimer and the mouth organ. But for his wife and two sons who loved fiction to a fault, there was always the public library, thanks to Andrew Carnegie, and the unrivalled radio serials of the dear old B.B.C. "Well, I'll go to the library!" his father would exclaim at any untoward issue, as if reduced to his last resort. His favourite listening was a military march.

While Brenan and his parents stirred their cups of tea in a jingling trio—even his mother, who had given up sugar years since when rationing began but still took milk—Brenan idly revisited their imposing built-in pinewood dresser. One more vestige of the recent Victorian past, it took up the entire southeast wall opposite the fireplace—open shelves hooked for cup handles, jutting butcher bench at work height and, under this, three deep drawers over an open ledge for more storage. The whole contraption stood freighted, top to bottom, with his parents' souvenirs of a quarter century together, everything from seldom-used fancy tea service complete with pot, jug, and bowl to biscuit barrel, vases, and small marble clock too faint to be heard against the Bavarian.

Here, at floor level on the ledge, sat his mother's precious Singer sewing machine in its gleaming arched carrying case and, directly above on the main shelf, the still stylish cabinet radio, Cossor 1934, battery operated, which was his father's unfailing concern. The husband took care of radio as the wife took care of sewing, and all other housekeeping—though this husband kept the brass polished too. Electricity had yet to supplant Victorian coal gas for lighting their part of the house. "When the juice comes on," said his father, "up goes the rent"; and Mr. Vartan was, as always, too considerate of their limited means to faradize them now. In each hallway and room—save the very smallest in which an oil lamp burned—gaslight would glow at the touch of a struck match once the sun went down, but only at need. "Don't forget my gas bill, you boys," his mother would plead whenever a globe was left burning in a room not in use. "I'm not made of money."

Here on the dresser, to right and left of the radio, the Bible had its place, accompanied by a wide range of bound commentaries issued by the Watchtower Society and presented to his parents in 1936 by the gracious Miss Bickley (of great family renown) who had once needed somewhere to stay briefly. She was the first Jehovah's Witness they had ever met, a pioneer evangel who, after a while in the Lord's work, went home and married a bank manager in Widmerpool. Brenan's mother had a way of taking to a young woman all alone in suburban London, as she herself once had been, and bringing her home to be cared for. This was strange because with her immediate neighbours around the heath and along the edge she tended to be more than a little reserved in manner. He wondered what, in his place, she might have made of Valija Didelis at the Merchant Hospital the day before yesterday.

"A regular cup of sergeant major's," his father said

appreciatively, "strong enough to make the spoon stand up in it. Yes, I will have another cup thank you, Mother."

She used a sensible floral cosy over the teapot, the secret of good tea being, while keeping it warm, not to rush it. "If I'd known it was sergeant major's you wanted, I'd have made it with Brooke Bond," she said in mock reproach.

While she was refilling his cup he added winningly, "What do you say we take young Mick for a last walk through the park before he leaves us? This weather's too good to miss." She did not, as he would have expected, object that on such an afternoon the park would be too full of folk for comfort.

"If you two will throw these tea things into the scullery," she said, "it won't take me a jiff to change my shoes, put on my coat and hat, and be ready." Both she and his father knew well that their son, who had hours to kill before catching his train, would not demur.

As they readied themselves for yet one more Sunday afternoon stroll, Brenan sat finishing his secret tour of the room. His favourite thing of all, perhaps, belonged against the flowered paper of the inner southwest wall, between the doors of the back hall and his bedroom. Here stood a high walnut sideboard or *chiffonier*, as his father would sometimes facetiously call it, mispronouncing the French like the old sweat he would always be. Crammed with the better china and cutlery for the nearby dining table, it displayed, together with wineglasses, tumblers, nutbowl, nutcracker, and an occasional bottle or two, three large translucent cut-glass shapes. Two were vaselike for holding flowers, newly picked or dried; the one in the middle was compotelike for holding fruit, fresh or, if necessary, artificial. His mother always did her "damnedest," he knew, to keep this cornucopia flowing. But for him the quaintest beauty of it all was in the noble pair of framed Constables in brown photogravure which set off the looking glass above the *chiffonier*. The *Corn Field* and the *Hay Wain*—these had been chosen for his mother by his father, when they first set up home together, to console her somewhat for the ghostly landscapes she had left behind in Suffolk. Though a little blind to colour, his father had the sketcher's eye and hand and taste. How many times as a child had he, Michael Brenan, been pulled across this room by the looking glass that reflected so much of it, only to find himself at a pool by a cornfield like the boy in the picture, lying prostrate slaking his thirst?

Having sat together at the screened fireplace and drunk tea, the three of them now went for their walk through the park, talking as usual on impulse and at long intervals, his mother the slightest of womanly figures in between his father and himself. She no longer wore gloves when out walking on Sunday. The war had put an end to all that. They went along the front of the heath in silence, past the pristine facade of Mr. Vartan's own Victorian pile, past the site of the Council's growing jungle of postwar apartments in the Corbusier manner, and the grand but crumbling drill hall of the Kent Rifle Volunteers, through the towering brick wall of the park at the southernmost narrow gate on Maze Hill, and into the haunted flower garden.

Many families in hushed tones or silence were taking the perfumed air together there, far enough from the bandstand to render its brassy strains but faint to the ear. *"Old Comrades,"* whispered his father approvingly once he had caught the tune. "My stars, what a mob," murmured his mother. In the grassy ways among the dahlia beds and tall tentlike cedars, all the deck chairs had been spoken for. Frequent sun seekers were now settling on little straight ones, those folding, slatted, wood and iron chairs in green found in gardens everywhere across England. The Brenans, however, were there to walk, not sit. They were "stepping it out," as his mother would wish. Each knew what an exception she was making for his sake this time. On their left they passed the deeply wooded, strongly fenced little park within a park where the King's deer were kept. At times a roe, less timid than the rest, would come to take bread at some kind person's hand. All along the fence, at breaks in the undergrowth, knots of children and parents waited in anticipation.

"I suppose you'll be seeing our John at Somersby tomorrow," Brenan's father said. "You must give him our best." Although he and Brenan's mother had once visited the college and met Huby, they would never be so forward as to send the Warden of Somersby their best. "Tell him we are still looking for a good square leg and mid on combined." He laughed, shaking his head. "Remember how, as a youngster, John hated to run fast after the ball once it had got past him?"

Brenan's mother said instead, "You be sure, Michael, to give John our very kindest regards. No talking about old cricket. My heart goes out to him, poor soul, with his mother in the state she's in."

"Isn't she convalescing at Torquay with Mr. Offord?"

"The trouble with colitis is that cancer will set in, as it did with sister Maggie. I shall be very surprised if Mrs. Offord is long for this world. Didn't you see her, before she went away?"

They were on the path that leads around the big ornamental pond, where in those days the ducks were not timid but the swans ferocious. They glided so peaceably in the brown waters yet, when people passed, they would maraud like pirates on the pond's enameled bank. This path led to the splendid avenue of chestnuts, laid out by Le Nôtre from the main gates to the Observatory, where stood a statue of Wolfe which still looks across the river as if from the heights of Abraham. "You know," said Brenan's father, brooding on the pond, its rushes, lilies, and solitary islet, "this could be the place to be interred— ashes sprinkled under one of these willows—if only the park high ups would agree." Brenan and his mother held their peace. Grandfather Brenan lay uncremated in an airy upland graveyard on nearby Shooter's Hill, and the burial ground was Roman Catholic.

They came at length to the avenue and crossed it with care, avoiding the couples who strolled slowly and mutually absorbed along each side path. One or two Sunday cars processed solemnly through the light shower of leaves. On the well-kept gravel in front of the Superintendent's house, families with toddlers stood feeding pigeons in a ring. Outside the gates a brisk trade in donkey rides went on and on and on. The Brenans entered the rock garden. This rather sepulchral defile would eventually lead them around a deep hollow, fearfully crowded with rhododendron, and out by the gate in the wall at the corner of Chesterfield Walk—on to the open heath.

"Now don't fail to send me your things to be washed each week," said his mother determinedly. "You can't afford laundry prices, and your good shirts could be ruined by those infernal machines. Besides, your father and I like to hear from you at least once a week."

"Oh, Mother, you don't want to wear yourself out washing and ironing for me at your time of life. I'll write you in any event. I'll even get Offord to write you. But please don't overdo things here. Try to take life a little more easily now that you have only Dad to look after.

"I'm worried about your health. You never see a doctor. Besides, Mrs. Wilson who does my room at Somersby likes to have laundry to take in. She's very good, brings us fresh eggs from her hens, and seems to need all the money she can earn. I can afford what little she asks; and you can be home free— and write to Patrick *twice* a week! Or, better yet, Dad can take you to the pictures to see *Now, Voyager* again." He glanced knowingly at his father.

His mother bristled. "I don't know what you're talking about. There's nothing the matter with me, I'll be bound. Nothing a bowl of slippery elm and early to bed won't put right, once you're off my hands. I can't for the life of me imagine what you think is wrong. A queer spell now and again is only natural at our age." She was seven years younger than her husband but would survive him by only one. The thread of life is at times finer than we know. "Besides, it's your father who likes Bette Davis. I like the Swedish girl who played a nun in *The Bells of St. Mary's.*"

Once out on the heath the mood changes. Even his mother, never one to relish a breeze, let alone gusts of wind, comes through the narrow gate and claps her hands in pleasure. "My heavens, what a sight to behold!" October is the month when the gulls return in force, the common gull, the blackhead, the herring, and the lesser blackback. Now their white shapes dapple all the green as far as the heath's western edge, limit of the Brenans' walk.

"Upwards of one hundred thousand," says the Open Air correspondent of the *Observer*, Richard Fitter, "roost every winter within fifteen or twenty miles of London . . . mostly on the open water, but a few sleep on the banks." None seem to breed here; they all come from the Baltic, lured by the promise of playing fields, rubbish dumps, and refuse wharves up and down the Thames.

"Gathering for their evening flight to some reservoir," said his father, giving them a wide berth as he led the way across the grass to Hyde Vale and the Point. "Your grandfather used to tease me that the year I was born, 1892, was the first that people fed the London gulls instead of shooting them for sport." He had been born in October and, as Brenan and his mother had already reminded each other, was coming up for another birthday, his fifty-ninth.

Crooms Hill, Hyde Vale, and the Point make the steepest and most densely wooded, as well as the quaintest corner of the heath. Suddenly little roads drop away between winding cliffs of cottage and copse down to Greenwich and the Thames. Looking along the Vale as they crossed to the Point, Brenan said to his mother, "I always think of John and Bella's first home as being down there at number 23 or thereabouts, don't you?" In recent weeks they had been following yet one more radio serial of *Our Mutual Friend*.

"Can't say it ever crossed my mind," said his mother absently, taking her husband's arm as if she might be tiring.

"Not far now, old girl," he said gently. "We'll find a seat at the Point and you can enjoy the view in comfort as long as you like."

And so they came to the little park of sycamores right at the end of the escarpment, looking west, where river and City, even to the dome of St. Paul's and beyond, come clearly into sight as if by fiat. There one looks in wonderment at all the things given, kingdoms of the world in a moment of time.

For some reason few people were here about, so the three at once found a bench to sit on by themselves. The view was all before them north and west over the tree tops as far as the eye could see—endless London, "its postal districts packed like squares of wheat." Upriver, now that the tide was out, the shining mud of the long-gathered, treacherous foreshore was marked only by gulls and stranded barges. This far inland any murmur came, not from the Thames, but from little dwellings among the silent factories and workshops below, plots of grey brick, mortar, and cement, roofed with slate and sending up, even on such an afternoon, the occasional wreath of smoke above the trees. They sat with their hands folded and said nothing.

At length Brenan said, "Can't we see your new office in Rotherhithe from here?" He had begun to regret that all summer there had not been a time for him to visit his father at work. His father shook his head. "And don't want to, if you know what's good for you." He said this in the same sad, mocking way that, when some minor misfortune befell a workmate, he would say, as if in wonder, "Only a young fellah, too."

Bill Brenan knew perfectly well how to disarm without undue offence. An eternal sergeant, he was especially good at this with his wife who, though generous to a fault, took offence too easily and too much. After one of her bouts of indignation in the middle of some shared kitchen chore, I have heard him— I, Patrick, and Michael together amusing ourselves in the best room—mollify her by crooning "I take offence too easily, I take offence too fast," and her say, helplessly but with a little laugh, "I know, I know; you don't have to tell me, I know."

Bessie Aspall, for all her failings of temper, was still a fallen angel, we each in our different way would have had to agree, some emphasizing the fall more than others. As her husband had been heard to admit, you could "go off" someone like her; but once she had taken you to her heart, she would never be the someone who went off you. This Billy had learned long since, and even I, and certainly Patrick and, best of all, Michael, who had caused her more sorrow, she said, than the rest of us put together. What in all the realms of possibility her fond rebuke alluded to I never learned—something to do with a difficult first delivery in the Shooter's Hill nursing home, Brenan said when I pressed him—but this couldn't have been the half of it.

Perhaps the most sorrowful time of life is when children who have grown up begin to go their own ways, taking with them what has become the chief joy of their parents' time together. There is no way in the world that a certain family happiness can then ever recur. For the parents at least, some soft music of being young and silly turns forever harsh and wintry—the sound of being merely part of nature.

Five years before, when the war ended, we younger ones had still been little more than thoughtless boys going daily to school and coming home to play. For the duration we had been, as only children can be, much more content with things than the grown ups could ever be. But by now any such fortune of war, if not forgotten, was long spent. My own mother, Vivien, having taken the second war even harder than the first—in which she, like Bessie, had lost a brother—was wasting away before our eyes. After my entering year at Northfleet, I had been seen off to France by her for this summer whereupon she, none too soon, committed herself to hospital care, leaving my father to fend stoically for himself, which he did. Off I duly went to Pau, francophile that I was, in thrall to "the attraction of a country in Romance," as Wordsworth saw fit to call it, conveniently forgetting Robespierre and the Terror.

Now I was making for myself, as was Brenan for himself, a new if even more ephemeral life in college—so much kinder than the army, of course, but no more like home. Family life at Heathdene, such as the Brenans lived and had allowed me to share, had all but run its course for him as well as for me.

Brenan—always the lucky blighter, as his mother would be the first to say—had at least spent this latest summer, however distractedly, at home with his parents. Day by day, month after month, on the idle stream of his private self, he had drifted further apart from the American girl he had come to know so well at college the previous year. A nicer person and better company than he had ever thought to find in the world at large, she had spent one whole academic session in Northfleet, much of it shared with him. Then, of necessity, she had gone back to be with her family and get on with her graduate student life in Alabama. Well-set Southern Baptists and provincial to boot, her father and mother could have had nothing but suspicion of their daughter's fancy for a penniless Limey undergraduate, who was also some sort of Roman Catholic. It was Billy, Bessie, and Justine all over again, only in reverse and in spades. To me the cream of the jest—which I did not share with Brenan—was that Marianne's pretty Southern drawl was, at moments, as close to Bessie's Suffolk brogue as any one could ever hope to hear from America.

Brenan and Marianne had fallen in love during the winter, as Christmas came on. In the midst of wind and rain for days on end, they had been surprised by some unforeseen mutual happiness. Being together suddenly made all the difference; this was the secret of such a happiness: wanting to be with the one who wanted to be with oneself. It was, he said, like finding a long forgotten sister with whom one's lost childhood might be recovered. Coming from him, in Northfleet, this was indeed a surprise, since at first glance up there on the Lincolnshire coast she had to be seen as an exotic—"foreign," as Bessie would say with a sniff. A magnolia, perhaps.

At the end of the college year they had not quite recognized how final their parting—she by way of Southampton and New York on the USS *America*—was bound in the circumstances to be. They began a correspondence back and forth through the summer; and letter by letter it soon became clear how little they had to look forward to as a couple. Writing from the heart, as if the previous year had never run its course, they were in actuality washed up on far different shores of the world and might, like Amélie and her lover, "never reach Venice together."

To do him credit, Brenan had already glimpsed the farcical aspect of any situation that makes two twenty-year-olds tragically unhappy. He had come up with one of his melancholy little poems on the topic soon after losing Justine. For those who love by the book, true love always has to be, as anybody knows, a tragedy. Who could not have foreseen that the very beauty of self which made Marianne lovable would also make her unreachable, since she could never deny her family—and he could never ask her to. It was only to be expected that the way of love and the way of marriage would not be the same. We musketeers knew well enough, thanks to Brenan, what the sages have to say about passion and society, De Rougement having recently come out in England.

Sitting beside his mother and father on a bench at the Point this Sunday afternoon, he thought wryly of Graves in the autumn of the first war asking his comrade Sassoon, who was in denial, "How would Old Joe, . . . the most understanding man in the Regiment, understand it?"—and then himself marrying Nancy Nicholson, whom his own father and mother would never in their lives approve of. Duty is right but love is better? If only everyone, the older generation, the others, could see through appearances to what really mattered most.

In the brightness of the sun's rays, cloud after white cloud was piling up before them to the west, but it would be hours before these turned gold and then red over the City and river. His mother stood up finally, saying, "Come on, father, let's see this boy off to school at the other end of the earth before it's too late."

"I can see myself off. Why don't you two stay here and enjoy the sunset? With that bank of cloud it's going to be glorious." Anyone's leaving home on a long journey would always mean his mother at the front door, too full for words, silently weeping.

"No, we'll be on our way as well. Your father and I will be going to Brother Childs's for Bible study this evening, I expect. What do you say, Billy?"

"Right you are," said his father evenly, turning his attention from the riverine distance.

They came out of the little park at the Point, looking east across the heath to the distant flank of Shooter's Hill half hidden by intervening trees and houses.

"You think of the world as so wide," Brenan said to his mother, "but it isn't—not always, and not as the crow flies. Think of that milestone in the churchyard up there on the hill, 'Ypres Salient 130 miles.' Who'd 'a' thought it? Only forty-odd leagues from here to where Dad caught his trench fever in '17? How far does that make it to down home Mickfield from here?"

His father did not cotton to the tone of such dangerous talk. They were crossing in front of Lansdowne Place, leaving to their right one of the heath's oldest pubs, the Green Man. "*Who'd 'a' thought it?*" he echoed. "Your favourite of all the pub names known to man, isn't it, Bess?"

She said demurely, "Don't you be so cheeky, my lad," looking down with the faintest of smiles. In the years when they were courting, it had been their landmark on long walks over Shooter's Hill into the Kent countryside.

Emboldened, his father went facetiously on, "My favourite is the Green Man." Then, doing a tour guide and a tourist in two different voices, he chanted,

> "'We are now passing the Green Man Hotel and
>   Tavern.'
> '*Why?*'"

Although it was long past closing and not yet Sunday opening time, his Baptist-born wife was not amused. "Why? Why? Because, as you well know, we have had licensing hours since the first war, thank the Lord. And none too soon either."

In the long silence that followed Brenan began thinking of Marianne, Miss Hollis, the one who had first introduced him to Valija in Highfield six months before. It was a while now since he had heard from her or written her. There she was in the land of smilax and scuppernong, learning to be a teacher, listening to her parents, praying, driving a Buick, occasionally dating some eligible young man of the Baptist faith, dreaming, perhaps, of a love never to be. And where was he?

What was it, this fine afternoon, that he had, as his mother would scornfully say, "on the brain"? Not so much Tievas, the stricken, uncomprehending face (to say nothing of Didelis); not so much Valija, the mild gaze, the way her mind moved, the secret sadness; but Marianne, her sudden smile, her openness to laughter, the kindness she seemed to have for everyone she met. He wondered idly about them all without reaching for any conclusion, stepping it out once more with his mother between his father and himself. Three could be a crowd, but not always. Parents and a child,or three children together, had the best of it. But then, after all, a stranger could come along and be the chosen one of the child, making two, not three, company. It was a complete mystery how love and marriage could sometimes go together and sometimes not.

And so home to Heathdene they went, this three, by the way they had come through the park and along the heath, each for the time being silent with his or her own thoughts.

Chapter Four

Night Train North

The glance by day, the whisper in the dark.

~Pope

He came from the Underground into the Pandaemonium of the main line station at its evening peak, ten minutes or so before the 7:35 departure. People—passengers, seers off, those meeting arrivals, inspectors, porters—trolleys piled high, nimble forklifts, taxis from the forecourt, cooing pigeons, an ample public address, noises at every level from murmur to shriek, the smells of smoke were milling about him under a vaulted glass roof. From the Euston Road outside, he knew, it all looked deceptively like some Victorian cartoon of St. Mark's minus the piazza. God bless Cubitt! But behind the facade, a maelstrom. As usual, his first impulse was to find the bookstall and browse quietly. Instead, lugging his two bags crammed with clothing and books, and juggling his folded trenchcoat over one shoulder, he found the booking hall, bought a ticket, and presented himself at the platform where his train stood waiting.

Long, particoloured brown and green, well-groomed,

sinuous, wily, it was the evening express to Doncaster and York, there to become the night train for Edinburgh and Aberdeen. He—he and Valija, so he hoped—would change in East Retford for Northfleet and the sea. He had come from home by 53 bus as far as New Cross Gate, and thence by Underground, and he was still in that slight suspension of faculties which suburban travel can induce—"not quite all there," in his mother's phrase. Hurrying up the platform, trying not to get too heated since he was wearing his gaberdine suit rather than crushing it into a suitcase, he began looking about for Valija.

He was also curious about the locomotive and hoping to see it at close quarters before boarding the train. Never a fanatic spotter like some of his schoolmates, he had picked up a little of the know how, and was secretly sorry not to remember more. "Railway research," musketeers like Offord had used to call it, to twit the more solemn initiates. "Double O nothing" meant the most humble of tanks, to be seen any day of the week shunting in the yards below the Edge. But this Eastern and Northern express would be pulled at very least by a "Two six O *Mogul*," if not by the new "Four six two *Britannia*," pride of British Railways, the swallower up not so long since of the old L.N.E.R. Wondering if older footplate men and guards had been as saddened by nationalization as his father had by post-war change in the G.P.O., he glanced back at the guard's van, noting that it was now too late for any more mail to be loaded on this train.

He went all the way up to the gleaming, hissing loco at the mouth of the terminus without seeing Valija. It was certainly not a *Britannia*—no characteristic deflector modeled the smokebox. It was a Two six two *Duchess*. The driver was still on the platform chatting with the guard, the fireman adding coal at an open firedoor, but the moment of departure would not be long in coming. What if Valija were not to be on this train tonight after all?

He retraced his steps quickly, looking into every compartment, which was not easy because the corridor intervened. Towards the rear, not far from the barrier, he at last caught a glimpse of her, seated alone in a far corner with her back to the engine, reading. She was not at that moment keeping an eye out for him. To his horror he realized that the well-appointed compartment which she had all to herself was First Class.

Dropping his baggage and trenchcoat on the mackled platform at his feet, he took off once again for the booking hall, calling as he went to an idling porter to please put them in the compartment with the young lady, and he would be back in a jiffy. "Cuttin' it a bit fine, ain't ye, mate?" the porter said glumly. But the barrier was not yet closed, and he took his chance.

When he arrived back with his new ticket, the carriage doors were being clapped to and the guard was about to raise his flag, but the train itself had yet to lunge forward into motion. A door was being held open for him by the porter, now intent upon earning a tip—"Thank ye, sir"—who did not go so far as to touch his cap. This last door closed, the train lunged forward. As he watched through the corridor windows, Platform Four and all King's Cross Station began gliding by on their unknown journey—pillars, vault, things and people all in motion—summarily carried off into the Euston Road. The thought occurred to him that this outing in Valija's company was already costing him more than his parents had ever spent on a whole weekend at dear old Frinton-on-Sea.

"There you are," she said, looking up from her book when he slid back the compartment door. "I thought you might come looking for me later, once the train had got going. Were those your things a porter just brought in?" His suitcase was flat under one of the seats, and his grip and trenchcoat were in the luggage rack. On either side of the compartment were three roomy seats placed *en face*, as the French say—though very far from in one another's faces. Each was furnished with armrests and a fresh antimacassar at head height; its upholstery, flowered plush, neither dusty nor worn, shone richly. No framed Pickford advert or photogravure of the "not to be missed" Grampians fretted the eye of a seated passenger. There were two mirrors and, reflected in them, two lights glowing under burnished lampshades. The floor was carpeted in deep maroon. Drapes hung at the window where an air freshened. He thought absurdly of Catherine Barkley in a hotel on the Via Manzoni saying, "'I've never felt like a whore before.'" Her hair, too, shone under the light.

"Hullo," he said, remembering to smile with his eyes, and moved forward to kiss her. Whose mother was it who taught him always to kiss the lady on entering a house? All that he could manage, ensconced as she was within two armrests and the table top she had raised in front of her to rest a book on, was a peck on the cheek. "The train isn't as crowded as one might think." He eased into the seat opposite hers and looked out of the window. They were plunging into the blackness of the Gasworks tunnel, while smoke from the chimney swirled past outside, wreathing their reflections.

"Only one stop, at Peterborough," he went on, "and then we change at East Retford for the 10:13 to Northfleet—but that will be a stopping train." Why was he behaving like the *pater familias* who had paid for her ticket?

She said nothing.

"You're seated with your back to the engine I see," he said.

She had looked back down at her open book. Beside it she had a little notebook and pencil. Now she looked across at him neutrally. "And what have *you* brought to read? Where's your Richard Jefferies?"

"I finished it at home last night. I was looking forward to talking with you now. I feel I've known you all my life but in fact know nothing about you"—she was giving him the raised eyebrow—"well, hardly anything. What are you reading?"

She held up a slim book in red library binding so that he could read its spine: *Richard of Bordeaux* by Clemence Dane. Why not some crochet to do as well?

"Is it any good? It's a play, isn't it?"

"It's not Shakespeare. I'm doing a thesis you know, on verbic extension in modern English; and my sample is all dramatic dialogue published in London during the '30s."

"That could be fun I suppose. Ben Travers and all that. We used to look for farces like *Cuckoo In The Nest* to read during the war. I told you that, didn't I?"

"Yes. But I shan't be coming to T for quite a while, being just up to D, as you see. I'm working through the B.M. Catalogue." Her heart-shaped face took on a slightly hard, tired look.

"Verbic extension? That's like . . . 'put up with?' As in 'up with which I will not put?'"

She gave him a grimace, mock offended, and opened her play at a previously marked page. They sat in silence while the compartment swayed and rattled reassuringly around them. The train had come out into evening sunlight, blinding their window with gold, and was gathering speed before plunging with a shriek of the whistle into the next tunnel.

"Have you really nothing to read? Isn't that a book up there in the pocket of your grip?"

"Yes. I usually have one or two about me, especially when I travel alone." He stood up and took down what she had in view, the new Eric Ambler, *Judgement On Deltchev*. He would have preferred to save it for a time when he could give it his full attention.

Settled back in their seats, they both read without interruption for some twenty minutes or more, while backs of tenements and yards full of cable drums rushed by outside.

Near Hatfield a restaurant car attendant came through, telling them that last seats for dinner were now to be had. He was followed by an inspector who asked for their tickets and clipped them with a flourish. When they were alone again, Valija put her work aside and turned to the bulging satchel on the seat beside her. She also had a large suitcase and a raincoat in the rack overhead.

"Will you have a little supper with me?" she said. "I packed enough for two in case you joined me."

Putting his Ambler aside, he said that he would love to.

She unpacked two paper napkins, one for him and one for herself, and two tiny fifty millilitre bottles. "Not what you are used to," she said, "but this is a Lithuanian picnic. I thought of bringing glasses, but on a train at this speed it is better to swig from the bottle."

He tried to read the label. "*Slyva vynas,*" she said, "from plums."

"Ah," he said, "related to Balkan slivovitz. Serious stuff."

She was unwrapping greaseproof paper from around what looked like a gourmet version of one of his mother's Mickfield sausage rolls. "*Pyragelis,*" she said, "not still warm, I am sorry to say, but fresh."

It turned out to be very tasty. They sipped the wine and savoured the little pastries contentedly. She had brought two for each of them and, as dessert, a small lemon curd tart. Bluestocking though she might be, she evidently had her domestic side.

"That is all," she said finally.

"Who would have thought rationing was still with us?" he said by way of praise and thanks. She was tidying the table top, folding their napkins full of pastry crumbs into the waste bin. They each still had some wine to finish. "Please have a cigarette if you would like," he said, "and excuse me if I don't have one with you." The compartment she had chosen was for smokers.

She nodded knowingly, smiling a little. "*Kupe rukantiems,*" she said. Why did mealtime always tend to take people back to their roots?

When she had lighted her cigarette, he said, "How about an after dinner poem for the train?" And when she raised her eyebrows as if to wait and see, he began:

"This is the night mail crossing the Border,
Bringing the cheque and the postal order,

Letters for the rich, letters for the poor,
The shop at the corner, the girl next door."

"More film poetry," she said, interrupting him, "and not even your own." She looked out of the window at valleys paved with rooftops swerving by. In the vicinity of Stevenage or Hitchen, somewhere suburban was being left behind and the move on to a high speed stretch before Huntingdon was in the making. "Had you no poem for Marianne when she went home to Alabama last June? Nothing of yours for that delightful young woman?"

Encouraged by their moment of intimacy at tea in Christy's the day before, he tried his luck at pleasing her yet once more with a poem written for someone else. "You won't think much of this," he said diffidently. But she only sat back smiling, smoking, and waiting like the confidante she was.

"It's called *Daisy Fay,*" he said unhappily.

> *"'Perhaps Daisy never went in for amour at all.'*
> *And on her blue lawns guests*
> *Among the heaven flowers grew*
> *Enamoured of the negro music,*
> *While she sat white gowned*
> *Below the flower tree and swung*
> *A gallows song: as Gatsby said*
> *That evening waiting in his car,*
> *Her voice was full of money—*
> *And yet undying on the air*
> *Those trumpets death pale hung*
> *All summer long."*

Valija finished her De Reszke Minor, stubbing it out in the ash tray nearest to hand. "So sad," she said. "So brief."

"I told you it wouldn't please you."

"Oh, but it does. Ah, Marianne. She is so *nice*. Do you hear from her?" The tone in which she asked the question implied that she, sadly, did not.

"Niceness is much undervalued. Lawrence in one of his poems may make fun of it as another English hypocrisy but Americans can be so nice, too—the Anglos, at least—and it sets them apart as good people. Deception and mistrust may be everywhere but in my experience they don't cancel niceness. People want to discard the word 'nice' because it is vague and sentimental, like the word 'real,' but there's no doing without it once one knows what it *can* mean. Every good quality has a true and a false function. To define true niceness is a work of dialectics, as in the *Praise of Folly*."

"What on earth brought this on?"

"It's too easy to get someone as nice as Marianne wrong," he said as if in excuse. "But let's not talk any more about my favourite people. Let's talk about yours. Am I ever going to meet your uncle? Tell me about him."

"You are baffled by her going away out of reach, aren't you?" She said it kindly, as she did most that she said to him. But he did not respond, waiting instead for her to respond—if she would—to his leading question. Outside, farms and fields and nightsheltering cattle fell away to the southwest. All was still clearly visible but daylight was beginning to fade.

"'Nice' is not the word for my Uncle Jurgis. He has many good qualities, and I owe him everything. He has provided for me as if I were his sister's only son. At heart he is a soldier— and niceness is not what soldiers are made of. But he is the nicest a soldier can be—so far as I am concerned—and simply the most interesting man I have ever met." She lapsed into silence.

"What do you suppose he is doing at this very moment?"

"What a peculiar question! I have no idea"—she glanced at her watch. "Let's say, working on a new edition of *The Silent Woman* somewhere near Cambridge?" She looked out of the corridor window toward the darkening east.

An attendant was passing by their compartment and Brenan

signaled to him to slide back the door. "Is coffee still being served in the restaurant car? Could we be served?" The attendant signified as much and Brenan looked at Valija, waiting for her to demur.

"What a nice thought," she said. And so they made their way up the train to the restaurant car together. As they passed a toilet she said, pausing, "You go on, Michael. I will find you."

When she joined him at a table to the right of the car, this time looking east, a waiter was hovering. The dinner sitting being over, the long, swaying car of tables under white cloths was all but empty. "Ye're not thinking of getting off at Peterborough, are ye, sir, madam?" said the waiter. They reassured him that they were not.

She looked out across the fenland at a fading view of brickfields piled up in the gathering dusk. "If this were France," she said, "a pot of coffee would be the nicest of thoughts. But since this is England, hadn't you better order tea?"

He felt a certain unkindness in her voice, but not for sure, and he did as she said. They sat in silence, watching the changing scene until their tray was brought. Then she did the pouring. There was lemon for her as well as milk and sugar for him. The tea, they agreed, was quite good.

"A magic journey so far," he said unwisely. "Compartment all to ourselves, supper together; it knocks Hannay and Pamela on Hitchcock's Highland Express into a cocked hat. Our own little *kupe rukantiems* all to ourselves,"—he made a mess of the pronunciation—"we might as well be married—all but the handcuffs." She did not find what he was saying at all amusing.

"You set far too much store by Alfred Hitchcock, Michael. He is an old creep—an old Catholic creep—worse than Graham Greene. Don't you remember Marianne saying so on the night of the party in Highfield last spring? You had been holding forth tipsily about silk stockings, Madeleine Carroll, and the Princess Flavia as the subjects of the trivium ... and your jaw dropped. No such heresy as that the *maestro* is a creep had ever before touched your trembling ears." She did not look or sound as if she were just teasing.

He chose the better part of silence, and sat brooding over their downhill approach to Peterborough. What he had been inclined to ask was why she remembered only the foolish things he said, his bad poems, his pedantic jokes.

Through the glass the somewhat muted spectacle of a main line platform galvanized by the arrival of an express then distracted and amused them for the while. One sight centrally in their view was a motley newsstall, placarded with handlettered headlines and still at this hour open for the sale of papers and magazines. He could have slipped off the train, made a purchase, and slipped back into his seat at the window with impunity; but what might a paper purchased on Sunday night in Peterborough have to say that would be news? One of the placards, meant to cry up a pictorial weekly which even his parents would not be caught dead reading, said, "Tievas To Northfleet By Sea." Still, it was tempting . . . .

Once they were on their way again—towards Grantham now—she offered him a second cup of tea, which he declined. For herself she lighted a cigarette.

"Nice place, Peterborough," he said.

"Splendid cathedral," she said, gently breathing smoke, "but with your taste in buildings, I should have thought Stamford would be the showplace around here."

"Never seen it," he said regretfully. "What do you think Marshal Tievas will do in Northfleet for two days? Are you going to be part of anything he does?"

"The big civic occasion, when Aneurin Bevan is expected to come from Wales, will be on Tuesday. The Chancellor will be at that, the banquet. But the Vice Chancellor has been so kind as to invite me to the farewell reception at his house on Wednesday evening. I should like to put in an appearance then, but the next day, as you know, I have to join Dr. Didelis on Ben Jonson business in Norfolk. It is going to be a hectic week, what with lectures beginning and tutorials, too."

"I have a tutorial with the VC myself tomorrow afternoon. There he'll be in his woodland chancellery, scanning my halting essay and giving me the benefit of his *impressions personelles.*"

"I thought you liked his work, especially the poetry."

"Oh, I do. I do. He's the best of the post-war bunch as far as I can tell. I just wish he weren't so—superfine."

"You care too much about his noticing you for yourself. To him you are just another student. His whole career has been perfectly self-contained. You notice it is Marshal Tievas, the historic European figure, who is visiting *him*, the minor English poet, not *vice versa.*"

"Minor poet *and* war hero, well-known for his classic memoir 'With Cloak and Dagger in Gdainys'—or whatever it is called."

She said nothing.

He noted with satisfaction that she was taking her time over her cigarette, in no great hurry to be back with verbic extension in the work of Elizabeth MacKintosh, *alias* Clemence Dane, *alias* Josephine Tey. Looking out over the violet land at hedgerows rising and dipping and farm houses as yet unlighted, he said, as if to himself, "Lincolnshire. Very flat . . . . Somewhere that way lies the little town of Bourne and the neighbouring village of Edenham where Frederic Manning once lived and wrote his poems, and *Her Privates We*, and other fine things. If ever we are able to travel in time as well as space—backwards, I mean—my first visit of all will be to him, there at the Bull in the early '30s, one summer's day when T.E. Lawrence stops by on his motorbike heading south . . . ."

"Michael, Michael," she said gently, shaking her head, "'this is the land of *lost* content'—not of *content*. What will you possibly say to them?"

"Very little. I shall just look, and listen, as long as they let me. Manning will chain smoke; whisky will be drunk—a single malt, I expect. If there is occasion I shall propose the health of Private 19022 of the Shropshires. At this point in his life he will look rather like the actor Claude Rains in Hitchcock's *Notorious*—quietly elegant, time weathered, dead within a year or two. I might even ask if he will let me see his *Golden Coach*, the Romance he never finished."

"I never have been to Bourne, and the only Mannyng I have read is *Handlyng Synne* by Robert of Brunne, the Gilbertine canon—which reminds me, Dr. Croker will be lecturing on it this term, beginning tomorrow morning."

"Are you sure? I was planning to go—I need all the help I can get with the Middle English dialects—but I thought he would be doing the *Ancrene Riwle* since it's set for finals, and *Handlyng Synne* isn't. You know, *a nonne may kepe no beeste but a catte*, and so on?" He smirked.

She was, for some reason, less than interested in his fantasy of starveling Dr. Croker and the anchoress's rule of life. "We shall see, shan't we?" she said with finality.

Eyes down, look in, he told himself in words that his father always used at any sign of danger from the fair sex or those in authority.

She watched in silence while he found the bill left by the waiter, fished in his trouser pocket, and counted out payment for their tray of tea in shillings and sixpences.

Whenever two young people first entertain the notion of being in love, trying to love one another or die, there comes a moment of mutual recoil, of wanting perversely to be alone, a stranger among strangers. But such a moment rarely comes when they are apart, out of one another's sight, or when they happen to be thrown very close together—as now. Standing up from the table, Brenan and Valija find themselves—at a lurch of the car—wrapt in one another's arms without having meant to be. Smiling, but saying nothing, they disentangle and move off down the swaying aisle, she to the fore.

Past closed compartments in First and Second full of faces and figures, they make their way along one vacant corridor after another. Out of the window, perilously spread, furnaces in the redbrick machine shops of Grantham glow fierily, their beds of coal burning, burning—even on so peaceable a night as Sunday. Every time Valija comes to a coupling she pauses for Brenan to reach round her and slide open the heavy door between carriages, and they pass through together, one behind the other. The third time she does this, instead of opening the door, Brenan looks her in the eye, then puts his arms around her and kisses her on the mouth. Where they are standing no one, even in the nearest compartment, can actually see them— though who knows who might be coming up on the other side of their unopened door? It is not in Valija's character to respond to anything with unease or surprise. She kisses him automatically in return. For a long moment the unrelenting express shakes and worries them into wakefulness. Enfolded and enfolding, she opens one eye only an inch from his and, as if conspiring with him, murmurs, "Not the place, Michael. Not the time."

At their compartment door he reaches to open it and is dismayed to see that the first seat inside, facing the engine, is now occupied. "Thank *you*, Peterborough!" he says under his breath, more for himself than for Valija. They go to their seats at the window and, without a word, take up their books and read on—uncomfortably aware of being seen without being watched.

Their fellow passenger is a tall, lean woman of their parents' generation, sporting brown tweeds and a green felt hat. She keeps her attention firmly on the *Illustrated London News*, except for an occasional glance out of their window at the gathered dark. The corner seat in front of her is occupied by a sizeable leather weekend case, waiting, as it were, for someone who knows his manners to lift it into the rack overhead.

Something about her starts him thinking of Mrs. Offord, John's mother—her air of knowing what is what, perhaps, though without the mitigating charm of being vulnerable. Brenan is one of those unfortunates for whom similarity signifies more than difference and the world is full of look alikes, the compensation being that he can usually see another person's point of view. This forbidding fellow passenger his father, who has a weakness for nicknaming, would simply write off as an "Iron Jaws." But then his father, as his mother has been heard to remark, "doesn't really *like* women."

Newark-on-Trent comes and goes suddenly in a cluster of gauzy lights and that change of pitch, of clatter, which only a hurtling station can cause. Brenan perseveres with his reading of Ambler. Eventually he arrives at a long passage of reflection on the treason trials in Eastern Europe that seems to call for undivided attention; so, with a sigh, he sets it aside. When Valija looks up from her reading and notemaking, he catches her eye and winks. Her left eyebrow rises infinitesimally.

As if they were alone, he says,

> *"Tag und nicht hat Ich gedichtet*
> *Und hat doch nichts gerichtet."*

She will have nothing to do with such nonsense. Without putting down her pencil, she says a little wearily, "I shall let *you* translate, Michael."

"I am reminded of old Meux at school in the Remove. He would look all round the room over his spectacles, licking his chops, and say in a sort of chant, *'Ver hat nicht gelesen?* Ah, Brenan, *auf Deutsch bitte; dann auf Englisch.'*"

In silence and expressionless she waits.

"Interesting verb, *ausrichten*. Has any number of uses, military as well as civil, as in *richte ihr einen Gruss von mir aus,* or *sich nach jemandem ausrichten*—to line oneself up with somebody as a target. Heine seems to be complaining that, though he has worked on his poem day and night, he still can't get it lined up right. Does poetry make anything happen?"

She twiddles her pencil. "I hope you speak French better than you do German," she says, turning back to her work.

Having tried to be clever, he can but feel crestfallen. "It's true," he says ruefully, "Housman is more one's cup of tea than Heine.

Into my heart an air that kills
From yon far country blows."

Their fellow passenger opens her travelling case and, without revealing any of its contents, deftly puts away her illustrated weekly. Then she spends the rest of the time until the upcoming stop gazing fixedly out of their window.

"Retford. East Retford. Change here for Gainsborough, Brigg, Barnetby, Brocklesbury, and Northfleet. East Retford next!" The ticket inspector comes up the corridor calling his news and, when he sees Brenan and Valija stirring, slides back their compartment door. "Change here for Northfleet."

Valija puts her book away, and starts buckling her satchel.

"East Retford, the town that Baedeker forgot," says Brenan gratingly, taking down her suitcase and raincoat from the rack. For some reason he all at once feels ill-tempered, out of sorts, absent.

"Thank you. I can manage," Valija says. Still some distance out of the station, the train is losing speed fast. Needlessly, they begin rushing their preparations to alight. He has taken down his grip and is tucking away his Ambler safely in a pocket. She is already on her way out of the compartment, making for a door at the end of the carriage. Are they, after all, no longer journeying together?

Brenan gets into difficulty retrieving his suitcase from under the seat where Iron Jaws is sitting. Embarrassed, she has to listen to the excuses he has to make. With both hands full, he takes flight and catches up with Valija and several other alighting passengers just as the train grinds to a stop.

Out on the platform, *terra firma,* the usual panurgency has broken out. An all but unintelligible public address points them up the train and over the bridge to Platform Two where the

10:13 is expected any minute. Starting up the stairs, she stops and looks back at him.

"Where's your trenchcoat?"

"*Jesus wept!* You go on; I'll catch up with you." He turns and hurries back down the train as fast as he can while she continues up and across and down to where a sprinkling of passengers already await their Northfleet connection.

She takes her place at the platform's edge, facing across an empty track to where the express stands fuming and chafing. Somewhere down to Valija's right, Michael is retrieving his *verlorene Regenmantel*. Opposite where she stands, a window on the express goes down, and a familiar voice calls softly across the track in Lithuanian, "Valija, is that you?"

"Antanas! Mr. Baltrušaitis, what in the world brings you here?"

In the lights and darks of the station his pretty face is a smiling mask. "Jurgis wants me to interview at York tomorrow. Tell me, is that your new English boy friend, Mr. Brenan, that you are travelling with?"

As soon as she nods and looks behind her to the stairs which Brenan will come down, Baltrušaitis turns away out of sight and the window goes up. It is quite remarkable what can be done with a mere platform ticket and a little initiative.

Making its first powerful manifesto, the express lunges forward. At the same moment the train for Northfleet shuffles discreetly into Platform Two. Evidently the now invisible express was not waiting for this local, a Retford original. Over the bridge and down the stairs scrambles Brenan, clutching both bags and juggling his folded trenchcoat over one shoulder. Valija sighs.

At every stop before Northfleet, groups of young people, most of them returning students, enter the train. Here, thinks Brenan, is where we see faces we know. It is curious how the boys as well as the girls dress up in their best to return to college on a Sunday night. Some look familiar, but none happens to choose Brenan and Valija's compartment, and no corridor connects theirs with the others. In Retford, they have failed to find any First Class carriage at all to go with their tickets. They are sharing a compartment in Second with a family of four returning, it transpires, from a weekend with relatives. The two young children, a boy and a girl, snuggle sleepily against their parents who whisper endlessly together, first about the weather—thunderstorms are forecast—then about work—the husband is an electrician in the docks—and finally about their relatives. Brenan and Valija sit side by side opposite this family and vegetate: the lighting makes it difficult to read. The country they are passing through slowly becomes more familiar and more vague. At one point he dreams he hears the cry of gulls.

After Gainsborough she stifles a yawn and asks quietly, "Have you ever visited the George Eliot places hereabouts?" He says he hasn't but would like to. If ever he has a car, there will be so much to see. Windmills, for example—more of them are to be found around here than anywhere else in England. There were once windmills on the heath at home he says. But one can always take a country bus to Gainsborough she says; a car is not everything.

'Oh, that reminds me. On Saturday at tea you told me about Guy Fawkes bonfires on the heath, and later in the Hospital library I came across a local history which went into detail about them. Do you know that in the 1860s the Greenwich mob would parade noisily past Our Lady Star of the Sea with the effigy before burning it in Washerwoman's Hollow as a warning to Roman Catholics?"

"Roman Catholics like you and me, you mean? Guy Fawkes long since lost any religious or political meaning in Greenwich—though the place did become a nest of Papists, I suppose, especially from Ireland."

"Hollow? Hole? Didn't you call it Washerwoman's *Hole?* Which is it?"

"What's the odds?"

Why are we talking like this, he asks himself. Why aren't we just enjoying one another? I want to believe that when

Tievas was being mauled in the chapel, Valija was sitting in the library reading *Catiline* unawares. But is this likely? Is it probable? *Do I care?*

After Brigg, on towards Barnetby, he feels the usual aura of *Orphée*—Orphée at the outset of his errand into Hades at the bidding of La Mort. It is a land of little more than level crossings, harsh-named halts (at which there is no stopping), gangs of workmen in the night. Then comes the solace of remembered level crossings from his own boyhood, below the Edge or out at Kidbrooke—afternoons spent with Patrick and later John, watching the gates close and open and the cargoes glide safely through for industrial Woolwich on the river, for residential Welling in the fields.

After Brocklesby they begin to anticipate entering the city, its spires and cranes, domes and statues, canals gray with industrial froth. Passing through semirural Stonham on the northwestern outskirts—tumbled graves around the church, the Dragon, a last level crossing before the terminus—they catch glimpses of Somersby, its slate and redbrick down below the tree tops. The train's whistle sounds.

"You will be seeing John tonight, won't you? For the first time in months."

"I shouldn't be surprised." All he wants to say is *Somersby*—ah, Somersby! According to Huby, the Browningites would have named it Spilsby but, thank Heaven, the Tennysonians prevailed. What he does say is, "Have you never visited Somersby?" And, when she shakes her head primly in rebuke, "Then you must. Come to tea on Tuesday." They both smile over what they think is their secret.

At the dark terminus, down the long cool arrival platform momentarily crowded, not far from the ticket barrier, Brenan thinks he sees someone familiar, not from the college but from Greenwich—the man who stood with Vaughan behind the railings at the Naval College that morning. But then the hatted, raincoated figure is gone as soon as glimpsed. Brenan says nothing to Valija.

Out in the station forecourt, they can see that the night sky is full of high white clouds, covering and then discovering a young moon. They smell the fish dock and the sea. Along towards the sidings there is a scattering of grain on the cobblestones. The Station Hotel bar and the Sailor's Return are both closed and dark.

It takes what seems a lifetime for a cab to come but, once it picks them up, it has them to Highfield in a flash. The college buildings for the most part cluster in the western quarter, alongside four hundred acres of common. Across its copses and clearings, Highfield looks south towards an intersecting avenue of approach to and from the Bargate of the old town and the docks below it.

Once stopped in the front drive of her well-lighted, bustling hall of residence, Valija takes charge. From the back seat she tells the cabbie that Brenan is to be driven on to Somersby; she pays her part of the fare and asks for her baggage to be put in the foyer. Then she opens the cab door and slips out, holding it open. Several of Highfield's young ladies are to be seen and heard in the foyer and at open windows, going about their pleasant business of being just back from the long vacation.

She gives him her hand in a friendly handshake. "Thank you, Michael," she says, smiling with her eyes.

"Quite a journey, Valija."

She nods in agreement. "Aren't you glad it's over?"

"Yes, but . . . ."

She has clapped the door to and turned away up the steps to the front entrance, intent.

End of Part One.

PART TWO

FROM LONDON FAR

Tower'd cities please us then
And the busy hum of men

~Milton

Chapter Five

A Guilty Vicarage

i

Matins with Lauds
~Book of Hours

I f one opens the 1951 *Calendar* of University College, Northfleet, and turns to the School of Divinity, one finds but a single name—that of Hubert Ethelwold Lacy, D.D. (Oxon). This denotes in one person three distinct identities: first, the Reverend Hubert Lacy, Chaplain to the College; second, H.E. Lacy, Esq., Professor of Divinity and Church History; and third, Huby Lacy, Warden of Somersby Hall of Residence for Men, South Stonham. Father, son, and holy ghost, as his less deferential charges were quick to point out.

The duties of the first-mentioned, the Chaplain, in a provincial redbrick college overseen by the Senate of London University (creation, he would growl, of "the godless Jeremy Bentham") tended to be at most ceremonial, infrequent, not to say perfunctory; and the duties of the second-mentioned, the Professor, proved all but nonexistent since the post-war influx of undergraduates to Northfleet had yet to include so many as two intending divines or church historians. But the duties of the third and last-mentioned, the Warden, were of another order altogether. These were such as made, in practice, a very notable difference to the quality, character, and distinction of life in the college—especially as far as the young men within his ward were concerned.

Dr. Lacy brought to Northfleet from Oxford—not Cambridge as mere proximity might have led one to expect—something of the boundless spirit, the *panache*, of the elder university. There, at Magdalen College in the 'twenties after war service in Flanders, he had been a brilliant late bloomer, much seen and heard in the Harold Acton set *et toute cette galère*. Less than half of the thousand and more Northfleet students, male or female, could elect to reside in any of the four college halls dotted about the western quarter of the city; the majority, men in Engineering or Navigation, lived either locally with their parents or in digs: competition for the privilege of a place in hall, especially in Somersby, was fierce. Under Dr. Lacy, Somersby set the pace for the rest of the college, socially if not intellectually—or so we who were residents believed. Manifestly, the most collegial way to house at Northfleet was in the somewhat flamboyant yet benign care of Huby. Known as he was to everybody by sight, in his cloaks and bands and buckled shoes and with his grand clerical manner, he was not a person whom anybody wanted to know better. Once he had netted you in conversation, there was no knowing when you might be let go. But for good or ill, ostensively he was Somersby Hall made flesh.

As to the fabric of the place itself, it befitted the college at large, being modest, decent, pragmatic, pleasing and, above all, modern. Designed and built in the functional 1930s, three-quarters of a century after the founding of the Victorian nautical institute out of which the college had grown, Somersby occasioned none of the crowding or other inconvenience experienced in Louth, its neighbouring hall for men. This had originally been designed as a family mansion by Hawksmoor, or so it was thought. Somersby was—and still is—redbrick, quadrangular, and cellular, laid out around geometric lawns and shrub and geranium beds, margined and intersected by well-kept gravel pathways. The quad could be entered front or back, east or west, through a high, double-gated arch in the facade, but only on foot and preferably at the east. There the Stonham Road put out a spur between the very different entrances to Louth and Somersby, forming a convenient little piazza for pedestrians and vehicles, before curving narrowly away to the north around the flinty, towered church of St. Matthew, South Stonham.

In those days, this quiet corner where city and country met, well off main thoroughfares, rarely saw vehicular traffic of any sort. Few undergraduates or members of the faculty ran a car or rode a bicycle. For special outings there was the hired closed car; and for going to the college library or lecture rooms or into town there were the municipal buses and Shanks's pony. Supplies were delivered to Somersby further along the Stonham Road at a tradesman's entrance which gave on to the kitchen yard and the Bursar's office. The front gates at the east were kept—open, most of the time—by a uniformed Head Porter, ex-Sergeant Major Powell, who worked from a little windowed office just inside the paved archway. He was a big, amiable, plausible Welshman from the village who could manage most situations that arose in hall, from the arrival of mail to grounds keeping to the occasional emergency that occurred among the resident faculty, the undergraduates, or the Bursar's women who cooked, waited at table, cleaned, and made beds. I realize as I write that, surprisingly, Michael Brenan and I, who were usually attentive to such matters, never managed to get Mr. Powell talking in detail about any of his twenty-one years' service in the army.

That fine Monday morning of October 11, it was by the half open Dutch door of his office, framed in notices, that

Michael Brenan passed, with a nod and a word, on his way to a lecture about either the *Ancrene Riwle* or *Handlyng Synne*. "We shall see, shan't we?" Valija had said coolly on the train the night before, meaning that she would be there to find out which it would be. He started briskly across the piazza, admiring as always from this vantage point the well-tended, tree-lined expanse of playing field just across the road. For the coming season, rugger and soccer pitches were already marked out. Nobody would be seen coming up to bowl for another six months and more. Within three weeks the tennis nets would be taken down for the winter.

"Mick. *Mick*. **Mick**!" Plump, diminutive, vociferous Huby Lacy came from the lychgate of St. Matthew's in full cry, his cassock proclaiming that he had duly celebrated the morning office.

Brenan turned back and they met within the purview of Mr. Powell where he sat at his window but out of earshot. *The dripping mill wheel is again turning.* "Hello, sir, how are you?"

"Where *have* you been keeping yourself? Still sporting those awful bugger boots, I see. I do hope you've been going to confession regularly during the vac. Whatever time was it when you got in this morning? I tell Mr. Powell not to lock the gates at eleven, as you are aware, but this means that anyone coming in later should always let me know . . . . I looked for you last evening. Your friend John was in hall well in time for dinner. That compatriot of your *ilk* from County Armagh has been here since heaven knows when—at least since Michaelmas! And we have a nice new American for you to make friends with, thanks to Senator Fulbright, Al Yates by name. I have put him on the third floor of E with your other cronies. Perhaps he will console you for the loss of last year's Miss Alabama . . . . I trust you left your parents in good health."

"Thank you, yes; thriving." He answered politely, without giving Billy or Bessie a second thought for the present. A world away from home, heath, and river, with Valija for company— thanks be to fortune!—he listened, and smiled, and said, and worried as little as was needed. Huby was obviously on yet one more of his tears, but meant no harm or not very much. What was on his breath was communion wine and, perhaps, a glass or two of Cockburn's sherry before breakfast. Huby the Preposterous, somebody in hall had once dubbed him, and the word had caught on. But *histrio* was a better word for him, the eternal undergraduate as actor. With a theatrical change of tone, he now began extemporizing *sotto voce*, there in the middle of the piazza, on one of his several announced themes.

"My dear Mick, I do wish you and John could be more of an *influence*, you know, on your friend and neighbour Arthur. He is in serious trouble. He has turned out to be a disgrace to the diocese in more ways than one. There's no other way of putting it, disgrace—with that *minx* Mrs. Purvey, of all people. Her making the bed is one thing, but hopping into it for a quick one with Arthur beforehand is *quite* another! I can't imagine what I was thinking of when I let the Bursar take her on."

This was troubled water that Brenan had no intention of getting into with the Warden of Somersby. Sally Purvey was, like his own Mrs. Wilson, one of the domestics, only much younger and, by all accounts, far more complaisant. He had a faint impression of a stringy, sour-looking blonde whose path rarely crossed his. She had a rocky marriage to a hard-drinking Stonham man, a poacher and a ne'er-do-well known as Long Will, who now and again obliged Mr. Powell with some heavy work around the hall, ditching and the like.

Brenan said vaguely, "I don't believe I've actually met Mrs. Purvey. Does she take care of all three floors of E block?" And then, before Huby could enlighten him further, he held out his hand. "Delighted to be back, sir. Forgive me if I dash. I have a lecture on the *Ancrene Riwle* to go to—set book, you know."

Huby held on to his hand. "You don't mean you're off to sit at the feet of my colleague the Scarecrow, who thinks that early church texts in English are just so much mediaeval grammar and syntax? Ah well, let's hope this means that for finals year you're settling down to be a swot before it's too late. Perhaps I shall see you after dinner this evening." Then he wheeled away into the Somersby arch, calling to Mr. Powell—something about a man from the Post Office who would be seeing to the JCR phone. On any one day, Huby, the free fisher, always had lines in at least half a dozen different pools.

On his way up the Stonham Road to where a green doubledecker for college and the city center stopped every quarter hour on Saltfleetby (pronounced *Sullaby*), Brenan mused upon the wreck of his fellow student Arthur Bresnahan. Tall, dark, disheveled, fey, Arthur was of Eire and the not-so-holy land of Eire. An odd man out among the youthful English midlanders of Somersby, a little older than most of them, he had been in hot water with Huby since the previous spring, his first at the college, when a loaded revolver had been reported—and found by Mr. Powell—in his room. Presumably, the weapon was a precaution he had taken against the jealous fury of Long Will. But what sort of excuse was this? Few of the interested parties knew Arthur well enough to realize what an unlikely suspect he was where any putative I.R.A. connection was concerned, though it was true that he led his life as if he did not expect to be alive beyond Thursday. Small wonder that he and the immortal Huby never saw eye to eye. To Brenan and Offord, Arthur was a figure of peculiar interest and fond concern, originally because he resembled some Celtic *eidos* of Michael himself, the near-Cockney. They would refer to him, as the Romans did to an Irishman, as *Scotus*, and sometimes—though not to his face—as Wandering Arthur. He seemed to have no family other than a married half-sister in Liverpool; and where such money as he spent came from was never clear. He did not acknowledge that, like so many older students at Northfleet, he was on a government grant. Perhaps he wasn't. Certainly, he was forever hard up and on the scrounge.

Arthur had been the first to greet Brenan when he had

arrived in hall the night before. No sooner had he found his key and opened his door, dropped his things on the carpet, turned on the low table lamp, and slumped into his chair by the window, than there in the doorway, lollygagging, stood Arthur, the pride of Armagh. Re-entry after the long vac always made Brenan feel more of a stranger in hall than he was: whose was that unfamiliar face in the quad—what'shisname, the president of the JCR? This unbelievably tidy room smelling of Mrs. Wilson's furniture polish, this empty cupboard, whose could they be? It would take a week or two of routine, of hebetude, to make such a clinical corner of D block his own, one that he enjoyed being in. For the moment, what he wanted most was to take a long, hot shower, fall into bed, and finish reading his new Ambler. Meanwhile here was Arthur, smiling his soft, wounded smile.

"*Thought* it was you, Michael, I saw slipping past in the night unbeknownst. How were the summer holidays?" He had a book under his arm, which made him look unlike his usual self. The degree he was doing, as far as Brenan could make out, was in Economics. But they never talked together about studies or the future, always about moods or meditations, what was on the wireless or in the papers, the racing results at Doncaster. Arthur especially liked to discuss the weekly Crazy Show on the BBC Home Programme, though the Goons proper had yet to come on.

"All too brief, Arthur, all too brief. How the hell are things with you?"

"I'll tell you. I just woke up from a terrible dream. You'll think I'm fanti, but listen to this. I was back home at the county fair, looking for a ride on the big wheel. The woman in charge, a right duchess by the dress of her, called me out first of the cluster that was waiting to take a chair. To start with, every chair was empty; she turned me right up to the top of the wheel and then brought me down again slowly while she filled up the half below me chair by chair. I could see all across the town and beyond, nearly to the border. When she had me down to the ground again, 'Out you come, Arthur,' she says. And when I refused, she had a couple of her gypsies throw me out of the fair ground. The funny thing was that then she started the wheel turning for the ride proper without filling my chair or any of those in front of me. There couldn't have been more than half a dozen chairs taken. When I asked her—as they were dragging me away—what she was up to, she said, as if quoting some folk tale. 'If Waynor have wrought well, well may it betide her.' How do you like that for a dream nobody wants to be burdened with?"

Brenan had not wanted to be burdened with it either, but he had said sympathetically, "Sounds as if you might be having woman trouble, Arthur."

"Not on your life, lad. I've been given my marching orders, and taken 'em, and I've met a new one from the old country, barmaid down at the Ship, near the fish dock. No, if it's woman trouble coming, I'm ready for it. This is what bamboozles me: I've no idea what *sort* of trouble to expect."

"Well, not every dream is prophetic. Have you asked John about it? I'm just going over to see if he's still up and about. If he is, let's ask him what Freud he say about big wheels." Brenan came to his feet, a little wearily. "What's the book, Arthur?"

Arthur had edged into the room between the foot of the bed and the low table. "That's a lovely light your lampshade gives," he said. "However did you come by a folderol like that?"

There were times when he was talking that he reminded Brenan of the young James Mason in films as early as *I Met a Murderer*— much scrawnier, of course, but with that air of being nobody's fool, an otherworldly, contemplative manner. "It was a gift from a French girl I knew here in my first year. Yes, I like the way it filters the light. You know, Huby says it looks like a souvenir from a brothel."

No mention of Huby was going to lead a conversation with Arthur anywhere. "Oh, the book, I was forgetting: the poems of William Butler Yeats. I noticed last year that you don't have your own copy. I thought you might like to take this one off my hands for ten bob. I'm running a bit short of change as it happens." It was the delicate rose coloured update on yellow paper of the 1933 collected edition, not mint but unmarked; and Brenan still did not have a copy of his own— he couldn't quite say why. After Eliot, Yeats was his favourite among the moderns. He liked reading the earlier single volumes in their green decorated cloth, but these were hard to come by except on loan from the library.

"Arthur, you can't part with your Yeats, for God's sake! I don't want to be the one to take it away from you. Let me lend you ten bob."

"No, thanks all the same. There'd be no telling if you'd be repaid. Probably never. No, it's better this way: the poems find a good home and I get the change without any strings attached. I'm obliged to you."

In some embarrassment Brenan had taken out his wallet, found a ten shilling note for Arthur, accepted the book and placed it in splendid isolation on his as yet empty shelves over the desk. Then they had gone to E block to look for Offord.

"I'm thinking John may have too much on his plate just now, poor fellah, to be wanting to read my tea leaves," Arthur had said as they climbed the stairs to the third floor.

"You mean Mrs. Offord's illness? Is she worse?"

Arthur nodded compassionately. "The hand that rocks the cradle kicks the bucket," he said, as if he were quoting the book of *Proverbs* rather than repeating a schoolboy joke about not mixing metaphors. Brenan said nothing.

There had been no light under Offord's door, no sound from his room, so they had refrained from knocking and entering. The whole block, indeed the whole of Somersby Hall, was unexpectedly quiet for the eve of the first day of term—even if midnight had come and gone. At the other end of the corridor, however, a door stood ajar and from within came lamplight and the sounds of a typewriter being used with gusto. In those days it was a rare college student who owned a typewriter. Quizzed on the associations of the word, Brenan would probably have answered "secretary" and Arthur "pawnshop." At a momentary loss outside Offord's silent door, they had caught one another's eye: then Arthur had nodded jauntily in the direction of the sound as if it came from a pub still open.

When they rapped on the door, a husky midwestern voice had intoned "Come" in a recognizable echo of Huby's well-known response. But when they entered, the rattle of typewriting persisted. "Let me finish this para, fellers. Make yourselves comfortable." The room was foggy with pipesmoke, every wall plastered with modernist poster art in museum reproduction and homemade enlargements of passages from *The Cantos*, complete with Chinese ideograms where pertinent:

> *Pull down thy vanity*
> *I say pull down*

> *But to have done instead of not doing*
> *this is not vanity*

And other sad sounds.

"Al wanted to put that one in the WC," said Arthur confidentially, "but the Bursar wasn't having any."

Brenan had never seen a Somersby room so untidily full of a number of things: the cupboard, standing open, stuffed to capacity with clothing and food; the low table furnished with enough bottles and glasses to be a bar; the floor and carpet littered with books and magazines in impromptu stacks. What on earth would Huby or the Bursar think? Arthur was appraising the drinks table.

"He'p yo' se'f to a snifter," the typist had said jovially. "'Fraid the ice is all gone."

"Don't mind if I do," Arthur had replied.

The typist had come to a stop with a flourish, stood up and turned to Brenan, holding out a hand. "Al Yates," he said. "You must be the legendary Michael Brenan. I've heard of you from more sources than one."

"Nothing good, I hope." Brenan had shaken the proffered hand. It was big and broad, with stubby fingers and workmanlike nails, as of one who had grown up working on a farm. Yates was not tall but heavy set, with thick brown hair cut very short, and wide hazel eyes in a fleshy, sunburned face. He looked at least as old as Arthur and almost as well-worn.

"The worst," he said, trying with a lighted match to get his pipe going again, "was that you had *The Waste Land* by heart. My mission will be to convert you from Ol' Possum to Ole Ez."

Brenan had felt, as when encountering Valija in the chapel that Friday, both flattered and suspicious. His new made friends seemed fated to know him better than he would ever know them—or, perhaps, even himself. He had said, sheepishly, "The only conversion I'm capable of, I think, is from poetry to prose, the more evolved, reasonable, mature form—and who knows how long that will take me. Unlike Pound, or Eliot, I happen to think that prose should be as well written as poetry."

"You and Bill Faulkner," Al Yates had said, grinning impishly. "Dragged kicking and screaming out of the nineteenth century."

"Are you doing English here at Northfleet?"

Al Yates had shaken his head. "Politics. Though I hope to take in a few lectures in English, Templeton's in particular—if he gives any. You're all so damned casual about announcing courses and class meetings over here."

This had reminded Brenan that he had a lecture to attend the same morning of that very day, so he had made his excuses and left his fellow students to their nightcaps together. "O sleep, the certain knot of peace . . . ."

When his bus to college came up Saltfleetby Road and stopped for him to board it, he was still musing, no longer on Arthur, or Al Yates, or Huby, but on Valija.

ii

Prime with Terce
~Book of Hours

In those days, a student on the Arts side at Northfleet, woman or man, spent most of a weekday morning in one or other of two imposing but mismatched buildings which faced off across lawns and an approach road right at the centre of the college. On the one hand, there was the library, under the same roof with lecture rooms and offices, including the Registrar's; and on the other hand, there was the student union. Scattered all about this central couple were the Science buildings—offices, labs, greenhouses, engineering shops—which in later days would be the nuclei of a fullscale University of Technology and the Arts.

At first view, the library and the union gave not the least token of having been designed one for the other. In that fashion of farfetched analogy to which Brenan was a willing slave, he liked to allude to the library as "Heorot" and to the union, rather differently, as "Joe Lyons." Indeed, the whole complex of college buildings randomly imposed upon an uncrowded residential suburb can only have looked from the air like so much salt, pepper, grated cheese, and bread crumbs lightly shaken out over a small garden salad. As usual, there was something in what Brenan said; but to my mind neither English nor History, both of which departments inhabited the library building, evinced any heroic fellowship of chieftain, minstrel, and spearman. All but the very senior members were consigned, for office space, to nearby wooden huts left over from the war, when the Royal Air Force had been in occupancy. Perhaps this arrangement was fair enough in the circumstances of post-war austerity, since most junior faculty were returned servicemen anyway, as was Templeton—though being Vice Chancellor as well as part-time tutor in English, he could afford to make an office arrangement of his own.

It must have been the narrow, pitch roofed bleakness of the library building that caught Brenan's fancy and made him think of the timbered meadhall in the *Beowulf*. In fact, the library's fortress-like appearance was probably some delayed Edwardian reflex of the Scandinavian American style of Henry Hobson Richardson's brownstone college architecture. As if on an afterthought or in mere contradiction, the union building on the opposite side of the road was all too indigenous—a cross between modern English town hall and *de luxe* suburban cinema. Blockish, of yellow brick, and windowless except at the back, it was complete with roomy cafeteria and spacious dancing floor—but no theatre. The dramatic society had to perform in a makeshift auditorium where most of the college rituals, including examinations and the granting of degrees, took place. There, behind the library, lay a mazy camp of more or less permanent structures, among them not only the aforementioned faculty huts but also a rustic book pavilion, courtesy of W.H. Smith & Sons, and a small, creaky gymnasium. But behind the student union, and fully overlooked from its floor to ceiling back windows, lay nothing but the denes and nettle beds of a long disused, muddy brickfield.

It was at a trestle table under these high back windows of the union that Brenan this morning sate, nursing a cup of cafeteria coffee and watching the brickfield path along which residents of Highfield Hall walked towards the library and lectures. His bus having delivered him with half an hour to while away before Dr.Croker began lecturing, he felt—having skipped breakfast in Somersby—ready for something wet, warm, and sweet that would keep him wakeful. On a first morning of term, there could be no student newspaper for him to browse on, so he sat and speculated idly—as it happened, on the word *cafard* and its possible relation to that catchy little number "La cucuracha." Cockroaches of the world unite. *Lost of course and myself owing a death.*

Before long he was joined at table by a pair of students he had known and liked in a vague, wondering way ever since those early days at Northfleet when he had met Justine—Elise Myer and Reike Handel—faces in the Underground or in Kensington Gardens along a high wall and spiked railings. He still had no clear notion of how they came to be a pair (though they evidently were one), where they lived, or even which degrees they were studying for. At a guess, he would say that Elise was doing Fine Arts and Reike doing Maths. Like himself, each was a Londoner—this he did know for sure—a metropolitan in temporary exile, one of a small minority up here in *ultima* Lindsey, which might as well be surrounded by sea, being in every other respect one of the several farflung British Isles.

Elise was vivid: a brunette, stylish in dress, plump, as were so many young women of that time, yet she was not quite so beautiful as she might have been. On the rare occasions when he was in her company, Brenan enjoyed it well enough. She tended to talk with him as if she were actually interested in what he thought—mostly about the West End theatre, some recent play by Christopher Fry or Jean Anouilh, perhaps a Sadlers Wells ballet. What she now said, once greetings were over, was, "Too much chicory in this coffee, Michael," as if it might have been his fault after all, but never mind.

Reike said, "*Camp* coffee *with chicory*," echoing the label of the most popular brand of extract—which Bessie, too, had been known to buy and use. He spoke perfect B.B.C. English, much better than any native speaker Brenan had ever known personally. Born in Berlin, Reike had finished school at Emmanuel in central London before coming up to Northfleet. What he usually talked to Brenan about, intently, passionately, was the music of Beethoven, especially the later quartets. Could it be Reike who had told Al Yates that he, Brenan, had *The Waste Land* by heart? He hoped not. All he could recall trying once to discuss in some detail with Reike was the *Four Quartets*.

Where Elise was vivid, Reike was very handsome: broad of face, cotton eyed, gleaming, much better looking than either Tom Conway or George Sanders on the covers of old *Picturegoers*. As Brenan had felt more than once in the presence of Elise and

Reike, looking at them smiling suavely and saying so little, there must be some pleasure, some happiness, he could share with them, if only he knew what. He wondered what it was they wanted, even from one another,what he could do with them, for them. What he had never in his life understood was this *what*.

Then he caught sight of Valija in black, making her way across the sunlit brickfield, and said, "Excuse me, I have a lecture to go to." Not forgetting to take his half full cup and saucer with him as far as the counter, he hurried out of the union to intercept her at the roadside.

Lectures in English at Northfleet varied notably in quality but not at all in kind. They were readings aloud of the lecturer's very own notes on a text, or texts, without benefit of performance or, on his part, any sense of public delivery. There was no conversation between him and his student audience, no mutual questioning—unless one went up afterwards to ask something, in private, as it were. When the fifty-minute hour was up, the lecturer folded his papers and books and beat a dignified retreat. The students, as best they could, would by then have taken copious notes. To know and use Pitman shorthand as George Bernard Shaw did would have been the most practical recourse to have, but no student Brenan knew had ever done so. He had started to learn how on his demob course in the army, but once the six weeks were over, and he was at home again and free to go to the pictures whenever he fancied, he let what he had learned of Pitman slip. It was the same with typing. Writing by hand, reading, seeing films like *The Third Man* were for him much more immediately pleasurable than practicing typing or shorthand, however useful these might prove to be in college. Who ever heard of a poet taking a poem down in shorthand as he was being visited by it? Or typing it up, except to please a publisher? Yet when thinking this, Brenan was reminded, as so often, of *Orphée*, which seemed to refute him. "*L'oiseau chante avec ses doigts.*"

Concerning lectures, Middle English language study, which was queen of the Arts at Northfleet, made the case in point perfectly. Croker the Scarecrow, M.A., D.Litt.(Oxon.), would stalk into the small lecture room—as he now did—without so much as a glance at the seated handful. Once at the lectern, papers all arranged, he would begin reciting in a dry, rustling voice like the wind among dead leaves. Reading fast, and at a fairly high level of abstraction—having written what he wanted to say more for his philological peers than for some poor undergraduate—he came across less like Socrates than like Worzel Gummidge. Emaciated, parchment skinned, wispy haired, stick wristed, with an overactive Adam's apple, he was nonetheless said by those who knew how to benefit from his learning to be, out of the lecture room, a friendly, kind, whimsical man with a charming wife and five children. Unfortunately, Brenan, the modern poet, was not one of his disciples, and suffered accordingly in marks, of which the Scarecrow, as Senior Tutor, was departmental keeper.

It at once emerged that Dr. Croker was reading to whomever it might concern his latest thoughts, not on *Handlyng Synne,* but on the *Ancrene Riwle.* Brenan looked at Valija and Valija looked at Brenan, she with raised eyebrow, he in triumph. They were seated side by side in desk chairs, and she would probably have to be looking over his copy of the text as the lecture proceeded. "Bevis of Hampton, meet Havelok the Dane," he muttered, incomprehensibly in a sinister tone.

When their paths had crossed just previously, at the road between union and library, his greeting to her had been a delighted smile but no word. Instead, he had reached into his jacket pocket, pulled out his little brownish yellowish set book of *Ancrene Riwle* selections and held it up, meaningfully, for her to see. Smiling back, she had reached into her satchel and taken out a copy of the big mud-coloured Furnivall edition of *Handlyng Synne* just to show him.

"Let's wager on it," he had said. "If you're right, I never darken your doorstep again. If I'm right, you come to lunch with me after this lecture."

"We are not still on vacation," she had said, but had gone along with him, holding hands while they crossed the roadway.

For this moment at midmorning, there were students and vehicles everywhere. "Whichever Dr. Croker chooses," she went on, "the Mannyng would be the better: more entertaining, never a dull moment, full of anecdotes—and, above all, versified in a local dialect." She had looked about her, as if to be reminded that this was Lincolnshire, nor was she out of it.

"In couplets?" he had said, but received no answer.

"Dialect is key," she had said. "Last night on the train you were talking as if there were no difference between a nun and an anchoress, and as if the *Ancrene Riwle* were in Chaucerian dialect. You ought to be clear about this: there is a difference; and the *Riwle* is in a thirteenth century northwest midland dialect,or so scholars think. Actually, it would be more interesting linguistically if you had been set to study an alternate version, in manuscript at Cambridge, which goes by the alias of *Ancrene Wisse*. As to anchoresses, they were solitaries, immured in cells built into the walls of churches. They watched the mass through a curtained window."

What on earth brought this on, he had wanted to ask. But instead he had said agreeably, "In our system, the set book, small, examinable, and cheaply in print, is the tail that wags the dog. But you can count on the Scarecrow saying at least as much about any alternate version and variant manuscript as about the set text itself."

Once again, in the event, Brenan was proving to be right. After a few throat clearing whispers about unknown authorship, uncertain date of composition, Latin and French versions, and dialectal variety among the English manuscripts, Dr. Croker came to the point. Leaving no time at all for any blandishment such as "finest little prose piece between Alfred and Malory," he started to crepitate:

Ancrene Riwle *being a book of rules for three Christian women leading reclusive lives next door to a church, its salient feature of interest to the historical linguist—and of difficulty, perhaps, for the undergraduate translator—would seem to be the morphology and syntax of its numerous* negative *sentences: statements or speech acts of what* not *to do. On almost any of two hundred and more pages in the modern printed edition, negative syntax such as the following is to be found:*

**For þi þ[et] wepmen ne seoð ow neʒe ham
wel mei don of ower cla ð beo hit hwit
beo hit blac bute hit beo unorne.**

*Since men do not see you nor you them,
it makes no difference whether your garment
is white or black as long as it is not ornamented.*

Those of you who happen to have the set text with you will be able to find this particular sentence on page sixty-nine, but for our present purpose it is not necessary to do so. All we are interested in is the structure of negation in an early thirteenth century English sentence, and how it may be understood and rendered into modern English. Let us consider a very simple negative sentence embedded in the one just cited:

wepmen ne seoð ow
men do not see you

The difference between modern and mediaeval negation here is twofold: (i) the modern has a periphrastic auxiliary word "do" in support, whereas the mediaeval does not; and (ii) the placement of the modern negative "not" is after *this auxiliary verb whereas the placement of the mediaeval negative "***ne***" is* before *the verb "***seoð***." As speakers of modern English, we may be confident that we understand and can translate such a mediaeval sentence. However, in northwest midland dialect (as in others from elsewhere), the syntax of a simple negative sentence sometimes includes* additional *negation, as in*

Nowher ne binetli hire . . . .
Let no one chastize herself with nettles . . . .

or as in

ne na keoruunge ne keorue ....
nor cut herself ....

or as in

Nest lich nan ne gurde hire
with na cunne gurdles
bute þurh schriftes leave.

Do not anyone [of you] gird her body
with any kind of girdle
except by confessor's permission.

*Here it becomes clear that in this syntax negatives were much more frequently used in the same sentence than they are in our modern system. It would appear that fewer restrictions than we are used to governed, not only where negatives were placed, but also how many were used. You will find that double and triple negative constructions are, as a rule, less frequent in our text than the single one with "**ne.**" Still, a question remains whether the double or triple negative is merely a free variant of the single one, or not. Does the double or triple negative perhaps denote emphasis as in our modern expression "definitely* not*"?*

Brenan found his attention definitely flagging after the anchoresses were forbidden to sting themselves with nettles. Out of the windows, a sunny midmorning sky with cumulus cloud beckoned. On his note pad he had written only one sentence: "Two negatives (or more) do not a positive make." He had rewritten it several times. Then he had paraphrased it in French. *Deux zéros—ou plus que deux—ne font que zéro.* He had hoped that Valija would be keeping an eye on his notes, but she wasn't. He looked covertly at her in the chair beside his, careful not to catch her eye. She had already covered more than a page and a half of her note pad with contiguous script. He discreetly began looking around the room at their classmates, all of whom he knew, more or less, and some of whom he quite liked. Sitting at the feet of Huby's colleague the Scarecrow there were four women and two men besides Valija and himself.

Almost in the centre of the room sat a young woman Brenan hardly knew but thought very well of; her name was Iris Jordan. Once in a while her path and his would cross, elsewhere than in lecture, at the new books shelf of the city's public library or at the municipal art gallery, which was interesting enough to have acquired several pieces by Wyndham Lewis and other moderns. He knew that she was someone to talk to, for a few sentences at least, about new books and modern art. But her manner when spoken to—by him, anyway—was, though pleasant enough, never encouraging. Iris was probably the most intelligent person in the room. Ordinary looking, plain of face, brown haired, a rolypoly, she was unmistakably the salt of the earth: sensible, sober, hardworking. She was as plain, and as fine, as the hen bird of a pair. Bessie would love her. Not only could she probably do a crossword in no time at all, but she also would never presume that any (let alone every) mother's son was about to fall in love with and marry her. He wondered where in England she was from. Like most young women, she had a certain mystery to her; hers was from the world of Stanley Spencer, not of Wyndham Lewis, that harsh world of war where Valija was from . . . and Tievas—yes, what about him, the Baltic deputy, this fine Monday morning?

The Scarecrow still crackled away at his lecture like a bundle of twigs on fire; and he caught Brenan's attention by whispering the name of Peterborough:

The so-called Peterborough Chronicle, *which is in a different dialect from northwest Midland, can be dated with some certainty, since it was presumably written at more or less the same time as the events it annalizes. The following sentence is from the annal of the year 1129, when every priest and deacon in England was ordered to get rid of his wife by St. Andrew's Day:*

> ***Ne frama nan clepunge þaerto na hafde mare.***
>
> *[He would] have no further claim to [his church, house, and home] at any time.*

Here the complexity of a simple negative sentence in Middle English becomes apparent. The sentence contains at least three negatives, yet none of them is the equivalent of the only negative we would expect to find in a comparable modern English sentence, "not," i.e., Middle English "*nawt*" as in

Ischoed ne slepe 3e nawt.
Do not sleep with your shoes on.

Or is the sense of this emphatic: "Don't you [dare] sleep . . ."? In fact, it is rare in Middle English to find the negative marked only by "*nawt.*" In the sentence from the Chronicle just cited, a further complexity may be involved: this is negation both in part (constituent) and in the whole of the same sentence (sentential). We should not suppose that this complexity does not exist in modern English; it does. Consider these two types of sentence:

I do not want anybody to see you. (sentential negation)

and

I want nobody to see you. (constituent negation)

In the first, the negative denies the whole sentence, that is the matrix, whereas in the second, the negative denies only a part of the sentence— an underlying somebody who becomes a "nobody." Notice, I say, the comparable complexity of the sentence from the Chronicle. Is the negation in "*ne . . . nan . . . na*" for the matrix or for only part of the sentence?

If we look in our early thirteenth century text for a sentence comparable to each of the two types of modern English negation cited above, we do find one. But in it both types are present together, sentential and constituent. The matrix ("**Nulle ich**") is negated, yet so is the clause ("**ne man iseo ow**") embedded as the direct object of the verb:

Nulle [Ne wille] ich þet nan iseo ow.
I don't want nobody to see you . . . .

Sitting over in the relative glamour of the sunlit side windows of the room, next to a girl whose name Brenan could not recall (though she and he always said a friendly "hello"), was the unignorable Louise Prendergast—daughter of a doctor, president of the Highfield JCR, good at tennis, fit and smart— in fact, good to look at all round. ("There is that Michael Brenan—consorting with a foreigner again.") He would dearly have liked to forget his brief encounter with Louise at the end of their first year, some months after Justine had gone home in gloom to Oran. Out of the blue, Louise had invited him to be her partner at the Highfield annual dance, *the* social event of the Trinity term, and he had been pleased to accept, though he had no designs on her—felt indifferent towards her might be the better way to put it. But a compliment is never wholly unwelcome. He had blighted that otherwise delightful evening of the dance for Louise—and for himself—by *not* wearing a dinner jacket. He did not own one and, for some reason, had simply not bothered to go into the city to Moss Bros. and rent one. When he showed up in the foyer in his customary suit of inky corduroy and gaberdine, even a black bow floppily tied could not save him from the unforgettable look on poor Louise's pretty face. *Boule Miche,* perhaps, but *never* for the Highfield dance!

Valija was now on her third page of notes, having written in larger script across the top of the page: "**Ye, mine leoue sustren, . . . ne schulen habbe na beast bute cat ane—** Michael, n.b." When he caught sight of this *billet doux,* she gave not the least sign of noticing, but kept on writing. The Scarecrow was sounding hoarser and more forbidding by the minute:

> *. . . Nawt ne makeð hire woh.*

Now should we understand this combination of sentential and constituent negatives to be saying

Nothing makes her angry

or to be saying

Something does not make her happy

or to be saying

Nothing does not make her happy

and if we do understand any one of these senses, what does it mean? Our Modern English grammar blocks sentence making such as this . . . .

Brenan's two male classmates in the room were seated apart but near the front, almost underneath the lecturer's glassy eye: David Pengelly, Kenneth Higginbotham. Neither meant much to him. Pengelly, a humorless Methodist swot, had come to college straight from a grammar school sixth form somewhere, and was steamrolling his quiet way through the curriculum. Higginbotham was perky. He may well have been ex-service— it was unclear—but if he was, the service had probably been Royal Air Force ground staff. He always seemed to be wearing invisible bicycle clips but never actually riding a bicycle; he knew what one was about to say even before one knew oneself.

. . . adverbials show clearly how the few restrictions on negative placement and negative incorporation affect meaning in Middle English. In modern English, the negation of "he will always change his home" is adverbial: either "He will never change his home" or "he will not change his home ever." But in Middle English, the negation may be placed at either or both of these points in the sentence as in

> **He ne schal þ[e] stude neauer mare changin**

*where the main verb is denied and "**neauer**" replaces an understood "ever."*

However, the complexity of negation in Middle English may still not be fully appreciated. In Modern English, the sentence "John always likes Mary" can be negated either as "John never likes Mary," or as "John doesn't always like Mary." One may find in Middle English sentences of this latter type in which the placement of the negative seems to be restricted, as in

ȝef ȝe ne mahen eauer halde þe time

if you cannot always keep to the [right] time [for saying your prayers.]

Here there seems to be an implied sense of "sometimes" which would not be found in "ȝef ȝe mahen **neauer** *halde þe time," where the adverbial negation implies not "sometimes" but "on no occasion."*

The fifth woman in the room, sitting nearest the door behind Valija and him, Brenan had no wish even to look at. Embarrassment at his *contretemps* with Louise two springs before had been nothing compared to his chagrin over a *gaffe* with this young woman, Mildred Sayre, the following term. Her severe good looks had never appealed to him much but, unlike Louise, she had invested heavily in an acquaintance with him, inviting herself to tea in Somersby more than once. In return, she had entertained him and John to a full scale dinner party for three at her parents' very presentable house towards Blechynden while they were away in Sweden. Having known Justine slightly, Mildred had used what she knew to have searching talks with Brenan about the French and their character as a nation. When a depressing postwar Rumanian novel called *La Vingtcinquième Heure* (first published in Paris) came out in English, she had bought a copy, read it, and discussed it with him relentlessly—knowing that he had been sent his copy by the sister of Justine. In retrospect, he fully realized that he had been the object of some sort of crush, but at the time he had thought—in so far as he thought about her at all—that she and he were just two undergraduates getting to know one another—not a couple starting a love affair.

Then he made the mistake of asking her out to dinner one

night at the Cowherds Inn, across the common—just her and himself—by way of thanks for the stagey dinner party. The evening went well enough; conversation kept coming round to Justine and how fascinating the French could be. But on the long walk home in the warm May night, he allowed himself, seemingly with her approval, to start talking French love theory, *d'après* Rougemont. As Arthur would say: he must have been fanti. He certainly forgot or misjudged whom he was with. He said things like "One isn't in love with a particular person but with the idea of being in love." When they finally turned the corner of her road, embowered in acacia, she stopped and said, "You don't have to walk me any further. Goodnight!" And while he stood there, surprised and wondering what to say, she slapped him sharply on the cheek with her gray-gloved hand and hurried away. To have been slapped by a girl one has never even tried to take a liberty with has to be some sort of record.

Now the Scarecrow was saying scratchily, as if nearing the end of a tether, that in Middle English, sentences which give commands, *imperatives*, have a scope of negative incorporation comparable to that of negative declaratives—as was obvious from one of the earlier examples cited this morning, "***Nest lich nan ne gurde hire wið na cunne gurdles***," which is both negative and imperative:

However, what is not so obvious is that sentences which ask a question, interrogatives, *also resemble imperatives, since in asking for an answer, they, as it were, command a reply. In the* Ancren Riwle *we find the question* "Do you love me?"

Luuest tu me?

We also find this question with an introductory interrogative, as in Modern English, "Why do you love the man or the woman?"

Hwi luuedest tu þe mon oðer þe wummon?

Once again, the Modern English use of the periphrastic auxiliary"do" is absent from Middle English, even when an introductory "why" is used. But what is present is an implied structure of positive *or* negative *reply which is also present in Modern English. In Middle English, this implication of a "yes" or a "no" involves, instead of the modern auxiliary "do," an* inversion *of the order of subject and verb. Presumably, there was some difference of tone added to this grammar of inversion, but if so, there are no known clues to its phonology.*

When negation was constituted in the interrogative sentence, it was structured somewhat differently, as in

> **Nult tu as ofte smiten?**
> Do you not want as often to strike [him] down?

Here, in addition to the reversal of noun and verb, we find an incorporation of the negative into the initial modal auxiliary "nult," which equals, of course, "ne" and "vult." Modern English, on the other hand, now has available the use of the tag question, "do [or don't] you?"

The Scarecrow fell silent, as if his latest incursion into the world of the children of men was at last over—God be thanked! No bell rang. He scrabbled up his papers and books but, before he could stalk to the door, he was accosted by Higginbotham and Pengelly, newly primed with questions to pose. The other students left the room unobtrusively, Valija and Brenan in tandem. Down the narrow corridor of lecture rooms and offices they passed into the foyer of the library building. It was high ceilinged but lighted only by electricity, an exchange-like hall busy with people. The two made their way across it side by side.

"How can you so much as hear one of those sentences without wondering what *human* situation it implies?"

"The linguistic structure of a sentence is itself quite enough for me to wonder about." She glanced at him as it were accusingly. "You really only read for pleasure, don't you? The pleasure of imagining?" He shrugged. When they reached the pavement of the approach road and Brenan veered away from the union towards Saltfleetby where the city buses stopped, Valija said, "Where are you taking me?"

"You'll see," he answered mysteriously. "What do you think English lectures would be like if there were women as well as men in the department?"

"Very much like what they are now."

"I wonder. We had a woman visitor from one of the Oxford Colleges last spring who gave an excellent seminar on John Donne. It was one of the very best courses I've had here—as good in its way as the VC's on Meredith, Hardy, Conrad, Forster and Woolf, which I used to see you at sometimes."

"Yes. I found Sir Marcus's lectures full of insights, most original, beautifully expressed. That Donne seminar would have been interesting too, I'm sure. But it was for second years—and by invitation—so I couldn't just drop in and, besides, I had my research to be getting on with. I still do! . . . Of course," she added mischievously, "our Marianne was invited to drop in, wasn't she?"

"This is what I mean. Mrs. Bromwich was unusually sociable, easy to approach, and treated undergraduates as persons of interest, even consequence. After her last seminar, she took us all to lunch—at the hotel you're allowing me to take you to today. So you see, what you lose on the swings, you gain on the roundabout." When he said this, he thought, for some reason, of Wandering Arthur and his dream; Valija's brief and no doubt phatic reply was lost on him. "Don't worry," he said, "you'll be back in Highfield by one-thirty. I have to be at the VC's for my tutorial by two."

She never did ask him *which* hotel, especially when they caught a bus and he paid for two tickets to the Royal Pier.

A fine view of the estuary and the North Sea opens out from the bottom of the High Street, where the Town Quay has stood since the early fifteenth century. A little away to the north of the Fish Dock and the new deepwater termini downshore, this quay is the waterfront of the Old Town below the Bargate. The chief features of the Old Town, including the Royal Pier, were decided in the late eighteenth and early nineteenth centuries, all subsequent mercantile and industrial development having been southwards. The Town Quay, however, still serves traffic to and from the Baltic countries, including the staple timber trade with Lithuania, Latvia, and Estonia. It was to the offshore moorings here that Brenan expected the Tievas flotilla from Greenwich to have found its way. A clear if narrow view of them could be had, he knew, from one of the windows in the upstairs dining room at the Dolphin Hotel.

"One more coincidence," Valija had said, when she first confirmed that this was their destination.

"One in every seaport in England," he had said in reply.

They walked into this unmistakably English coaching inn through the main doors which gave on to a cobbled archway leading to and from the High Street. The reception desk and the several bars and snugs on the ground floor were unusually busy, partly perhaps with visiting press and radio people. It was a little early for lunch, but Brenan found a waiter and enlisted his help in getting upstairs to the table with a view.

"You should be able to spot the presidential yacht from here," said the waiter, seating them at a small table in the southwest corner of a spacious room full of whiteclothed, well-appointed tables of all sizes, most of them as yet untaken. He glanced out of the window. "There she is, if I am not mistaken, the *Dolphynas* and escort, just off the Royal Pier, this side of that Norwegian cruise ship. I'll send up the luncheon waiter as soon as we start serving. Here is the menu. What would you like to drink?" Valija ordered soda water and Brenan a pint of the house mild and bitter. They duly looked out together at the harbourscape, gray and gusty, with clouds gathering to break the sun's gleaming. At anchor in the middle distance, the *Dolphynas* looked toylike.

"That she blows," said Brenan. "Have you ever seen her before?"

"Only in photography. What a cockleshell compared with some shipping to be seen even in this modest harbour."

"Yes, he's a man who likes to do things his own way, your President, isn't he?"

"Marshal Tievas has always had history on his side and the rest of the world against him."

"Have you ever met him in person?"

"Never. He has little to do with the academy or the arts in Gdainys. All I know of him is what I've been told."

"What do you make of this *Englandreise* of his? Why has he let it turn into such a disappointment for everyone involved—even for him?"

"I simply don't know enough about it to say. I haven't seen a Baltic newspaper for weeks. What do you know about this visit of the Marshal's that might explain it?"

"Yes, young Brenan, what *don't* you know about it?" An amused Welsh voice from behind, echoing Valija's question, was all too familiar to him. "You seem to be doing the legwork for an eyewitness history of the Tievas visit."

"Why, Mr. Vaughan! What a surprise! I did wonder if Northfleet might not be next on *your* list." He got out of his chair to look Vaughan in the face and shake hands with him. "This is Valija Didelis, who is studying at Northfleet. Valija, this is Inspector Vaughan of Scotland Yard. He's an old army acquaintance of my father's and lives along Westcombe Edge— in the most interesting piece of architecture after Vanbrugh Castle."

"So you know the heath, Miss Didelis, as well as Northfleet?"

She nodded, smiling and offering her hand in a quite unEnglish way. "I have visited Greenwich," she said neutrally.

"We're about to have lunch," Brenan said. "Won't you join us?"

"Thank you, I should like to, but I have another engagement. I thought it was you I saw come in downstairs. Let me sit with you until your lunch arrives." He swung a chair round from the next table and seated himself; Brenan subsided into his chair.

"Miss Didelis, are you related to Dr. Jurgis Didelis of the Baltic Embassy in Holland Park?"

"Yes, he is my uncle. Do you know him?"

"Only by name and reputation. We have never met. He sounds a very interesting person, with more than one calling besides literary scholarship. Have you been in contact with him recently?"

"Yes. I am going to join him at a conference on Thursday. I haven't actually been in contact with him since last week. Term is now beginning, as you know. We have all been going our several ways as the long vac has ended"

"Where are you going to join him, may I ask?"

Valija looked at Brenan as if she had a question for him to answer. "A house called Theobalds"—she pronounced it in the eighteenth century way with two syllables—"near Holt in Norfolk. It belongs to Professor Stephen Rawlings of Caius College,who is chief editor of the New Cambridge Jonson."

Vaughan thanked her with a nod. "Your uncle seems to be out of contact with everybody just now. Perhaps I shall have the pleasure of meeting him this week in Norfolk. You don't happen to know a visiting student from Gdainys named Draugiski, I suppose?"

"Yes, I've met him in London at our embassy. But I can't say I know him. He should be traceable through the embassy— if you wish to contact him."

"Of course, like your uncle. Now let me leave you to your lunch. Nice to have met you, Miss Didelis. You, I'll be seeing, young Brenan." A waiter had arrived to take their order. Vaughan faded away among the tables as unobtrusively as he had materialized. Valija ordered a cheese and tomato salad and Brenan a bloater with toast.

He said, "I'm sorry if he grilled you. My father says he's a 'tec in the Special Branch."

She said, "You are hardly to blame. One is always reluctant

to talk to the police about relatives or friends; it's only to be expected."

They looked out at the *Dolphynas*; on and around it there was no sign of any coming or going.

iii

Sext with Nones
~Book of Hours

When Valija alighted at the stop nearest Highfield, Brenan remained in his seat on the bus. One moment she was next to him in the front window seat to the left of the driver, another and she was gone from view among other passengers and the bus was jolting forward. Why did he have this sudden panicky sense of loss when she left? No one took her place beside him. She had said thank you for lunch, smiled a friendly goodbye, and moved out of sight. *How beautiful it is, that eye-on-the-object look.* And he was left in this mingled, troubled, lost flow of mind. He felt ashamed, a fraud, an impostor. What he wanted most was to confide in Valija, to have her confide in him, and at the same time to let Vaughan know what he knew. Why had he kept this wretched secret to himself for three whole days now? What good did keeping such a secret do? Was it so dangerous that he could not share it either with a girl he had fallen in love with or a policeman his father respected and admired? Waves of contempt for himself washed up against what till now had been a steady swell of elation. "What the hell," he said to himself defiantly.

The bus carried him in a snaking curve around Stonham and into the high lying, built-up, but heavily wooded promontory beyond Blechynden where the Vice Chancellor, Sir Marcus Templeton, had his private residence overlooking both estuary and city. Inevitably, it was referred to by the undergraduates— as Vaughan's more modest venture into planned housing on the Bauhaus model was by the DAC—as "the bunker," but

Brenan preferred to think of it as the Vice Chancellery. The two bunkers had almost nothing in common. Not, he told himself sarcastically, that he had to choose. This one kept its head down, prone in several acres of coastal pine woods, seldom rising to a second storey, full of surprising angles and balconies, all weatherworn concrete yet well-windowed and naturalized with creeper and shrubbery. Brenan appraised it uneasily as he came round a bend of its long driveway, having dropped off the platform of his slowly climbing bus right at the gate. "*Embarqué*," he said to a stone pine in his Simone de Beauvoir voice.

Templeton figured largely in Brenan's imaginary life— unduly, for someone he had never been alone with more than twice before. He had sat happily absorbed through several departmental and public lectures on poetry and fiction which Templeton had given during the first year of his Northfleet appointment. Every word of Templeton's limpid prose and verse that had come under his eye Brenan had read and admired—except the famous Baltic memoir, which he had only glanced at and found to be little more than an episode in a rambling narrative of war service in Europe and the Far East. If only he had known then how curious he would before long become about anything concerning Tievas. When Templeton had been appointed Vice Chancellor, his war record of public service had naturally received more attention than his youthful promise in *belles lettres*: a slim book of poems from Faber and a slim volume of essays from Chatto.

Any recognition from the press and the nation had been all to the good of the college which, as their centenary approached, looked forward to being chartered as a university. The Earl of Auldcaster, who was official visitor and would become Chancellor, and the city fathers of Northfleet had all been most gratified. Recently, however, Templeton had settled into an academic phase, publishing occasional lyric poetry in the *Listener* and research in *Essays in Criticism* as well as lecturing and tutoring busily in the college English department. His duties as Vice Chancellor were hardly onerous. But now the Tievas visit threatened to subject him once again (if only briefly) to public notice as a Name. It was a question whether Northfleet would have been honoured by a visit from Tievas at all, one time student or not, if his first and best Boswell had not also happened to settle here. Brenan would not have been at all surprised to find himself this ominous Monday afternoon treading on the heels of some city reporter with initiative casing the site of Wednesday's reunion.

The narrow front door of the Chancellery stood open and, when Brenan touched the bell, Templeton's dry voice called him across a paved hall to the huge booklined study with iron spiral staircases rising to a mezzanine. After Shelley, E.P., the *faux* mediaeval craftsman, was, he knew, the *paragone* in this workshop. The tag from Ole Ez that ran fleeting through his mind was *vocat aestus in umbram*. Templeton's voice, like his Mediterranean look and quiet manner, was of its kind perfect, wholly at ease with itself and with others—in so far as they mattered at all. It was both dry and mellifluous: it spoke of deep feeling, rare imagination, and superior judgement. He wore slate grey tweed and twill as if the combination had never before occurred to any man. He had a shy, infectious, heartless smile.

"Have a seat, Mr. Brenan. You're right on time." He had an ingenious coffee-maker of Italian design on a low table in front of the armchair he sat in. He said, "I thought we might drink some coffee to help us through the after lunch *spleen*, what?"

This was the pre-war Balliol College aspirated "what?" to which there is no proper response. Brenan said, "Thank you."

"The last time we met you had tried writing on Marlowe's poetic drama—*Tamburlaine*, as I recall—and found it difficult, which is understandable. Blank verse tragedy is hard enough to appreciate without being overlaid with Marlowe's several eccentricities, brilliant as they may be. Now you have taken on Shakespeare's *Antony and Cleopatra*, which gives you a great deal more than *Tamburlaine* does to respond to and enjoy. Next time, I want you to try one of Ben Jonson's major plays, *Volpone* perhaps. You'll find a question about *it* on my list on the department notice board." He handed Brenan an elegant white cup and saucer containing about four mouthfuls of black coffee.

"As to this try"—he picked up Brenan's five-page handwritten paper and leafed through it—"you made much more of a go of it this time, didn't you? Very lively, all the love psychology. It was evidently a matter that meant a good deal to Shakespeare; it released in him some of his finest poetry. But let me warn you about his later plays. They are a great temptation for student and teacher to talk about whatever happens to be topmost in one's mind. 'All things to all men,' don't you know? But for someone in your position, giving in to such a temptation can be dangerous. Try to let the play you are studying itself decide your approach, not some prior interest of your own which the play happens to trigger. De Rougemont— I've read his book—it's heady stuff: it gives one the illusion of all manner of different works falling into place in a certain cultural pattern. Now, *Antony and Cleopatra* may be, among other things, one of the world's great love stories; and not merely a tragi-comedy of middleaged sex. But *Romeo and Juliet* it is not."

In the midst of his elegant, incisive sentences Templeton always seemed to Brenan to be sleepwalking like some Pharaoh—say, Akhenaten rapt on his eternal frieze. Wasn't this how Sassoon had looked to Owen at Craiglockhart in October '17 or was it to Rivers in New Court at St. John's, Cambridge, after the Armistice? No conversation being called for, the hieratic tones continued, a voice reciting out of a cistern or empty well. "Everything in the earlier, younger play exists to . . . to discriminate the love passion from what surrounds it, . . . to make real the actuality of passion. We are not asked to judge it, to conclude that Romeo should have taken *thought*, should have paused at some point. To do so would be to falsify the experience that Shakespeare's poetry offers. In *Anthony*, there is incomparable dramatic language, all the psychology of sex, but none of this secret religion of love. Cleopatra's secret is merely sexual.

"Now the one love tragedy by Shakespeare that De Rougemont deigns to mention in *L'Amour et l'Occident* is, as you know, *Romeo and Juliet*. Why do you suppose this is?"

Brenan had swallowed his coffee and could see very well where such a question was leading. He liked his paper about De Rougemont, if not about Shakespeare, too much to see it shot down in flames with his own help. The putative Albigensian source for heretical passion interested him as little as did the closing Genevan sermon on Protestant divorce. It was the mystical reading of the Tristan myth, the drinking of the love potion, the mutual obsession with death, that he found endlessly fascinating. The thought recurred to him that Templeton was Roman Catholic. "I see the point," he said. "Next time I'll try to be more of a New Critic and take my bearings from the poet's metaphors rather than from psychology. I actually do find the critical approach in a book like *The Well Wrought Urn* satisfying and very helpful, my sort of thing . . . ." Having lulled his opponent, he seized the time to riposte.

"But, Sir Marcus, may I for a moment change the subject completely and ask your advice on another matter—a personal matter—which has been troubling me lately? It may even be of some national importance."

Templeton assumed the quizzical, slightly amused expression which was all too characteristic of him in any situation. He nodded dubiously. "No more of the psychology of young love, eh? All right, of course. What is it?"

"I live in Greenwich, and last Friday afternoon I happened to be visiting an old chapel in an almshouse across the heath when I saw something very disturbing—a man who looked like Marshal Tievas was being restrained, violently, by four men. They lugged him away, apparently unconscious."

"What did you do?" The tone was mild astonishment.

"Nothing. I was up in a dark gallery and they didn't notice me."

"Skulking, eh?" Again, the mischievous smile. "Did you notify the police?"

"No. The Marshal appeared on television as promised that evening and, when I went back to the chapel, there was no sign of him or of his attackers, so what was I to tell the police?"

"What, then, are you now telling me?"

It was like trying to come to terms with one of those sleek *quattrocento* heads in a Florentine portrait—no dice, let alone any dialogue. Brenan said, "But the case is now altered. Since Friday, the Marshal seems to have totally queered his own pitch, politically, without any good reason. Tomorrow he has to make one more public appearance. This might be the time to find out whether the man on the *Dolphynas* and the man in the chapel are one and the same—or not."

"And I, no doubt, am the man for the job. Why are you any surer now than you were on Friday that something has to be done?"

"On Friday I didn't doubt that it was Tievas in the chapel. Perhaps I should have made more allowance for its being a double. In any case, my evidence disappeared and I had nothing to report but an unlikely story."—

"The finest Elphberg of them all, what?"

—"The story is no more likely now. But I thought you might be interested to hear it, since the political situation in the Baltic seems to be getting so much worse. And you will be meeting the Marshal in person tomorrow or Wednesday."

"You've done right to tell me your story." Somehow Templeton did not look quite so pleased or so gratified as he sounded—perhaps because he was as ready as Brenan for this slightly sour session to be over. "I will see to it that what has to be done is done. Meanwhile, you won't need my telling you to keep your suspicions strictly to yourself, will you? Especially if you find yourself in the company of our guest students from abroad."

Brenan thought of Valija first, then for some reason of Al Yates. He did not think of Arthur. The tutorial was patently over. His paper on *Antony and Cleopatra* was handed him without further comment. He was seen out.

He found himself at the end of the drive, heading for the nearest bus stop. Nothing had changed; everything had changed. His feelings were still in turmoil. Having tried to little avail to unburden himself to Templeton, now he had to confide in Valija. "*Mein Irisch Kind,*" he muttered. "*Wo weilest du?*" What was to be expected of Templeton anyway? The several conceivable consequences of having finally told him his secret danced about in Brenan's mind like an Italian goalkeeper facing a penalty kick. Where he was crossing the tree-lined road a pebble large as an egg lay on the crown of it. He turned and sized up the wooden vice-chancellery gate which stood wide open. No one was about. Then he took the penalty kick as hard as he could, making sure to lift his right toe a little so as to catch the stone on the thick crepe sole of his shoe and not hurt himself. The stone smacked into the near gatepost with a sound like a shot and ricocheted down the drive. The sound seemed almost to echo among the trees. "Where is the damned goalie when I could use him?" he snarled.

Highfield Hall still sits in humble Omdurman Road, round the corner from the sub-post office in Khartoum, behind tall redbrick walls, its third and fourth storey windows gazing south across the elm tops of the common and north to where the brickfield has since given place to more and bigger college buildings and newer walkways, stepped, railed, and concreted. Highfield's one time air of almost conventual gentility has long dissipated, leaving it no better and no worse than many another well-planted, much remodeled, late Victorian, urban hostel for contemporary youth doing contemporary degrees. In 1951, access to the young ladies residing in hall was monitored by a student receptionist, who kept a register of all visitation at a desk near the wide front door. Monday was not normally an afternoon when visitors might be received but, when the annual garden party had to be postponed by reason of the Tievas banquet the next day, the Warden, Miss Ellen Lightbody, M.A. (Cantab.), proclaimed a modest exception: as on Wednesdays, visits might be made on this day also between 3:00 and 6:00 p.m.—a proclamation which even Brenan had noted. When he took the bus back from Blechynden to the common, he did not at once look for his Stonham connection but began walking along a footpath under the elms towards Highfield Hall, thinking fondly of less clouded afternoons not so long since when he had crossed the grassy heath at home. His thoughts of it were of Valija as well, Valija seen as if for the first time under the cupola, Valija kissed at the gates in the sun. The story of his heart had become the very thought of her, whom a week before he had not the least thought of. Now he must take her in his arms and hear her tell him she loved him too.

The girl on duty at reception, immured but visible through an open *guichet,* was the one who had been with Louise Prendergast at Croker's lecture, the one whose name he could never remember. She must have been doing a general degree because the book she was reading was a set text in French, the *Atala* and *Réné* of Chateaubriand. Brenan said, "Hello. Don't you wish you were in Alabama, too? 'Moon of Alabama' by Kurt Weill *d'après* Chateaubriand?"

"Hello, Michael. Are you here to see Valija Didelis? She hasn't put your name down for a visit today."

"Hasn't she? Perhaps she forgot. She hasn't put anybody else's name down, has she?"

A reluctant smile. A shake of the head.

"Do you think I could go up and see if she meant to put my name down for a visit today?"

Another reluctant smile. A shrug. Back to *Atala.*

"What's her room number this year, please?"

"Still thirty-nine."

When Valija acknowledged his tap on her door and he opened it, she looked anything but pleased. "Michael," she said, "this is too much!" She sat in front of the window at her desk and, by the look of it, was still searching for verbic extension in Josephine Tey's stage English. "You must be careful never to wear out your welcome." She put down her pencil, stood up and came across to the door, not smiling affectionately.

"May I speak some words with you, *por favor?*" he said with sudden formality, echoing Jose Rodriguez.

"We are *not* in one of your favourite films," she said, closing the door behind him and indicating that he should take the armchair. She went and sat on the edge of her bed across from him. It was littered with pages of script and notecards and a few open books.

"No, we are not," he said ruefully. "Just think, you and I never have seen a film together."

She looked at him levelly as if he might be a stranger after all. "But we have gone through a poem or two, haven't we?"

So this was how the *consolamentum* took place. If they had been in a Browning poem, he might have tried to strangle her.

And all her hair
In one long yellow string I wound
Three times her little throat around.

But all he did was sigh inconsolably. *What shall we do till nightfall?*

She waited in silence.

He started again.

"There is something I simply have to let you know, Valija, and not by telephone. I'm no good on the phone."

"And, of course you are not expecting to see me about the college tomorrow—or to entertain me to tea in Somersby after all?"

"It's something I must tell you now."

"How was your tutorial with the Vice Chancellor? Did he like your work this time?"

"I think not. His view of *Antony and Cleopatra* seems to be that the key to its poetry is middleaged lust."

She gave a little hiccup of laughter.

"I never thought I would say this, Valija, but I would much rather have had a tutorial with you this afternoon than with him. You must realize that in these last few days I have fallen hopelessly in love with you. That is why I am here uninvited. You are always in my thoughts every hour. I can't not think of you, even if I want not to—which I don't. I have to see you whenever I can. Your eyes, your hair, your smile, your voice— the thought of you is with me wherever I go and I am always looking to be wherever you are." He was telling her the truth about how he felt, but he could see that this was not being welcomed or even well received. He broke off.

Her hands did not move from the edge of the bed where they rested on the coverlet to either side, as if bracing her. She was wearing the same black serge dress with white at the throat and wrists that she had worn to lunch. She looked at him with the kindest of her several sad smiles. "Michael, Michael, Michael, you are alarming me. I know what you are saying: if I don't take pity on you, you will die. You think I should be pleased; and I am, because your company has been a pleasure to me, a delight. But what do you expect in return for this confession you are making? That, like Juliet, I will marry you in church tomorrow if only you make the arrangements— whatever my uncle's wishes may be? What do you *really* want when you speak like this, with such passion? After all, there *is* no obstacle, is there? We're here in Highfield. This is not a book or a film we are in, is it? Tomorrow is another day."

His gaze dropped to the wellworn carpet under their feet, to her small black sensible shoes. Had he any idea of what he really wanted? He had wanted the VC to take Tievas off his mind, and what good had wanting that done him? "I want to be with you," he said sullenly. "I want you to want to be with me."

"Is that all?" She reached out both her hands to him, taking his, and drew him towards her. He came forward out of the chair and went down on his knees in front of her.

She gently rested his head on her lap and stroked his hair.

"I have been thinking what a man of the world you are, but you haven't yet stopped being a little boy as well, have you?"

"There's no right answer to that question," he said, and came to his feet, and she stood up with him. "May I kiss you?" he asked.

She put her arms around his neck and gave him her warm, spontaneous kiss. "I think you should go now. Starting out with a kiss on an express train is enough to give anyone false hope. We can try again tomorrow."

So he went, wondering how much store should be set by her saying there was no obstacle between them.

About half an hour after Brenan left, Valija had another tap on her door. This time she was wanted on the telephone. Downstairs she went to the corridor outside the Matron's office where the kiosk used by all student residents stood: the receiver was off the hook. She was careful to close the folding door and give herself privacy. "Hello?"

"Valija? Antanas. *Salut.* I have an important message for you from Jurgis. When I talked to him today, he asked me to phone you for him. He is very busy, moving about all day, and he wants to be sure you get this message in time.

"He is keen to have a word with your friend Mr. Brenan this evening. I don't know what about—Ben Jonson business, I suppose. I didn't know that Jurgis knew him, did you? Anyway, it is important that Mr. Brenan call Jurgis at this number—Holt 35218—between seven-thirty and eight this evening. Have you got it—35218?"

She said that she had it.

"Do you know Brenan's number?"

She said that she did. He lived in Somersby Hall and could be reached on the JCR phone there.

"Good. Will you please phone him this evening at seven-fifteen and ask him to call Jurgis at Holt before eight. It is important to catch Mr. Brenan at seven-fifteen. He should be at dinner, then, don't you think?"

She said that she thought so; and that she would be sure to do as Jurgis asked.

Antanas rang off. Wherever he was phoning from—York? Retford? Northfleet? Merewell?—she could see that pretty boy smile of his. On the way back to her room she thought amusedly that Michael might be right after all and that there was a Jose Rodriguez at work, keeping an eye on them.

iv

Vespers with Compline
~Book of Hours

An evening meal together was the secret of the common life in Somersby then. Every day except Saturday, a few minutes before seven, Mr. Powell would come out into his echoing archway and ring a hand bell. Undergraduates not already gathered in the Junior Common Room, where the BBC news (followed once a week by the Crazy Show) could be listened to, would make their way there or at least as far as the wide corridor between it and the refectory— each presentably dressed in his academic gown, if not always in collar and tie. *I am an Arcadian, . . . he is a Utopian.*

Huby made an absolute point of ritual dining in hall; procession, blessing, and return. On the hour, we would all troop into the refectory and stand against a bench by one of six long blond tables. Then, up at the high end, on the dais, doors to the Senior Common Room would open and in would swan Huby, followed by Dixon, Doyne, and Whitaker, resident faculty, shadowy figures at best, ones that would do "to swell a progress, start a scene or two." As I remember, guests at high table were rare; and in this respect the Monday evening in question was unremarkable.

Huby intoned the grace as usual in one flowing word— **Benedicite. Potum nostrum filius dei benedicat. In nomine Jesu Christi domini nostrum. Amen**—the seniors seated themselves; every undergraduate settled to his bench;

and in came the serving women with soup in big silver tureens on dining trolleys, one per table. Huby ran a tight ship in most things, though the order of the day was always niceness, the English niceness, especially with social inferiors. One phase of his refectory ordo that always made me wonder was its closing. There was no formal dismissal: at any time after the main course had been served, one might look round and note empty places. At high table, the faculty usually stayed for dessert before adjourning to their common room, as did most of the undergraduates, but there was no practice of waiting for the Warden himself to recess before leaving the table oneself. As soon as he did leave—and Huby was not one ever to linger at anything he did—the busy women, anxious to be off home, would swoop to their clean up and dissolution occur in five minutes or less. Some men might on occasion repair to the common room afterwards, but most returned to their rooms and their own devices.

On this particular evening, Brenan and I went into the refectory with Al Yates, whom we had been visiting in his smoky, overstocked room. We three settled, after grace, at one of the top tables under the high windows giving on to the quad. At the end of the table, to ladle soup and pass plates and so on, we happened to have portly, amiable Clive Mansell, President of the JCR, who fancied himself as a batsman but was now, of course, out of season. The talk started with his choice of new books for the common room library. It emerged that he had just spent the entire budget (not a fortune, to be sure) on the recent, very handsome, Chatto and Windus edition in green cloth and gold lettering of the collected works of Aldous Huxley. Huby had been appalled. "Why not the complete works of Mrs. Humphrey Ward, Clive?" he was reported to have said in outrage. The hubbub throughout the refectory, the coming and going of the serving women between kitchen and table, the general bonhomie, made whatever any of us said indistinguishable at high table. We could gossip freely, even about the Warden himself.

"What's wrong with Huxley?" said Cook, the Engineer from D block, another cricketer. "I thought he was about as much of an egghead as a novelist can be. One of your favourites, isn't he, Michael?"

Brenan couldn't stand this sort of parlour talk. He slurped his mulligatawny. "*Point Counter Point* is an interesting read, but I haven't a clue about the Complete Works. It's always the same with anthologies and libraries—it's a choice; someone has to make it, and one man's meat . . . ." He looked down the table at the friendly Economists from C block, Broadbridge, Croft, and Secombe and the rest whose names I forget. He probably hadn't spoken with any of them since the June before. "Seymour, have you been to *A Place in the Sun* yet? I see that it's on at the Regal."

"We went last night. Don't miss it. The girl is smashing. Unreal. Elizabeth Taylor."

Croft, good natured, slightly wistful, a few years older than most of us, having spent more than two years in the RAF as aircrew, seemed to find undergraduate life slow, if not interminable. He was one of the very few in hall to keep a motor car somewhere handy, a battered 1939 Triumph. He said, "Elizabeth Taylor's must be the most beautiful face ever in the history of the screen, don't you think?"

"Cleavage out of this world, too," said Secombe.

"I thought it was the cutting, the editing, not the *mise en scène* you Economists went to study," said Brenan. "They say there are more dissolves in this one than even in a Hitchcock."

Secombe just grinned. "Why don't you tell us who directed it, Michael?"

"The most beautiful face ever on the screen," I found myself saying, "has to be Vivien Leigh's about ten or fifteen years back, before she went to America—fell for Laurence Olivier and went to Hollywood."

"If you've seen *A Streetcar Named Desire*," said Broadbridge, "you'll know that *that* face has gone with the wind."

"More choices," said Brenan. "You're all anthologists—or librarians."

The empty soup dishes had gone their way and the meat had been served. At Mansell's end of the table, comparable loose talk had been going on with Case and Phillips, who were in Classics, and with Smith who was another Generals student, like Mansell.

"Talking of beautiful faces," said Croft, "has anyone noticed that Elizabeth Taylor is a dead ringer for the girl Bellamy married last year?"

"You're right," said Secombe, "but don't you want to put it the other way round?" Nobody took him up on his quibble.

The Bellamy affair had been the scandal of Somersby the previous spring—and Huby's heaviest cross in living memory. Fair haired, urbane, pursy, with a most charming manner, Bellamy had been the only one in hall who could address you as "old boy" and get away with it. Spoiled by his mother, who was rich and widowed, fawned on by undergraduate women, adored by his college clique, he had spent every weekend of term away from hall and never once warned Huby or signed out in the refectory book. He would arrive back late on Monday or early on Tuesday, park his mother's Wolseley on the piazza (against an explicit rule), and wait for Huby to have Mr. Powell find him and make him move it. He was never caught in the act of whatever he did, including study. He would give alcoholic parties in his expensively furnished den in F block to which young women of the college, and sometimes of the town, were smuggled in. News of such excesses always came out afterwards—to us *hoi polloi*. Huby, who believed that the only discipline worth enforcing is self discipline, could only let his displeasure at such bad form be widely known, and simmer.

The full extent of Bellamy's brilliant abuse of Huby's hospitality had become known only in late May after finals week. Before then, most of the college had been at least vaguely aware that an unusually beautiful, nubile, lively young woman named April Hershey had run away with the Bellamy stakes that season. What Huby had been enraged later to discover was that, halfway through the term, April had walked out of

Glen Eyre Hall without a word to her warden, gone through a registry office wedding with Bellamy at the Northfleet town hall, and been living with him thereafter *in* Somersby—until after finals, that is, when he further distinguished himself by taking a First in Physics (which says very little for last-minute preparation). The arrangements which had enabled April to enjoy connubial residence in F block all during the weeks up to and including finals, as well as to slip in and out with Bellamy on weekends, had to be counted the acme of his several clandestine accomplishments at Northfleet. His cleaning woman in F block, whoever she was, must have been a jewel.

April had been in her first year, briefly a student in Politics. Hers was the face that Croft now compared to Elizabeth Taylor's, about which comparison Secombe, as usual, quibbled. It was Mansell, still rankled by Huby's remark about Mrs. Humphrey Ward, who said unkindly, "It looks as if this year's Bellamy might be Arthur Bresnahan."

Al Yates, whose first impulse at table was evidently to eat and listen rather than talk and eat, said, "Yes, where *is* Arthur, *rex futurus et quondam*? Doesn't he ever sit with us at dinner?"

I answered flippantly that he would never be caught dead within close range of high table and always sat somewhere near a door so that he could duck out early unnoticed by Huby—or so he hoped. We all looked across the commotion of the room to the far end but Arthur was already nowhere to be seen. The main dish—boiled beef, mashed potato, and carrots—was almost dispatched; the pudding trolleys were at hand—stewed plums and custard. I remember glancing at my wrist watch. It was about seven-twenty.

Between the refectory and the JCR, the corridor runs north and south, connecting the quad with a narrow side lawn under the perimeter wall. Just before it ends at French windows giving on to this lawn, the corridor opens into an alcove. Here, handy to the common room, stands the telephone kiosk for the use of undergraduates. On fine evenings, a user will lean comfortably against the kiosk door, talking or listening and looking idly out of the open French windows at the lawn, the redbrick wall, and the line of rhododendrons along it. At one point in the wall, a single tall iron gate of black railings, always locked, offers the telephone user a narrow glimpse of the Stonham Road and the playing fields beyond.

It was at this point in the wall that, a little after seven, Ciabuvis backed the van carefully on to the verge of the road. By opening the rear doors, Baltrušaitis gave himself an uninterrupted view through the gate, across the lawn and through the windows of whoever used the Somersby telephone some twenty-five yards away. He stretched himself out in the sniper's position, prone, angled, braced on his elbows. He rested the muzzle of the .303 against the tongue of the door lock on the off side, looked along the sights, and took aim.

From the driver's seat, with the engine running, Ciabuvis said anxiously, "Is the window still open? There are too many damned variables in this operation."

"Have faith, Šiauli, have faith. The window is still open. The lights are even on. I could knock the receiver off the hook with one round. You know what the poet says:

> *Through a machine-gun's sights . . .*
> *Only efficiency delights you."*

He was in his element.

Behind the near side door, through the scrub lining the road, he was invisible to any passer by. The van was backed on to a little patch of very shallow ditch which had clearly been parked on more than once before. To anyone who was curious, it would explain why a van was drawn up on this, the wrong side of the road. Outside Somersby, Stonham was not much more than a lane and, at this hour, one little used by drivers or pedestrians. Behind the wheel, Ciabuvis kept his eyes busy searching the windscreen and offside rear mirror for any sign of approach from the village or Saltfleetby.

At last the phone in the kiosk rang, and went on ringing until a woman, obviously irritated, came out of the kitchen and answered it. For Čiabuvis' benefit, Baltrušaitis said, "Now she's gone to give Mr. Brenan his last call to action." They waited.

A tall dark young man in an academic gown came to the kiosk and took up the receiver, turning as he did so to face the French windows. The sniper's bullet took him flush in the temple, knocking his lifeless body right back into the kiosk.

Having ejected the used cartridge case and cocked the rifle again, Baltrušaitis put it down beside him before pulling the van doors shut. "Go!" he said.

Čiabuvis swung the van on to the empty Stonham Road and drove fast towards Saltfleetby. As Baltrušaitis climbed into the seat beside him, he said, "What must Valija be thinking right now?"

"One more breakdown—courtesy of Post Office Telephones. Let's hope she has the presence of mind to hang up fast and try again later." The sniper looked at his watch. It was seven-twenty.

During dessert, Mary, the maid who waited only on high table, suddenly appeared beside Brenan and said, confidentially, that Dr. Lacy would like to see him after dinner in his study. No one at our table, except perhaps Al Yates, took any special note of this confidence. It was well established practice for the Warden to invite one or other of us—his several favourites—up for a glass of port and conversation after dinner. "Don't think twice about it," I had already told Al Yates. "Huby is no rapist and, anyway, Brenan has to be hetero the way a bird has to sing. You may be favoured yourself one of these evenings. Have you tried Cockburn's port?"

Huby and the rest of the faculty soon left high table; at ours we did as most of the other diners were doing and drifted out of the refectory for the evening. Al and I went our way across the quad to E block and Brenan went along the south path to Huby's lodging. This was on the upper floor in the southwest corner, and approached by a staircase all its own. Brenan tapped on the study door and Huby's voice gave a very fair approximation of Al Yates's intoning "Come" the night before.

"Ah, Mick, I am glad to see you back in the land of the living. Do sit down." Huby always acted as if his invited guest had just happened to drop in after dinner for a drink and a chat. "How did you find the lucubrations of my colleague on the *Ancrene Riwle* this morning?"

"I had difficulty following them. Dr. Croker assumes a linguistic sophistication in his students which I simply do not have. What he sees as a surface structure related to a deep structure, I hear as only a line in a poem, play, or novel."

"You are not alone in having difficulty seeing what the Scarecrow sees. Have a little Cockburn's to soothe the **inwit** of unknowing." He poured from a decanter and handed Brenan a glass of port. His own glass stood as yet untasted on the desk behind which he sat.

"You come from Greenwich, don't you? Something that Croker may not have mentioned about the *Ancrene Riwle* is that the French manuscript, thought by some to come before the English, once belonged to a woman named Eleanor Cobham, who was the second wife of Duke Humphrey, builder of the original Greenwich palace in the 1430s. The woman who gave her the manuscript wrote Eleanor's name and the word "Plesance" in it. You can see for yourself in the library at the B.M. In 1441 Eleanor Cobham was indicted for witchcraft. The manuscript was badly damaged by fire at Westminster in 1731 but has been restored."

Brenan could but listen curiously—as so often when Huby held forth.

"This is your last year in Somersby now beginning," he went on, changing tack. "I am going to ask you to accept the responsibility of being Block Responsible Student in D block; you know what duties are involved."

Brenan said that he did. They were in practice minimal. The appointment was mostly honorary. He wanted to say, "Cook would be a much better choice than me," but he didn't.

"When you go downstairs, look in on the Bursar. She will give you this week's tea, sugar and butter rations for everyone in your block, and you can make yourself known as this year's BRS by distributing them."

Brenan signified that he would do so.

"Thank you for being ready to be of service, Mick. Now you see that book on the table by your chair. My order from Blackwell's arrived today, this book included. I want you to have it and enjoy reading it often." It was the recent Oxford Standard Authors edition of the complete poems of William Wordsworth, revised by De Selincourt. "I have written your name on the fly leaf."

Brenan could only accept it with thanks but a slight uneasiness. "People keep giving me guns," he thought in the voice of Humphrey Bogart. But a new complete Wordsworth was something he was glad to have.

Then there was a tap on the inner door of the study which led to a corridor, to Huby's bedroom and bathroom, and eventually downstairs to the kitchen. It was Mary again, the Warden's personal maid, neat, proper, shy as ever. She was evidently much distressed. "Oh, Dr. Lacy, excuse me—the Bursar sends her compliments and could you please come down to the JCR telephone at once. There's been a dreadful accident and one of the young gentlemen seems to be dead."

Huby and Brenan both gaped at her for a moment.

Huby said, "Of course, Mary, of course. I'll come at once. Mick, you enjoy your port here and browse on your Wordsworth and I'll be back as soon as I can. Please do not go, or speak about this to anyone, until you have spoken with me!" And off he went with Mary down the inner corridor.

Mystified but not as yet much exercised by what he had heard, Brenan did as he was told. He made himself comfortable in the high-back winged chair near the window, drank his port slowly and read the 1850 revision of a poem only recently added to the Wordsworth corpus as "The Ruined Cottage." At one point in his reading, when "the first nippings of October frost" were mentioned, he fancied he heard distantly the urgent bell of an ambulance on call.

It took the better part of an hour for Huby to reappear. He bustled back into the study, not distraught, but obviously under strain. A dire emergency had brought out the former regimental officer in him. He dismissed Brenan at once—almost as if he had forgotten why he had asked him to stay. "Now, Mick, you must get along. No doubt I shall see you in the morning. Something terrible has happened to your friend Arthur. He is dead—God rest his soul."

Brenan looked suitably stricken.

Huby did not miss more than a beat. "An ambulance has already taken his body to hospital and I have had to notify the police. The JCR phone will have to be out of bounds for a while but I want as little notice as possible taken of this ghastly affair. You must say and do *nothing*, you understand, about what you have heard here? No one else in Somersby, except the Bursar and some of her women—and, of course, Mr. Powell—seems to be aware of what has happened. I expect you to be absolutely secret about it, for the time being at least."

"I understand, sir," said Brenan, his thoughts and feelings racing. "But what did Arthur die of?"

Huby studied him, eye to eye, apparently for any sign of panic. Seeing none, he said as if conclusively, "A bullet in the brain."

Brenan went back to his room, thoughts in a whirl, not knowing what to think. Absurdly, he felt less grief for Arthur than fear for himself. Why? It was shameful, this constant self reference. He would have liked to talk the thing over with someone, Valija, or Offord, or even Vaughan, but to do so was too dangerous, given Huby's interdict. With Huby, the good repute of Somersby, the virtue of silence, always came first—

always. For the first time in ages, Brenan was reminded of the death of Tom Loach, his godfather.

In the March of Brenan's first year at Northfleet, a month or two after Justine had returned to Oran, he had come to the end of his instruction in Roman Catholic doctrine at St. Edmund's on the Avenue and was ready to be baptized—a stage of life he had kept secret from his parents to save any distress on their parts. Father Hetherington, his confessor, made no more bones about the baptism than about the rest of Brenan's conversion. He had come to terms, a little sceptically, with the situation as presented to him. "You have a godmother lined up," he said, referring to the mother of Justine, who had written to him signifying her willingness to sponsor Brenan, even after her elder daughter's unfortunate experience with the English winter. "But you need a godfather, preferably someone who can stand up for you on Tuesday next. Isn't there a Catholic fellow student of yours in Somersby whom you could ask?" Even if Arthur Bresnahan had been in hall then, he would not have been a suitable sponsor, having no noticeable religion of his own.

Brenan had asked the advice of Huby, who was also a little sceptical, but for different reasons from Father Hetherington, and who, as an Anglo Catholic, could afford to be charitable. "Your co-religionists, Mick, are rather thin on the ground in Somersby—especially practising co-religionists—but I should say that Tom Loach is your man. A Chemist, he lives in H block. You don't know him? Oh, I'll say a word in your behalf." So Loach had stood up for Brenan on a wintry morning in late March. But between the two of them no chemistry whatever had thereafter occurred.

They never exchanged a word about being or becoming a Roman; they never once had a drink together or even a meal, sitting together in the refectory. Loach never visited Brenan in his room and Brenan was never but the one time, momentarily, at Loach's door in H block—on the evening that he found the penciled scrap of paper in his pigeon hole saying, "I will be there on Tuesday." Brenan had never before met anybody who, at least to begin with, did not want to know him better. There seemed to be nothing about anything, Brenan's baptism included, that Tom Loach needed to know. *I cannot remember / A thing between noon and three.*

He was from Liverpool, a scouse, as the army would say; and when meeting him face to face for the first time, Brenan had thought of Cpl. Leary, also from Liverpool, with whom he had once been detailed for escort duty. It was a best battledress, rifle and bayonet job: they were sent to Sheffield to bring back a deserter under arrest. The corporal's only concern had been how to include an overnight at Liverpool in a trip from London to Sheffield and back. Brenan had no recollection of the deserter himself, except that he had been duly delivered to the provost, but he could see young Cpl. Leary once again to the life in Tom Loach. Lumpish, pasty faced, unfocused, anaesthetic, he told you nothing, gave you nothing, waited for you to be gone. Brenan had been saddened to find that there was such a man as this in Somersby, too, and that, as fortune would have it, he was going to become a spiritual relation.

Then, a month or so later, when Loach had been nowhere to be seen for several weeks, Brenan mentioned him to Huby and was told, in as many words, that Loach had been found in his room dead, a suicide, and nothing more was to be done or said about him, except pray. To Brenan such a consummation had seemed hardly conceivable at first; but before many days had passed, he found himself accepting it in a Somersby spirit—not life in the hereafter, not life as it may be the year after next, but life in the here and now, to be made the most of:

> *. . . that is all*
> *Ye know on earth, and all ye need to know.*

Huby had eventually made him one of those welcome gifts of his, the recent translation of the New Testament by Ronald

Knox, suitably inscribed. *M. John Brenan. XXII June MCL. VII ante Kal. Jul. St. John Fisher. HL.*

Not that the Tom Loach of his first year had been anything like the Arthur Bresnahan of his second! Except for one thing— the cruel order of their going. *More servants wait on man than he'll take notice of.*

Brenan tried to compose himself by reading in his new Wordsworth, the 1850 *Prelude*, but to no avail. He put out the light of his table lamp, which not twenty-four hours before Arthur had found lovely, and looked at the bookshelf where his new copy of Yeats's poems still sat in splendid isolation, now deep in shadow. He tried to pray. One prayer for Compline that he might well have said, but did not, since it was as yet unknown to him, was "Lord, take me out of the net that they have secretly set for me." Outside his window, a cloudy, gusty North Sea night had come down. He took to his bed and slept fitfully.

Chapter Six

Inspector Hornby Investigates

i

The Other Half-Rome

~Browning

Neither Arthur's death nor the advent of Marshal Tievas much altered the routine of this Somersby Tuesday for most of us. Lectures, labs, tutorials had not been canceled in the Marshal's honor, so faculty and undergraduates tended their garden much as usual. If they thought about the Visit at all, they assumed that the authorities and the politicians were seeing the great man on his way through the world in customary fashion with surveillance and speeches. The city newspaper, the *Argus*, had made as much as it could of the event, in anticipation, by means of photography and a Monday supplement. But what had shifted overnight from cosmopolitan London to provincial Northfleet was not a sunburst but the eye of a growing storm in Baltic affairs. And this East-West imbroglio it was not easy, even for a provincial paper, to represent as good news. Nevertheless, a traditional civic banquet in the historic Audit House opposite Holy Rood church in the High Street, his Lordship the Mayor with aldermen and borough councillors in attendance, and a spectrum of politicians from the Earl of Auldcaster to Mr. Aneurin Bevan, Minister of Health and M.P. for Ebbw Vale—these are the staple of newsmen's chaffer; and the *Argus* that came out on Monday evening no doubt had done its best to magnify them all by putting them into one basket (*scilicet* fiasco) with the Marshal.

So far as I was aware this overcast morning, no one in hall was paying much heed—least of all the Warden whose thoughts must still have been almost exclusively of the violent death of Arthur. In his own mind he seemed to have already solved the puzzle of who had done what and why, and was now chiefly concerned with how the doing of justice might best be tempered by discretion. Huby managed to keep the appalling fate of one of his wards extremely quiet, both in Somersby and in the city, mainly by refusing to discuss it with anyone but the police officer in charge of the case, and by browbeating anyone else who happened to know about it into a politic silence. No undergraduate (not even Brenan) and only three of the domestics, plus the Bursar, Mr. Powell, and Huby, had actually seen the body before it was carried off to the city hospital the night before.

This was the secret of Huby's success in keeping curiosity to a minimum, the ignorance of almost everyone else. When the police arrived on the scene, there was no *corpus delicti* in place, and all they could do was cordon off the end of the corridor where the kiosk stood and begin asking questions. In the absence of a death weapon, it was not perhaps unreasonable that an ambulance had been called before the police were notified. Huby and his Bursar, Miss Robertson, a severe Scot, had put up a very plausible front for Inspector Alan Hornby and his assistant, Sergeant Cass, when they arrived from the new station house, down by the Bargate, where there had been an inspectorate of police since the time of Sir Robert Peel, patron of law and order under the young Queen Victoria. Deep spoke to deep, gown to town, and the Warden and the Inspector soon began to see eye to eye.

Outside Somersby, Huby's success in keeping curiosity to a minimum was owing to the total preoccupation of the *Argus* and its readers with the Visit. Civic controversy had arisen long since over whether and, if so, where the Baltic deputy (as his English opponents liked to call him) should be honored in this fair city. The mayor, aldermen, and councillors, constituting a doubtful majority of Labour votes, would on the whole have liked to see the hero of Gdainys feted in the Guildhall segment of the brick and concrete Civic Centre, begun in the 1930s and completed after the war. But when Jurgis Tievas had briefly been a student at the college just after the first war, the seat of government and business had still been in the eighteenth century Audit House. This columned and pedimented stone building, which had most improbably survived the blitz on Northfleet in the second war, was the civic centre that he remembered. Of course, most Tories who had a vote on the question would have preferred not to fête a Communist dictator and cat's paw of the Cominform in either place. But a majority of trimmers from both parties had, as usual, fastened on "the middle course" and found in favour of the Audit House, which was actually far too small and ill-furnished for any such function. Even the BBC decided not, this time, to try to cope—at least, not by television. It would be possible to follow the ceremony, like any show at the London Palladium, by means of radio commentary and well-placed microphones.

The great question Where, after keeping readers of the *Argus,* not to mention its staff, agog for a week or two, had allowed Huby to have the last word at the Vice Chancellor's Michaelmas luncheon for administrative colleagues. He had said that, since Marshal Tievas would not be paying his respects at Holy Rood across the High Street before dining at the Audit House, he, as Chaplain of the College, would not be paying *his* at the banquet. Church and state would yet once more have to agree to differ. Such civic controversy, however, had largely been lost upon returning undergraduates, including Brenan and myself, whose eyes were on the prize of new lectures, better marks in tutorial, and the best autumn term yet. I was currently fascinated by the *Eighteenth Brumaire* of Karl Marx and busy ransacking it for a longer than usual paper for my tutor on Louis Napoleon. Even Brenan, who had returned to Northfleet uniquely well-fitted to take an interest in any aspect of the Visit, apparently found himself otherwise engaged than with the logistics of civic banqueting—or so he later gave me to understand.

If I had not been tapped by Huby on my way out and asked to help the police with their enquiries into Arthur's death, I suppose that the shadowy presence in hall of the Inspector and his men would have been lost on me also, as it was on my fellows. But, as it happened, this became for me the morning of what I would remember as, not the Visit, but the Quiz.

"John, John, good morning, good morning, I have a very great favour to ask of you. Come with me to my study for a moment, please." He was dressed today with his usual unfailing care, but this time in a rich suit of very sober grey worsted and, needless to say, impeccable clerical collar. I walked beside him—in unwonted silence—across the quad and upstairs to his lodging. Ordinarily, he would have had something baleful to say, I feel sure, about the armful of Marxiana I was carrying. From the foot of his staircase, the door of the Senior Common Room could be seen along the corridor and, as we climbed, I noticed a man in uniform come out and go towards the Bursar's office and the kitchen beyond.

In his well-furnished study, Huby had me sit in one of the deep armchairs, but he remained standing with his back to the fireplace which was carefully laid but unlighted. "John, there is something very troubling that I have to tell you. But first I must swear you to absolute secrecy. Speak to nobody but me about what you are now hearing—except perhaps for Inspector Hornby, as I will explain."

My first, alarmed thought was of Mother—could she have died? But why should her life or death be of concern to the police? I was at once reassured: "When did you last see Arthur Bresnahan?"

I said, truthfully, that I had not seen him since Sunday night in E block, where he had been in the kitchen when I made coffee, and had joined me for a cup in my room before going along to see Al Yates at the other end of the corridor. All day Monday I had not set eyes on him, even at dinner when I had actually looked for him, without avail, in the refectory.

"Ah, John, I have to give you the saddest news of your friend and neighbour Arthur."

As usual when conversing with the Warden, I waited in silence, unable quite to believe my ears.

"He died last night in mysterious circumstances. His body was found in the JCR phone booth after dinner by one of the serving women." Huby watched me while I digested this grotesque news.

"But what did he die of?"

"A head wound. Bullet to the brain, by the look of it. But from what weapon—whose weapon—we have as yet no idea. This is why the police are investigating. They are the ones that you can help me with, if you will. They need to question people who knew Arthur well and can suggest why he was killed. You were as close to Arthur as anyone in Somersby—other than perhaps *one* person, I should add. You both lived on the third floor of E all last year. I hope you will volunteer answers to any questions that the Inspector who is in charge of the case may put to you."

I did not much like the sound of this. Being with Brenan a devoted reader of detective fiction and seer of crime films, I knew that the closer one is to the victim, the more suspicious of one the police will be. But what could I say? That, appalled as I was at Arthur's death, all I really wanted was to be left alone to deal with the trauma as best I could? What I said to Huby was that the police were empowered to question anyone who could help them with an investigation and that, of course, I would tell them what little I knew.

"Well, this is the point, John. I knew you would see it at once. Inspector Hornby is being most considerate by not setting us—and the college—in a roar by questioning *everybody* and propagating heaven knows what mass of rumour. Most of your fellows have nothing to tell him, anyway. If anyone does, you do."

"Am I the only one who is being questioned?"

"You are the first undergraduate to be asked officially about Arthur. There may be others, depending on the Inspector's good judgment. We did contact the last member of the JCR to use the kiosk before Arthur, but he had nothing to tell us except *when*—which was well before dinner."

It was interesting to speculate on how the Dickens Huby had managed, discreetly, to isolate the one in question among so many possible users. If Arthur had been killed—as opposed to killing himself—then anyone and everyone within range around the time of death would have to be suspect. In principle, the *who done it?* was prodigious. From the approach that Huby, presumably with the Inspector's approval, was making to me, it could be inferred that even I, close to the victim as I may have been, was not seriously suspect. In return for helping with the enquiry, I was being given the benefit of any doubt about my innocence. Still, to me, the situation did not exactly feel cosy. "Can you tell me if the police have a serious suspect yet? What's the motive?"

"John, let me save what I may have to tell you for another time and take you down now to hear what the Inspector has to say."

I stood up and we left the study; but as we did so, Huby murmured in his old familiar preposterous way, "*Cherchez la femme*, John. *Cherchez la femme.*"

Inspector Hornby had been given the SCR to use as a Crime Room, but he and his men, the Sergeant and the Constable, had hardly transformed it. They had, on the contrary, fitted in comfortably, I could see, at the table, behind the desk, and in the armchair, where Dixon, Doyne, and Whitaker normally took their ease with the Warden. The Constable was not in the room when I entered with Huby. He introduced me to the Inspector, an elderly, elegant figure who spoke with a very slight Midland accent. After a polite word or two with him, Huby withdrew, and Hornby then introduced me formally to the Sergeant, who was a little shorter but not much less elderly then he. Their quiet, kindly acknowledgment of me seemed to make it clear that I personally was none of their particular business as investigators of crime. At his suggestion, the Inspector and I settled at opposing ends of the comfortable window seat with a view of the quad. There was no one about just then. I could see the blushful euonymus across the lawn under Brenan's window in D block—spindle tree my mother liked to call it. The Inspector said, "Mr. Offord, tell me why anyone would want Arthur Bresnahan dead."

As Valija had said to Brenan at the Dolphin the day before, one is reluctant to talk to the police about friends, but it is only to be expected that eventually one will have to do so. I told the Inspector that Arthur's life away from Somersby was pretty much a closed book to me, that our relation in hall was one of comrades rather than friends, brought on by circumstance—even if this was not harsh, as in the army. We had simply been fellow students together; his room was across the corridor from mine; we had mutual companions. As I said this, I found myself thinking guiltily how much less Bresnahan had meant to me, as friend or comrade, than Brenan.

I said that Arthur had been a likeable, playful, but somewhat melancholy person, who seemed always to be looking for something in life that he did not have—comfort, companionship, love. I said that I believed implicitly that he was kind, straightforward, and no more violent than the next man. I did not believe that he was political, or fanatic, or capable of much cruelty—any fanaticism he had was that of a dreamer, not an activist.

"Mr. Offord, I know all about the revolver found in his room, and about his alleged relation with Mrs. Purvey. What do you know at first hand, what did you actually see of them together?"

I tried to take my time in answering: "I noticed last term that they had struck up a special way of being together, of talking and joking when she came to clean. Arthur would start singing 'Sally in our Alley' to tease her. Mrs. Purvey is not a very playful person, as you may know, but Arthur could make her smile. She seemed to take to him, and he to her."

"Did you ever see them kiss, or embrace, or in bed together?"

"They would be careful not to be seen in any such . . . connection—for everybody's sake. But Arthur was a late riser and once or twice last term as I opened my door on the way to lectures, I happened to catch Mrs. Purvey slipping quietly into Arthur's room. Of course, I didn't check to make sure that he was in there at the time, but that was my impression. Once I did hear him say, 'Why, Sally, what a happenstance!' or something of the sort. Of course, it *was* her job to go into each room and tidy up."

"Do you know Mrs. Purvey's husband, Long Will?"

I had a flash memory of the actor Robert Newton when young, in a pre-war English village film called *Poison Pen*, striding down a black and white lane to his cottage, loaded shotgun at the trail, hellbent on executing his accused wife, played by Jean Kent. "I might know him if I saw him in the Dragon, but have never met him."

"All right, Mr. Offord. That's all for now." We came to our feet in the gray north light of the window on to the quad. "I'll let you be about your business. I see you have some hard reading to do." He was looking at my Marxiana. "Thank you for your help. I gather you did your service in the I.Corps. Being debriefed must seem like old times, eh?" He said this without a smile. "What you have had to tell us may come in useful as testimony, so if you will stop at Sergeant Cass's desk on your way out, he will collect your autograph."

I left Somersby without seeing Huby again that morning. I had a distinct impression of being the cat's paw in an ongoing incrimination of Will Purvey which was just feasible enough to have police approval. I wished I had had the presence of mind to ask the Inspector, while he was being collegial, whether or not the bullet that killed Arthur had been recovered. I could not believe that it had not. It and the *post mortem* and the statement of the serving woman who had fetched Arthur to the phone must all have clarified the case considerably, either for or against Long Will. I thought sadly of Sally Purvey, sour look and all.

Inspector Hornby and his men, Sergeant Henry Cass and Constable Malcolm Eccles, made no further impression on me at the time; I saw no more of them on duty in Somersby following Arthur's death. But several months later, after Brenan had taken me into his confidence, I took the trouble to look them up and find out a little more about them and their part in the case: the Inspector and the Sergeant I found at the big station Above Bar, and the Constable, perhaps the most approachable of the three, in Stonham village, where he lived and had his pint at the Dragon. In June, 1952, it gave me a murky sense of satisfaction to discover that, admirable as they were as policemen, not one of them had ever actually caught up with Michael Brenan in person, who was unquestionably the clue that mattered most in the Bresnahan case.

It still does my heart good to think of them duly questioning me this Tuesday morning of the Visit at Huby's instance, when he so recently had put Brenan—who knew everything anyone could ever need to know about the case—in purdah, as it were, in Coventry, perhaps, and on his honor not to tell. Small wonder that Huby fell out of love with our Michael for a while when the full story came out. Inspector Hornby was one of those cultivated police officials that people these days so much enjoy reading (and writing) about in crime fiction. Not that the type does not go back a long way—at least as far as Sergeant Cuff and his roses. I do not know that the Inspector had a passion for opera or wrote poetry, but I would not be surprised if he did. I can just see him, in life as well as in a book, treating the Sergeant to a *bon mot* after I had been debriefed. He would have settled in the deep leather armchair by the fireplace in the SCR—a chair that was by custom Huby's—and regaled his colleague and friend of twenty-five years with his best thought on celibacy in Somersby. His sergeant might have remarked that every time they had seen Dr. Lacy since the evening before—several times—he had been dressed differently, and the Inspector answered that "fashion may wear out more apparel than man," but so does ceremony.

He was one of those quiet, wry speakers who seem not to be saying anything especially clever or funny—certainly not by design—until one finds oneself amused. Laughter out loud does not come to all of us; but there was a tone, a humour, to what little the Inspector said that made me envious of the Sergeant and the Constable in their ease of working with him. Over the years they had fashioned a mode of being on the job together that was truly collective. It was made possible by believing that the job was worth doing, by wanting to do it, and by not expecting much success or reward. With Hornby in charge, they knew when to push and when to stop pushing. Rank and file were the parameters of their working life, deference and discipline, but these made possible a community of being in which, if not equals, they were always comrades. Ego was somehow not an impediment to getting the job done as well as could be expected in the circumstances. The investigation of crime cannot be a happy calling. Sometimes I suspected them—Hornby in particular—of a self-serving cynicism in their ease and efficiency; but not for long: and I have never ceased to wonder at how in the Bresnahan case, without being right or even knowing enough, they managed not to be wrong and not to do any more human damage than had already been done. They were the Grant, Billings, and Dearlove of another *petit bourgeois* tragedy. "No need to black a dead man's name, *Sir*."

"When Mal gets back with word from the Dragon," said the Inspector to the Sergeant, "I expect we can lay this Purvey lead down for good and take up the search for person or persons unknown without delay." Dr. Galletly, the medical examiner, had put time of death at between seven and eight o'clock and confirmed that the cause had been a single entry-and-exit wound to the head, more or less instantly fatal. It had been Constable Eccles who located the spent .303 round deep in the JCR wall behind the kiosk and dug it out, late the night before. "I wouldn't put it past Long Will to have knocked off a Lee Enfield when he was demobbed from the Pioneers," he had said, "but I'd have thought he had too much cunning to use it for a murder where the bullet could be recovered."

Henry Cass sat in the inner corner of the room under mitred bookshelves at a big handsome desk which offered everything he required for record keeping except a typewriter. He was the slightest in build of the three and the most articulate, but a certain sly diffidence kept him from saying much or giving rein to his active fancy. Where Hornby was elegant, he was inclined to be dapper and even more taciturn. He had been the one chiefly responsible for questioning Sally Purvey and the other serving women who had found the corpse. No one appeared to have actually witnessed the shooting itself.

"All we need to know," said Cass grudgingly, "is who made the phone call. Everything else will follow. But where do we start enquiring about that?" Sally Purvey had been the one who answered the phone, and she swore that the caller had been a woman, 'a foreigner who talked slurry, ran her words together, probably Irish.' When she had asked to speak to "Mr. Bresnahan," Sally Purvey had jumped to the conclusion that this was Arthur's new girl friend calling him, the barmaid at the Ship. Subsequently, several trustworthy witnesses had stated that the young woman in question had been busy at the bar without a break from six till nine: so clearly she was not the caller, as she herself vehemently insisted.

When Cass had told Sally Purvey that she had been mistaken about the caller, she had protested, "But when I went into the refectory and threw it up to him, Arthur himself thought it was that tart! Who else could it have been with such a brogue—and wanting to speak to *him*?" She had thought for a moment and then said, "Of course, that phone is forever breaking down. The line is that scratchy and faint sometimes, you can hardly make out what anybody is saying." Throughout her questioning, she had withheld any sign of how she felt about Arthur's sudden death. If we were in an Agatha Christie, thought Cass, she might herself have faked the call, shot him with her old man's .303, and then hidden the rifle ingeniously to hand—all while the other serving women were busy clearing the main course.

Getting out of Huby's armchair, coming across the room and perching on Cass's desk, the Inspector said. "We can't expect to trace a tuppenny call from some other public phone box to this one, but I wonder if Post Office Telephones have anything at all to tell us about it. Mr. Powell says that a maintenance man was here only yesterday morning, checking. Why not have a word with them?"

Cass signified that he would do so. "Let me wait and see what Mal has for us first." To pass the time, he looked appraisingly about the room. Outside, the occasional student passed along the quad between flower bed and lawn. "Home away from home, this student hall, eh? And still a scene of homicide. That Bresnahan must have been a fish out of water here. The very air helped finish him off. Imagine being accepted into a place like this and then taking up with a skivvy like Sally Purvey." He shook his head.

The Inspector waited, as if ruminating on what the Sergeant had said. There was a domestic silence in which the wall clock over the mantel audibly ticked. "The Seven Deadly Sins say it all," he finally observed. "You know I was brought up a Roman. My mother used to say that to avoid the sins, you have to remember them: pride, covetousness, lust, anger, gluttony, envy, sloth. Then, as a sort of *aide mémoire,* she would say, 'Police come last and give everybody suspense.'"

"I don't think I've ever heard you tell this one before," said Cass. "The air here must be getting to you, too."

Before long, Constable Eccles came back into the room. On his way through the kitchen he had picked up a tray of midmorning tea and biscuits for three. "Compliments of Cook," he said. As they served themselves, he confirmed that Will Purvey was off the hook for the shooting. Half Stonham had seen him in the Dragon from six till closing.

"Dr. Lacy will be discomfited," said the Inspector. "Now you, Henry, can talk to the telephone people. I will find Mr. Powell and see what else I can get out of him. He knows more about what goes on in this place than all the others put together. You, Mal, can see if we have missed anything in the vicinity of the phone box and beyond."

"Right, sir. I'll go over the ground outside the wall, too. One thing Long Will said to me last night was that if *he* had been sniping the bugger—his words—he'd have got him through the little gate in the side wall."

ii

Did I only know what Charlie
did not know he knew?

~Kipling

When Valija came to tea with Brenan this Tuesday afternoon, I was there by invitation. He had lunched with me in the union after a morning lecture—on *Paradise Lost* for him, on the French Revolution for me—and we had caught up a little on one another's summer doings. He wanted to hear about

Pau, St. Pé, and the d'Argelès. Had I come across any relics of
Dornford Yates and his set in exile there? What about Paris on
my way home? I wanted to hear about Heathdene, Greenwich,
and the Festival of Britain on the South Bank. How had he
spent his summer? He gave me kind greetings from his parents,
but he could not tell me much that was current or substantive
about mine. They had a way of keeping their troubles to
themselves—as had the Brenans. I had forgotten until he asked
about him that Dornford Yates was my father's favourite author
and that, when I had not responded to the Berry books as well
as I might, young Brenan had been called into the circle. He
had been more responsive, ready to have the occasional fan
talk that my father had been looking for. I realized sadly that
in Pau I should have kept an eye out for relics and then written
my father a letter of Dornford Yates lore. Not that he was as
much of a fan nowadays as he had been before the war.

After lunch, on our way back to the library, Brenan had
said, "Come by my room at three-thirty and meet Valija Didelis
again. She's coming to tea. You remember her—at Miss Hollis's
party in Highfield last term? I got to know her better taking
the same train up here on Sunday night. You'll find her
interesting." This was so like Brenan. I had yet to meet the
woman he did not find interesting. I smiled and accepted the
invitation. Why Marianne was called Miss Hollis, when she
had so long been on friendly, Christian name terms with us,
was because she, like Arthur, had a role in our imaginary world
of names and legends—she because of her very proper
Southern Baptist upbringing in Montgomery and at Judson
College in Marion, Alabama. Somersby was far, very far from
Hartfield but Marianne had been our Mr. Knightley, familiarly
known and loved by no mere Christian name. Our favourite
Miss Hollis story concerned a sporting though reluctant
agreement she had made with the college dramatic society to
play the Conjur' Woman in a production of *Dark of the Moon*.
Though hardly from the hills of Kentucky where the play is
set, Miss Hollis had still been the only speaker of a true

Southern dialect in the whole cast. For all of them, she tried, on request, to be voice coach. When first night had come and gone and the inevitable review appeared in the Northfleet *Argus*, it heartily congratulated the company on a brilliant interpretation of a difficult script, but deplored the attempt at so *inauthentic* an accent by the actress who played Conjur' Woman.

I had accepted Brenan's invitation partly because I was curious to hear what he might say, in polite conversation with his new girl friend, about Arthur. It never crossed my mind that Valija would be the one to say something about him first. Over lunch, though Brenan and I had had a table all to ourselves, we had each kept Huby's secret from the other, as we had been enjoined to do. Neither of us knew what, or even if, the other one knew about Arthur. From listening to Huby the evening before, Brenan still supposed that it was a suicide that had occurred. I knew better than this, thanks to Huby, but had not as yet the slightest notion of any Baltic connection in the murder. It was Valija, of course, who must have known almost everything about Arthur's death and the Tievas visit. But she, too, seemingly did not know she knew.

"Not here yet." Brenan was fiddling with tea things on the low table when I dropped in decently late. For the occasion he had spread on it one of Bessie's large linen tray cloths embellished with cornflower motifs, embroidered by one of the Mickfield aunts. To eat, there was Hovis bread and butter, honey, and a chocolate Swiss roll. Tea would be made later on a sortie to the kitchen downstairs. Milk and sugar stood waiting. Brenan's room, number twelve, was in the upstairs near corner of the block, facing south into the quad and far from the main entrance.

"'Stands the church clock at ten to *four*?' Why don't you walk down and meet her at the gates? I'll put the kettle on while you're gone." There was no explicit rule of access to Somersby for women visitors. Provided it was visiting time, they might walk in under the arch without Mr. Powell's seeming even to notice, and make their own ways to their hosts' unlocked doors.

"Valija can find her own way here well enough." He flopped into the Morris chair by the window and I sat down on the bed which was suitably draped with a fawn afghan familiar to me from the slip room at Heathdene. "Do you know, she has a personal invitation to the VC's reception for Marshal Tievas tomorrow night?"

"So what? I gather from Al Yates that all foreign exchange students are invited. Proper thing, too. She's a Baltic national, isn't she? Personally, I'm just as happy not to have to go, aren't you? Tonight's shindig at the Audit House is the one not to miss, I should have thought. What will the great man say this time, having put his foot in his mouth—in everybody else's mouth—already?"

The door stood ajar. Someone tapped on it. It opened and there was Valija in a grey dress and sensible brown shoes. "Excuse my lateness," she said, "I went into town to Tyrrell and Greene's to get these from their bakery,"—she handed Brenan a little box of pastries (they were petits fours)—"and it took forever to get a bus back. The banquet tonight has the town by the ears." Her command of English idiom always astonished me. I remembered her at Marianne's party saying to Reg Croft, "What is the English for 'drunken bum?'" She was one of those speakers of a foreign language who are idiomatically perfect but never able, for whatever reason, to pronounce it quite like a native.

"You remember John Offord, Valija," said Brenan, by way of acknowledging my presence. We were all on our feet now, making a small, fully furnished room seem smaller than it actually was.

"Yes. Of course." We shook hands, Valija and I. "Michael has been telling me more about you—all of it good."

"Where would you like to sit, Valija," said Brenan, "on the upright one or in this armchair?"

She looked about her, as if for the first time since she had entered. "So this is your room," she said, moving past me, standing by the bed, to look at some small framed reproductions of paintings by Paul Klee that Brenan had put up, now that he was back, to relieve the beige drabness of the walls. His cupboard doors were discreetly closed. All along the window sill, books were shelved and, above the desk, his new Yeats no longer loomed solitary but was one of as many volumes as there was space for. Yet more books and papers were stacked on the desk top, where the lamp whose light Arthur had admired stood flounced but unlighted. It was a modest, unassuming room, all brown or beige with a little red here and there.

"I'll sit here, thank you," Valija said, having come around to the desk chair, turned inward to face the tea table. She thus sat between Brenan and me, and her face and hair were sidelighted from the window.

"Let me run down to the kitchen and put the kettle on," Brenan said, when I had settled back on the bed. He had left and returned to his chair before Valija and I had found anything much to say to each other.

"Michael," she said, "I have something vexing to tell you— if John will only excuse my talking shop for a minute while the kettle boils." I nodded and smiled, charmed by her manners. She did not miss a beat. "Last evening my uncle, Dr. Didelis, wanted to have a word with you—presumably about Ben Jonson business; I really don't know why. He wanted you to telephone him at a number in Norfolk before he left on a trip somewhere. I telephoned you here in Somersby to tell you this but, would you believe it, I could not get through. Your JCR phone was either engaged or out of order all evening—at least until it was too late for you to catch my uncle before he left. I hadn't thought to arrange a fall back number for you, so now we have to wait till he returns to Holt. Let me give you the number there." She handed Brenan a slip of paper from her purse. "It is where I expect to be joining him on Thursday, as you know—Professor Rawlings' house. But before you thank me, let me tell you, Michael, I had no idea previously that my uncle knew of your existence. Had you?"

It gives me no pleasure to recall that I sat listening without much interest to Valija confess to having called Brenan on the JCR phone the previous evening. After the discovery of the body in the kiosk, while the phone was off the hook, as it must have been for hours, any number of innocent callers could have tried and failed to get through to somebody in hall. I had no reason to suppose that it was Michael Brenan that Valija and a phantom sniper were collaborating to kill and not Arthur. So far was I at this juncture from being the amateur detective that it had not yet occurred to me to see whether, and if so how, the crime scene at the end of the JCR corridor was still "out of bounds" to everyone but the police. Brenan, I took for granted, was even less curious than I about the spot where Arthur happened to have made his quietus.

Brenan listened to what Valija had to say, I recall, with some mystification but no evident distress. He appeared flattered. "All I know about your uncle is what you have told me," he said to her. "I have never set eyes on him or spoken with him. What on earth can he want of me?" At this question, perhaps, a shadow of the faintest of clouds passed across the inmost landscape of his mind. But he was at once distracted by a cry of *kettle*! from the kitchen below—the voice sounded like Cook's—and he hurried off with pot, packet, and spoon to make the tea.

While he was out of the room, I kept Valija occupied by asking her casually who her uncle was and what he did. When Brenan came back with a steaming pot, the tea party proper began. We ate and drank everything there was on the table, except the remains of Brenan's weekly butter and sugar ration. There was plenty of talk between mouthfuls, but there were no more surprises. We talked of my travels in France, of films seen, of Valija's research, of the Visit; and then I made my excuses and withdrew. Left to themselves, Brenan and Valija cleared the tea things, did the washing up, kissed, cuddled, and said sweet nothings for a while—these were the days before the Pill; and then it was time for her to go.

On the way to the bus stop, they drifted back into talk about her uncle's interest in Brenan. To her amusement, he said that Jose Rodriguez must be at work, keeping an eye on them after all. This time she did not see fit to remind him that they were not in one of his favourite films. But not long before her bus drew up, she said, "It really is too bad that I wasn't able to speak to you during dinner last evening. A woman did take my call but, just as it seemed that you were coming on the line, there was a clatter of some sort, then silence. Eventually I just had to hang up. Was it you? What happened?"

"Nobody told me I had a call. I was nowhere near the phone all evening. I can't think what can have been going on. But . . . ."

"Goodbye, Michael. Thank you so much for tea. It was very nice. See you in the morning!" And the bus carried her off to Highfield.

On his way back to Somersby, past the playing field where rugger and soccer teams were both practicing, he found himself yet once more in a whirl. I finally tell the VC about Tievas, he said; Valija phones me concerning Didelis and can't get a connection; then in the phone box poor Arthur blows his brains out. What in God's name is going on?

iii

Across the yellow realm of stiffened day
~Meredith

No news may be good news, Vaughan, but if so why do I feel you're keeping the best from me? There has to be more mischief afoot up there in Lindsey than you are letting on. There couldn't be as little as you say, not with the Marshal at anchor off the pier, Templeton keeping house on the hill, and all those reds, whites, and pinkoes gathering in the osier isle. "We heard them noise," as the poet says. We hear them noise. The D.A.C. was in his saturnine mood today.

Those bloody Balts with their folksinging, country dances, village music, is none of them up there petitioning the Marshal to undo the revolution, or at least do it right? They are all your look out, Vaughan, now Holland Park has become too cribbed for them. You are the one to let us know where they are flocking. You know what the Commissioner would say (he did Sir Harold in a slightly different voice): *"Catch the idea on the wing to sedition or disorder." Where is Didelis? Where is Draugiski? Where's old Garas? What's more, where are the Russkis and where are the Cousins? Especially the Cousins. They must be in the front row balcony for this show, craning to see whether 5 and 6 and the F.O. have finally lost it—complete failure of nerve since Burgess and Maclean made themselves scarce.*

I wouldn't put it past the Cousins to have one of their friendly part-timers in place at the college there, would you? One of those superannuated exchangers they like to put over on us. Or perhaps Caius is their pigeon hole this time. A bit out of your way, Cambridge, I know. But, Vaughan, you really must try keeping me more up to date than you are doing. Tout à fait au fait, *as the Frogs say* . . . The line goes dead.

Coming down by car from the high ground at Merewell, through winding lanes and long, sere roadsides towards Fakenham and Lynn, Vaughan never once gave Connie a thought. They had honeymooned hereabouts when she was twenty and he thirty-four—by the sea at Blakeney, above the moorings. Told how to say the notorious local placename of Stiffkey, she had giggled like a schoolgirl. "Pity your name isn't Stu, darling, instead of Gil," she had lisped in her Madeleine Carroll voice. "Then we could spell it S-t-i-f-f, couldn't we?" She was always in some sense with him wherever he was sent. But today, as he turned the wheel and bore northward with the sea somewhere over to the right, his first thought was of Gus, back at the Yard North in that starchy office overlooking the Festival ground, and the nagging taskmaster he had lately become.

This particular fishing expedition was turning out to be worse news than even Vaughan's own enemies along the

Embankment might have hoped for—if they knew of it, which a pound to a penny they did not. Who the devil *did* know what the hell was what this time? It was the nicest of conundrums. Phoning in this morning as per usual, he had kept quiet about the headline which he had come up with last night in Holt and Merewell, fobbing the old man off with small talk about Northfleet, as if Lloyd and he had not left the city at all yesterday for points south. Thanks to young Brenan and his eye for a foreigner, Vaughan had at last picked up a loose thread that ran from Didelis to Rawlings right back to Templeton. At present he was hoarding news of it for a cyclone shot that would blow Gus back in his chair, perhaps this evening after the banquet when least expected. They had agreed on a later call than usual. The banquet might be the moment of truth, if anyone were going to knock off the Marshal this time round, now or never. But Vaughan doubted it. He had the feeling that what mattered was, as always, something different going on elsewhere—only this time he just happened to have more than half a mind what and where. It was too bad that by mentioning Caius Gus had brought in Rawlings as a player, confirming a suspicion of Vaughan's own before he could report it. The whole cock and bull set up shaping in his preconscious around the name Didelis hardly bore thinking about.

This Merewell ramble yesterday should have been a picnic. It could have broken the case if only the Holt police as well as the public hadn't to be kept in the dark about everything new to do with the Marshal. The one thing Gus had been up front about was not confiding in the Constabulary, or the local Branch boys, or anybody, not in Northfleet, not anywhere. *This is not your usual Hammer and Sickle business, Vaughan. You're back with S.O.E. in the field, no short cuts. Do it all by yourself.* Evidently the old man was once again indulging himself, fishing someone else's stream for the fun of it; at Vaughan's expense, too, testing him as if he were some tyro like D.A. Lloyd instead of the oldest of hands serving out his time in the field, a colour sergeant in the trenches. So here he was, now that things had at last got moving, half blind, with one hand tied behind his back, scrambling in darkest Norfolk. Lloyd could say as much, of course, if not more—though leaving that young weasel in a ditch with only a .32 and no wheels was something Vaughan believed he could live with. Lloyd's predicament would be a gentle reminder for Gus, whenever he was told about it, that he had flatly refused a third man and a second car for a job that cried out for both. More keeping the circle closed at any cost, the circle of those who knew what was supposed to be going on: Vaughan could but wonder how in the first place Gus of all people came to be one of those who knew.

At a cross road in a shower of dead leaves the signpost said that the way to Lynn lay well out of sight of a *tour abolie* called Castle Rising. But he took no notice, giving not a thought to Walsingham, away to the east, where twenty years before Connie and he had been enchanted by another local spirit than Our Lady. At a Feminist rally in the village hall, an impaneled woman had said to the chairwoman, who was refusing to let a man speak from the floor, "It's all right, Mary. He's my husband." Connie and he had giggled together helplessly that night until he shut her eyes with kisses. In those days she had made him feel young at heart again in spite of the first war. "It's all right, Mary. He's my husband," she would say thereafter on every appropriate occasion.

At Theobalds in Holt yesterday afternoon, after racing down from Northfleet, Vaughan had scored a hat trick. Lloyd had done little more than drive, but Vaughan had outdone himself chatting up the housekeeper, Mrs. Tydeman. All the nice girls love a policeman, especially unidentified as such and in plain clothes. She had stood in a white work coat at the foot of the front steps as their Wolseley turned into the tree-sheltered drive. A caterer's van from Cromer was just pulling away. Yes, for the present, she had said sweetly, *she* was in charge of the premises and their furbishing.

You'll be gentlemen for the music at the castle on Thursday. I'm afraid the master won't be back till then. He's in Cambridge tonight, and tomorrow he goes up to Northfleet for the big send off. Vaughan had agreed amiably that music at the castle was indeed what Lloyd and he were there for, and expressed concern at all the work it must mean for her. *Bless your heart, yes, a mountain of work, but at least the master has hired cleaners from Sheringham to do the castle, so things are well in hand.* Vaughan had given her one of his phony visiting cards and assured her that Lloyd and he were not unexpected early arrivals at Theobalds. They were putting up in Brancaster where there was a golf links. *Oh yes, most of the guests for the music will be coming from elsewhere. Here at the house we shall have only the master's sister, Lady Elizabeth, and Sir Marcus, and a doctor from the Baltic States and his niece, and the three musicians. The rest will be meeting at the castle Thursday afternoon for the music. If only the weather lasts. I do hope so, for the master's sake. He has put so much into bringing the Friends of Merewell together.* Vaughan had said that they must not impose on her a moment longer. He and his friend were wondering if the castle could be viewed at all that very evening. She had said she didn't see why not. It was only three or four miles away, towards Sheringham, and no one was in residence nor had been for donkey's years.

Before they left Holt, he had called old Binnie in Files, who confirmed that Stephen Rawlings of Caius was indeed somehow connected with MI5 as well as with Ben Jonson studies. There might even be some overlap between the Friends of Merewell Castle and the Aldeburgh how-do-you-do. But nothing was on record yet about any musical picnic under the dome on Thursday for movers and donors in the campaign to bring the castle into the care of the state.

By the time Vaughan and Lloyd had located Merewell, circled the clearing once on foot under the trees, and returned to their vantage ground not far from the car but well within the padlocked gate, darkness had fallen. Within the mausoleum-like pile there had been not the least sign of occupation. Lloyd had been his usual junior-knows-best self. What price a padlock, if, by clipping it, they could drive right up to the terrace steps? Why not march up to the front door and break right in, there were four front doors to choose from in this pretentious ruin? But Vaughan's circumspection had been immediately rewarded and by a genuine epiphany.

Down the darkened lane outside the gate had come headlights and the sound of a vehicle. An Austin van had turned in and pulled up, and a man had jumped out on the passenger side. Before he could unlock the gate, he or the driver or both had spotted the Wolseley parked under the pines to one side of the entrance. A cry of warning had been given. By then Vaughan and Lloyd had been pelting towards the van, waving and miming "Halt!" They were all too clearly visible for a moment in its blinding headlights. At once it backed away without a shot being fired; the passenger hopped in, and it disappeared down the lane even faster than it had appeared, this time with its lights off.

In all the wooded rides and farm tracks around Merewell, Vaughan and Lloyd had been unable to catch up with their quarry. Eventually, frustrated, they had taken a breather at an all-night pull up on the Norwich road and reviewed tactics. In any such stand-to Lloyd could be trusted; his judgement would be sound. They had agreed to return to Merewell and reconnoitre the castle itself in case the van driver and his mate had circled back and entered during their absence. This time they had left the Wolseley well away from the entrance and found an approach from the south along the cliffs, where the trees grew closest to the terraces. Having crept up the steps without being challenged, they had broken into the pantheon and, guns drawn, looked round in the near darkness with their torches. Nobody seemed to be about, so they had left as they had come.

Access to the basement by the spiral staircases had been firmly blocked by cast iron covers flush with the floor and bolted from beneath. "Like bloody man holes," Lloyd had said, sulkily. From outside on the ground, the four huge garden doors had proved impregnable, but nothing indicated that the basement was any more occupied than the pantheon or the dome. "Merewell *machts nicht,"* Lloyd had muttered. Back at their new vantage ground, a sandy ditch running under the exposed roots of an enormous oak, they had made themselves as comfortable as they could. Lloyd stoically laid in some of the clobber from the car, groundsheet, water bottle, field ration. One hour off, one hour on, they kept an uneventful watch on the castle until midmorning, when Vaughan left to phone Gus and drive back to Northfleet for the banquet. Lloyd had agreed without demur that someone ought to stay and pick up the new lead if any such chance occurred.

Skirting Lynn and crossing the lowlands of the Wash, while church after church rose blandly at him out of the marsh, Vaughan began wondering what Lloyd must think was going on anyway.

Each had been briefed individually by Gus, and no confidences or impressions had since passed between them. Lloyd was not one to allow much intimacy, let alone condescension from a mere senior. Public school boy, university man, up and comer, he had managed to marry Gus's only daughter. Less brainy than Vaughan, he took much better care than he of his professional standing and social acquaintance. Courting opportunity, keeping his own counsel, taking no vulgar risk, he would quietly convey that he had somehow overtaken Vaughan, or Dai Morgan, or whomever he happened to be with on the track they were all following at the Yard.

In a young colleague, Lloyd's air of cool competence had at first been for Vaughan reassuring, even likeable. But now, after more than a few partnerings, it had become a little sinister. If there were a clean and a dirty end to any of the sticks they had to pick up, Lloyd would be sure to get the clean end. Vaughan knew he was not the only one in S.B. to have noticed as much. Lloyd's neatness, his modesty, his tone, all that he so smoothly said and did, was part of some carefully composed personal success story. Left in the ditch at Merewell, watching for unspecified arrivals at an apparently empty pile, he had given his usual knowing half smile when Vaughan said, "I did my best on Saturday to talk the old man into giving us support and another car." It had not been contemptuous or even unpleasant, this smile, just confident that whatever response was called for, his would be the superior one. To Vaughan, when a partner in the field was less worried than he, it meant that the partner knew something he did not know. For Lloyd, the works and days of dirty hands all seemed to be part of some damned perpetual W.O.S.B.

Vaughan wouldn't have put it past Gus to brief him less fully than he had Lloyd before they started out on this fool's errand. Where he stood in the old man's liking was not something he had any illusions about. It was just that he would rather think about Gus than about Lloyd any day, even if the one gave him ten times as much grief in a month as the other did. Funny thing, that, how one's seniors, whatever their faults, were so much more bearable than one's juniors. It must go back to school, where those younger than oneself hardly seemed to exist except as shadows. It was only the masters and prefects, or classmates and those ahead of one, who were substantial and were loved or hated, recognized and remembered. Later on, in the real world, if a junior drew himself up and looked in at a window, as it were, shades of the ivory tower still seemed to be drawn against him. Lloyd, for instance, could never be more than a faint annoyance compared with Gus.

As D.A.C., the old man had always treated Vaughan a little more than fairly—till now. Together they went back a long way before the second war and the posting to Bletchley. In 1927 they had each, at a different rank, made a name for himself on the Arcos case, when the missing War Office papers had never been recovered from those legendary armoured safes, but plenty of incriminating Bolshevik documents had. *There are no political police in England* Gus still liked on occasion to say with great emphasis. But this Tievas to-do was something quite different from the usual. It was as if the old man were at last daring him to find out what they had both better not know. It was a test that could not be passed, only to a greater or lesser degree failed, one of those Californian investigations in which the client already knows who has done what and hires the shamus to *not find out too much* (as Connie scornfully put it when they first saw *The Big Sleep* together. It had been at the Warner, Leicester Square, on her demob leave from the W.R.N.S.).

Glimpsing Boston Stump across fields and rooftops, he was reminded to stop at the next pub and snatch lunch before it was too late. Settling back to the wheel, he decided to have his first pipe of the day. Driving onehanded, with more caution than previously, he continued to think of Connie. When left to his own desires, he always came back to her. The road took him up into the wolds where the wind could be heard whistling above the sound of the car's engine and it was no surprise to see on the hills and in the vales green outcrops of pine and fir. This was aerodrome country. "We could have so much fun if you didn't have to be a detective," she had said when he called her from Holt and the question arose of his being home for her bridge party on Friday. "Why can't we give it all up?"

He still liked Connie more than anyone else he had ever met. Once, when he had asked her to marry him, he had been hopelessly in love with her. Now he was in his early fifties and she was thirty-nine—actual, not statutory thirty-nine. It seemed less and less likely that she would have a child. So far as he knew, she was acceptant of her childlessness: no pilgrimages to Harley St.; no prayers, unless he was mistaken; no complaints. But more and more she had become expectant of him for company at home. "I don't know why you can't be an attentive nine-to-five husband like Thom Callender or Chris Delaney." She made less and less allowance for the loss a policeman's wife may have to take. His duties, on the other hand, the call on him as embodied in the D.A.C., took no account whatever of any concern he might have as a husband. He kept his place in the competition for rank by being ready always to behave like an unmarried, younger man. As yet he was unready, unwilling, to give up the game—even for Connie.

The Special Branch, more than most services, tended to become a married couple's whole life together. For better or worse, it was the only family either he or Connie happened to have known since their childhoods. Both were sole survivors, under the too common rule that, from generation to generation, all flesh is grass. At first she had taken to his career as if it were an added thrill in her life. She kept her own job as a secretary at the Empire Marketing Board. "It's no good your standing there looking middle aged, Gil. I'm no ministering angel." But after a while she found that conspiracy, or anticonspiracy, "kissing over the phone," as she called it, was not so much fun as expected. Then the second war broke out and gave them both something more than their marriage to be getting on with. It was afterwards, when they settled in Blackheath at St. Mary's, that from time to time—especially when some vexed I.R.A. case came up—she would allude to his finding himself a *cleaner* job than this one, to their making a fresh start.

The countryside he now passed through remained dry, but clouds were gathering in the west; and a storm appeared to be on its way across Kesteven behind him and out to sea. At Louth, he would have liked to take a look at the new R.A.F. Flying College nearby. In the old town, a tall spire, elegant red brick and roof tiles, all for the present meant nothing to him. It was Northfleet, his room at the Dolphin, a hot bath, a stiff whisky, preludes to an evening on duty at the banquet, that beckoned.

Templeton in the pier glass of his dressing room at Blechynden watches himself tear a black tie from around his starched wing collar, readjust both of them, and begin again for the perfect knot. *I am damned if that wretch Stephen is going yet once more to get my goat.* Rawlings has just telephoned to cancel his appearance at the banquet this evening. He is needed at Merewell instead. But tomorrow he will be here as promised "for the Restoration and to see Cromwell off the premises." *What a pain, what a goad the creature always is. The last time was in that dewy flower garden at Greenwich, on our way back from the all-night consult at the Naval College. With his usual infernal insolence, he lets drop that Didelis insists after all on having the change made here, at this house. So he has given him my word that it will be. How this can have come about without my scotching it . . . . Hadn't I listened enough times to the pair of them go over the plot in excruciating Jonsonian detail? By his account, it was during my only absence from that reeking closet in eight long hours, towards the end, when I freshened up for the return to Whitehall, getting into my camouflage, as Elizabeth calls it.*

Templeton loops his folded tie and, with the node held firmly in place, begins the difficult trick of threading—or is it unthreading?—the other end. "Didelis drinks himself into a stupor on your wine, but it's Tievas who is poured back aboard the *Dolphynas.* The Old One will be tickled to death when you break it to him." *Now see little Stephen jockey himself into position for dropping out tomorrow, too. The sensibility, as even his mother says, of a shoe salesman. It will be Elizabeth and I who end up delivering Didelis back to Theobalds. What will she have to be told? "The thing we know of but we do not know." . . . Why do the Old One's dream operations always turn out so badly? If only this whole charade were done with already. Inefficiency, extravagance, and yet for the first time in history (save the mark!)* **bloodlessness.** *Try telling the Catholics of Lithuania that their sacrifices under Stalin will be more acceptable than the Croats' under Tito. Why on earth would anyone listen to Didelis and believe what he says enough to act on it? The only use Stephen was expected to be, other than to scout bolt holes for the henchmen, was to keep the Baltic play actor on the same page as the rest of us. . . . Thank God it is Auldcaster and not I who must do most of this evening's responses.*

Templeton flexes his newly modeled black tie with a certain

nonchalance. *Why were we in a park among cedars and dahlia beds? Because at that hour of the morning no train was due, and rather than sit at the bottom of Maze Hill we walked to the village station, a twisting mile of silent grasses. Stephen always knows the best way and the shortest cut. "The heel on the finishing blade of grass."* . . . *That boy from nowhere who was here yesterday bleating about* Antony—*or was it* Caesar?—*he seems to know as much about what is going on with Tievas as anybody. "What ye have spoken in the ear in closets shall be proclaimed upon the housetops." If it were Stephen he had gone to confession to, he would be dead in a ditch by now . . . Six o'clock . . . I wonder where Elizabeth is, in her getting dressed . . . . One thing to be said for Elizabeth, one of many, she never surprises me and is never surprised.*

iv

Κύριέ μου, σὺ οἶδας
Sir, you are the one who knows

~Revelation

Dinner in the refectory this evening went very much as usual. Brenan sat with me and our fellow students in Classics, Economics, and Engineering, well in view of Huby at high table with Dixon, Doyne, and Whitaker. A familiar, discreet hubbub obtained. What we gossiped about I now forget, but I doubt if it was the death of Arthur, the incursion of Hornby, Cass, and Eccles, or the entertainment of the Baltic deputy concurrently going on at the Audit House. These occasions were already to Somersby at large as if they had never been. When pudding had been served, Mary, looking every inch her discreet self, appeared at Brenan's elbow and murmured that Dr. Lacy would like to see him after dinner in his study. Brenan thanked her with a shy smile, and glanced up at Huby in acknowledgement. I can still see the Irish set of his pale eyes and smooth cheekbones as he did so. Dinner then dawdled to its usual ragged halt.

He and I drifted out into the quad and stood looking at the gathering clouds. He said, "'Nothing but waves and winds,'" and I knew that he was grieving in his own way for Arthur.

"What are you going to do?" I said fatuously.

"Do?" he said, and he did not look me in the eye. "I am going to remember him always as d'Argelès—for you, for the mountains, and for *Orphée*. If in doubt, cite *The Waste Land*."

What was there to say after that? When he was stretched or troubled as he now was, Brenan could be offensive, showing a hard, offhand side that was not otherwise to be seen. I said, "How about the Queen of the Waste Lands? It was interesting to see her again. I must say academic life in England seems to agree with her."

Brenan made no answer to this. "I'd better go and see what Huby wants," he said.

This was the last I saw or heard of him for several days, if not a week.

It turned out that Huby was in one of his moods. He moved about the study with a glass of port in his hand, having poured Brenan a glass, asking edgy questions and then answering them. Brenan sat in the upright chair in front of the desk and waited politely for a moment when he could take his leave.

"Mick, who is the young lady you had to tea this afternoon? I don't recall having seen her before. Does she live in Highfield? I presume that she is one of those D.P.s from eastern Europe, deserving people, as the Minister likes to call them."

Brenan regaled Huby briefly with one or two things he knew about Valija.

"She would have been introduced to me, no doubt, if the Chancellor's banquet for Tievas hadn't caused Miss Lightbody to cancel the Highfield garden party." His facial expression implied that a response from Brenan was expected.

"The garden party has only been postponed a week, until Monday. No doubt Miss Didelis will be introduced to you then. If John and I had known you wished her to meet you, we would have invited you to tea this afternoon. You know you are always welcome to drop in."

Huby savoured a mouthful of his Cockburn's. "Precisely," he said, a little thickly. His study looked north, and because the evening light was failing early he put down his glass and bustled over to the windows, where Brenan sat, and began drawing the curtains with a flourish. Then he went about the room turning on lamplight in well-chosen places. Everywhere became pleasantly comfortable, even though the woodfire remained unlighted. But there was no music. In those days, in this situation, nobody would have expected any.

While Huby flitted about, Brenan looked at the handful of new books stacked on the low table by his chair. He picked one out and said, "*Conclusive Evidence?* I thought you never read detective stories, sir, not even from Gollancz."

"I never do. If you look, you will see that the book you refer to is a family memoir by a Russian emigré, written somewhat in the vein of Proust." Brenan glanced at it; the author was unknown to him. "This one came out in New York I see."

"Yes. There is a very kind young man who handles my account at Basil Blackwell's and keeps an eye out for what may please me, even if it does come from our former colony."

Brenan's eye lighted on an opening sentence and followed it for a few lines: *In thinking of my successive tutors, I am concerned less with the queer dissonances they introduced into my young life than with the essential stability and completeness of that life. I witness with pleasure the supreme achievement of memory, which is the masterly use it makes of innate harmonies when gathering to its fold the suspended and wandering tonalities of the past.* "I see why you are reminded of Proust—or at least Scott Moncrieff," he said. The bait remained untaken.

Huby eventually settled into the high-backed, upholstered chair behind his desk. "Precisely," he said again.

"May I ask, sir, why you aren't at the Audit House banquet this evening?"

"My dear Michael, you know very well that my advancing years and priestly duties mean that I must be to bed with the nightingale and up with the lark. Besides, it is all wrong for the visit of a professed atheist to be allowed to disrupt the calendar of a Christian college. Entirely wrong. Look what has happened to Convocation this year. It could have been held yesterday without creating the least conflict with the Great Man's Visit. It is always a mistake for church and state to try to be cosy." It was the postponement of the Highfield garden party, an event at which he was by custom the cynosure, that lingered foremost in his thought and rankled. He was well-known for arriving on the minute, talking nonstop to as many guests as was feasible, and leaving early. His signature trick was to pen and mail a note of thanks well before attending a party, so that it would be delivered to his hostess or host with astonishing promptness.

"Most of the people of Baltija are still Christian, of course."

"Very likely. But tell me, whose feet were you sitting at this morning—together with the serviceable Miss Didelis? Would it be my colleague's from Edinburgh, who is not a Caledonian? Professor Brillingham, the distinguished Miltonist?"

"Yes, it would—except that Miss Didelis wasn't there for some reason. Perhaps she thought she already knew in sufficient detail how integral the epic similes are to *Paradise Lost,* and how well they epitomize the whole poem."

"Ah, the wind was in that quarter again, was it? 'Small night founder'd skiff' and all that. Well, the Professor is a very sensible, downright man, you know; and I am glad *you* were there, with or without Miss Didelis, to hear what he had to tell you. I trust you took copious notes. He has his doubts about you, Mick, as a serious student of English. I don't have to tell you this. Long ago, when you were looking for a way to study at the Sorbonne during your first long vac, he told me, 'That Brenan, he's a bit of an *aesthete.*' I tried to remind him, of course, that some of our best literary critics have been aesthetes. But your work in tutorial may have begun to reassure him.''

Brenan let his tarnished record with the head of English at Northfleet lie for a few beats. Then he said, "What about the death of Arthur Bresnahan?" As Bessie used to say about Michael in other contexts, he could be bold as brass for the time it takes to ask a question.

"What, indeed, about the death of your friend and neighbour Arthur?" Huby emptied his glass and set it on the silver tray with the decanter. "While you finish your wine, Mick, let me retire for a few minutes. Then you can come in and talk with me about Arthur while I undress for bed."

So it was going to be one of those evenings. Huby would toddle off across the corridor into his bedroom, leaving both doors open behind him, go around his huge Victorian bed, duly turned down by Mary, and into the little dressing room or lavatory on the southeast corner. (We never discovered which it was, or whether it was both.) As his guest, one would finish one's port in the study and then venture across the corridor into the well-furnished, softly lighted bedroom, which was more like a small theatre than a boudoir. The windows of the facing wall, giving on to the side lawn and kitchen yard, would be heavily curtained from ceiling to floor, and here and there along walls stood benches or chests with upholstered tops. The lower end of the room, where a whole wall of handsomely bound books loomed, would always be unlighted when one saw it in the evening, whereas the upper end, with the huge bed, would be resplendent in white and blue.

Just inside the open bedroom door, against the wall, another upholstered bench stood a few feet from the foot of the bed. Brenan came in and seated himself here, waiting to be acknowledged.

"You must forgive me for keeping you waiting, Mick," Huby called from the dressing room and/or lavatory. "It has been such a long, tiring day and I am not getting any younger." Then he pranced into view, completely naked, on the far side of the bed, a silver haired, pale bodied, corpulent but immaculate little man of sixty-five and more. It looked to

Brenan as if he might be doing a skit on the new Charlie Chaplin film that was widely reported to be in production with Claire Bloom.

He had a special routine for this part of the ritual. He would pause, as if a thought had struck him. Then in a single gesture he would dip the second finger of his left hand in a tiny jar of some salve or unguent that stood on the dresser and quickly anoint his anus. His crimson silk pyjamas would be waiting neatly folded on the dresser top. He slipped into these gracefully enough but, like a little boy, left the skirt of the top tucked into the bottom. Then he would bounce into the splendid pillowy bed and pull the clothes up to his chin, rather like Christopher Robin. It is not easy to say what expressions came and went in his face while he went through this routine. He was no Baptiste, but they were always rapt, always benign, yet mischievous. "What a pity one can never get Huby going on the poetry of Cocteau," Brenan once said to me, when we were gossiping.

Tonight, Brenan was in no mood for mischief. "*What about the death of Arthur?*"

"Mick, Mick, Mick," Huby sighed. "What can I tell you? This is the most terrible thing that has ever to my knowledge happened in Somersby Hall. The less said about it the better. I trust you will respect my confidence in you if I say: Arthur is dead; his next of kin has been informed; she will be making the arrangements for his burial. The Constabulary are doing all they can to discover who murdered him, but—"

"*Murdered* him?" As he broke in on Huby's grudging elegy, Brenan came involuntarily to his feet. "I thought you said yesterday he shot himself!"

"No, no, he was shot by someone from a distance with an army rifle, from somewhere on the Stonham road apparently. The bullet blew his brains out. It was not, however, a village crime of passion, as one might suppose. The police are looking into Arthur's connections with Eire now. It is all a ghastly mystery—"

Brenan recognized the shock of fear in every part of himself, as if once again he were in the chapel parlous, and transfixed.

"Are you feeling well, my boy? You look awful. I do wish you would sit down."

"Thank you, no. I must be getting along. Thank you for the port wine and conversation." *I am not what you supposed but far different.*

"Thank you, Mick. I trust you will soon feel better. Remember, this matter is strictly between you and me. Not a word to anyone else."

Brenan let himself out of the Warden's lodging and went straight along to the JCR telephone. It had started to rain steadily, the downpour hissing on the gravel path between lawn and flower bed or shrub. From behind the closed doors of the JCR came the sounds of a BBC variety show. At the end of the corridor, the telephone kiosk stood empty, looking much as it always looked, a little cleaner perhaps and more polished than usual. In its rear panel against the wall there was a new, neat patch, handiwork no doubt of Mr. Powell. A sterile smell arose from scrubbed floorboards. Otherwise no sign remained of this having been the scene of a murder. The whole alcove was well lighted, and through the closed French windows giving on to the side lawn all was blackness, making their panes a looking glass on the verso of which raindrops beat and trickled. Averting his eyes as from a phantom, he shut himself firmly into the kiosk.

As he turned the pages of the town directory, his hands were atremble. Assuming that the police had set up a duty phone at the Audit House for the banquet, there was just a chance that he could speak to Inspector Vaughan pronto. He picked up the receiver with his right hand and listened for the tone; with his left he put two pennies in the slot; then he dialed the number he had found in the directory. When a gruff official voice answered over some tumult in the background, he pressed button A to make the connection. As usual, the tumbling of the pennies, the split second of disconnection, was vertiginous. But then he was through and, to his astonishment, hearing within a minute or two the cool dry tones of Gilbert Vaughan himself.

"Mr. Vaughan, Michael Brenan . . . Hello. Yes. I am calling because Dr. Lacy, the Warden of Somersby, has just told me that a student with a name rather like mine, who looks—looked rather like me, was shot with a rifle and killed here last evening by someone unknown . . . Why would anyone want to shoot me? Because on Friday afternoon in Greenwich at the Merchant Hospital I happened to witness the abduction of a man who looked like Marshal Tievas. It was done by four Balts in the chapel. I got away unnoticed, I thought, but this shooting of Arthur Bresnahan—"

"Mr. Brenan, I do wish you had reported your suspicions to me at once on Friday."

"So do I, now, but then I had nothing to go on, no support for my story whatsoever."

"And you had Miss Didelis to think about."

"But on Monday afternoon I did report my suspicions to Sir Marcus Templeton here in Northfleet when I had a tutorial with him. Five hours later Arthur was dead in this very kiosk."

"You're taking quite a risk telling me this, aren't you, young man?" There was a pause in the conversation. "I suppose you want me to go up to the guest of honour here tonight and ask him if he is the real Marshal Tievas or not. I might do that. On the other hand, I might not. But in either case you can count on hearing from me. Thanks very much for the tip. Keep what you know to yourself." The phone went dead.

Brenan was left feeling empty and with none of the sense of purpose that sometimes goes with being empty. If only Vaughan could have told him he was needed at once at the Audit House to confront somebody. Leaving the kiosk, he caught sight of himself again in the watery French window looking, his mother would say, like a sheet, like death warmed up. *On Wenlock Edge the wood's in trouble.* He wondered what to do.

He wanted most of all to talk to Valija, but for the moment this was out of the question. By her own admission she had some part in the killing of Arthur. Whether innocent or unaware of what was involved or not, she deserved to be heard out, face to face, not questioned over the telephone; this meant tomorrow, not tonight. At this hour of the evening Highfield was impenetrable by a man, unless he was Heurtebise or Kamikaze. Brenan thought of Valija saying at tea in his room this afternoon, "My uncle wanted you to telephone him at a number in Norfolk. I telephoned you here in Somersby to tell you this but, would you believe it, I could not get through." Why would she risk telling him this if she were guilty of helping to try to kill him or even aware that whoever answered her call had been killed?

He felt in the breast pocket of his jacket for the piece of paper she had given him, took it out, and read the number: 35218. "Sait-on ce qui est poétique et pas poétique?" he said to himself in his Orphée voice. He began to feel less empty, less shaky. But he could not remember when he had ever felt so all by himself in the world, keeping his own secret. At this moment, there was no one he ought to turn to or confide in. "Keep what you know to yourself," Vaughan had said. "Not a word to anyone else," had said Huby. Even the VC had said, "Keep your suspicions strictly to yourself." Brenan now thought what he would do. He would go back to his room and play the game, the one he played only when deeply in doubt. With his old red one-volume Peter Alexander edition, he would play the *sortes,* seeing with closed eyes what Shakespeare had to tell him at the stab of a finger. The last time he had played, when dispirited at Marianne's return to Alabama, he had landed in Verona and Juliet had said to him, very sensibly, "What satisfaction canst thou have tonight?" His mother, he knew, would never approve of such "demonism." Nor would the pious Miss Hollis, whom he had once tried to talk into playing with the Bible by her Highfield bedside. "What shall we ever do if we turn up 'Then Judas departed, and went and hanged himself'?" When he had said "Try again," she had said, "And what if we turn up 'Go, and do thou likewise'?"

But what the hell? Where were they all when he needed them?

He plunged out of doors into the pelting rain and raced for D block. Now the night was black as well as torrential. Most windows around the quad seemed to be dark, as if his fellow students were either elsewhere or asleep. Ten o'clock, and Somersby already benighted? He ducked into D, where no one was about, and went straight to the blindingly white bathroom to dry his head and wipe off his jacket and trousers. As usual after a drenching, he felt flushed and vigorous.

When he climbed the stairs and strode along the empty upper corridor to his room, his mind was almost at ease. In its unlighted corner his door stood as usual, closed but unlocked, its panels void of any information but the number twelve. Anyway, he thought comfortably as he turned the handle, the tea things are all cleared away and washed up, thanks to Valija.

Switching on the icy overhead light for a second to see where his table lamp had been put, he flinched as if struck in the face. Not three feet away from him in the Morris chair at the window, a man sat slumped. The man looked a little like his father, but more like Offord's, though older. He was smiling. In his right hand he held, not a gun, but a small green book taken from those lined up on the window sill. It was apparent that, while waiting for Brenan to return from dinner, he had been reading; but as daylight failed, he had closed the book and sat drowsing in the dusk. He looked a little too old to be dangerous.

He said, "My name is Garas, Vytautas Garas, Colonel, retired, Baltic Counter Intelligence. Do you know, Mr. Brenan, how lucky you are to be alive? Do you know where Marshal Tievas is at this very moment?"

"Yes, I do. No, I don't. Where is he?"

Instead of offering his hand to seal the introduction, Garas facetiously gave Brenan his own little green copy of *Howards End*. "This friendly old novelist of yours from Cambridge likes to advise people, 'Only connect.' Don't you think it is time we had a talk, you and I?"

In the near darkness they stood eye to eye across the low table, both a little dazzled by the flash of overhead light which Brenan had caused. They might have been sixty and twenty year old generations of the same being. Brenan lay down his book and turned to close the door behind him. "I do think so," he said. "Have a seat, won't you?"

Chapter Seven

Offord Elegizes

1

Yea, she hath passed hereby,
and blessed the sheaves.

~Manning

Since I began Brenan's story a few months back—a
few months *et toute la vie,* as the painter Vernet says of
such an investment—all other concerns have fallen away. Work,
other people, play, food, none of these matter to me as they once
did. It is as if, after all, I were born on purpose to write this "likely"
tale which is not my own but a friend's of forty years ago. I await
with impatience my impending retirement from dreary meetings
with administrative minds, from the endless marking of student
screeds, from preparing and delivering lectures which (to me at
least) no longer matter. When, oh when, will I be free to do what
I most like doing with all my day: remembering, identifying,
imagining—emptying out my memory? Only towards the end of

a seventh decade of being alive have I at last come upon my truest (and most feigning) vocation: the historicizing of young Michael Brenan and his blessed anecdote.

In the actual telling of it, I now arrive at where it would be much better if he were writing it himself, because for him and me the ways abruptly diverge. Not for the only time in our young lives (though, as it turned out this time, not for long) he took the road less traveled by and I, having trouble of my own, took no notice. At the moment, that rainy first Wednesday of Michaelmas term, I might have said, if asked, that it was I taking the other way, turning aside to look death in the face, while it was Brenan who took no notice. For to me, suddenly, the saddest and most terrible of losses was happening: my mother was dying. I say "suddenly" because one's mother's death, signal or not in premonition, must in the event always strike one as inconceivable—as well as unacceptable. How could such tragedy be happening to *me*?

When I arrived from Paris the previous weekend, *via* Babs's London flat, there had been a letter from my father waiting for me at Somersby. The handwriting I knew so well yet in those days rarely saw—careful, upright, brisk; the sentences always calm, official, "unflappable," as Babs liked to say—did not at once alarm me. Mother had been patiently concealing her perhaps fatal colitis for some years: and at this point her not writing me one of her dutiful notes of good news, encouragement, and advice was not necessarily ominous. Looking at the envelope as I took it from my JCR pigeon hole that Sunday, I thought I could see—as still I can—my father seating himself impulsively at the little cherrywood *secretaire* which was properly hers, there in the parlour at Heathdene, whipping out his black Waterman fountain pen, unscrewing its shiny top and placing this on the other end, inspecting the nib, and with a sigh drawing the pad of white Basildon Bond towards him.

But as misfortune would have it, this particular letter had been penned, not at home, but at the Regina Hotel, once favoured by E.B.B. in (to quote Muirhead) *la coquette ville de Torquay:*

8/10/51
Friday

My dear Son,

> *You must excuse the delay in letting you know how things stand. Once you left Pau, we were not sure of your whereabouts, or that you would see or hear from Babs before arriving back at college. We have tried not to make her unduly anxious, as we have you.*

> *But the sad fact is that your Mother's health has once more collapsed, this time here at the Regina; and the doctor says that she should be moved into hospital, preferably near home. Naturally, she feels she would be better placed at Blackheath in care of Dr. Villiers than anywhere else; though what he or anyone can do for her at this stage is not easy to see.*

> *Your Mother is as stoic and brave of heart as ever, trying always not to burden others with her trouble. We both send you our love and every good wish for the new term's work. Next time you hear from us we should be at Heathdene, where you can always give us, or we you, a ring if necessary.*

Your loving Father

The next morning I telephoned from the JCR kiosk (not as yet out of order at the whim of some Baltic death gang), but got no answer. Thinking no news might be good news, I waited to hear from either my father or my sister. On Tuesday evening, while Brenan was having audiences of one sort and another with Huby, Vaughan, and Garas, I heard from Babs. It was by way of a telephone call straight to the Bursar in her office. Miss Robertson kindly made one of her very rare excursions to E block, crossing the teeming quad in the shelter of her small beige umbrella and prudently having put on her black galoshes, to let me know personally that Mother was on the danger list at St. Alphege's Hospital in Greenwich, and I should go home "forthwith" to be on call. The shock of this news put any further consecutive thought about Brenan, Arthur, or Valija out of my mind for the time being.

Trust Babs to go straight to the seat of administrative efficiency at Somersby. Before Huby had time to look up from matins on Wednesday, Miss Robertson had my permission to leave college granted and my seat on the 8:15 a.m. train to King's Cross reserved. She was one of our favourite figures of myth, Brenan's and mine, second only to Arthur, though her role was somewhat less versatile than his. Brenan always adverted enviously to the crammed shelf of Stevensons in some red octavo Edinburgh edition which she kept high above her neat desk in the narrow office near the kitchen. "What do you bet she's never taken any of those down to read since God knows when?" he would begin. Her father, we presumed, a retired sea captain, had made her a gift of them just before she came south to work for the Sassenachs, his own treasured collection which had survived typhoons with him in the China Sea. Before she left, he had taken her out to tea for the last time at Cranston's and . . . . This was Brenan's scenario, of course. I had a different one; I forget what.

Seated in a steamy second class carriage of the train from Northfleet, which this time went through Lincoln on the way to Peterborough, I read without much curiosity, I remember, not the *Eighteenth Brumaire*, still my craze of the moment, but the morning's *Manchester Guardian*. Marshal Tievas in his speech the night before at the Audit House banquet had managed once again to take press and public by surprise. "Baltic Deputy Eases Into Role As Overseas Lecturer." Having the time before, in Greenwich, annulled any hope of Baltija's joining NATO, he this time, on provincial and more personal grounds, became all sweetness and light. It was, said the *Guardian,* as if his rebuff of the West and his endangerment of Baltic autonomy by stirring unrest in Gdainys, Vilnius, Riga, and

Tallinn, and along the Russian and Polish border had simply never happened.

Tievas had commended himself to his audience by confessing to nostalgia for times past when he, too, had been a resident, all too briefly, of "the most important fishing port in the world." He quoted verse from of all things *Mr. Punch's History Of The Great War:*

> For there's wild work doin' on the North Sea ground
> An' it's 'Wake up, Johnnie!' they want you at the trawlin'
> (With your long sea-boots and your tarry old tarpaulin);
> All across the bitter seas duty comes a-callin'
> In the winter's weather off the North Sea ground.

Reading from a script, as usual, he had on this occasion contrived to make his English accent less rebarbitive than before. And as to town and gown, he displayed a most gratifying, if unexpected, acquaintance with local history.

Unlike most redbrick colleges or universities, Northfleet was not a mere by-product of the Industrial Revolution, endowed by visionary machine masters to meet a future need for a more educated managerial class. On the contrary, the original college built Above Bar represented a mild reaction against industrialism, started by the scion of a wealthy eighteenth century family of vintners. An eccentric, he founded his institute of scientific, classical, and literary studies specifically for a cultured minority "knowing little and liking even less of the new age of docks and railways." Although of necessity modified over a hundred years of industry, this pristine vision, said the Marshal, should never be wholly ignored. The forthcoming university of technology in Northfleet, which he welcomed into being, should be also an academy of the arts, classical and literary, fine as well as applied—open albeit to the children of the proletariat as well as of the bourgeoisie.

Tievas was on fairly safe ground here; and so he was when,

in thanking his hosts for their generous hospitality in times of severe and widespread post-war austerity, he alluded easily to flush times in the eighteenth century when, the Audit House ablaze with torches, a mayoral banquet might dispose of numberless gammons, beeves, turkeys, rabbits, chickens, ducks, pigeons, and umpteen dozen bottles of wine, not to mention "hogsheads of claret tipped into the conduits for all to drink." He trusted that to *ultima* Lindsey, as to the many bare corners of Europe, prosperity, if not prodigality, would before long return.

I suppose I should be embarrassed to record that, while preparing to take a First in History at Northfleet, I remained unaware that a *coup d'état* of European proportions was in process under my nose—especially since, at the moment, my best friend from boyhood was being briefed and debriefed, as a uniquely well-informed witness, by none other than Colonel V. Garas, formerly of the *Baltijos Kontržvalgybininkas*. I can only plead that none of my mentors or examiners ever evinced any more awareness of what might be going on than I—not to mention the press and the public. And for my own part, my mother's fatal illness was quite enough to distract me for the present from any but familial concerns. I suppose if I had remained in Somersby Brenan might have confided in me there and then, once Garas materialized and started enlightening him. "Do you know *why* poor old Arthur bought it on Monday night?" he might have begun . . . . But as it was, I spent most of Wednesday morning and afternoon entrained, drowsing unhappily about Mother.

Nowadays I waken at first light, now and again with someone from my far off past vividly present. It is as if I have been dropped in on unexpectedly, here in this ninth floor eyrie of mine in the new Louth Hall—not in the flesh (I usually see or hear nothing), but in the spirit. As I surface in the dim mill pool of sleep, my thoughts are taken over by one or another lifelong familiar. Lately it has been Brenan, or Huby, or Valija, but today, the third of March, 1999, to my astonishment it was my mother, Vivien Offord, née Conway, my father's wife. She came in a shape I have not actually seen her in since the '30s—except once when I was spending the night at Heathdene just after she died. As then, she now smiled and spoke to me.

My big bed here in Louth lies at very much the same angle to a deep bathroom doorway as my little bed at home used to lie to my parents' bedroom door. Aslant this, there as here, the grey morning light falls deceptively from a tall rear window. Outside, there only a fathom down, here fifty, the garden tends to lose itself in mist and rain. My mother wears her silky, floor length floral dressing gown, all "greenery yallery Grosvenor Gallery," as Babs used spitefully to say. The flowers Mother is moving out of my room for the night may be hyacinths in a bowl, or gladioli in a vase, or even a sheaf of winter cherry— the light is too poor for me to tell. Time of year is also uncertain; probably it is the everlooming late autumn. As she glides into the shadow of the doorway, she glances back over her left shoulder and, seeing my eyes open, smiles her sad smile and murmurs, "It's all right, Johnny. Just go to sleep."

My old room was directly above Michael's but less narrow than his and with a much loftier outlook on the well-tended back lawn and its ornamentals. I cannot now recall where, when he came of age to have a room of his own, Patrick slept. Could it have been in the alcove made by the removal, when war came and shelter space was needed, of our much-loved, interconnecting, winding stair? Or was there for him yet another niche or nook somewhere in the Brenans' well-compacted home that I do not remember? Now I shall never know. (This irreversible passing of some fact, some homely detail, once as familiar or findable as one's own face, out of mind forever, is, it seems to me, perhaps the cruelest of all the tricks of time and age, this side of death.) Mother, god bless her, would never have wanted to know where any of the Brenans happened to sleep. To her all that mattered in the world, in real life, so to say, was pretty well confined to our own commodious (if much converted) first floor flat, which at a glance might indeed be taken, part though it was, for the whole of Heathdene.

Vivien Conway was a child of the west country whose family had farmed and raised horses for two or three generations near the market town of Hereford. Cattle and fruit were always the more reliable investment in those cathedral-graced environs; and the Conways never prospered. Vivien grew up unfulfilled in the Welsh marches, dreaming on *A Shropshire Lad* and some implicit beauty ever more about to be. That lovely little album of poems became a token of the bond that grew between her and my father, a Hereford solicitor's son, once they met at a Christmas party and began seeing one another in 1910. Mother could sketch in her own words the actual places unforgettably named in Housman's limpid songs, and would sometimes do so to amuse me when I was a very little boy at the dairy in Sydenham. But her true dream landscape, I slowly learned, was never the farms of home but an unforgiving sea (which she had hardly ever actually seen), swirling, pounding, misting, under a dark grey sky, with far off foghorns sounding longingly. Something in her life had, from earliest childhood onward, always been missing, lost, wrong.

It took years after she died for me to discern the true shape of Mother's melancholy life. From being an avid, graceful girl she had gradually gone on to become the severe, greyhaired, sad eyed woman I knew at the last, without ever finding the other, the only one, who would confirm her own sense of self. First her mother, then her father, neither of whom I knew, failed to be the soul mate she was seeking. For a few golden years she did seem to find him in her elder brother John, who died at Suvla Bay with the Royal Horse Artillery in 1915. By the time she was seventeen, his gift of love and understanding had already enabled her to find for herself a lover and eventually a husband in my father, Charles Offord, but not happily, not for long.

Father won her heart, I believe, by his equable but deeply idealist temper: round the world under sail before the mast at twenty, then one of Lord Kitchener's first hundred thousand. But he could not hope to keep from her that sense of loss, mere loss, as the true story of life. His wounding and near death at La Bassée, from which he never fully recovered, bound her to him forever—a lung sufferer still smoking a pipe—yet fed her secret anger at the terrible unfitness of things. She gave birth to a daughter then, my sister Babs, and fourteen years later to a son, me. As was her way, she would reach out to each of us in turn from the bottom of her lonely heart, but neither Babs nor I could ever be the one she really wanted. Alone in her dream, she worked on her Chopin, tended her garden, beautified her home as best she could on my father's limited income, and searched the women's novels of the '20s and '30s for some spirit she could recognize as kindred.

At Heathdene from 1938, she kept very much to herself. My earliest memories of her there are almost all interiors: at the piano she is playing and I stand near, not much taller than the raised stool she sits upon, enthralled, enveloped by such a tone and volume of pure sadness. On the yellow divan in her bedroom she rests with one of my books open, gazing out of the window at the Vartans' apple tree in bloom, while I try to decipher for her one of the rhymes that I have by heart:

> *Jonathan Jo*
> *Has mouth like an "O"*
> *And a wheelbarrow full of surprises . . . .*

My only outdoor memory of her from those days, except for summer holidays at Hunstanton or Torquay, is an afternoon excursion by 75 bus (Father would have the Austin Seven at work for the Ministry) to Woolwich Common to see the Royal Artillery horses in training. We broke our journey in Charlton, just beyond the village at the point called Little Heath, in order to visit Maryon Park. A dreamlike green knoll in the wastes of suburbia, it then overlooked, and presumably still does, the River Thames at Blackwall and all its industry. Islanded among the park's narrow gravel walks and lawns are several unusually dense clumps of copse entirely surrounded by heavy wooden railings of an insistent rustic design. The most sinister enclosures I ever saw on open land, they form a sort of zoo, not of captive fauna but flora. When thirty years later at a cinema I glimpsed this unhappy stretch of suburban parkland, with its two incongruous tennis courts, in the opening sequence of Antonioni's surreal English film *Blow Up*, I knew it at once, alien as it was.

Mother showed me the view from this pastoral upland and then took me across Charlton Road to a spiffy little retail branch of the Home Farm Dairy, the very firm that Father had until recently managed the stables for in Sydenham, and bought me a glass of ice cold milk. I wonder if this shop is still there in Little Heath. It was, I suppose, just another shop, but to my young eyes unimaginably cool, hygienic, finished in stainless steel, "a . . . pleasure dome . . . those caves of ice." Even the shop assistant—or should I say dairy maid?—wore white like a nurse or, perhaps, white and black like a parlour maid; and the milk she dispensed from a huge refrigerator—still rare in English households then—was positively frigid to the hand and tongue and belly. Set back from the thoroughfare in a terrace of singlefronted grey brick houses with careful gardens, the dairy was entered and exited by way of several well-scrubbed stone steps and a sloping garden-sized forecourt of tiles, which met the pavement a little like a magic carpet of dull reds, whites, and blues.

Mother then took me back across Charlton Road and on the next bus to Woolwich barracks with its noble buildings, triumphal arch, towers, open squares, paved paths, and riding ring. ("Can be compared," says Pevsner, "only to St. Petersburg.") All around for an acre or two to the south, against encroaching roads, street lamps, and suburban villas, a grassy common reached out over a ha-ha ("Not exactly Offa's Dyke," said Vivien) and past the Rotunda, a metal replica of the huge tent in which the victors over Napoleon were received in the

West End in 1814. We were here, Mother said, to see the horses, not the guns. A scene by Degas it was not, but army horses moving, mounted men, limbers rolling have always for me tended to wipe the eye. Yet the most vivid single image I have from that whole afternoon spent sightseeing with Mother is merely of the grasses on the common, their fullness, greenness, softness, rippling and waving and nodding, crowds of them overhanging the black asphalt edge of Ha-Ha Road, which seemed to lead nowhere.

I remember wondering afterwards if Mother would ever again take me out to Woolwich, or somewhere else; and later, when she did not take me anywhere at all, why she had taken me there of all places that March afternoon. So much about her was incomprehensible to me at the age of eight or nine; at my age now there is still much about her that remains so. "Your mother," my father once said to me in confidence, "has no time for ordinary things," as if this explained her. While I was a child, she was unduly kind in her own way, discovering in me an innocent with whom the lost child in herself could commiserate. I was more fortunate than Babs had been fourteen years before, because with me Mother read, not her own stringent masters, Carroll, Ruskin, and MacDonald, but gentle newcomers like De La Mare and Milne. With me she listened to the Children's Hour, then in its prime, and herself heard for the first time of Toytown and Worzel Gummidge, and was finally apprised of the charm of Zenda. For her the naïveté of childhood was a temporary refuge from the faithless world of men and women. But eventually some lonely hurt of never having known for long enough the love of anyone, from her parents to her children, must have told upon her. More and more she masked, with detachment, any sense that it was she who was flawed, her grief at the ugliness of things that could not be assuaged.

The first war broke her spirit but the second finished her as a survivor. Horrified by Hitlerism as she was, she never could quite set her jaw and say, however embarrassedly, "We can take it." Somebody else had to do that. Where was the pattern of those spartan young redcoats of Housman's when she really needed it? But for thirteen years she did serve doggedly in one cause that was very much her own. "What keeps your mother going," said my father, "is that border war of hers with Old Peebles." Mr. Peebles and his men were a bit like the war itself in forcing us—though Father and I personally needed no forcing—into a certain accord with the Brenans, another way of being neighbours. "That old devil Peebles was about the place again today," Mrs. Brenan would observe to her husband and sons in my hearing, "but John's mother gave him a proper earful as usual."

F.C. Peebles & Son, Builder and Contractor, kept his cluttered yard and workshed not far from the new Roxy Cinema in Old Dover Road. Bustling, distracted, not quite credible, a little man in a bowler hat and dusty three-piece suit, he was retained by our landlord, Mr. Vartan, to keep Heathdene in reasonable repair. He and his gang of three, Ted, Charlie, and old Mr. Grant, would come down on the fold several times a year in the name of undeferred maintenance—more often during the Blitz. Their overloaded handcarts bearing his inflated legend would barricade the wide gravel walk of our tidy front garden. Piles of material would appear here, there, and everywhere, under tarpaulin. Tins of paint or varnish would be found stacked under walls. The makings of cement or concrete would overflow sedum or stonecrop along the rock verge of flower beds. One or the other of our quiet homes would then become a frantic, pungent, noisy scene of Peebles' men at work, hollering among themselves, smoking their vile fags, upsetting everything.

Mrs. Brenan herself, genius of the front garden, was never so indignant at such depredations as Mother, perhaps because the basement flat was less frequently the ostensible beneficiary of them than ours was. Certainly, Michael and Patrick's mother had a soft spot for grandfatherly old Mr. Grant the carpenter, who could be a godsend when the plumbing failed, and for

Charlie the clownish plasterer, painter, and wallpaperer, whose loose smile and wisecrack were irresistible. Ted, idiot son of the boss, dreaming he was foreman and fancying himself jack of all trades (especially anything electrical) was another matter altogether. When he was not in evidence, she would make tea for the other two and join them in gossip while they drank it in her kitchen. My mother saved her ministrations, which were most severe, solely for Old Peebles, the elusive, evasive, egregious gaffer. Year after year she carried on a spirited defence of Heathdene's former glory against his despoiling of the property in the name of improvement. "Let me assure you," I can still hear her say to him, "what your men are doing here is not *at all* what Mr. Vartan—and I—have in mind." She spoke the name of our benign landlord in such a tone as her parents might have used of Mr. Asquith; and ever since I have been unable quite to free my image of Lloyd George, that great manager, from a certain aura of Old Peebles. First it was the preservation of floral tiles in the former conservatory at the back which became our kitchen and bathroom. Then the fine moulding of the ceilings of drawing room and dining room, parts of which had become bedrooms: how could it be repaired, or even restored in spite of partition? Always there was the preservation (given the advent of electricity) of Victorian fixtures, the proper discreet disposition of modern appliances. "What you are doing here, Mr. Peebles, let me tell you, will not do at all, not by any means, not at all."

Time and chance being on his side, Old Peebles had his way in the end. Unremittingly, the pre-war finery of parquet, wainscot, dado, sconce, pocket door, and column disappeared. After the beveled and stained glass had to be replaced, Mother's final and saddest defeat was the loss to the front garden of the ornamental double gates in carved wood painted a pagoda red. One of them lost its hinges owing to rust and stood for the worst of the Blitz propped against its pillar, half hidden by a laurel bush. Not long after VJ Day, the other one keeled over and Old Peebles finally intervened, only to carry them off forever. "Is there to be nothing left," Mother had Father write in a letter to Mr. Vartan, "between Heathdene and the gutter?" Her unworthy adversary was a classic case, politically speaking, of the mercenary whose cruel power derives from being called in by the prince to serve his people and who can defraud both at will if only he has the *virtù*. Whereas to Mother he was the spoiler of the taken town, to Mrs. Brenan he was merely the spectre of raised rent. She proved wrong, thanks to a very understanding landlord, but Mother, to her continuing chagrin, could only prove right about the unrelenting spoil of things.

Now that I come to think of it, Michael and Patrick and I probably started our whole collection of larger than life figures about whom stories could be made up with Old Peebles, Mother's Nemesis—not the goddess but a mere middle man. I remember being called in to the slip room with Michael one day to share Patrick's discovery, in the Penguin Modern Painters *Stanley Spencer*, of an ominous domestic vision all too true to life, entitled "Workmen In The House." "Mick, Johnny, just take a gander at this."

Turning in between those still ungated pillars on the left side of Vanbrugh East this rain washed Wednesday afternoon, having made my way from King's Cross by tube and bus, I look up at the old facade for the first time in nearly six months. How diminished it seems. Not a window open or uncurtained, nothing but silence emanating. For the first time in my life I am hesitant, a little fearful to be entering here. For this once more at least I can go in and find the old familiar furniture in place, if not the face I look for. There will be word from Babs waiting somewhere to tell me what to do next. Father must be at work and she too, unless Mother is in so dangerous a state as to call for visiting all day. Like Father, Mr. Brenan will be at work, but maybe Mrs. Brenan will be about the house, doing her usual things. I am suddenly visited by one of those stray thoughts that come, I suppose, to everybody. I think of Patrick, somewhere in Germany. If only *he* should happen to be home on leave this week.

The two top storeys of the house, tenanted again since the war ended, have the look of being occupied, though not of anybody's being in just now. The Fevershams who moved here in '47 are all but strangers to me because of my absences in the army, in France, or at college. Archie, a teacher of Maths and violin at Colfe's, and his *bravura* second wife, Gwen, have twin boys under school age, plus an adolescent daughter from his first marriage. He is an Oxonian, suitably eccentric, and Gwen is very much his wife, though a bit Bolshie. My impression—largely secondhand—has been that they are not at all easy to know, not for Michael and Patrick's parents, not for mine. "Stuck up," I have heard Mrs. Brenan call them.

I walk the wide gravel drive and climb the six broad front steps. Today wet leaves are everywhere underfoot, making smooth surfaces slippery. There was a time, I suppose, sixty years back when in rough weather a horsedrawn carriage might have pulled right in—a bit of a squeeze perhaps—and stopped here at the foot of the front steps. A hansom cab, if one were to be found this far from town, could certainly have done so. Then, there might have been horse manure at hand for the flower and vegetable beds at the back.

I let myself in through the double front door with the wellworn key marked Vaun that has been with me since before I left school. Through the glazed inner doors the carpeted hallway, leading everywhere within, smells a little musty. A note from Babs, tucked into the frame of the hall tree looking glass, tells me to take Father, when he gets home, to dinner at Mrs. Barnes's, a nearby guest house, and then to the hospital by seven-thirty. Babs will be there to meet us.

I put my grip down by the dressing-table in my bedroom—which I see Babs has been making use of—and go wandering through the other rooms looking for traces of Mother. By her bed stands the bookshelf I know well, lined with the names of her many comforters: the Lehmanns, the Jamesons, the Holtbys, the Delafields, the Bowens, the Brittains: dusty answers, cloudless Mays, South Ridings, provincial ladies, deaths of the heart, testaments of youth. In the drawing room on her piano a collection of Chopin rests open at the E minor Prelude.

Then, to my surprise—and (I must admit) relief—the front door bell rings. A little tentatively, or is this only my fancy? Could Mrs. Brenan be at home after all, have heard me move about, or perhaps seen me come in, and slipped upstairs now to give me a welcome on this *sad occasion dear*? If Mother were here, it would not be like Mrs. Brenan to make a call instead of waiting to be called on. But Mother is not here.

I open the front door and there stands a pretty young woman in a long navy blue raincoat with a hood. She has blue eyes, fair hair, and is smiling shyly. Over one shoulder she has a traveling bag on a strap. She looks a little surprised to find me here, though not unpleasantly so. Her eyes say that she recognizes me for who I am. I, too, feel sure that we have met somewhere before. But who is she?

"Hullo. You're John Offord, aren't you? I'm Janet Feversham. My parents live upstairs. I've just arrived from the Radcliffe for a forty-eight hour visit and no one's at home. I don't have a key. I was hoping your mother might have one. She and I were chums before I went away. She used to keep one from the time when our flat was empty."

"Won't you come in, Miss Feversham? I'm afraid Mother isn't here; she's been taken to hospital. But if she has a key to your flat I expect it's on the hook in the kitchen. Let's look."

"Oh, dear, don't let me be a pain. I am so sorry to hear that about your mother. The old trouble. I was forgetting. So sure that she would be pleased to see me. I must try to visit her while I'm here. At St. Alphege's?"

"She's on the danger list. This is why I'm here in the middle of term."

"Oh, God . . . ."

"Put your bag down and come through to the kitchen. We'll see if your key is to be found."

"I always enjoyed sitting out here in the daylight with Vivien under this glazed roof, especially when it rained of an afternoon and she wasn't able to do her gardening. I would be home early from school, putting my bike away under the side steps, we'd get talking, and she would ask me in to sit with her until Gwen came back with the twins. I never was very reliable with keys."

"Is this the one you are looking for? Or this?"

"Thank you . . . . Oh no, these are both Yales. Ours is a Vaun, I am pretty sure."

"Yes, like ours. Looks as if we've drawn a blank. I can't think where else Mother would keep a key but out here. We can have a hunt if you like."

"Never mind. It was just a thought. Thank you for being so helpful."

"Miss Feversham, why don't you wait here till your mother gets home? Take off your damp coat and sit down. I just got in myself and was about to make some tea. I'd be glad of your company. Father won't be home for an hour or more."

"That *would* be very nice. Thank you, I will. Let me help with making tea. I think I know where things are kept. You know, Gwen is not my mother: she's my stepmother. Mother lives in Sevenoaks, all alone now. She's not very well. I usually visit her whenever I can get away from Oxford. But this time I felt I ought to visit Archie for once."

"You don't get on with your father's wife."

"She's a bitch. My last year or two here, before I left school and went into nurse's training, were miserable.—Though I was probably a handful myself at fifteen. I liked the twins well enough, but Gwen can be impossible."

"How do you find nurse's training? I did a couple of years' National Service myself. Wasn't exactly a vacation."

"I was lucky to get into the Radcliffe, I suppose, being a bear of very little brain. Archie's connections helped. But I do find it terribly hard—too much work on the wards, too much reading for classes. Physiology is torture. No time to oneself. Very strict rules. I'm in my second year now, thank goodness."

"Life gets harder and harder to deal with, doesn't it? I have been lucky so far in the way things have gone for me since I grew up. But the more I have decided for myself the less happy I have been, compared to when I was a child and had very little say in whatever happened to me. When would you say you were happiest?"

"When I was nine or ten, perhaps; for a year or two before and after that. Before Archie and Muttie broke up. We called her that for *Mutter* in German. Her father, my grandfather, was English but her mother came from Coblenz. During the war we lived on a little farm near Binsey. Archie was in the army, a cryptographer. It wasn't a working farm but we had several horses. We all rode. I learned to take care of horses, and milk the cow. I think then I was happiest. Horses are my darlings. The best company there is. Only things at Binsey didn't last, not for Muttie and Archie, nor for my older sister and me."

"(Will you have some more tea?) Where is she now?"

"(Yes, thank you.) She's in Canada, Toronto, married to a Canadian she met over here at the end of the war."

"Times change so fast. If Mother doesn't recover, or even if she does, life here at Heathdene is all but over for us. Yet we've probably been happier in this house than anywhere."

"Vivien used to tell me about life at the dairy in Sydenham. She had some happy memories of that. But her own girlhood in Shropshire seems to have been the best time for her."

"Yes, Hereford, actually. She and her brother had all the western marches by heart, just before the first war came."

"Your father and Vivien are going to retire to Stokesay, aren't they? I remember her showing me snapshots of the village. She was very taken with a war memorial in the churchyard, a sandstone figure of a soldier backed by a dolphin. Isn't it strange how one treasures such quaint memories, especially when they are shared?"

"You and Mother must have been close for her to tell you about that. I had no idea."

"She often talked of you. It was while you were overseas doing your National Service."

"I can't say that to me she ever made any special mention of you. But now that I know about this . . . *liaison*, Miss Feversham, I shall have to ask her all about you. Isn't it strange how two people such as you and I can be neighbours for years and never exchange a word? How well do you know the Brenans?"

"Please call me Janet, Mr. Offord. I hardly know them at all. Mrs. Brenan made herself known to me when we moved in and has always been kind when we've spoken. She's a woman in an apron. The family keeps very much to itself, as you must know. When Patrick was still at home, he and I would say 'hullo' in passing. He seemed very nice. I'm a rather simple, straight forward person. There won't be much for Vivien to tell you about me."

"You never saw *her* in an apron, I bet. What did you two talk about mostly?"

"Oh, I don't know, all sorts of ordinary things. She would tell me what she was doing with her plants in the garden and in the greenhouse and frames your father gave her. Old Mr. Bridges, you know, the gardener from the garage next door, he would advise her about any difficulties."

"I know old Bridges all right, Miss Vartan's gardener. He always tells you the Latin name for whatever he's talking about. He knows his stuff. We used to call him Adam after the cartoon in the *Sunday Express*. Horticultural hints, you know?"

"Who is 'we'?"

"Oh, Michael Brenan and Patrick and me."

"Miss Vartan is very kind, but awfully vague and highly strung, isn't she? Some sort of near St. Vitus' dance, do you think? Gwen bullies her shamefully on the telephone about maintaining the flat, which is really her brother's responsibility. She must be hopeless at giving old Mr. Bridges directions. No wonder he likes to slip through the side gate of an afternoon and join Vivien in her little greenhouse when he can."

"So you and Mother talked about gardening. What about reading? Who's your favourite poet?"

"Oh, Lord, you're just like Vivien, wanting me to talk like a book. You mean *after* A.A. Milne? Well, I liked several we read for School Cert., but now I don't remember their names. My first crush was on Rupert Brooke. I still have his *Collected Poems* somewhere. Vivien tried to broaden my taste. Told me I should stop choosing poets by their looks in the frontispiece. My last crush was on that Battle of Britain poet who wrote

> *Do not despair*
> *For Johnny Head in Air.*
> *He sleeps as sound*
> *As Johnny Underground.*

What is his name?"

"Pudney, John Pudney—"

"Oh, isn't that the twins and Gwen I hear climbing the side steps? Squabbling as usual. I'd better be off. Thank you so much for having me to tea, Mr. Offord."

"Please call me John. Let me hold your coat. You don't know that a treat it has been to have company and get to know you a little. Here's your traveling bag. Mustn't forget that."

"How would you like us to have tea again tomorrow? My turn this time, if you're free. I'll ring down at noon to find out. We could go across to the village to Christy's. I shall be ready for a break from Gwen and the twins by that time. And you can give me the latest word on Vivien's progress."

"I should like that, Miss Feversham—Janet."

"Good. See you then."

"See you then. Oh, Lord, it's started raining again."

Father came home at five-thirty and we spoke our sad greetings. After a quick gin and It we went across to Mrs. Barnes's on the corner to eat the modest dinner she was serving her other paying guests. Then Father got the car out from the garage next door, where Old Bridges and his wife had their tiny upstairs flat, and drove me to the hospital. Rain was still falling. St. Alphege's stood where it still does, a huge grey brick barracks but without squares or uniformed men on guard, down on Trafalgar Road just below the Edge, well within the purview of the Vaughans's white bunker. Babs met us at an unmanned reception desk in the lofty, gloomy, hushed entrance hall. "Here you are at last," she said. "Let's go up and be with her."

The moment I saw Mother, ashen of face, emaciated, inert, bound within the crisp white sheets of a hospital bed, I knew how near to dying she was. Having been forewarned, I now was shocked into recognizing the actuality. As we entered the small bare single room where she lay, she opened her eyes and seemed to know me. Her lips parted but no words came. She raised her right hand a little in deprecation, as if to say that I should never have left college and traveled all this way only to see her in such a state. I cannot say that she smiled; she seemed not to have the strength.

A uniformed nurse—no Janet Feversham—came in with chairs for Father and me. Babs already had one by the head of Mother's bed. He and I settled down on the left hand, he between her and me. There was one curtained window, but the walls still closed oppressively in upon us. Neither Father nor I ventured to greet Mother with a kiss, even on her forehead, or to take her listless hand in one of ours. "Mrs. Offord is in a great deal of pain, I'm afraid, and heavily sedated," the nurse whispered. Minute by minute, some intolerable distress of body, if not of mind, was distancing Mother from us and from the whole world. None of us, not even Babs, knew what best to say or do. "Not a word all day long," she muttered. We sat in silence, watching the thousand tiny shifts and twitches of Mother's body under the bedclothes tell us over and over again of the pain she must be in, despite being deeply drugged. She said nothing, and I, looking into her shriveled face, knew neither where nor how to find her.

Time stood still, as the saying goes, but the saying is untrue of this time. To stand still is what one asks time to do when life is at its kindest: *carpe saeculum saeculorum*. But when it is at its most devastating, what time does is to race unheedingly by. This evening at Mother's bedside, hour after hour passed as if unmarked. Only by the little movements she made, the rustling, did we know that she was still, in some sense, with us. Towards midnight the nurse came back and suggested we go for a walk downstairs, or even home and wait to be recalled. "Doctor says there's no telling how long Mrs. Offord may last like this." We told her we would wait downstairs, the cafeteria being long since closed. The entrance hall was all but deserted, a gallery of shadows. We walked aimlessly about, saying little.

Eventually the nurse came and found us in a corner, seated and silent. "You'd better come quickly," she said. "Doctor says there's a change for the worse." We hastened back to Mother's bedside, but no one's haste could ever again make any difference to her now. All movement under the bedclothes had quite ceased. Her parchment face, the nose beaklike, the jaw slack, pointed up from the pillow like the blade of an axe. This could not be Vivien. She herself was gone. "I'm so very sorry," said the nurse. "Let me leave you to yourselves for a while. Then Doctor will come and speak with you."

Father and Babs and I, sleepwalkers, it seemed, together in step for the past several hours, each took a seat by the bed and sat looking at Mother's corpse. Still none of us gave her a kiss. Father and Babs sat stonily, suffering in silence, but I found myself all at once dissolved helplessly in tears. Flooded with them, on and on, hot salt tears, and wracked by sobs, loud sobbing, I had not wept since I was a child and then never uncontrollably like this. "Soldier boys don't cry," Mother used to say. Taken by surprise but not, for some reason, ashamed, I felt that, having lost Mother forever, weeping was the least I could do for her.

I did not excuse myself to Father or Babs, not even afterwards when I could have. Nothing was said when I collapsed in grief. They merely went on looking concerned, neither kindly nor unkindly. Babs, I knew, must be in deep distress herself, needing as she did to know just how Mother felt about her, but never being able to find out now. Father handed me a fresh white handkerchief from the side pocket of his dark flannel suit. After the doctor had spoken with us, chiefly Father, about what little remained to be done for Mother, we went back to Heathdene and sat in the parlour for a while looking sadly at one another and making desultory remarks. Father poured a glass of brandy for each of us. It was then, as we seemed to be easing back into our own lives, into a new life without Mother, that the final blow fell.

It came out of nothing, nothing definite that I was aware of, except, of course, Mother's having just died. Father was saying that he doubted if the cremation she had asked for in Bexleyheath would be feasible before Monday but, meantime, there was plenty needing to be dealt with about the house. Without thinking, I said I hoped the cremation could be arranged for Saturday because I needed to be back in college for Monday if at all possible.

"How bloody selfish you always are!" Babs burst out at me, her face dark with anger, her eyes like flint. "It's always been the same, all your life: *Johnny first! What's best for Johnny?* You've never given a damn for another living soul, not even Mother. Never here when she needed you, always gone, always abroad. Now she's dead, and you can't even be here to see her poor body burnt to ashes. Well, let me tell you, Mother never loved you. She saw from the first how deeply selfish you are, and she gave up. You like to think that she and you had a special relation, you loved her and she loved you. But it wasn't so. I know for a fact that she gave up loving you long ago."

Now I had finally seen Babs in a fury. It astonished me. In my hearing she had never before even hinted at anything like this. Her most severe rebuke had always been an angry silence. I was astounded—not at the truth of what she said, for I did not believe a word of it—but that my own sister would come out with such a cruel farrago and Mother not two hours dead. I was appalled.

I looked to Father, settled in his accustomed armchair, for some sort of intervention, but he took no notice, gazing at the Phillips radio receiver on its little table in the corner as if what he had heard was of no more concern than a sound flash from a BBC play by Priestley. I did not look at Babs. I came to my feet, set my empty glass down on the buffet, and left the room, saying, "I'll sleep on the drawing room sofa tonight." In the front hall, I looked for my raincoat and, having found it, walked out of the house.

Outside, it no longer rained. High overhead, huge grey clouds scudded across the sky. The moon was almost full. Everywhere glistened. I felt suddenly free, and went on walking out along the heath for an hour and more, my mind blank except for an occasional detail that caught my eye. Nobody else but drivers of the solitary benighted vehicle seemed to be about. I went all the way under the park wall from the war memorial past the main gates to the corner of Chesterfield Walk. Here, where four roads meet, two of them little more than a lane and a footpath, stood the shabby tea hut where long distance lorries on the North Kent run could pull over for a while, and their drivers find char and wads for sale and pass the time of day. Now the duck board they gathered on, rafted in the roadside mud, was empty and the usually open, well-lighted counter shuttered and dark.

It struck me as I passed that in all ten years spent as a youth about this heath, crossing it often twice a day on foot or by bike, I never once stopped here for refreshment or even thought of doing so. Indeed, if I had been set to describe it, I should probably have visualized a coffee stall on wheels, like those more elegant ones seen in the West End, Victorian bathing hut-like vehicles at which a Leslie Howard might first encounter his Eliza. This one, I saw, was nothing but a sordid, over-sized Punch and Judy booth, set like a tub on its own bottom and not, for the time being, even open. No massive transport marked Bowater Lloyd, crammed with enormous spools of newsprint for the City presses, waited while master and mate took cuppas and leaks—these latter in the very proper rustic redbrick convenience at the head of Long Pond under the willows just across the road.

Not even the weed of sorrow sprang at these four cross ways. I left the sad tea hut behind and struck out across the grass going parallel with Goffers Road as far as Whitefield's Mount. With its fronded trees, toy escarpment, and lagoon-like pond, it always seemed as if it might be some desert isle— which tonight at this hour it certainly was. Whitefield and Wesley once preached to the multitudes from its modest heights and Gladstone later electioneered, but what always drew me back to it was the thought that some eighteenth century landscapist, looking northeast, had apparently been able to see all the way from here to Blackwall Reach. *Let observation, with extended view . . . .*

The heath I knew had, from the first, been blinkered and all but overbuilt already with bricks and mortar and tarmac. I came around the little mount and the margins of its pond and stopped in front of a solid outcrop of trees and buildings edging the Vale and filling it. They will have been begun, even before the windmill went down, by Victorian golfers who needed a club house. Now there was a whole hamlet here, a would-be village without the Village. Here stood sinister Mill House, which Brenan claimed John Buchan must have had in mind in *The Power House* when he sent Edward Leithen to Blackheath looking for a retired East India Merchant named Julius Pavia. Myself, I always think the white house over to the north on Crooms Hill a more likely point in question. The only textual clues are *villa* and *White Lodge*.

Having strolled along to the very point of Talbot Houses, I stood looking east across the chartered heath to where, in the damps and mists of distance, St. German's Place and the Paragon converge on the Merchant Hospital. Out of the faint miasma of it all, car headlights were coming fast towards me down Duke Humphrey Road from the gates of the Park. I waited where I stood at the granite kerb, wondering. The car was "another matchbox," as the Brenans would say of any Austin Seven but Father's. It slowed and swerved into Talbot Place, stopping for me on the wrong side of the road with its nearside door opened. "Hop in, old chap," said my father. "Your mother would not want you out on patrol at this hour of the ack-emma, no matter what Babs says." A little touch of Dornford in the night—as now I can all too easily acknowledge. I hopped in.

As it happened, Mother's cremation could be fitted in by the Bexleyheath undertaker on the Saturday, and I returned to college for Monday's lectures. Father spent Thursday putting Mother's simple estate in order, and Babs closed her meagre correspondence with friends in the west country. While I was out to tea with Janet Feversham, Babs took it upon herself to sew a little black triangle of mourning on to the upper sleeve of every jacket of mine that she could find. On the Friday, she went back to work, and that night slept in her own flat (in Finchley at the time).

There were only the three of us, she, Father, and I, at the crematorium the next day. Janet told me at tea on the Thursday afternoon that she would be with us but for being due back on duty at six on Saturday morning. I wonder how her presence would have been taken by Babs and Father. The crematorium was more like a small private theatre than a chapel, except for the seance's being in the middle of the morning. The one undertaker present was, in his dark serge suit, the soul of discretion. There was no music. At the podium, Father said a few well-chosen words about Mother—her beauty of spirit, her love of nature, her kindness—to an audience composed of Babs and me, silent and pale in our most sober Sunday best, but very comfortably seated. He recited from memory both stanzas of Housman's *"Parta Quies."*

Mother's coffin then moved, as if of its own volition,

through the curtains at the rear of the stage and into the furnace, as the undertaker had said it would. Later, in the foyer, he presented Father with a little metal urn of ashes. I had an urge to cry out in agony with Laertes, "Must there no more be done?" But I had learned my lesson: there must not. And so we drove home in the Austin Seven.

I felt at the time that I had lost the future company, not only of Mother, but also of Babs. But this was not to be. After Mother's death, she and I soon drifted back in touch, much as before. Ten years later, she and I were still together on Bredon Hill for the final mingling of Father's ashes with Mother's.

> *These two by the stone wall*
> *Are a slight part of death.*

Babs stayed in Father's cottage at Stokesay, and I weekended in Tewkesbury with Janet at the *Hop Pole*. But I never tried to share with Babs my friendship with Janet. This friendship became a great comfort to me, even though neither Janet (I think) nor I turned out to be the marrying kind.

It was Brenan who, when I told him back in Somersby the following week that Mother had died, came out with the best epitaph for her that I ever heard. Brenan and she had aways by some mysterious means managed to recognize and salute one another in spite of all the intervening spaces; they knew their own. "She never found her Merlin," he said sadly.

ii

> *My life had stood—a loaded gun*
> ~Dickinson

While I traveled home to Heathdene this Wednesday of Mother's death, Inspector Vaughan was returning to his appointed scene in deepest Norfolk. The morning lowered on him all the way from Northfleet, grey and with unrelenting drizzle. At Merewell under their chosen white oak, he found his partner, young Lloyd, bivouacked in the ditch and chafing at inactivity.

"I thought this bloody trench poetry went out with your war, Gil."

"What's the good word, David?" Vaughan answered.

Things had happened at the castle while Vaughan had been away. The previous afternoon, for as long as daylight lasted, a squad of cleaners and caterers from Sheringham had laboured in the first floor pantheon, preparing it no doubt for the promised musicale. No sign that the base court was in use had come until very early this morning, when the dark green van had finally reappeared, backing in—"pretty sharpish," Lloyd said—at the huge east door. Since then the whole castle had been quiet as a tomb. He scrambled up out of the ditch and stood by the gnarled trunk of the oak staring across the clearing.

It looked to Vaughan as if young Lloyd had spent too many hours in solitude recently, cultivating the melancholy side of his character. He seemed to feel obliged to affect some heroic impatience with playing safe, to scorn the shelter of a parapet. Perhaps he wanted to have his cap knocked off as soon as possible by a spent bullet. Then he would be safe for the day. Just a little wet with the rain.

"Don't you think we ought to drop in on these birds pronto?" he said accusingly. "Now they've regrouped, they'll be taking off any time."

"Let me tell you something. At least one of these birds is a regular sharpshooter. On Monday evening in Northfleet he picked off a key witness at fifty yards with one round. Only it was the wrong man, as luck would have it."

"Key witness to what?"

"Never mind now. I'll fill you in later. We ought to cut down on the chance of being spotted in the open by coming from opposite directions and keeping our heads in the grass. You make your way round to cover on the other side of the castle from here. At eight on the dot"—Vaughan checked his wristwatch and so did Lloyd—"we'll both move in, down on all fours but as fast as we can. I'll meet you on this side of the terrace at the door we jimmied last time."

"Back to No Man's Land, eh? Okay. What if the manholes are still bolted down?"

"We'll deal with them when we have to. Off you go!"

By some quirk of fate—thanks, presumably, to the gang's being busy with their preparations to depart—both Vaughan and Lloyd made it all the way to the terrace without being spotted, uncomfortably wet but unharmed. They let themselves in to the newly cleansed pantheon, furnished now as for a chamber concert, yet quite empty of anyone. Vaughan stood in the center, gun in hand, keeping an eye out on every windowed side. Lloyd hurried round the floor trying the closed stair well covers. When the third one he tried gave a few inches, he breathed "Bull's-eye." Vaughan as well as he knew that their moment had come.

From the basement floor fifteen feet below sounds, together with a whiff of exhaust, floated up: doors opening or closing, muted voices calling in altercation or command, an engine idling. "Now or never," Vaughan said and Lloyd, without looking at him, jerked the cover fully open and started down the narrow spiral stair, gun in hand.

No sooner was he far enough down to be able to see all round the basement than two men came at him from the nearest of its several grotto-like doorways, shouting and firing. The taller one, coming from behind, carried a rifle at the hip. The shorter one in the lead, armed with a Sten, fired a burst right at Lloyd. When the bullets took him all across the upper body, he shrieked and groaned and slumped in the staircase, his gun clattering on the treads below.

Vaughan, starting down behind him, at once reversed himself and went head first, holding the rail with one hand and firing with the other. He emptied his whole magazine into the two men before they had time to target him above them. While they died on the floor in a heap not far from Lloyd,

Vaughan hung in the staircase by his toes, like some tree sloth, and reloaded as fast as he could, cursing furiously.

Over in the east door, which now stood open, he could see the van all ready for getaway. Another one of the gang, who seemed not to be armed, had just finished loading. He turned with a grimace to watch, horrified, the scene of sudden slaughter not twenty feet away. Vaughan heard him scream at the driver of the van and, as it began to pull away out of sight, saw him dive into the cluttered back and close its swinging doors. By the time Vaughan could get out on to the terrace to take a view, the van was nowhere to be seen, the decayed castle and its overgrown clearing standing silent and unremarkable in the drizzle.

Vaughan trembled. He satisfied himself that, at least, he was not going into shock. As usual in such moments, he began to follow a very simple routine, just putting one foot in front of the other. "Too old for this sort of stuff," he grumbled, taking out his whisky flask and swigging. The thing to do was to report to Gus at once.

Making himself go indoors and down the fatal staircase was harder than he thought it would be. He checked the crumpled bodies of young Lloyd and the other two and found them all repulsively dead, eyes glazed, teeth bared. A pool of their drying blood seeped into the lichens on the floor. Otherwise, the gang appeared to have left things in the basement much as they found them, vacant and mouldy with the smell of time past.

He secured the fallen .32 and .303 and Sten, and carried them off to the Wolseley a hundred yards away, where it was parked under a wild hedge of beeches. He did not stay to search the basement or any of its grottoes and corners, thinking, as he closed the east door behind him, there would be time for doing this later in the day.

The D.A.C. received Vaughan's telephone report with unaccustomed neutrality, even the news that his own son-in-law had been killed. He uttered no more than a mouthful of terse sentences. "So you are still on the track, Vaughan? Stick to it. Two of the four managed to make off—with their precious cargo, apparently. Go back to Northfleet now and see if they don't show up at Templeton's this evening. Forget Merewell. I'll have the Removers in and everything back to rights by noon. No more sudden deaths, if you can help it."

Vaughan left his isolated crossroads kiosk near Holt, curiously unresolved whether or not he was being watched. "Wind up," he told himself guiltily. He ducked into the Wolseley and yet once more headed north, thinking no more than he had to about anything.

Chapter Eight

Exeunt Severally

i

The one Brenan could not speak highly enough of,
when he told me about the Tievas affair eight months
later, was the Colonel. He was the hero of the hour, Brenan's
Ulysses. I heard more about the virtues of Colonel Garas—and
less about the misdeeds of the Didelis group—than I needed to
know to understand what actually occurred. Colonel Vytautas
Garas, *B.K.Z.,* appealed to Brenan as being a rare compromise
between the Baltic *gravitas* and the English unseriousness of manner.
His mother had been a colonel's daughter from Cheltenham and
his father a true Balt from the Teutonic provinces, serving over
here in the Polish diplomatic corps during the latter days of the
Old Queen and the reign of Edward VII. *Bin gar keine Russin,
stamm' aus Litauen, echt deutsch.*

Vytautas Garas the younger had grown up in England and lived here much of his picaresque life. Over the years he had become well-assimilated in more than one native English *persona*. At twenty he had made captain in the 2/Royal Fusiliers on the Somme when the Hindenberg Line was being broken— a fact of which he was inveterately proud. Immediately postwar, he read Greats at Corpus. Ten years later, he was established in the intelligence service of the emergent capitalist republic of Lithuania. At what point he crossed paths with the Secretary-General of the Communist Party, Jurgis Tievas, Brenan could not say. "Sometime between the wars, of course. But you don't often come across a gent like the Colonel who has gone from Georgian romantic to Communist mercenary and not missed a trick of the *fanfarone militar*." In the early years of the second war he escaped from occupied Baltija only to be reintroduced there as an underground agent by S.O.E.— "to no great effect," said Brenan, echoing his mentor, as he often did. Never having met the man myself, I am inclined to think Brenan besotted, as he could on occasion be.

They spent the early hours of Wednesday in his room, hashing out in whispers and with the light off what had gone on, so far as they could tell, in Greenwich, Merewell, and Northfleet over the past long weekend. Then they planned an intervention at the VC's bunker that night which would, they believed, undo the Didelis plot. However, what ye have spoken in the ear closely shall not always be proclaimed upon the rooftops, St. Luke notwithstanding. Why Brenan would trust Garas right off the bat was that he recognized him, almost at once, as the somnolent old gent in the Fox Under The Hill checking unobtrusively on the Marshal's television appearance on Friday night. "Mr. Brenan, you're looking at me as if we've met before—and indeed we have, early on in this masquerade. I am at a stage in life when I can put on fifteen years and a stone or two in weight with impunity, if I have to. I am currently operating solo, you understand; a certain mutability is sometimes indicated." With his walking stick, pork pie hat, riding mac, tweeds, and crisp, well-shaven features, he could for the present be taken for one of the many retired army officers at large in the land—which in some sense he was. "So, I should also be much obliged if you would share with me exactly how you first came to be interested in the, ah, *identity* of Marshal Tievas." Like every Balt in the case except the Marshal himself, Garas spoke unexceptionable idiomatic English, and seemed to enjoy doing so.

To Brenan, how *long* ago that Friday now seemed when he had failed to make Mackie credit his tale of mayhem at the Hospital. Here it was, in demand at last, the very first news his midnight caller wanted to hear, an invitation not to be missed. So he delivered his third such *obbligato* within thirty-six hours, this time being copiously circumstantial. "Yes, Colonel, I do see the resemblance. I told myself then that you must be some 'decay'd Turkey merchant' from the Hospital, lately cast adrift in Blackheath. You had me snookered. Let me tell you exactly what I saw in the Chapel. It can't get me into much more trouble than I'm already in, can it?"

"On the contrary, what you know could still be the death of you. We have neither youth nor age in common, you and I, but a certain, as it were, disability. Our enemies, and also those who might be our friends but aren't, have no further use for us except as dead men, knowing nothing, having seen all. But we could, if so inclined, perhaps be of some use to one another. You are a student who already knows too much. I thought on Monday you had paid for your curiosity with your life until I realized that it was your friend who paid while you remain one of Luck's darlings. And what am I? My life has stood an unopened book, an unpublished poem. In my profession I am what is known as a mole—what's worse, an old mole. Are you familiar with the term?"

"Yes. I know:

> *All but blind*
> *In his chambered hole,*

Gropes for worms
The four-clawed mole."

"Ah, yes, a toilsome mole. I am a man who likes to talk,
Mr. Brenan, especially with a man who likes to talk poetry. It
rarely fails to raise the tone of whatever is being said." At this
point, Brenan later told me, he realized that Garas was a fat
man in a thin man's body.

Garas himself then knew little for sure about the crime
and its secret cause but, being of an observant turn of mind,
he suspected the more. His suspicions had first been aroused
that Friday morning at the Naval College, where security
arrangements struck him as, to say the least, eccentric.

That night at the Fox, he had been alarmed at the tenor
of the Marshal's television broadcast which seemed, if not
reckless, then delirious. Noticing that for some mysterious
reason it seriously disconcerted the only other pubgoers who
happened to be watching, he decided, *faute de mieux*, to try
keeping an eye on them. They led him at once to Valija
Didelis and, by association through the Embassy, to her
uncle, his little "department," his colleague Rawlings of
Caius and, by an inspired guess, to Merewell Castle itself in
time to track Baltrušaitus and Čiabuvis all the way to
Somersby. "Small wonder," said Brenan in retrospect, "that
the old boy felt he didn't need Forster telling him 'Only
connect.'"

I must not forget how close I once felt to this meeting of
minds of theirs in Brenan's room eight months before, when
finally I sat where he once had, on the shawled bed, and
listened to him reminisce from the Morris chair by the window,
where Garas had once sat while an October rainstorm emptied
itself outside. "So you saw the Marshal plain," said Garas
gravely, by way of summary. "Suppose you next surprise me
with your best word on his present whereabouts and—if any—
his future."

"What's this, some Socratic dialogue? Don't I get to ask you any of the difficult questions?"

"Later, Phaedrus, later your turn will come. For the time being, indulge me. What's doing with the Marshal?"

Brenan saw from the first that he needed Garas as he needed no one else in the affair, not so much for the answers he could give and the quiet of mind they might bring, as for the need Garas himself had for Brenan's active assistance. This time there would be no injunction—as there had been from Vaughan—to do nothing, whatever he knew, to sit on his hands. He said, "Ever since seeing him in the Chapel, my hunch has been that Tievas is a prisoner and his double is making the speeches. Since these have been disastrous, the double must be an enemy, not serving the Marshal at all. Where he is being held prisoner I have no idea, but probably he will be brought back to the *Dolphynas* before it sails tomorrow night—tonight rather—when the great impersonation will be over and the damage done. In Gdainys, Vilnius, Riga, Tallinn, already fighting in the streets.

"The trouble with such a hunch is the question *cui bono*? What's the purpose of such a cruel hoax? Who on earth could hope to get away with it here in England? This isn't Ruritania."

Garas smiled. "Have you asked your little friend *panelè Didelyte* if she could answer these questions for you?"

"I haven't yet had time. Dr. Lacy only tipped me off to Arthur Bresnahan's murder an hour or two ago. I hope to see her today."

"Ah, yes, your spiritual adviser, the Warden. Not much use in a crunch like this, I should imagine. What little I've seen of him makes me expect him to say 'snackems' and 'drinkipoo' if he takes to you. I am truly sorry for the loss of your friend Bresnahan."

"Don't underestimate Huby. He knows whose business he is about. Yes, I'm afraid I do have as yet to come to terms with myself over the death of Arthur. Thank you."

"In time of loss, keeping busy can be the best medicine.

Let's go back to your question *cui bono?* One answer to 'Who could hope to get away with it?' is 'Only an enemy with friends in very high places.' This is what we evidently have here."

"But how could that be? Both the Labour government and the Tory opposition would rather see Tievas in power than the Russians."

"Save this thought for a moment, and finish spelling out your hunch for me. Soon after he comes ashore at the Naval College, the Marshal is taken prisoner and whisked across the heath to the Hospital. His double makes the crucial speech that night, and next day at the conference aborts any provisory Anglo-Baltic *rapprochement.* That night he goes back aboard the *Dolphynas* and sails for Northfleet on the Sunday tide. Who *is* this double, able to carry off such an impersonation? Who does your intuition tell you he has to be?"

"You want me to say 'the play actor, Professor Didelis,' but I don't even know if he looks like Tievas."

"The other Jurgis. Yes, I have made it my business to know what he looks like; and I say, 'Shave him, and he could be the Marshal.'"

"On the television screen, how did he look to you? There were plenty of medium close ups, even if the focus was a bit soft."

"The play actor had some tricks of expression down pat, some Byelo-Russian traces of accent, the old man's tempo. But let me tell you, the Marshal is my C-in-C, from wartime in the field, and I have a feeling about my C-in-C . . . . That man in uniform on television was an impostor. I know a forgery when I see it."

"If so, how did he dupe his bodyguards and ship's officers on the *Dolphynas* when he went back on board?"

"Ah, this is the cream of the jest. Because the Marshal had promised himself a sea cruise in the presidential yacht, putting in at Greenwich and Northfleet only, his wife and his usual bodyguards were left at home. The yacht, which is by way of being his latest toy, has its own naval crew who can also serve as bodyguards, though as yet they have seen little of the Marshal in person. The captain and the first officer, fairly recently recruited and already favourites of his, are both Englishmen— Scots, actually, and ex-Royal Navy. Evidently, they are, in some sense, double agents. Not that they needed to be turned. This cruise, you will see, was an opportunity simply not to be missed by his former admirers over here."

"What do you mean, his 'former admirers'?"

"Before I tell you, finish telling me all you know about the other Jurgis. You never met him?"

"Never. All I know is what Valija has told me: former Baltic Division under the Germans, liaised with the Partisans, Professor of English at Gdainys, connected with the Ben Jonson school at Cambridge, cultural attaché to the Baltic Embassy, has a following of four ex-service graduate students from Gdainys whose names I forget . . ."

"Plus a beautiful, enigmatic niece who may or may not know all about what her uncle is up to."

"Yes, this is an urgent question for me. How little could Valija possibly know, having said and done what she has? Could she be innocent, a sort of alibi or figurehead for the others?"

"One thing you can be sure of. In a life like hers the *need to know* has been enforced without fail. Of course, the *need to know* is, in effect, the obligation *not* to know."

"You think that, when she called me and I picked up the phone, she might not have known one of the group would be snuffing me out on the instant?"

"I suppose it's possible. But, to move on, see if you can answer for yourself what the former admirers of the Marshal, from Baltija as well as here in England, could possibly be up to, discrediting him in the eyes of the world, and especially of his own people."

"This is where I keep drawing a blank. Why would anyone in the West want to destabilize Baltija and give Stalin an excuse to take over?"

"Look at the world picture. The U.S. has never been ready

to toe the line for the Baltic peoples, not since 1919 anyway. In the struggle to overmatch the Cominform with NATO, the U.S.—together with the U.K.—has come to a point of having to choose between securing Baltija and securing Jugo-Slavia, the two 'fifty-fifty' spheres of influence confirmed just before Yalta by Churchill, Stalin, and Roosevelt, when the War was not yet Cold.

"Look at the map of Europe and you'll see that for the West there is only one strategic choice, short of an atomic war: secure Jugo-Slavia and let Stalin try to secure Baltija. I shan't be surprised if, in the next year or two, it is Marshal Tito who makes a state visit to England by sea."

Jug, Jug, to dirty ears. "So Tievas, just as he veers of his own will towards England and the West, becomes expendable? I can see that. But the Labour government, Churchill, the VC, the FO, would they all agree to ditch Tievas in favour of Tito— and all to satisfy Washington? It takes a bit of believing. There's a lot of history there. You are the one to know how much."

"The FO, after the ignominy of losing Burgess and MacLean last spring, 'owes Washington big time,' as the saying goes across the pond. Templeton only does what Churchill says; and what does the Old One say? He says: 'This postwar aberrancy of Labour politics abroad and nationalization at home has proved to be a flash in the pan. The time is here—almost— for the Conservative Party under my leadership to resume power at the will of the electorate. Eden and the others and I will show the world how a muzzledloader can and should be made to fire. Meantime, any adjustment of the world situation such as mollifying Washington, giving Stalin enough rope to hang himself with, making Labour's foreign policy look silly, is much to the purpose. I am confident that my old comrade in arms Marshal Tievas would be the first to agree that, once a war is over, *political* expediency rules—though betrayal of a friendly power, however expedient, should never be *seen* to be done.'"

"Phew! You certainly know how to paint one into the big

picture, Colonel Garas. It all sounds likely enough. But in such a tricky situation, all sleight of hand, diplomacy, no final solutions, why should I (or my friend and neighbour Arthur) be sentenced to death?"

"I hope you and your fellow students of literature still read Kipling. He is my favourite among the moderns, and never to be ignored when answers are being looked for. Listen to this:

> *Ah, what avails the classic bent*
> *And what the cultured word,*
> *Against the undoctored incident*
> *That actually occurred?*

I know you deplore the purposeless death of your friend— as I myself do. But is this the moment for us to try to psychologize a Baltic death gang, Professor Didelis' little department? He no doubt has less control over it than he would wish. When it was realized that you had seen the four of them recapturing the Marshal (by the way, how *did* they come to realize this?), someone panicked perhaps and tried to wipe clean the slate before their mentor saw it. It is of the essence in such a conspiracy (all sleight of hand, as you say) to *keep* the secret. Or, perhaps, someone merely seized the opportunity for more mischief even than had been foreseen. Who knows?

"We don't yet know the full consequence of what the gang and its sponsors are trying to do, including kill you. But don't you think that, instead of theorizing about them, you and I ought to be trying to stop them dead in their tracks?"

"I do. I do." Brenan found himself caught up ecstatically in a dream of action. "And isn't tonight our last chance to do so—at the VC's reception? There should be a moment when the false Tievas and the true Tievas are both under the same roof. All we have to do is take control and bring them together under the eyes of neutral witnesses. At that moment the hoax will fail; the secret will be out."

His interlocutor forbore to warn him against the trap of his "All we have to do . . . ."

For Garas, vividly attentive in the nighted room, this response of Brenan's must have brought a not particularly promising session to a most gratifying climax. "*Now* you're talking, Michael Brenan! There will be plenty of neutral witnesses. Templeton will have invited a few of his county friends, but most of his guests will be college people like you. The constabulary will be there and will be neutral, concerned only with the Marshal's safety but—handy, dandy, which *is* the Marshal?

"You and I will, of course, be outnumbered, four or five to one if the gang is there, what with Didelis and his body guards, Rawlings, and Templeton. But we will have the advantage, if not of surprise, of being ready to make a scene, of having nothing to hide."

"Who is Rawlings, again?"

"Oh, another of these Cambridge academics in transition between books and guns—or guns and books. We will have to act impromptu, wait for the right moment and seize it. Nothing can be planned until we're there in the actual situation—except not to lose track of the false Marshal and not to miss the true one's arrival. Presumably, he will be unconscious. The play actor will have gone through the Marshal's usual party routine, I imagine, of drinking himself unconscious on *starka*. We shall have both a waking dormouse and a sleeping one to catch hold of and exhibit to the partygoers side by side."

"Not quite the manner in which the Templetons are accustomed to entertain, the Slavonic vodka orgy, would you say? The VC is fastidious; and Lady Templeton likes a certain decorum to be kept. Why ever, do you suppose, it was decided to make the switch at the bunker during their reception? Why not aboard the *Dolphynas* or on the Town Pier during the early hours?"

"For this particular *coup*, to be unremarked, to be

'carrying on regardless,' seems to be important. The police, the Special Branch, the civil authorities, the press, the public—none of these can be privy to the conspiracy. Incidentally, the Special Branch will also be there tonight, no doubt. Life has to appear to be going on as it normally does, even during the final *monstrum* of Didelis turning back into Tievas and *vice versa*.

"And, for this purpose, where else is so safe and private as a guest room at the Vice Chancellery, especially while a semi-official reception is being given? From the beginning, it has been the *modus operandi* to use a certain public busyness, bystanders ignorantly milling, to screen the covert action. Think how, at the Naval College, the original abduction was handled. There are theatrical imaginations behind the tactics of this *coup*, doctors of letters, bloody academics, who are secretly sorry, in some part of their beings, that the fires of open war have once again died down.

"No, I think we can assume that this reception for the Marshal is precisely where he will be produced, behind the scenes, before being shuffled aboard his yacht. If we're wrong in this, then one of us will just have to wing the play actor while he's still in uniform, or perhaps poison his cup and have him taken to hospital, to wait until the Marshal can come into his own again."

Brenan said to me later, "You have no idea how chuffed the Colonel himself was to be back in the field, as he saw it. He was beside himself, 'figuring away at force' once again. Given his retirement, working alone, keeping an eye on things from a sideline, he could really only relish this disastrous *Englandreise* of the Marshal's as a turn up for the book, *Trent's Last Case*."

To Garas, he now said, "The witching hour seems to have gone to your head, Socrates. What kind of knockout drops do you think of using?"

"Nothing would please me more than to treat the play actor to a glass of strychnine, compliments of the Marshal. Have you considered what five days of ruthless sedation will have done to him, poor devil?"

"Not really. It doesn't bear thinking about, does it? A king 'wasted by sickness.' By the way, speaking of winging the play actor, do you have a gun I could borrow for the time being, and in case I run into Arthur's assassin?"

"When we get to my car later today I'll give you a .32 and some ammo, if you'll remind me. You've done weapon training, I suppose."

"Only .303, Sten, and Bren—and grenade. I failed WOSB, so small arms never came up. But I expect I can manage a .32."

"You were too young for the real war, of course. When I was your age, things were easier. I was commissioned in the Royal Fusiliers. Your father's war too, no doubt. There is a very fine Great War book about the Fusiliers in France by someone who is now Professor of History at Leeds University. Do you know it, *A Passionate Prodigality* by Guy Chapman?"

"I've heard of it but never read it. One of these years I'm going to read all the good Great War books. *Her Privates We* by Frederic Manning is my best ever, for the time being."

"Ah, yes, Manning, an Aussie, wasn't he? Tried to write in the style of Pater. An aesthete. Too rich for my blood. I think great writing has to have the common touch."

"You're right, of course, but the common touch may not be what makes it great. Shakespeare and Kipling both have their secrets, their esoterica, their allusions, as well as all that charms the ordinary reader. It may be the complex of several different appeals that makes for greatness. By the way, are you another Baltic admirer of Ben Jonson?"

"Not on your life. I wish I knew some of the ancient authors as well as he did but, as to sensibility, he leaves me thinking merely what a clever bastard he must have been. But back to business, what about your new friend and neighbour Yates, from across the pond. Could he be C.I.A. at some remove?"

"Good question. It hadn't occurred to me. He's a Fulbright Scholar, of course. So much of American cultural outreach seems to come from Washington with strings attached. Just think, if he is a spy, he must have been sent to this farflung corner specially to keep an eye on Templeton and the Tievas connection."

"Don't try to second guess yourself. If you formed a different impression, so be it. Leave second guessing to the political journalists and historians; they do it so well, our benefactors."

"This is what I tell my friend Offord who's doing Political History here. Where would he be—where would they all be— without revisionism? Undoctored events are as rare as originality. About Al Yates, I do know that he will be at the reception tonight, its being an international occasion. Offord, on the other hand, will not be there."

"We shall see what we shall see. Have you told any of them what you know?"

"No. Only the VC and Inspector Vaughan."

"Well, that will do for a start! Who is Inspector Vaughan?"

When Brenan told him, Garas said, "The pilgrim who spoke to you and *panelė Didelyte* at the Dolphin Hotel on Monday. But don't tell anybody else, not even your little friend, who will also be there tonight. Try to get some sleep now. Carry on regardless. I'll be waiting for you at 8:30 p.m. near the west gate, where the lane takes that curve away from the stream. My car is a Hillman." He stood up a little stiffly, back to the window, darkening even further what little light came from it.

"Oh, be sure to dress in a dinner jacket. Even as gatecrashers, we don't want to let the Templetons down. You can manage that." He picked up *Howards End* from the low table where Brenan had laid it down and returned it to the space on the window sill. "Don't be afraid. Whatever happens, we'll see to it that nobody thrashes you with the flat of a sabre and buries you under an avalanche of books."

He came to where Brenan now stood by the bed, shook

his hand while looking him calmly in the eye, opened the door, and was gone. Outside, it was still raining.

ii

Of love, that never found his earthly close,
What sequel?

~Tennyson

At one point, I asked Brenan outright what his true feelings for Valija were. He answered that, once you fall in love with a woman and are recognized by her, you never quite get over it, no matter what. In those days he was very much at a distance from Valija, in retreat, but he still spoke as if the secret they had shared—or failed to share—made her unforgettable, at least by him. So far as I could tell, he mostly kept his own counsel about any woman he was in love with, behaving as if he were the adept, I not as yet even an initiate, and the secret only to be hinted at.

When, somewhat later, I went for high tea with Valija, somewhere off the Edgware Road, I could hardly question her about moments of truth in Brenan's tale—moments between her and him, I mean—for fear of betraying how much he had told me about the fatal official secret. This fear was particularly frustrating in that Valija's own part in things was not really well-represented in his account. He could hardly be expected to speak as well for her, I suppose, on the spur of the moment that night in Somersby, as for himself. Yet over the years, her untold tale has come to seem to me of more interest, perhaps, than the one he told me—untellable, unimaginable as hers might turn out to be. *Should my shadow cross thy thoughts . . . .* If only the women in poems could have been given their own voices more often. *Kommt denn die menschen stimme nicht zu euch?*

It was never difficult to see that, unlike him, I was not going to fall into some cauldron of subjective emotion over a woman, *odi et amo*, etc., etc., as he had done more than once in his young life. He seemed to know no better way, having beheld her as if for the very first time, than to plunge blindly in, once and forever and even unto death. I recall hearing his father say to him during his first infatuation at sixteen, "You don't have to see your young lady *every* evening, you know, Mick." De Rougemont and D'Orczy—and the rest of the romantic authors who made up his inner life—they had much to answer for.

In the case of Valija, a charming, intelligent, kindly, mysterious foreign woman, this particular way of recognizing how special she was, this trying to love her strictly by the book, though perhaps youthfully irresistible in him, was bound to prove, sooner rather than later, abortive. She and he had far too little in common and far too much pulling them apart. But for him in 1951, at the age of twenty-two, it was not possible to see this. "I was as much in love with Valija," he said later, "in spite of everything, as I have ever been in love with anybody." Then, as an afterthought, he added, "With Miss Hollis, it was, as you know, quite different. *Steadfast love.*"

So in retelling his brief tale of going to see Valija this Wednesday afternoon, for the first time since certain terrible facts had dawned on him, I must once again rely more on imagination than on History. He did say that it was the worst tea party he had ever been to. Then he made one of those farfetched associations of his, which have always charmed me—if not all his friends and mentors. This time it was not so much a prolepsis as a *non sequitur:*

Crossing the brickfield from the library, after a lecture by old Tailleferro on Swift, without Valija, and lunch in the union, still without Valija, all I could think of, for some reason, was my father and Mutiny On The Bounty. *Before you came to Heathdene, he once took me to see it at the Gaumont, Lewisham, just the two of us. It was one of the first films I ever sat through; I was seven. Some parts of it terrified me, even more than the cabin scene in* A Night At The Opera, *when the sea rushes in through the porthole. (Mother had taken me to see this at the Roxy the year before.) That night I could not sleep for the sheer anxiety of replaying in my head certain scenes of keelhauling, flogging, and other cruelty. You remember how it was—for instance, when you and I first saw* Fury *early in the war, that woman whirling a firebrand, the nightmare of family life.*

When everyone was in bed and asleep, I started crying and calling out to be comforted. As it happened, that Saturday we had guests staying over, one of my unmarried aunts and her friend Tom. She was sleeping in the main bedroom with Mother (and, I imagine, young Patrick), and Tom in the slip room. Father and I had Morris chairs made down like deck chairs in the best room. When I called out, he got up and came over to see what was wrong. How those Morris chairs did creak! When I told him he said, kindly, "We mustn't make a scene at this hour, must we, old chap? You know, those Jack Tars under Captain Bligh knew when to take it and when to give it. Remember how they were on Tahiti with the friendly natives. They were all in clover by that time."

Then he went over to the tall glass fruit bowl on the chiffonier *and fetched me a banana, like the one that the pretty native girl lays on Clark Gable's bare chest when he is asleep. "There," he whispered, peeling it for me, "have a banana. Don't think about being keelhauled. Think about being on the beach in Tahiti." So I ate the banana and fell sound asleep.*

This, I gathered, was how life's terrors, such as the murder of Arthur and Valija's probable complicity in it, were to be dealt with. Sometimes you lose; sometimes you win; then you die anyway. The beauty of it is all in the imagination, in this instance his father's. For me now, in my retelling, however, the person whose imagination begins to be of most interest is Valija. Rather than her knowledge, which was considerable, what made her mysterious was what she did not know, her ignorance. Think how confusing it will have been for her, trying to imagine, to *realize*, the whole truth, when Brenan first popped his offhand question about Arthur.

Valija expected him, having received a call at breakfast time asking if he might come. Her room, though crammed with useful and decorative things, was scrupulously tidy; and she, coiffed and carefully made up, was softly elegant in a light blue dress that buttoned down the front. No sign of tea things was visible. When she said, "Come in," answering his knock, she was standing at the window, looking down on the damp, glistening beds of grass among gravel walks and herbaceous borders. Here, on Monday, the postponed garden party would, weather permitting, be held.

He came in, closed the door, crossed the little room, and kissed her gently on the mouth, holding her at the waist. As usual, she returned his kiss without hesitation. "Thank you so much for letting me come, Valija; I just *had* to see you. There's something I must ask you."

"You are most welcome, Michael. Not always. But now you are. Tell me, what is so urgent? You look as if you might have missed a train." She went on letting him kiss her and kissing him back, with her hands resting lightly on the lapels of his corduroy jacket. But she was not quite tall enough to be comfortable in such an embrace for more than a minute or two.

"You look perfect, Valija. *Cette robe vous sied très bien.* You *are* perfect."

She gave a little laugh of deprecation. But was she not indeed as perfect as anyone could reasonably expect her to be? She at least aspired to the condition of being perfect. "Don't try to speak French. I like you best in English. I like kissing too. I'd like to do more of it. However, do you not feel that true love, especially an *amour passion* like ours, calls for something beyond mere physical contact, beyond touch? You know, the *sleeping* sword." (What a piece of work is woman.)

"Debatable, *I* would say. So would Sir Philip Sidney." There spoke M.B., the eternal Eng.Hons. student.

"Things between you and me have happened so fast since Friday. I blame myself for being too intimate with you, too personal too soon—especially since I am prone to give those I care for too much and then expect too much in return."

"I don't know about that. You strike me as acting very

reasonably, expertly in fact, just for the sake of it, for your own satisfaction, not only to be pleasing to others—to me."

"Should I be flattered at your saying this, Mr. Brenan? Let's catch our breaths, shall we? Come and sit down, like a nice young visitor from Somersby. Stop trying to sweep me off my feet, and tell me what's troubling you." She led him by the hand to the centre of the room. The armchair had been moved over towards the corner of the carpet, high back toward the door, and the straight chair at the desk turned inward to face it, cosily.

He did what she asked and they sat together *en face*, all but knee to knee, in the middle of the carpet. The little comfortable room was full of afternoon light. On the walk up Highfield Lane from the brickfield, he had decided, prudentially, to broach only the matter of Arthur with her, not the matter of Tievas at all. No great reckoning was called for. He needed to know immediately no more than whether or not she had tried to help kill him.

"Have you heard about the shooting of my friend Arthur Bresnahan at Somersby on Monday night? I don't know if it was reported in the *Argus*, what with all the excitement about the Visit. He was found dead in the JCR telephone kiosk just after dinner."

While his question hung in the air, all the composure of her face, of her hands, of the way her body rested in the chair, disintegrated. Alarm washed over her and through her. Certain moments of her recent life, with and without Michael, must have passed before her eyes, certain voices sounded in her ears, saying certain things. Was she drowning? His gaze soon fell uneasily away to her sensible brown shoes, to the patterns in the Axminster carpet under her feet. He could not bear to look at her dismay.

Visibly, she collected herself, her thoughts evidently racing. She and he were both sleepwalkers, duly met, and now bent on waking one another. "I did hear someone at dinner last night refer to a suicide in Somersby, but I thought nothing of it, having just visited you and your friend John for tea. You are the only ones I know in Somersby."

"Didn't you say that you tried to phone me during dinnertime on Monday? Someone picked up the phone, there was a clatter, then silence. You had to ring off. That could have been Arthur getting shot. That *was* Arthur getting shot, wasn't it?"

"My God, Michael, what are you telling me? What did you say his name was?"

"Bresnahan. Who knew that you would be phoning me? Your uncle?"

"Yes, and Antanas Baltrušaitis, who is one of his students and who gave me the message from him to give you. Why should Dr. Didelis or Antanas want to have you shot?"

"Why should anyone want to shoot Arthur Bresnahan? Yet, someone did. He is very dead. You told me yourself that your Baltic friends are a knot of vipers."

"Oh, yes, but that was a manner of speaking. I am sorry, terribly sorry, for the death of your friend, especially if I somehow had something to do with it. But I cannot believe I did. What possible motive can you think I had?" Her question hung in the air now, but he only shook his head wonderingly and waited for her to continue.

"Thank God it was your friend and not you who died. I couldn't bear losing you like that. In the war I lost everyone who means anything to me, except my uncle. To have met you, Michael, and then to lose you at once, somehow through my own fault—it would be too cruel. It would be enough to make me want to end my own life. I have been there before, let me tell you. It is really too much!" She broke into silent weeping.

The sudden collapse of her sense of the rightness of things, her unmistakable misery, was enough for Brenan. It seemed much more likely that she had not tried to have him killed than that she had. At the Hospital on Friday and everywhere they had met since, including here and now, there had been something guileless—reserved, but guileless—in her responses to him. Would he even have suspected her in the first place if she had not herself innocently confessed to trying to phone him on Monday night? He reached out to her consolingly and she came into his arms and onto his lap, still silently weeping.

There is something very intimate about weeping, when it is shared and neither hatred nor anger is present. It can bring a couple together like children in a rare moment of innocence and trust, an enchantment, as of Psyche comforted by Eros.

Valija eventually ceased both weeping and being silent. Brenan began making her little blandishments once again; he went on comforting her with caresses, without being rebuked. More at their leisure than before when standing in the window, nestled in her armchair, they whispered together and resumed kissing. Slowly, by indulging herself in a search for bodily pleasure, she found her way back to self-possession, though this was now much mollified by the new pledge to Eros and dream.

"Where is it you really want to touch me, Michael?" When he told her, she sighed and stood up in front of him. Then she undid her dress. Before she sat down again on his lap, she said, "Let's slip your jacket off, shall we?" and they did. "It is quite warm in here."

"I've been dying to know just what you wear under your street clothes," he said. "You always look so neat and proper; it is an enigma, what you are in *déshabillé*, or even how you might be brought into it."

"And how *do* I look in *déshabillé*? You know, there is a quaint English version of the word, 'dishabille,' if you would care to use it." Under her dress she wore a camisole in light pink, a little suspender belt for her silk stockings, and one or two other flimsy things. "That," she added, as he felt his way about her, "undoes with two little clips at the back."

"You look much more vulnerable than I've ever seen you but still very neat, undisheveled, though wandering." To himself he said, Dare I eat a peach? The most telling evidence, the clincher, of her innocence, would be her telling him what she now thought about her uncle and the fate of Tievas. But this, in the circumstances, was far too much to expect. She would have to broach a matter which she had yet to think carefully and make up her own mind about, a matter which could only re-open the question of how much she knew when she did what Antanas said her uncle wanted her to do. He decided not to ask what he should do about phoning the number in Holt she had given him.

"I like attention to detail, don't you? Observing the niceties, noticing the finer points. Oversight, vacancy, emptiness of outlook are not for me. You have nice hands, Michael; they make me look forward to being touched where you said you wanted to touch me." She had a sullen red spot on either cheek but she was still cool and calm with a sort of dewiness. Her eyelids were heavy. "Why don't you kiss me *here* and touch me there." She shifted lightly on his lap.

He was content for the present to do whatever she said. One never knew what would come of a *séance intime* such as this. She laid her head on his shoulder and he could tell by the tone of her voice that her eyes were closed.

"When I have fears and doubts and questions which keep me from falling asleep at night, I reassure myself, failure or not, that whatever I have done in my life, I *had* to do. Then I meet someone new, you. Anything seems possible again; and I put myself out to please, to entertain."

"You *are* very pleasing, Valija, wonderfully pleasing. Who wouldn't find you most entertaining to be with?" He kissed her on the lips. Most of all, Wandering Arthur, he thought.

She kissed him back and sighed. "Because I am straight-talking, measured, deliberate, others take me to be harder, crueler, colder than I am. No doubt, I am to blame for this. But serious trouble always makes me lose confidence in who I really am, makes me lose courage." She sighed again.

After a while, she said, "You know, Michael, your D.H. Lawrence in *Lady Chatterley* is such a perfectionist. At a lovely moment like this, I am sorry to have to say there is serious doubt that I ever have one of those *quelquechoses* at all. You couldn't be kinder to me than you actually are being; I enjoy your attentions very much. But I am afraid nothing more is going to happen to me just there."

After she brought me from Vilnius into Germany proper, when the war was still in the balance but my family had already been broken up and taken away one after another from 1939 on, my aunt was killed in an air raid on the railway terminus, and I was left all alone in Berlin. I was a very young nineteen. That winter the German authorities recruited me into the Arbeitsdienst *and I worked on the production line in a munitions factory and lived in a cold, draughty hut in a camp. Then my uncle Jurgis, my last surviving relative as far as I know, pulled strings and I was transferred into the* Luftwaffe Nachrichtendienst *as an English translator. A posting came through, and I found myself blessedly in transit from the camp, the squalor of industrial outskirts, the bombed city, the shortages, to beautiful Rügen Island in the Baltic.*

On the train going north, my seat was in a very crowded first class compartment. But as the day lengthened, I was left in it all alone with two S.S. officers and their Schaferhund. *Why it had not been consigned to the* Dienstwagen *I do not know. Perhaps the S.S. was a law unto itself. Yet these two young men, not out of their early twenties, were well enough behaved. They spoke to me in a friendly, unofficial way—we were all in uniform, of course. I was blonde, German-speaking,* bürgerliche *if not* vornehmene. *They had no reason to suppose I was only* Brudersvolk *and not* Herrenvolk. *In fact, their behaviour towards me was quite correct.*

As dusk came on, I was foolish enough to take notice of their magnificent dog, crouched obediently on the compartment floor. I attracted his attention. Whether it was something I did or said, or whether one of the men somehow communicated with the dog, perhaps inadvertently, I don't know. I remember only that at the moment the smell of the Baltic

Sea began to be in our nostrils, the dog growled and sprang on me as if I were prey or some escaping prisoner. He was huge, and he was all over me. It was terrifying. I have never been so far out of my mind with fear and horror before or since.

The brute did not bite or draw blood, though he scratched and bruised me with his paws and teeth and tongue. He tore at my clothes; and the final horror came when I realized that what he was trying to do was bestialize me, as he must have been trained to do. To their credit, the S.S. men seemed as outraged as I. They leapt up in a flash, screaming commands, and beat the animal mercilessly into submission with a metal leash and a swagger stick. Their apologies and their concern were abject. But unharmed, physically, as I was, in that flash while the beast was upon me, I was mentally scarred for life. All my misery was rolled up into one obscene act which, when I have my worst nightmare, I awaken to.

Brenan remembered much that Valija told him about this and that. But whether or not it was this very afternoon that she told him this about the Alsatian dog, he was not sure. It was certainly related to all else that she then gave him to understand about herself. How many other obscenities she had conceivably been part of between 1939 and 1945, and after, he did not ask. When she made him her sad confession about pleasure deferred, all he said to her, reflectively, was, 'Not a short fuse, Valija. No fuse at all.' And he kissed her. What does one do with a woman in an intimate moment but kiss her?

She slipped out of his arms and off his lap onto the carpet and came to rest half kneeling with her elbows on his knees. "You poor boy," she said, "wouldn't you like to do Something?" It was the German *Etwas;* and he knew from her slightly mischievous expression what she meant. "If you have one of those things," she went on, "and are careful not to give me a baby, I wouldn't mind."

He told her regretfully that he did not have one of those things; they did not come in jars like lollipops at the confectioner's. At the solemn chemist's shop Above Bar they were an embarrassment to ask for; and life was unbeautiful enough without them.

She did not appear rebuffed or offended. She touched him gently between the legs, where she had been sitting and where he still shone. She said sadly, "I could not bear to do it for you with my mouth, as Welsh women do. I just could not bear it. But I will touch you with my hand if you like."

"I thought it was French women, not Welsh. What do you know about Wales? However, speaking of French women, do you suppose Odette and Swann made love in the ancient Roman position, but lying in bed? There seems to be some reason for thinking so. Could this be part of why Swann says at the end that she was not his type?"

"I have no idea, Michael. What possible difference could it make to you and me?"

"Everything makes a difference. And nothing makes any difference. οὐ φροντίς as T.E. Lawrence liked to say. Take your pick. I know it doesn't help the situation to say such things, but they seem to be true all the same."

He took her hands gently in his, kissed her lightly on the forehead, and urged her to stand up. She did; and he came out of the armchair and took his jacket from where she had laid it folded on the bed.

Outside in the corridor and all through the quiet hall of residence, an annoying electric buzzer sounded. It signified that high tea—the visiting day alternative to an evening meal—was about to be served in the dining room downstairs.

Valija began straightening her underclothes and buttoning up her light blue dress. She glanced at herself in the small mirror hooked onto the door of her clothes cupboard. She patted her long blonde hair into place and restored the makeup on her lips.

Brenan slipped into his jacket. He said, "Excuse me, Valija, if I don't stay for high tea. I must pick something up from Moss Bros. in town before they close. It's very important; otherwise I wouldn't miss having tea with you for the world.

"Thank you for everything, for letting me come to see you this afternoon, for putting my mind at rest about—well, you know about what. Thank you for the *cattleya*." He was trying to be nice. He had moved to the door and taken the handle in his hand.

From the mirror, she turned on him, suddenly infuriated, her face a mask of pain. "What do you *mean*, you won't stay for high tea? Where on earth do you have to go that you need new clothes for tonight? I was sure you would stay to tea. I put your name down as my guest. How can you do this? Is it because of what I told you? Oh, I can't bear it! I can't bear to lose *everything*!"

To his further astonishment, in this sudden fit of passion, she flung herself full length on the floor, toes drumming on the boards, fists beating on the carpet, and moaning, "Oh, oh, oh, if only I could do it! If only I could make myself do it! If only I liked it!"

She had gone—the nymph departed—into some agonized tantrum or trance all of her own. He for the moment—the sad shepherd—was completely forgotten, abandoned. So this was the stormy sea of love, the wind tossing the waves, lifting you high before letting you fall back into the depths. He felt ashamed. He felt useless. His impulse was to try to comfort her once more but, all things considered, it was probably better simply to leave and do whatever he could for her another time. He was hopelessly out of his depth here.

On the bus into town just before the shops closed, he felt in the pocket of his jacket and found the small box of chocolates safe in its crisp white paper bag—Black Magic, one quarter lb. only—bought, with all the coupons he could rustle up, to give Valija, but forgotten in the moment of visiting. Now he visualized her accepting them from him, saying (if only he had thought to offer them on arrival) "Oh, Michael, you shouldn't, you really shouldn't. *All that rationing allows* . . . . I am not Marianne, you know, to be won over by the right kind of sweets."

"Don't you believe it," he mouthed miserably, as his bus

ground on past Our Lady of Grace, past Tyrrell and Greene's, towards Moss Bros. The Black Magic must have gone soft by now anyway.

iii

> *[S]eldom can it happen that something*
> *is not a little disguised, or a little mistaken.*
>
> ~Austen

Garas was waiting in the Hillman near the west gate when Brenan slipped out of Somersby at eight-thirty, his leaving unremarked he hoped, his evening clothes concealed under his trench coat. He never wore a hat—did not own one. He carried nothing. Dinner in the refectory had been uneventful. He had managed to avoid sitting with Al Yates, who had come to table already resplendent in black tie under his robe. No one Brenan sat with so much as mentioned the big show that was looming over his day's end. At high table, Huby had for once seemed mercifully oblivious of him.

The South Stonham evening was, as so often, spring or fall, dank. Leaves hanging on the trees—and there were still many—dripped moisture. No bird sang. The sky threatened yet more rain. Debonair in homburg and dark topcoat, Garas reached across from the driver's seat and swung the near door open, the engine running. "Up the line," he said by way of greeting, "but not to death. Not this time. Let me make a few matters clear to you, while we drop up to dear old Blechynden on the bluffs."

"I've a few things of my own to report," said Brenan, settling uneasily into the death seat.

"Fire away then. There's a .32 in the glove compartment there for you to carry. You'll see it's holstered as well as loaded. I suggest you strap it to your right leg under the trouser and practice quickly pulling it out while we drive and talk. Please, do nothing with it that I wouldn't do." Together with the gun there was a small cardboard box of extra ammunition, which Brenan put away in his dinner jacket pocket.

"Thanks." What, he wondered, has become of Arthur's notorious .38. Inherited by his next of kin, the half-sister who lives in Liverpool? "I went to see Valija Didelis in Highfield this afternoon. She was flabbergasted when I told her what happened in Somersby on Monday night—genuinely upset, or so it seemed to me. She talked as if she were quite unaware of any conspiracy. I didn't mention the Marshal, of course, and nor did she. I learned nothing about him except that she seems to know rather less about what is going on than even I do."

"I trust you took every advantage of your superior position. It is a rare opportunity when the woman one is involved with knows too little rather than too much."

"She did leave me with the impression that I'd given her some very painful thinking, or re-thinking, to do; and I suppose I had."

"It will be instructive to see how she carries things off tonight."

"We said nothing about the suggested telephone call to her uncle in Norfolk. So when I came back to Somersby, I tried the number she gave me on Tuesday and asked if I could speak to him. Who do you suppose answered? Rawlings. He couldn't help me, needless to say, since the good doctor was on the road and not expected there at Theobalds until tomorrow. But he took my name and number and said he would let Didelis know I had phoned. All very ordinary, if highly mannered. However, it must mean that Rawlings himself won't be up here tonight at the reception."

"Good. One down, too many still to go. Unless he is arriving later with the gang and the Marshal."

"Yes. It also occurs to me that not all four of the gang may be needed to handle the Marshal's delivery in the van. We may have only two of them to deal with at the bunker."

"Maybe." The Colonel looked thoughtful. "Where is your friend who was with you at the Fox and later at the Hospital on Friday night?"

"Well on his way to Aden in an oil tanker, as far as I know. He wasn't persuaded that to be in England now is more helpful than to be at sea."

"'How can I help England,' eh? We could use him tonight, whether for England or not. Those Scots are always the best in a scrimmage."

"By the way, Colonel, I've been turning over your account of what we're trying to throw a spanner into tonight. I can buy everything you say about the Marshal's return except one. Suppose we were to fail and the operation were to go forward according to plan. The real Marshal wakes up tomorrow or early Friday on the *Dolphynas* or back in Gdainys and he realizes what has been done to him. He orders his bodyguards to seize the captain and first officer and force them to tell the world . . ."

"That he's been made a fool of, politically? Wouldn't Uncle Joe lick his chops to hear that? My dear boy, again you raise a question which it is fruitless to speculate about. God knows just how the captain and first officer would manage the Marshal's return to consciousness, his disembarcation, his resumption of office. God knows whether or not he will find his wife and bodyguards and inner party waiting for him in Gdainys anyway. Whatever he does, whatever we do for him, the die has been cast. Power has already changed hands. All we can try to do for him is to begin his return and his exoneration here in England tonight."

All along the rising way from Somersby to the bunker, Garas regaled Brenan with the fruits of a day's reconnaissance. He had come across a little used secondary approach to the bunker from further up the Blechynden Road leading down through woods to an indoor garage at the rear. This, he guessed, would be where the gang delivered the Marshal, probably at some time between ten and eleven. He would be carried up a stair directly from the garage to a bedroom above. There the play actor would be waiting, no longer feigning drunkenness and quite ready to make his further exit with the gang in the green Austin. The Marshal would be left lying on the bed, sodden with drink, soon to be helped back aboard the *Dolphynas* by his captain and first officer.

"The number of those privy to all that will be going on," Garas said, "is bound to be minimal. I can't see why Rawlings, the brother-in-law, won't be needed to lend a hand. His absence means that Templeton will have to supervise at the rear of the house, while his wife sees the rest of the guests off at the front. They will be mostly gown rather than town—your mob—the mayor and corporation had their moment last night. The keeling over of the guest of honour and his retiring to a bedroom will be a signal for the other guests to go, embarrassed at the great man's having made such a spectacle of himself. But what can one expect of a Communist Slav anyway?"

"Where will the police be while the VC's subterfuge is taking place?"

What police there were at the bunker, Garas supposed, would be deployed sparsely at the front and north side where everyone, including the play actor in a Rolls Royce (courtesy of his worship the mayor), would arrive and park before entering. In the north drive, east of the breakfast room windows and the kitchen area, a barrier had been set up to discourage any further incursion. So far as the guests went, the empty indoor garage and rear approach were beyond bounds. The Templetons' own car, a Riley, had been parked on the north side, at the barrier, where it stood blocking the way round to the east. Templeton would no doubt have seen to it that this whole eastern approach to the house was no concern of the police in their duties tonight.

Passing the main gate, which stood open, Garas and Brenan saw no sign of the reception, no gate-keeping constable, no late-arriving guest. There was no sound of hospitality from up the long winding drive. They would be the latest guests to arrive before the prisoner of Merewell himself unwittingly consummated the charade. According to Garas, it was being staged in two continuous acts: first, a formal dinner party for the select few, including the false Marshal; then, towards nine, the reception proper, when the many others invited would arrive for refreshments, to mingle and to meet the great man before he sailed.

"Quite the *domaine* Templeton has here," said Garas, as it were enviously. "There must be four acres of woodland, and the house itself is much roomier than at first appears. The layout is the work of some German designer now in California. Nine units of living space, all clustered round a central foyer—they can be opened out into larger spaces by sliding the inner walls. It's as much French as German in feeling. You say he saw you in his study on Monday. This would be unit four on the southwest corner. Tonight it will probably be opened out to form part of the reception area with units three and two plus the central core and the breakfast room on the north side."

"Some of those walls must have been open when I was there on Monday, including the one between the drawing and dining room. That was where the great effect of space within a quite small building came from. Now that I think of it, I could see right across to where staircases went up to a mezzanine."

"No doubt. The Vice Chancellery is a most ingenious little box of tricks. Tonight, I imagine the guests will settle down in groups here and there, one of them around the play actor, though the idea is no doubt a continuous *va et vient*. When the play actor retires to a bedroom, it will be up onto that mezzanine at the rear, above and beyond the main floor. You'll have to shadow him and I, let's hope, will already be within reach of the Marshal himself, once he's arrived. Imagine our all coming together at his bedside and you and me taking over at gunpoint. We'll march them back out to the mezzanine, making whoever carried the play actor carry the Marshal, and present them to the departing company—especially to the police, the Chief Constable, and Colonel Seton of the county yeomanry. I've asked a newspaperman I know from the *Guardian* to try to be in at this finale."

"I should think Inspector Vaughan will be putting in an

appearance too," said Brenan, "whether by invitation or not. The question is, whose side will he take?"

"As with most of these covert actions," said Garas, "you can count on nothing happening quite as expected. We shall have to wait and see. But let's be sure about one thing. Once I have got you in and circulating, we must work like a doubles team, apart but always aware of where the other is. You must stay close to the play actor until he makes his move and then move with him. I shall be keeping an eye on Templeton at all times, waiting for the Marshal to be delivered. We are gate crashing from the rear, by way of the garage. We won't go upstairs but filter into the party along the kitchen corridor. This also leads to a downstairs loo. Behave just as if you were one of the invited. Try to enjoy the occasion, but drink nothing alcoholic. There will be some people you know and like among those present, including *panelë Didelyte*."

"If you were posting your best man to keep an eye on things," said Brenan, "where would you put him?"

"There's a skylight over the central hall in front of the mezzanine, where the roof rises over the upper floor. Looking down, one could see much of what goes on—though not in the bedrooms, of course, and not at the rear of the house where we shall arrive."

Then they were there, turning off into the woods, quietly dropping down the leafy ride out of gear and leaving the car parked under low-growing branches as soon as the house itself came into view. "Take your mac off and put it in the car," said Garas, tossing his own hat and topcoat onto the back seat. "We don't want to look like the late arrivals we are." Rain had held off but night was falling. Houselight and a faint hum of festivity came across the dusky service area and into the trees. In this quarter, nobody seemed to be about. All the guests' cars were out of sight, parked round the other side. The garden terrace to the south was deserted, though splashed with light from the paneled windows of the dining room.

Garas, nodding encouragement, led the way towards the garage door which was open.

Elizabeth, Lady Templeton, opened the kitchen door and, followed by an older woman, stept out into the corridor— almost into his arms. "Why, Colonel Garas, you *have* managed to join us after all! I'm so glad. Mark seemed to be sure you were out of the country. Mother, you remember Vytautas Garas. He gave the talk at the embassy last year on Miçkiewicz, his *Pan Tadeusz* in English translation."

She found it a chore to be entertaining her mother and her friends and the college people—almost as tiresome as having to sit next to the mayor and aldermen's wives last night at the Audit House. Tonight was a deliberately dull affair she had had to lay on for Mark. None of the county people, the Auldcasters and their set, could be here, only the Setons and the Wynn Hargreaves, for God's sake. The Great Man himself was turning out to be rather a bore after all his previous notice, giving most of his attention to getting squiffed. However, one could take quite a fancy to the young Didelis woman, very neat in her crimson taffeta party frock, clever as a cartload of monkeys, and talented into the bargain. And now, here was old Garas from the embassy, an unanticipated pleasure; she had always hoped to run into him again, not very Baltic at all, really.

"And your daughter, madame," Garas was saying gallantly to her mother, not taking his eyes off his hostess, "gave the finest recital of *dainos* I have yet to hear in England."

"*Labas vakaras, pulkininkai,*" she murmured indulgently, giving him her hand while her mother just stared. In his out of fashion cut of dinner jacket and with his fine head of silvery hair, the old boy was a charmer and, for all her superiority, Lady Templeton could on occasion be induced to purr. "And tonight we have Dr. Didelis' niece Valija here who knows your old songs and dances as well as anyone could wish."

Her sublime gaze settled on Brenan, who stood rigid at his

protector's shoulder, a decent figure thanks to Moss Bros. "Now, *you* are a familiar face, too, one of my husband's young men, but I'm afraid I don't know your name. Let me introduce you to my mother, Freda Rawlings." To Brenan's dismay, it was Iron Jaws from the Peterborough train on Sunday night, now suitably dolled up for the party. What must she and Valija have made of one another at the dinner table? She eyed him disapprovingly, appearing not to make the connection at once as he did.

What had not been evident on Sunday was something a little *farouche* in her, under the waxen propriety, a certain disarray of coif and straying of the eye. Tonight he would never have guessed that she was the mum of a dish like Lady T. From now on he would have to look at his hostess somewhat differently, as he already did her husband, *unser Gastgeber*. And where, incidentally, among all the to-ing and fro-ing, was *he* to be discovered? Not an encounter Brenan looked forward to.

Garas and he made their polite noises of introduction as the four moved down the corridor towards the reception and its whirlpool of voices and faces. There can be nothing more frightening, as Borges says in his review of *Citizen Kane*, than a public assembly of persons, a party in a little palace, "a cordial atmosphere of frank and spontaneous friendship." This was the only corridor in the whole carefully calculated house, this "machine for living in," as Garas had at one point called it; and directly ahead of them, ineluctably, lay the seething, centreless labyrinth of reception.

A crowd of more than fifty was now intimately disposed about the Templetons' foyer and its adjacent rooms, under an oblong echoing skylight. Most of them, whether on their feet or seated in the occasional piece of straight furniture, either chattered or listened fixedly, glass in hand from which they drank or not, as seemed to them fit—none more freely than the marginal group standing at the empty fireplace around the unmistakable guest of honour, the only one there in military

dress. When Brenan first spotted him, he was holding his glass
up and laughing, about to drink. His two henchmen in dinner
jackets were discreet, unobtrusive, but very much at hand. He
had his small audience all before him, in the palm of his hand,
as the saying goes. But where was the VC?

"By the bye, Mr. Brenan," Lady Templeton was saying, as
if the thought might have struck her earlier—they were all
four poised on the brink of where her kitchen corridor became
her crowded foyer—"aren't you the one Miss Didelis was
talking to me about at dinner? Her uncle has been trying to get
in touch with you on Ben Jonson business. She seemed to think
that you, too, might be in Holt tomorrow, where we shall be at
my brother's. If you are, *do* come to lunch. The house is called
Theobalds; it's on the Sheringham road. We are all going to
hear a chamber recital afterwards at Merewell. You might care
to join us for that also. Valija is such a charming young woman;
she deserves some company of her own age."

Garas was looking amusedly at Brenan, and his hostess
noticed as much. "You, too, Colonel, of course," she said
kindly. Brenan and Garas both bowed their heads in polite
acceptance.

"My son Stephen and his eternal Ben Jonson business,"
said Iron Jaws gloomily to nobody in particular.

"We'll expect you both at midmorning then," said her
daughter unnecessarily.

Garas had been glancing interestedly about him, more at
the installation itself than at the preoccupied throng before
them. Under the dimly lighted mezzanine to his immediate
left, there on the other side of the generous if unlighted hearth,
the play actor was still in spate. As Garas watched, the elegant
figure of their host moved catlike across the mezzanine and
down the winding stair where he took a place among those
nearest his bibulous guest of honour. From where he had come
out of the shadows above the undarkened tumult of the foyer,
and now where he settled on the further edge of it, a pair of
uninvited latecomers being graciously received by his wife and

mother-in-law would not as yet have been at all obvious to him. Nobody else seemed to be noticing them either.

As a party, of whatever genre, this one was not of the kind at which guests are much diverted by seeing *who* has been bidden to come. Determined as they each might be to keep the feast that had to be kept, these motley guests could not dispel a certain air of *de rigueur* and *déjà vu*, of determination verging on the indifferent.

"Fascinating house you have, Lady Templeton," Garas said unctuously. "Such unusual design, even for the post-Bauhaus. It never offers quite the same aspect twice, does it, outside or in?"

"How kind of you to say so, Colonel. Yes, it is *interesting*. We worked it all out before the war, you know, with an architect Mark became friends with at Princeton during his year there. Would you care for a little tour, a few of the finer points?"

Garas said he would. It seemed that Brenan and her mother were not included in the invitation, but Lady Templeton did not immediately make off with the Colonel. "Our Richard," she said proudly, giving the name a German sound as in Wagner or Strauss, "of course wanted to *begin* with the double garage of all things. But we managed to get round him, thanks to the lay of the land. It's not as if he couldn't outdo himself on everything else—so *we* feel, at least."

Garas nodded, absorbed by her every word.

"It's the glimpse of the old harbour below the woods that everyone raves about. That is best seen from the little roof garden above Mark's study—but we can't go up there now. The view I love best is of the uplands through the woods from the breakfast room here, when the sun is rising. One can't see much now, the daylight having dropped, but let me at least draw the curtain for you."

She began moving with Garas towards the north windows, taking no further notice of her mother or Brenan. "Labour saving was our guiding light as well as integration of design. *Not* merely corner windows, as Mother likes to pretend. The whole house is built on a single concrete slab."

Her mother now moved distractedly onto the reception floor in their wake, leaving Brenan alone to his ill-considered devices. She was making for a trio of older women of her own stamp, quite unfamiliar to him, who had come to rest like migrant birds by the severe built-in furniture of the breakfast room. They stood there, looking about them, as if they might be waiting to be seated by one of several serving women busily crisscrossing the crowded foyer—a long wait, Brenan judged. Seeing her duly settled into this group at the eating nook— "Bridge Players" by Henry Moore?—he resolved to move forward before he became a liability.

Gritting his teeth, he began to unwind round the room, anticlockwise, keeping a sharp eye on the guest of honour until at last arriving in front of him, the play actor, and if all went well, in front of old Garas and our taciturn host, too. Above the babel, he could just hear Lady T over by the north windows saying ". . . hollow like the walls, and so allowing for central heating" and old Garas, ". . . wondered what you did up here when it rains and is bitterly cold; you have such high ceilings with this open floor plan . . . ." Most of the self-absorbed, highly articulate clusters of guests lying all before him comprised at least one face he could put a name to.

First of all, to his dismay, came Professor Brillingham, the Miltonic inquisitor, in close company with—surprisingly— young Dr. Anstruther in French, as well as Mrs. Brillingham and two very distinguished-looking couples yet to be identified. The talk must not have been going well for Brillingham, who really liked to lecture rather than converse, since he greeted Brenan's approach with unwonted *brio*.

"Why, if it isn't the umbrageous Mr. Brenan!" He glanced sidelong at the couples flanking him. "Let me introduce one of our several English Honours students, Michael Brenan, formerly of the Roan School, Greenwich." Then he murmured, as if these names were of even less concern to Brenan than his to them, "Sir James and Lady Wynn Hargreaves, Colonel and Mrs. Seton."

Would it help, Brenan thought, for you to know that I am unlawfully armed?

"What on earth do you mean, Horace," interjected Mrs. Brillingham noisily, "accusing our nice Mr. Brenan of *umbrage*?"

"Good to see you, Michael," said Dr. Anstruther, taking his hand unobtrusively and with a reassuring smile, while the Brillinghams went on with their little routine for the gentry's benefit. "I wondered if you would be here," he whispered. "How have you been?"

"*Umbra*, my dear. *Umbra*, not umbrage. Mr. Brenan *haunts* my department, rather as the young Andrew Marvell must have haunted Milton's at the Latin Office."

"Professor Brillingham," said the Chief Constable after a pause, "wherever did I get the idea that *umbra* means *un*invited guest?" He eyed Brenan kindly and with equanimity. Even in a dinner jacket, however, Sir James cut an alarmingly thuggish figure. His wife, on the other hand, *petite* and smiling, was pretty as paint. They were both in the postprandial mood of those chosen few at the reception who had dined with the guest of honour before the others, *hoi polloi*, arrived.

Taken aback as always by the total unamiability of the Brillinghams, Brenan would have liked to move on immediately. It was for him this sort of party—very peripatetic—except that Anstruther was that rare thing, a friend on the faculty, whom he had seen nothing of since before the long vac and whom he always missed seeing more of.

The Colonel of the Lincolns, a saturnine presence despite his lady's buxomness, now offhandedly delivered the Brillingham's punch line for them. "The Roman poet Horace, what? In the *Sermones* or the *Epistolae*. Uninvited guest as *umbra*." For some reason, as he said this, he looked meaningfully at Brenan rather than at the Chief Constable.

But Brenan, immersed in his own world of self, was not rising to the social moment. To him it was all a dream too bad to be believed. What am I *doing* here? Yet how many times, when drowsing over a book in the slip room at Heathdene, had he fancied himself here, in this very house, scintillating among the Templetons' guests, on such a night?

"On second thought, Mr. Brenan," said Professor Brillingham, "it's really no surprise that you're here, is it? Sir Marcus is the one member of my department whose tutorial questions you will always choose to answer—unless we give you no choice."

How bored with life you must be, Brenan thought, to be busy twitting me when you could be making time with our host there and the Hero of Gdainys himself—or at least his brilliant understudy. He glanced away over the troubled sea surface of the reception, looking forlornly for old Garas and Lady T. At a drinking of the stifling wave on this scale, one could never know how near or how far rescue actually was. Suddenly he found himself eye to eye with a guest who had just plunged away from the guest of honour's circle only to be washed up at once against himself of all people.

"Michael, my boy, well met! First splash I have been to in a long time where the guest of honour drinks harder than I do. These Balts know their business, let me tell you. This *starka* of theirs certainly separates the men from the boys. Where's your glass, man?" It was the ebullient, transatlantic Al Yates of Fulbright fame, apostle of Ezra Pound.

His voice then fell, as if he might be in some error. "Why, Dr. Anstruther, good evening to you, sir! You must pardon my frankness." He took no notice whatever of all the others in the group. "Will you forgive me if I snatch our Michael away? I need him to introduce me—none too soon either—to the ravishing Miss Valija Didelis over there. Having heard it from the horse's mouth, I want to listen to the distaff side."

"By all means, Mr. Yates, what better reason?" said Anstruther agreeably, turning back to the Chief Constable and Lady Wynn Hargreaves, who were still resolutely smiling.

"A sort of Melusine," Valija was saying in her quiet and knowledgeable way to the women she was with. Miss

Lightbody, Warden of Highfield, and Miss Pryce White, the Registrar of the College, being elders, were seated in two straight chairs, while about them were gathered, with Valija, Louise Prendergast, her friend the nice girl whose name Brenan could never remember, and one *bona fide* overseas student, Charalambos Menelaou from Greek Cyprus *via* Somersby Hall. Al Yates and Brenan came down on them, there by the entrance to the foyer, with the former blurting out, "What's a Melusine when she's at home?" in his recently acquired Huby voice.

She said nothing, but she fixed Brenan with her beaming smile, as if he were not to blame for the people who pick one up at parties; and the rest of the group turned to him in polite expectation. Valija was, as Lady T had noticed, even more striking as a blonde in crimson than in her usual black and white. There was still a certain flush on her, as during their afternoon *séance*, but now it was softly glazed like some bride's or ballerina's. Among these provincial ladies she stood out like the other Baltic guest, an exotic. He saw how tactically she had stationed herself, though not a guest of honour, at the other pole of the reception from the play actor.

"What a surprise to find *you* here, Mr. Brenan," she said evenly, after waiting in vain for him to speak first.

"Always a pleasure to be found by you, Valija. May I present Al Yates from DePauw University in Indiana who's living in Somersby this year on a Fulbright." Brenan made himself look all round the little circle of faces so as to exclude no one.

Valija took him up on this, saying, "How do you do, Mr. Yates" and introducing each of the others to him in order of seniority, including Hazel Cartwright, whose name Brenan was relieved to be reminded of. He had the feeling that Louise was regarding him, dinner-jacketed at last, with mingled emotions.

Al Yates stood his ground for these introductions, holding on for dear life to his half empty brandy glass. Beads of sweat pimpled his brow. Then he moved heavily over to Valija's side, displacing Lucky Menelaou, whom he already knew well enough from Somersby to impose upon. Lucky, the Kid from

Nicosia, as we called him, wore a quaint doublebreasted white dinner jacket which, with his immaculate head of crisp black hair, made him look rather like a band leader. Smiling his easy smile, he turned and joined Brenan in addressing the mesdames Pryce White and Lightbody, as was only proper. They were muttering nervously to one another as some women do when one of the men at a party shows signs of having drunk too much. These two at least had no glass in hand.

"... I hear Dr. Didelis of the Gdainys *Barocktheater*, the famous Jonsonian, is your uncle," Al Yates was braying to Valija. "What's more, he's in England right now. How come we don't have the pleasure of his company tonight?"

Brenan would have liked to hear Valija's *riposte*, but Miss Pryce White already had most of his attention. Her severe expression put him in mind of Lady T's mother, only it was much better focused.

"Such a great pity Dr. Lacy couldn't be here this evening," she said. "An historic moment for the College." Lucky Menelaou went on smiling sunnily.

"Dr. Lacy has great difficulty with the separation of church and state," Brenan heard himself saying. "It will be some time before a Communist Field Marshal lures him out after vespers."

"But Marshal Tievas," said Miss Lightbody, frowning, "is anglophile through and through, an old comrade of Sir Winston's and a distinguished alumnus." She sounded aggrieved. "By the way, everyone seems to be addressing him tonight, not as 'Marshal,' but as 'Mr. President.' He *is* the President of the Baltic States."

"Yes, I noticed—'*ponas Prezidente*' whenever possible, people reaching for an occasional Baltic expression when ordinarily they would use French. *A la guerre, comme à la guerre,* I suppose. Not one of Dr. Lacy's pastoral teachings, as it happens. He is far from prompt, you know, when it comes to rendering unto Caesar." Miss Lightbody and Miss Pryce White both looked a little abashed. Louise and Hazel looked aghast. Brenan decided to temporize. "As to representing the Somersby

SCR, Mr. Doyne *is* here somewhereabouts." He turned and looked over at the deans and college faculty who were clustered between him and the President. He saw Garas, no longer in the company of gracious Lady T, accepting a brandy glass from one of the serving women—no more than a length or so behind his host's turned back.

"So much the worse for Mr. Doyne," said Miss Pryce White in her most sybilline manner.

Hazel Cartwright, in a kind but hopeless try at raising the tone of things in this Highfield group before it was too late, wondered aloud how Michael was finding Dr. Croker's new lecture course on the *Ancrene Riwle*. "I saw you on Monday taking copious notes for once," she said coyly.

"Not easy to know where it's all leading, is it, Hazel?" he answered. He could hear Valija, a little to his left, beset by Al Yates, saying ". . . heartbreak there may be in the *Pisan Cantos*, but isn't coherence always the first casualty on any of Pound's expeditions . . . ?" "Excuse me," he said to the Highfield ladies as a group, "while I go and pay my respects to Mr. Doyne now," and he drifted away feeling a little like flotsam that no castaway had any use for.

This was the *oddest* of parties, if one looked at it as a party. No one save the guest of honour, his henchmen, and one or two mavericks like Al Yates or the subaltern in the Lincolns seemed to be drinking much, or eating. There was no open buffet or side bar for those—by far the majority—who had not been at dinner; but a handful of local women in aprons kept busy between foyer and kitchen serving such drinks or *canapés* as were asked for. Almost everyone seemed to be talking more or less nonstop, neatly balancing glass and/or napkin, without much caring to whom so long as he or she were in earshot. It was as if some apocalyptic news of which Brenan was unaware had been broadcast previously and was now being excitedly discussed.

Less intermingling of the various caucuses was going on than he had at first supposed. Yet this was still some sort of conference, in that every now and then a delegate or two would end up, if only briefly, at the presidential council under the mezzanine over on the right, where the great man in his nonchalance was the acknowledged focus of all, the impressed and the unimpressed. Was that not Brenan's own eventual destination? But not quite yet, thank goodness.

Meantime, nothing happened. No one was going anywhere. What everyone was politely waiting for, even the uninitiated majority, was the President's own exit—as, indeed, was Brenan himself. One should never reckon without the English sense of duty, of what *ought* to be done, a sense in which he normally was rather deficient. According to Garas' timetable they might have as much as an hour to kill before going into action. And already he had frittered away two opportunities to become safely enfolded for the time being with his hourkilling elders and betters. He could hear Brillingham as from afar, now busily maligning RB's "lurid poetry."

A nearby gathering of college deans, faculty, and their wives, together with some of the more formidable foreign students, Esterhaze, Du Planty, Bauer, here on the drawing and dining room fringe, was probably his last haven in the whole room. Even to the uncongenial Doyne, a doughty mathematician whom he hardly knew, it would never occur that he, Brenan, ought not to be there. Templeton had invited three deans in the President's honour, Science, Arts, and Engineering, and a professor or two in the Social Sciences. Having done their best with him at the dinner table, they could now in good conscience become engrossed in shop talk: trends in finals results, seeing that the college was soon to be a university; the upcoming annual presentation of the usual external London degrees in the Guild Hall; and so on.

After exchanging a dutiful word or two with Doyne—"Too bad Dr. Lacy couldn't be with us"—Brenan settled into seeming deeply interested in this deanly debate, standing still among virtual strangers, hanging on to every word, letting time go by, as it will even in purgatory. Before very long the professors of social science—not one of whom Offord had ever made personally known to him—steered the talk deftly from college affairs to national: how a new university might fare under the change of government which seemed imminent, now that nationalizing coal had flopped; and so on into less and less untroubled waters . . . .

By ten o'clock, however, he was more than ready to move on.

Then mercifully Garas came to fetch him into the presidential circle. "Same drill as we said," he murmured, "once the moment comes. Templeton is playing this very straight; we may as well play along." Gently, unobtrusively, avoiding people's eyes, they made their way through the foyer, Garas first, then Brenan. At one point Brenan paused and looked up through the indirect lighting and the dim skylight to the dark night sky beyond. On the instant, moving clouds parted and there was a little moonlight. At the top of the frame, a man in a trilby hat and a raincoat became visible, looking down, either grinning or grimacing—but only for the split second. It was Inspector Vaughan at last.

Arrived at the mezzanine, Brenan looked closely and with eager interest at the President, now sprawled at his ease in one of the Templetons' built-in sofas that framed the fireplace. Silver mane a little rumpled, truant lock fallen across the right eye, splendid pale gray uniform jacket unhooked at the neck, brandy glass in hand, eyes alert, he was enough like the fugitive in the hospital chapel either to confirm or to deny what Garas and Brenan believed about him—and not much like Joseph Conrad ca. 1907 at all, as Valija had once allowed. Behind him stood his stern but amiable captain and first officer, Ingraham and Frazier, pleasantly engaged in conversation with the Warden of Glen Eyre, Dr. Eileen Aitken, and one of her foreign students, a young Frenchwoman by the look of her. On the sofa facing him sat his hostess and Valija, and behind them stood his host, elegant, inscrutable as ever. The infinitesimal nod of recognition which Templeton gave Brenan when Garas presented him could have meant anything—except, of course, vulgar delight.

The President chuckled. "So this is your henchman, Colonel? He looks too young to be in any liberation movement except . . .—how do you say?—*Olsteriu.*" Valija said, "IRA." "Yes, Mr. Michael Brenan, I am glad to see you here. We sons of small nations have to look out for one another. I am an admirer of ancient peoples who . . . endure, and who remember their *dainos* . . . . *Kaip angliškai dainos?* Folklore?" This last was addressed to his hostess, who simply nodded encouragingly. His accent in English was harsh and only approximate, the words a little slurred by the *starka* he had put away, but he was entirely intelligible because he threw out whatever he said clearly like an actor. Brenan wondered if the decanter from which he was being served would prove on investigation to hold, not *starka* but some stage substitute.

"In a very old province of my country, where the dialect now is almost . . . outlandish, Samogitia, in the north, they have a saying about a young man called Michael who at night would turn into a wild bloodthirsty bear, *lokis*, preying on beautiful young women:

> *Miszka su Lokiu*
> *Abu du tokiu.*"

He looked at Valija, inviting her to translate, which she did:

> "Michael with Lokis
> Both are the same."

She looked enquiringly at Garas who responded at once with a quick laugh like a sigh. "Ah, *ponas Prezidente*, we must, as the saying goes, 'not expect too much of Samogitia.'"

"Like silly Suffolk here in England," added Brenan, unhelpfully.

The President finished his glass of *starka* with a flourish and, while it was replenished by the serving woman at hand, cried, "Where's your glass, Michael Brenan? We will toast your namesake the bear and my former colonel of spies." Glasses were found and filled; and a slightly bemused circle of old and new acquaintance, which now included Al Yates and Lucky Menelaou, complied with the guest of honour's wish. He said, "You were not always known as *Lokis*, were you, my dear colonel? When our great war of liberation was at its most desperate, my captains in the field knew you as *Kurgis*, the mole. Why? Because when your help was called for, there you would always be, underground, working for final victory."

If this was Didelis the play actor, Brenan thought, having tasted his first brandy of the evening, then "the good doctor," as Rawlings called him, was not only outdoing himself in performance but had really done his preparation too. What must Garas be thinking now? What Valija? As the group around the President settled after the toast, it at once became clear that he was only now getting into his partygoing stride.

"*Lokis* is not a folk tale that I . . . how do you say? . . . set much store by, Mr. Brenan. I doubt if there is anything similar in your Irish tradition. But my favourite is the tale of *Boudrys*. Tell me if in Ireland you have anything like this:

In pagan times, when the knights of Vilnius were at war in all three corners of the world, Russia, Germany, and Poland, old Boudrys called his three sons together in his castle courtyard. 'This year, my sons, I shall not go to the war,' he said, 'but you three shall each prove the valour of our line in a different foreign field. One of you shall go with Olgerd against Russia and bring back ermine skins, brocades, and many roubles, seized from the merchants of Novgorod. One of you shall follow Keystut against the Teutonic cross-bearers and bring back their precious amber, their cloths of rare sheen and colour, and their priests' vestments ornamented with rubies. And one of you shall cross the river Niemen with Skirghello into Poland and bring back, not the base tools of the ploughman, but lances, swords, and bucklers—and a beautiful young woman to be my daughter-in-law.

'For of all our captives, the women of Poland are the most beautiful and the most playful. Half a century ago, when I was young, I brought back across the Niemen a lovely captive woman who became my wife, your mother. Dead though she is, I never lay eyes on the other side of the hearth without seeing her.

'May the gods of Lithuania protect you all three.'

Here he paused, inclined his head to his hostess, her charming guest and, behind them, his host, and emptied his glass of *starka*. Brenan, looking round at Garas, wondered who, if anyone, knew where this new narrative turn in the order of things would lead.

Well, summer gave way to autumn; autumn gave way to winter; snow fell and the campaigners came home. In the midst of a heavy snowstorm, the first horseman appeared, a precious burden under his black felt cloak.

'Is that a sackful of roubles from Novgorod?' asked Boudrys.

'No, father. I have brought you a daughter-in-law from Poland.'

A second horseman appeared, out of the snowstorm, a precious burden under his black felt cloak.

'Is that a cargo of amber from the coastlands of Prussia?'

'No, father. I have brought you a daughter-in-law from Poland.'

When a third horseman appeared out of the snowstorm, sheltering a precious burden under his black felt cloak, old Boudrys had already begun calling for a feast in his castle hall and bidding his liege lords to three weddings in one.

A ripple of amusement ran through the listeners, who had increased in number while the President held forth. From a few of them, there came a shy patter of applause which obviously gratified him out of any proportion. But just before he came to the end of his tale, something had happened all but unnoticed by any but the initiates, Ingraham and Frazier, Garas and Brenan. A serving woman had come from the kitchen and whispered to Templeton where he stood behind his wife and Valija, and he had slipped away, as it might be to answer the telephone. Brenan watched Garas ease his way towards the kitchen in pursuit.

From the play actor, however, there came no signal that his own exit falling down drunk might be imminent. On the contrary, he came to his feet without staggering, set down his glass, murmured something for the ears of his hostess and Valija only—they nodded in agreement—and began moving out from the hearth into the foyer with his arms spread wide, shepherding the number of guests who had closed in to catch his telling of the folktale. When he came to centre stage, under the skylight, he stood and looked at the audience he had surrounded himself with. Only a very few of the dedicated fifty and more had so far slipped discreetly away from the reception. Meantime his hostess, having supervised the sliding back of the wall to her music room on the right of the mezzanine, sat down at a grand piano, and was showing Valija a book of music. Dr. Aitken joined them, sitting down by the pianist, ready to turn the pages as they were played.

Brenan found himself standing, astonished, at the foot of the lefthand staircase, not far from the kitchen corridor by which he and Garas had come in. Neither Garas nor Templeton was anywhere to be seen. Nor was Al Yates. But the boys from the Dolphin were both being visibly attentive to their lord and master from a tactful distance. It was obvious that this musical interlude had been previously agreed upon by the performers. Perhaps at dinner Lady Templeton in a moment of enthusiasm had said to her two Baltic guests, "Let us bring the evening to a close with a folk dance"; and her husband had seen no reason to demur.

"My English friends," began the President, waiting for silence, "my kind friends, before we part and my delightful . . . *pertrauka* in your fair city is over, let me give you by way of thanks and as a souvenir of friendship this relic, a little treasure from my own nation's past. Our hostess, Lady Templeton, an accomplished performer as you know of Lithuanian *dainos*, has graciously consented to play and *panelė Valija Didelyte* of Gdainys University to dance for us . . . the Lithuanian *russalka*.

"This is an ancient celebration of domestic union, often performed at village weddings." He drew himself up majestically, stamped his left foot, and clapped his hands with a sound like a whip. One of the serving women brought him his Prussian blue military cloak, which he flung about his shoulders. "*Russalka!*" he cried.

The piano burst out *allegro presto*, filling the foyer with melody. Valija moved as a dancer, now barefoot in scarlet, across the empty floor to where he stood swaying slightly. Three times she circled him. When there came a pause at the end of the introduction, she was standing with her back to his, facing east, and he west towards the mezzanine. The company was now hushed, curious, and concentrated on the two ill-matched figures posed under the skylight.

In her sulky alto, Valija announced, "A *russalka*, ladies and gentlemen, is a water nymph native to those deep black pools of water which beautify the forests of Lithuania. She rises from the very depths, wreathed in smiles, and captivates by her charm any journeying prince who should happen to behold her." As she spoke, the President and she both circled slowly, back to back, so that no part of their audience was not addressed. When they came to a stop she was now facing west and he east. She eased up her crimson party dress at the hips until her knees were free, saying, "To do this dance properly I should be wearing a full pleated peasant girl's skirt." Then the piano struck up once more, a kind of uncanny waltz, and she began to dance alluringly around her partner.

She did so lightsomely, showing that she had once been trained as a dancer and was still well-practised. Dancing seemed to come naturally to her; she was one of those born performers who, the moment they appear before any audience, take on a new and more graceful life of the body. The strange music, in her embodiment of it, became a vivid story.

The russalka *fascinates the prince by moving round him ever faster in one long crescendo and accelerando. He reaches out for her again and again, never moving his feet but swaying like some great-rooted tree in a storm. She always slips between his arms and beyond his reach until at last, with the music at its climax, he manages to embrace her. The music stops. He kisses her. She twists away, leaping in the air and striking him a fierce blow on the left shoulder. He falls lifeless. She watches him slip slowly into the pool of water at her feet.*

The President improvised what was evidently a slight variation on this traditional story. When he finally held the mischievous nymph in his arms, before she could escape, he kissed her only very chastely on the forehead. But Valija still uttered a sharp little cry, twisted away, and struck him fiercely over the heart. Among the onlookers there was appreciative laughter to be heard as the great man sank to his knees and fell prone at her feet. She briefly assumed a pose of conquest before dancing away to bring the pianist, Lady Templeton, out on to centre stage to be applauded. The President, shrouded in his blue cloak, remained for the moment prostrate.

Brenan felt his heart begin to beat wildly as he realized that this could be zero hour. On his right calf under the trouser the gun weighed like a clog. There was polite clapping of hands all around him. He saw Templeton, Ingraham, and Frazier hurry forward and kneel beside the fallen President. Templeton was speaking to him urgently, and the other two were helping him to his feet. Lady Templeton and Valija were joining them, and the polite clapping was increasing as the audience began to close in. The President raised his hand in acknowledgment, saying laughingly, "Nymphs of Lithuania are amazons."

Brenan looked anxiously about for Garas and found him suddenly at his elbow, having come down the stair from the darkened mezzanine. "It's no go the ambush, Michael," he growled. "The real Marshal won't be showing here tonight after all."

"What the devil? How do you know?"

"I've listened to our host receive the good news from his brother-in-law by phone. Not a happy moment. You see him over there now, having broken it breathlessly to the play actor and his henchmen. Does he look happy?"

"The VC never looks happy." Out at stage centre, the host and hostess were seeing off their guests, the great and the not so great, through the front hall which opened out of their foyer and into the blustery night by their narrow front door. It was one crowded, excited, occluded scene. In the whole vortex of it, Valija was invisible. The sound of car engines igniting and the beams of headlights began to come in from the northwest driveway.

"We should keep tabs on the play actor. Let's scarper through the music room now, and see if we can catch up with him just down the road. Chop, chop." Garas was as undismayed as ever.

No one seemed to notice them repair in haste to the southeast patio. As he went out into the darkness a little nearer than Garas to the foot of the spiral stair from the roof, Brenan stubbed his toe against something soft and heard a faint groan. Stopped in midstride, he peered down incredulously at the crumpled body and unseeing face of poor Al Yates. A second groan satisfied him—perhaps too easily—that the American was the worse, chiefly, for strong drink and he hurried on, horrified, along the path that Garas was taking back to his Hillman. Its engine was already running when Brenan fell into his seat and slammed the door.

"Tantivy," said Garas, backing out on to the steep ride and accelerating uphill before turning his lights on.

Down on the Town Quay, which was all but deserted, they sat in the parked Hillman under a cobbled archway and saw the presidential party safely delivered to the end of the Royal Pier, where the tiny launch from the *Dolphynas* waited bobbing in the waves. From nearby railway sidings came the desultory noise of night-time shunting. Between the bunker and here, there had been no conceivable occasion when the real Marshal could have been secretly restored and Didelis dispensed with. The harbour water was very choppy, but the tide was high and, as Garas and Brenan helplessly watched, the launch was inboarded, the anchor upped, and she sailed for the open sea.

When the police escort swept by on its way back to the Bargate, with a figure that looked rather like Inspector Vaughan slumped in the back seat of one of the two cars, Brenan said, "Did your man from the *Guardian* ever show, Colonel?" And when Garas did not reply, "I wonder if the VC is watching all this from his roof garden up there on the Blechynden heights."

"How did you like the party, Michael?"

"It reminded me of guard duty—only more dangerous."

"What we should both be thinking about now," said Garas severely, switching on the ignition, "is taking Lady Templeton up on her kind lunch invitation to Theobalds tomorrow, lunch with Dr. Didelis—and a *concertante* afterwards in Merewell." He glanced at his wristwatch. "It's nearly midnight. We can't go in these duds. I'll pick you up at, say, five-thirty near the west gate. You'd best hang on to that .32 for the time being.' 'Appy cum peachy?"

Brenan nodded, smiling.

And so, yet once more to Somersby and to bed.

End of Part Two

Part Three

Converging On The Sea

Over some wide-watered shore,
Swinging low with sullen roar

~Milton

Chapter Nine

Morning After

i

A muffled cry on the other side of silence
~ George Eliot

N ow suddenly she was awake, out of dormant
turmoil into momentary panic at not knowing where
she was. The mountain of crumpled eiderdown, the earthenware
hot water bottle gone cold, shadows everywhere, a family portrait
on the facing wall of some young soldier in Victorian dress uniform,
floorlength drapes sealing the windows at either end of the room—
everything huge, larger than life, heavy footed, yet very domestic
as in childhood . . . an empty fireplace with ornate marble mantel,
more than one plush armchair, armoires against the walls, a
consular desk under the far window, two walls of leathery
tomes . . . but no lavatory *en suite.*

She knew one was somewhere to be found through the

only door to this enormous room and well along the gallerylike corridor at the rear of the house. And didn't she also seem to know that right here at her bedside in this grand mahogany commode there stood—of all things—a well-scoured floral chamber pot? A Mrs. T—something quaint sounding and East Anglian—fresh complexion, sweet face, in a housekeeper's dress, had told her so, elfishly, the night before, on their arrival . . . Lady Templeton, Sir Marcus, herself, everyone worn out, sleepwalking, she cramped from being curled up in the back seat of the Riley.

The wall facing, with its chimney midway and no windows, was not an exterior wall, yet it had no connecting door to the next room either. On the other side, she now remembered, was the so-called west wing, semidetached except by way of the downstairs conservatory, an apartment where Mrs. Rawlings sometimes stayed—and on this occasion the Templetons themselves. "I'm going there now, through the wall," Lady Templeton had said. "Don't be frightened. Make yourself at home. I'll come and find you in time for breakfast. This is one of those rambling old places where every room feels like a fresh start. Call me 'Elizabeth,' why don't you, and I'll call you 'Valija.' *Schlaf gut, meine kind.*"

This was Theobalds, of course, Mr. Stephen Rawlings' place near Holt, where Uncle Jurgis should—all being well— arrive for lunch today. But all was not well. He wouldn't arrive here at all, would he? The little travel clock on the other huge bedside stand was her own. Here was the empty tumbler from which she had taken a draught before dropping off, knowing how troubled her sleep was going to be. Cold damp air moved through the dusky room in currents from window to window. It was not yet seven. She would snuggle down in her nest of high-piled bedclothes, letting the delirium she had washed about in all night sweep over her yet once more . . . in question after question after question—about Jurgis.

How could the man in Marshal's uniform at Blechynden

yesterday have been her uncle? He had not even looked very much like him—at first. She always thought of Jurgis as he had been on those summer holidays before the war at the old family farm in leafy Medentiltas, when she had been a schoolgirl and he, as yet unbearded, still youthful looking. Would her Jurgis, Mother's younger brother, her own last hope of family happiness, ever use her like this? . . . as part of some sordid conspiracy which he had never so much as hinted at in her hearing? If he would . . . then why leave the Templetons' in such a guilty last-minute rush without a word to her?

I simply do not understand, she burst out in English to the listening shadows. I simply do not understand *why?*

Who but Jurgis would have known he could count on her, at no notice at all, to dance the *Russalka* with him in front of fifty people? Lady Templeton certainly would not. Nor Marshal Tievas. Before his out-of-the-blue request at the dinner table, no such notion seemed to have been incubating in their hostess' mind. Only afterwards it became her own. *Improvizacija!* A musical interlude to carry everyone easily along and away. Lady Templeton's kind of thing.

What a catastrophe it could have become, too. Luck had been with them, the Marshal half seas over yet never putting a foot wrong. Or perhaps not really half seas over. Perhaps the *Russalka* had been his only way of at last taking her into his confidence, in public, just before sailing for Gdainys and God knew what consequence.

What on earth can Jurgis think he is going to accomplish in Baltija by parading as the Marshal?

In these dark days, what good does it do to wonder? Why feel betrayed when the scholar and man of the theatre once again unmasks himself as soldier and spy? The war is over; the war has come again, and this time in the guise of peace. Whatever Jurgis was up to, it smacked as always of melodrama. She could see him, in his armchair at the Bayswater flat, shaking his head and smiling on her in self-mockery, saying *"Tiek daug*

Shakespeare, *tiek daug* Sartre, *tiek daug* Orson Welles, *visa melodrama.*" He would expect her implicitly to trust him to provide. When she really needed to know that he was there for her, he would be. Then she would hear from him, but not before. And certainly not today in time for lunch.

What made her hope against hope that the *coup* he was part of was not *contra* the Marshal? Who was Tievas to her, after all, or she to Tievas? Let Jurgis have his way. Yet one knew that the world's leaders of all stripes, Churchill, Stalin, Tito, sometimes used a double in dangerous situations. Perhaps Jurgis was merely doubling *for* the Marshal. It didn't seem so likely given the most recent insurrections at home, but could one ever be sure what any news like that actually meant?

How curious Jurgis had never before struck her as resembling the great man in looks, beard or no beard. But the breadth of forehead, straight nose, firm chin, strength of feature—all must look much the same to an unfamiliar eye. To most English people, of course, one middleaged Balt in uniform would look and sound very much like another. She herself was one of the few people alive who could be confident that, in the flesh if not in reproduction, a certain face really was her uncle's. But last night, when the moment to decide came, how confident had she been?

What could she have said to him, then and there, anyway? My life, my lord, *stands in the level of your dreams?* Theatre enough already. Among the happy few who, in this case, would know a hawk from a handsaw were *die Zwergen*—devil-may-care Antanas, sinister Juozas, Uncle Tom Cobbleigh and all, and all. They would have to be part of whatever subversion was going on around Jurgis—not this very morning, perhaps, in mid-North Sea, and presumably nowhere near him in public until the impersonation was over. But sometime, somewhere.

At the Hospital in Greenwich last week, they had said never a word in her hearing about the Marshal. She had walked about like an innocent, suspecting nothing. Weren't they all supposed to be professional scholars busy in seminar, their curiosity reaching no further than their research, no matter what current affairs might signal? Even when Jurgis left on Friday, ostensibly for the Embassy, nothing had been said about the Visit. She had been their mascot only, their alibi if need be, their fool. They had their nerve.

She found her thoughts drifting away to, of all people, the shadowy Marschallin—as her not many admirers liked to call her—poor Birute, *ponia Tieviene,* somewhere back in Baltija. Would *she* not, if the occasion ever arose, recognize the given face and figure as, after all, not her husband's? . . . *What is it they do when they change us for others?*

A knock sounding on the only door was followed by the sweet face of the housekeeper saying, "Good morning, dear," and hoping she had been comfy in the night. "Her ladyship said you'd like coffee, not tea. I hope this is right." A crowded tray with pot, jug, bowl, and saucer and cup big as a basin was placed handily on top of the mahogany commode. The coffee smelt reassuring, deliciously French.

Valija smiled her thanks. So much for the night's dismay. The housekeeper did not draw the curtains but switched on the bedside lamp instead, as if it were not yet daylight outdoors. She said, "If there is anything you want, all you have to do is ask. Mrs. Tydeman is my name, you remember." Instead of disappearing at once, she went and stood by one of the armchairs at the fireplace.

Valija sat up in bed, thankful that she was wearing warm pyjamas, and poured herself *café au lait* while it was still warm. She noticed that the night before, when she had dropped her underthings into one of the bedside drawers, her stockings had been left draped over the plump back of the chair where Mrs. Tydeman was standing. *They also serve* . . . .

Ever so gently, Mrs. Tydeman smoothed the stockings with her skinny hand. "Long time since we saw silk at Theobalds," she said, "in stockings at least." When Valija said nothing, Mrs. Tydeman said, "Shouldn't have thought they were much to be seen anywhere anymore, specially not behind the Iron Curtain."

"They certainly are not. This is my last pair. You see how much mended they are. I keep them for high days and holidays only. My uncle, Dr. Didelis, when he could, liked to spoil me. Still does."

"Oh, 'the good Dr.,' as Mr. Stephen calls him. Yes, he'll be arriving in time for lunch." She went on smoothing the stockings. "Beautifully mended, I see. You didn't have that done hereabouts I'll be bound. You should be careful not to leave them out like this—even the ants love to get into them. You need a little satin bag."

"I have one, Mrs. Tydeman. I do have one, but we left Northfleet in rather a rush and I forgot to pack it."

"Never you mind, my dear. You'll be putting them on before we know it, won't you?" Her eyes took on a faraway look. "Miss Elizabeth used to wear silk stockings when she was a girl at school and the General was still with us. That was before the war. She would come home here in the dead of winter and, in the morning, I'd find her sleeping in her silk stockings with bedsocks on top."

While Valija sipped her coffee, which was delectable, Mrs. Tydeman moved about the room straightening things on surfaces such as the mantelshelf and tabletops until she arrived back at the door and was ready to slip through it. "I expect you miss having your mother or your big sister to keep an eye on you," she said, her hand on the handle.

Why do women of a certain age still tend to treat me as if I were not yet twenty-one, a little sister who needs spoiling? And not only English women? In Gdainys the landlady will start weeping if I sing to myself while tidying up the room. "Mrs. Tydeman, when the war was over, do you know, my mother was nowhere to be found; all the family but my uncle gone. Now I find it hard to remember her face."

"Oh, my word how sad! Not a photograph? No memento? How cruel life can be! The world's a huge thing." She lingered at the door looking for the bright side. "Her ladyship tells me you danced like an angel last night at her reception. I wish I could have been there to see you." When Valija only smiled in return, Mrs. Tydeman went on: "I'll have your bath drawn in no time, my dear. All that old geyser of ours needs is a knowing hand."

A knocking sounded at the draped bay window near where she stood, interrupting her and startling her guest. "Only the wind," she said matter-of-factly, "swinging the big sycamore about. *Wind in the morning, sailor's warning*. It'll be rough seas on the fishing run th' day.

"You come along as soon as you've done with your coffee and you'll find everything you need. Her ladyship wants to take you down to breakfast at seven-thirty."

At Theobalds breakfast is served in the long dining room to the right of the spacious foyer. In all the fireplaces coal fires smoke, yet the circulating air remains damp and cold. From the dining room buffet, on which breakfast awaits in chafing dish and warmer, one can see through the screen of slender pillars across the foyer to the drawing room and also up to the foursquare gallery with its central descending staircase. Since the remodeling in Queen Anne's time, the foyer has been open all the way to the second storey, where gallery, balustrade, and vertiginous candelabrum look severely down. The morning light at Theobalds, though welcome, is not a playful seaside light as in Northfleet.

Lady Templeton leads her guest to the buffet and then to the dining table, which is laid at the near end for four only. They eat like birds from plates half empty to begin with.

"Let's not wait for Mark. There's no telling when he'll be down—or my brother. He's managed to put my husband in the foulest of moods. I'm so glad you've taken a fling with the kedgeree—one of Mrs. T's specialities. Nothing would do, when we finally got to bed, but for Mark to go and rouse Stephen—to talk about the reception. Things Baltic mean so much to Mark. He tends not to realize *everyone* doesn't feel the same way as he and I do. Then Stephen kept him up for more of the night—going over today's agenda, of course.

"Do you know, I have yet to meet your famous uncle Jurgis—famous in Stephen's Ben Jonson book, anyway. I am so looking forward to seeing him."

"Is Mrs. Rawlings not here with you? It was such a pleasure to meet her at dinner last night."

"Aren't you kind to say so. No, she has a place of her own in Peterborough. She chose to go straight home and see to her dogs and cats and flowers. She's not much for books or politics; and she certainly doesn't care for chamber music.

"But I know you will enjoy meeting our three musicians— Stephen's trio from Aldeburgh. They should be here in time for lunch. The 'Sons of Boudrys' Mark and I are going to call them after hearing your President's story last night. They are three of a kind. You have never heard Haydn played so . . . *devotedly*—the Haydn Beethoven took lessons from."

"Yes, I can't wait to hear the concert, and to see the castle for the first time. Sir Marcus has so many fascinating interests: yesterday, host to Marshal Tievas; today, the first concert at Merewell since who knows when. Do you suppose Lord Byron ever had a taste for Haydn?"

"I wish I knew. He had pretty ordinary eighteenth century tastes under the rogue male manner, didn't he? We really owe this Haydn concert more to my brother than to my husband. But you're right, Mark does have more sides to him than one. When the government changes—as it will very soon, now—I shan't be at all surprised if Winston finds something else for him to try his hand at. Meantime, he seems content, writing and lecturing. It's Stephen who is the tearaway though. 'A fellow that lives in a windmill,' as Mark likes to say, '*without* his heart being lodged in a woman.' Don't you love Congreve? Best there is after *The Importance.*"

"Having heard of him so often from my uncle, I am very keen to meet Mr. Rawlings. It was such a disappointment not to see him at the reception."

"Yes, 'twas—specially when you made it so special by your dancing. I still don't know what it was that kept him, either here or in Cambridge.

"He certainly missed a great chance to meet the President, too. Isn't it curious how we seem to live in one another's pockets yet we all have different blind spots? Stephen has never met the President, who means so much to Mark, and Mark has never met your uncle, who means so much to Stephen. And I have never met your uncle, who means so much to you, and you have never met my brother. It's like a silk handkerchief time has got at."

"Yes, last night at the reception someone asked me why my uncle wasn't there and, though it had never occurred to me that he would be, I was hard put to say why not."

"He doesn't have anything at all to do with Northfleet, does he? Except through you, Valija.

The holes in our networks—yours or mine, I mean—mostly come about because the men in our lives *like* to keep each other guessing. It's the male thing—oneupmanship. Ever since the war Mark has been one of Winston's young men—he was on the phone to him only this morning, urgent as ever about something hush hush—yet Stephen, I know, has yet to be so much as introduced to the Old One.

"Happily, you and I have come to know one another in spite of them. I am so looking forward to our doing more together with your folksongs and dances. The President said last night that you have a fine contralto, as well as being a dancer."

"I wonder where Marshal Tievas can have heard that about me."

"These men in politics, my dear, have a way of picking up anything and everything in case it should come in useful. Their antennae are different from ours. My brother Stephen never ceases to . . . . By the way, speaking of your Embassy, I should tell you that I asked Colonel Garas and that young man who was with him to join us here today if they could. You did say your uncle would like to talk with him, didn't you?"

"I did. Thank you for remembering. His name is Brenan, Michael Brenan. I can't imagine what my uncle has in mind for him. Michael doesn't seem to know either."

"He's one of Mark's young men in Eng. Hons., isn't he? Rather a handful, I gather. Something gave me the impression that you and he—I don't know how you say it in Lithuanian—*vous vous entendent bien, tous les deux.*

"How did you come to look twice at him?"

"Oh, it was one of those happenstances. I saw a poem he had put in the student magazine. A few lines of it I just couldn't get out of my head; and I was foolish enough to tell him so."

"Ah, yes, it's one thing to be charmed by a poem and quite another to tell the poet so in person, isn't it? He's less likely to let go of *you* even than of his poem. That was my mistake with Mark. I loved him for a line he wrote when he was twenty."

"*The thing we know of but we do not know?*"

"How on earth did you guess?"

"Michael Brenan is always quoting it. But whatever is that . . . chanting coming from the gallery? It sounds like someone praying."

"Don't be alarmed. It's only Stephen, coming down to breakfast. When Mark and I are here, he likes to process about, singing that awful *Paternoster* of Auden's—just to get Mark's goat, or so he hopes. We've never given up the old religion, you know.

"I'll introduce you, and you can keep him company at breakfast. I'm afraid I must excuse myself. Mrs. T. needs my help desperately in arranging lunch."

ii

Sir, no man's enemy, forgiving all
But will his negative inversion, be prodigal:
Send us power and light . . . .

~Auden

And deliver us from my brother-in-law the magnifico, *his superior expectation, his frowning on your poor parasite Stephen.*

Ask him where in hell he gets off, blaming me for the cloddishness of henchmen—they were the good doctor's choice of an emergency room staff, not mine.

If Marcus had only made sure that they put paid to the right customer up there in Northfleet on Monday . . . and had seen to it that they didn't drag the Special Branch back here with them afterwards . . . then it wouldn't have mattered a damn whether the Marshal kicked the bucket yesterday or not.

He could just as well have been poured lifeless aboard the Dolphynas *last night, and his sad demise announced today at sea.*

Instead, here's my noble kinsman the Vice Chancellor at his temper's end over one corpse too many that nobody cares to discover—the friendless body of unburied man, *as he does not forbear to intimate.*

Where was he *when Gus Gilbert's boys picked up the scent in Northfleet and came sniffing round the castle? That's when this whole bloody contraption went off the rails.*

Marcus is in my *debt, though he'll never say so, for letting him know the worst at once—even if it was at the last minute—why should I be the one to dig the Great Man's grave, last night or today?*

Was it my fault that the Removers took till late evening to clean up after the fracas, *managing even so to overlook the* corpus delicti?

Is it not, sir, enough that on Tuesday in the wee hours, without anyone's being the wiser, not even Mrs. T, your servant saw Tweedledum and Tweedledee safely to earth here at Theobalds—still oblivious, of course, of having topped the wrong man?

He's the one Marcus ought to be settling the score with, that Cockney

Peeping Tom, not me: 'Od's my life, I'll have him . . . poisoned. Where does he eat?

What a blessing I was wise enough not to go back with those clods yesterday to face the music at Merewell!

Who were the casualties? Who drove away? This may be what Marcus cannot bear not to know, but you, sir, know that I can, very well.

Providence Strikes Again, *I tell him. When a* political *nonevent like this one fails to come off as planned, the only thing to do is act innocent, wait and see.*

Let the Old One's tragicomedy make its own sweet way, mysterious as ever, right to the bitter end.

> *Prohibit sharply the rehearsed response*
> *And gradually correct the coward's stance;*
> *Cover in time with beams those in retreat*
> *That, spotted, they turn though the reverse were great . . .*

Muscid, self-important, prophetic, the master of Theobalds makes his way singing boldly along the gallery from his bedroom, down the staircase, and into the dining room. Here he kisses his big sister good day, introduces himself to her beamish guest from Gdainys, and begins his breakfast.

"Now, darling, how did you sleep? Like a top I trust. Where's Marcus himself this ominous morning?"

"Ah, Stephen, the morning—dark and drear after all those fine days, I'm afraid."

"You don't mean you *know* it's going to rain on our picnic this *après-midi*? Tell me not now!"

"Marcus must be still at the telephone. You did keep him up till all hours, didn't you? What on earth did you say to him to put him in so filthy a mood? Now I want you to amuse Miss Didelis for me, please, while I go and see if he would like something on a tray. Then I must talk with Mrs. T about lunch."

"I am not in so angelic a mood myself as I might be, sister mine."

"You two begin your academic powwow while I'm gone, why don't you?"

"So we meet at last, Miss Didelis—or may I call you 'Valija'? The good doctor has spoken to me about you more than once. He should have been here by now, don't you think?"

"Mr. Rawlings, where do you suppose my uncle is coming from today? Since the start of term I have quite lost track of his movements. From our seminar in Greenwich he went off on one of those sudden tours of his and, for the moment, we lost touch."

"Haven't a clue, I must say. Weeks ago we made our plans to meet here today. That was when he proposed your joining us from Northfleet. The last I heard from him was in a cover note with his page proofs, posted in Greenwich during that seminar."

"It must be such a relief to you, Mr. Rawlings, to have copy ready for the printer at last."

"It is. It is. So you, too, Valija, are of the tribe of Ben? Your uncle gave me the impression that you'd be with him all the way through the editing of *Catiline His Conspiracy,* do your part in a pinch, what?"

"As amanuensis only. But, yes, it is some years now since I began doing assignments for him on the translation he made, you know, for the stage in Gdainys. Did you ever see a performance?"

"Can't say I did. Can't say I've ever set foot in sunny Gdainys—though it certainly seems to be where all the action is just now. Did you play a part on the boards? Sempronia, perhaps?"

"No, I'm afraid not. The company stayed true to precedent—it was all male."

"Of course; what could I be thinking of? Though your uncle seems to rate you so highly, I can see him dressing you as a boy just so that you could play a woman!

"By the way, in case he doesn't show up this morning for

some reason, will you sit in for him as editor of the new *Catiline?* We should move forward with the agenda at once, now that *The Silent Woman* is out of the way."

"I can certainly do that, if you wish. But is there any reason to think he won't be arriving at any minute?"

"Well, I expected him long before this—last night, in fact. Who knows *what* there is reason to think? We should get started as soon as we can anyway, good doctor or no good doctor. My sister's luncheon guests will be here before we know it—mine, too. By the way, what do you know about this Baltic colonel and his protégé, the undergraduate from Northfleet? Anything I should know?"

"They were Lady Templeton's guests at the reception last night. I know Michael Brenan quite well. Sir Marcus is his tutor. But what my uncle had in mind for him here I haven't the least idea."

"No reason to suppose that he wanted him sitting in on our Ben Jonson business anyway? One more of Elizabeth's causes, no doubt.

"Let me go and see if I can corner my brother-in-law for fifteen minutes of his valuable time. You must do your utmost to be reassuring in your uncle's absence. We're proceeding chronologically, as you know, which is why we got *The Case Is Altered* out of the way early rather than late. Now we are into the cream of the crop. I am hoping to talk Sir Marcus into taking on *Bartholomew Fair.* He is a quick study, and I am determined not to let this edition drag on like the New Shakespeare—poor old Dover Wilson still wondering thirty years after what Q would say. I have *The Alchemist* well in hand myself. Our question is, always, how do we upstage Herford and Simpson on any given day?"

"Mr. Rawlings, while you go for Sir Marcus, let me fetch a notebook from my room. My uncle will want a full account of everything that goes forward."

iii

Haunted by ill angels only

~Poe

She was clearer than ever by lunch time that Jurgis would not materialize here at Theobalds today, not in time for "preprandials," not at all on this particular occasion. After the short, prickly conference around the library table, after her hasty induction as co-editor of the New Cambridge Jonson, she felt she knew that neither Rawlings nor Sir Marcus seriously expected him to arrive. Indeed, they both seemed more than willing that she should be the one responsible to them, the one they were responsible for, should any question arise. Sir Marcus would make a final commitment to *Bartholomew Fair* when he had looked further into the textual situation. Otherwise, any progress to be made on *"His Conspiracy,"* as Rawlings called it, would be up to her . . . and, of course, Jurgis. She came away from the meeting with an absurd impression that, if anyone was in her uncle's confidence and would hear from him before long, it was she.

These were men she must never allow, under any circumstances, to take her up, never herself try to cultivate, even professionally. They were so finical in their own interests, and yet so bluntly uncaring of anyone else's. Either all business or all self-protective banter, they made her know what it was she loved in Jurgis, elusive as he could be—and even why she had looked twice at Michael Brenan. To be seen, really seen, to know that one is really seen, if only sometimes, makes all the difference between being alive and being nothing among men. The song of the ruthless is then for the present stilled.

Outdoors, through the gallery windows at the front, the light of day stood baffled by a shade of clouds. What little of the garden could be seen from this view lay inert beneath a shroud of autumn. Yet once more on her way from the enormous room, before turning down the stairs, she lingered awhile, looking first out at the dimness of the morning, then in at a bookshelf she had previously noted of Middle English editions and commentaries.

Here she found a marginalium that, listening on Monday to Dr. Croker's lecture about the *Ancrene Riwle*, she had promised herself to revisit:

> . . . *may yowe note manie wordes mere English wch nowe be forgotten and Inkehorne terms in their places / As* **Inwitt** *for Conscience / . . .* **Domelick** *for Iudiciall /* **Licamlick** *for Corporall /* **Dedelick** *for Mortall . . . .*

Downstairs, crossing the central floor at a good clip, Mrs. Tydeman answered a ringing at the front door. And who should be shown into the foyer with a flourish but Colonel Garas and Michael Brenan? The Colonel sported a suit of grey tweed and a tie with a dash of yellow to it, Michael a navy blazer she had never before seen him in. Last night in black tie, this morning in brass buttons, the butterfly was certainly coming out fast.

Both he and the Colonel looked eager for the fray. But what, for them in relation to Jurgis, Sir Marcus, or Rawlings, could the fray be? Something to do with Marshal Tievas and his safety, with Jurgis and his double dealing. Seeing Michael again—after, it seemed, so long—raised a question whether he could conceivably have been on police business at the Hospital that Friday, acting on some official inkling of the Marshal's abduction. On Monday, at the Dolphin, he could as well have been expecting to be bumped into by Inspector Vaughan as not.

Now it was Lady Templeton who glided from the dining room to welcome the newly arrived guests. Her easy laugh rang out while she was still hand to hand with the Colonel. This at once brought her brother from the dining room where, the long table having already been laid with gleaming white cloth, crystal and silver, Mrs. Tydeman and her girlish help were beginning to be busy between sideboard and kitchen. Rawlings came bearing what looked to be a glass of sherry; it was for his sister, and he stayed to introduce himself at some length to his guests. For several minutes straight he took self-satisfied charge of the conversation. Then he went back to the dining room, having asked, no doubt, what was to the Colonel's taste and to Michael's in the way of a drink before luncheon. Delicious smells had begun wafting from the kitchen and sideboard.

From where she listened at the east corner of the gallery it was impossible to catch what was said below in the foyer; Lady Templeton and the Colonel were rattling away together to Michael's obvious amusement. For the moment she allowed the book in her hand to reoccupy her attention

    ... *Ealderlick* for Principall / *Flugol* for Fugitive ....

Rawlings arrived back from the dining room with a drink for either guest; it looked like white wine for the Colonel and CampariSoda for Michael. Mrs. Tydeman also appeared, right on his heels, and with apologies she interrupted the hospitality. "The master" was needed at once, together with "her ladyship," to deal with some domestic emergency or other below stairs. Left to themselves, the Colonel and Michael turned nonchalantly away, glass in hand, as if to look out of the bay window at the garden.

She watched the Colonel make a murmured remark and saw Michael grimace. Together they poured their drinks neatly and in unison, but not quite unobserved, into the potted earth of an exuberant parlour palm.

She heard herself gasp; whether with amazement or fear she could not have said. Her hands holding the book trembled. Michael said something out of the corner of his mouth and clownishly patted himself on the right shin. He liked echoing his father; she could imagine his saying to Garas, mock sententiously, "Better two heads than one," or something of the kind. A likely pair, they now moved over from the window to the hearth, nursing their empty glasses and without so much as a glance up into the shadows of the steep gallery. Unimpressed, they stood together and contemplated a huge Victorian landscape in oils which badly needed cleaning.

"*Panele Didelyte*, are you finding what you are looking for?" It was the sleek, saturnine Sir Marcus on his way down to luncheon in the same dark brown gaberdine that he had worn at the library meeting. He always reminded her, somewhat improbably, of the beautiful young Benjamin Disraeli. This morning he had the close-shaven look of a man in command who has just been through a night of bombardment, a little less than his former self.

"Yes, I am. But it's not Ben Jonson, I'm afraid. My eye was caught by this Early English text because Dr. Croker mentioned it on Monday." She closed the book and reshelved it so that he could see the title on the spine.

"Ah, the linguistic angle. Always lying there in wait for us." He was being affable, taking notice of her kindly now in the requiescence of things. Were all his gnawing questions answered? "I think if I had it to go through again, *Beowulf* and all that, it would be this Cambridge man Chadwick who had my attention, bringing in Old Norse and the other Germanic cultures." He tapped a book which she had yet to read on the neighbouring shelf of Anglo-Saxon studies. "But he'd not be much help to you with *Catiline*, would he? Now that is a play I have never felt the . . . imaginative thrust of, never quite known what to make of as poetry, don't you know?" He was politely calling on her, as if in seminar, with a question.

"My uncle always says it's in the way Jonson conveys the fascination of pushing people about as if they were chess pieces, the practice of politics rendered as poetry. I think he's right."

"Hmm, more of the Machiavel as mask of the poet, the

Marlowe touch, eh? He was a hard case, Jonson, no doubt about that." There came a silence which finally she broke.

"Well, you will at least have his lighter side to deal with in *Bartholomew Fair*, if you so decide."

"Yes, I shall. I certainly shall. Let us go down together, Miss Didelis. Before we know it, Mrs. Tydeman will be beating her gong."

At table, when the host and his guests had seated themselves, there were four chairs empty. A certain zone or middle ground gaped between the two ends. "Not to worry," said Rawlings impishly, "our fiddlers three are never on time till they begin playing, and Jurgis we can count on to surface only when he sees fit. *Mangez, mangez!*"

Valija congratulated herself on being seated at Lady Templeton's left and not with Rawlings and Sir Marcus at the other end of the table as Michael was. She would be able to follow any conversation there as closely as she cared to. Looking at Michael two empty chairs away on his host's *right* hand—the Rawlings humour again?—she happened to catch his eye and received in response a neutral, perhaps wistful, smile. They had done no more than exchange a greeting when she had come down from the gallery with Sir Marcus.

She was a little surprised to find herself regarding Michael with what could only be termed indifference. *Or all the same as if he had not been.* It was Colonel Garas, this rather seedy fellow countryman right across from her, whom she was at present more curious to know what to make of. To have taken Michael, of all people, under his wing . . . *why*, in God's name? A less likely Paul and Timothy it would be hard to imagine. If the point of interest were something Michael had happened to see or know about Tievas and Jurgis, wouldn't a brief inquisition have sufficed? Why recruit him into the *BKZ*? How soon birds of prey had gathered against Jurgis and his purpose, whatever this might be.

The Colonel was continuing what seemed to be a serial exchange with Lady Templeton about the design of her house in Blechynden, now by comparison with Theobalds. "A very palimpsest of styles," he was saying unctuously. "A Jacobean redbrick manor, enlarged in both wings and at the back, converted to neo-classic in Queen Anne's time with the addition of a stucco facade and columns for the front door—and here indoors this elegant opening up of the reception area; so much unexpected height and depth—it is always interesting, don't you find, when some greatness of concept is confined within a smaller room? And then furnished in the late Victorian manner."

"You are most kind to say so, Colonel, as always. This time I feel that your Baltic flair for baroque is doing the talking. My brother Stephen has a standing joke about Theobalds: if anyone shows signs of being positive he will say owlishly, 'Not by Hawksmoor, you know.' This usually leads to a change of subject."

Mrs. Tydeman had placed a flask of white wine before both host and hostess. Now she placed a huge tureen of soup before Lady Templeton, who began ladling and passing plates of it down the table. It was a fragrant, steaming tomato bisque. Noticing that he himself had become the subject of his sister's conversation with Garas, Rawlings called out, "Colonel, be so good, will you, as to pour that Folle Branche for the ladies and yourself."

While filling the glasses as he was bidden, the Colonel murmured in a somewhat oracular manner, "There are moments of great luxury in the life of a secret agent." He glanced amusedly at Lady Templeton.

Still lending an ear to what was being said at this end of the table, Rawlings asked, "Whose *bon mot* is that, Colonel? It sounds as if it might be Willie Maugham's. But I can't say I remember where it comes from."

"I am not aware, sir," replied the Colonel, "that I was *quoting* anyone." Lady Templeton gave a little sigh of amusement whereupon all six settled down to the enjoyment of soup and

French bread. She then tried taking up the subject of Lithuanian folk motifs in Pushkin, but without much response.

Before long the one taking a marked interest in the Colonel, across the table from corner to corner, was Sir Marcus. Between the two of them some sort of *entendu*, if not *entente*, could immediately be felt; it was palpable, the old soldier coming to terms at lunch with the corrupt staff officer. While Rawlings carried on a desultory exchange with Michael about Redbrick *vs.* Oxbridge, the VC, as Michael liked to call him, though not to his face, quizzed the Colonel about their war in the Baltic.

Those who met Sir Marcus socially tended to be all too well aware that he had once been Churchill's chosen envoy to Tievas and subsequently had immortalized the partisans in print; and this awareness he was himself accustomed to take for granted. "In '43," he observed drily, "our paths never crossed, yours and mine."

The Colonel said, "No, not even here in England, not for the duration. When there's a war on, does the right hand ever know what the left hand is doing? Probably not." He smiled.

"There is always a war on," said Sir Marcus.

The Colonel inclined his head in acknowledgment. "In '41, when the R.A.F. dropped me into Courland, I went to earth in occupied Lithuania—as you heard the Marshal himself recalling last night in his own inimitable way."

Sir Marcus waited while the unspoken hung in the air and the Colonel went on. "Like Dr. Didelis, whom I very much hoped to meet here today, at last, I was not in the field with the partisans. I was part of a fifth column in occupied Baltija."

"You never saw forests deeper than those I was dropped into," said Sir Marcus pensively. "Nor marshes less traceable. You could lose a division in them and not know where to look for it."

"How right you are. A man or a woman would go in one month, and when he came out you might swear he was someone else. Even Tievas. Especially Tievas."

Sir Marcus smiled his wry, enigmatic smile. "Went in a

Communist organizer and came out Marshal of the people's army. A hero of our time."

"Yes, the war was such a wonderful transformer of persons. Look at Winston. He went from being a man in the wilderness to being the saviour of his country, practically overnight, thanks to the course of events."

"No good deed goes unrewarded, however. The British people caught up with him in '45 with a vengeance."

"I've always liked that story of the lady who was dining at the Savoy when she heard that Winston had been voted out of office. The only time I ever actually heard him speaking on the floor of the House—and he proved truly senatorial—he was praising the very design of the place for being so conducive to two-party government. But what the lady at the Savoy said on hearing the election results was 'Why, the *country* will never stand for it!'"

Sir Marcus broke into a little sighing laugh rather like his wife's. "There are few creatures more dangerous," he said, "than an Englishwoman who knows she is in the right—unless it be an American."

This time it was the Colonel who waited while Sir Marcus went on. "It's the Cousins, you know, that Attlee's government has been so careless about. They, and not the Soviets, are where the prevailing wind blows from. Winston, when he comes into his own again, will be clear about this."

"Well, it certainly does look as if he has a new lease on life. While Uncle Joe, the younger by several years, of course, seems to be losing the struggle with illness and death."

Where, a moment before, both Lady Templeton and Rawlings had been in voice at their respective ends of the table, there now came a random silence into which, whether by chance or not, the Colonel dropped his next question. "What do you make of it, Sir Marcus, this . . . *Russalka* of his with the Marshal these last few days—or Tievas' with him, perhaps I should say?"

For the instant, Valija found herself the unexpected focus

of all five pairs of eyes around the table—and for five different, though all unwarranted, reasons. But there was nothing material for her to say to what she knew was the question of the hour. Sitting on the fence—stuck on the fence, thanks to Jurgis— she could only look down in silence and spoon her soup.

Sir Marcus took his time to answer. He had the trick of wellbred nonchalance down perfectly. "Stalin has for some time been at that stage of life when he can trust no one's account of any situation but his own—his own presumption of it. Especially nothing that his intelligence services tell him, even when it happens to be the truth. Indeed, if it were not for the greed of *our* traitors, who importune him, he need never reconsider British policy again. He has always believed the best of Tievas and thought the very worst of Winston; that is all he knows and all he thinks 'he needs to know."

Valija fumed inwardly. "To Hell with them, and you, and your wisdom!" she wanted to cry out. "What's to become of Jurgis?"

"Tievas is a great survivor," Sir Marcus went on blandly. "What the truth is concerning his actual ambitions, who knows? But when he arrives home today or tomorrow, what will determine everything else for him is how well he manages his domestic troubles. Neither Stalin, nor Truman, nor Winston— let alone Attlee—wants the Tievas regime to collapse or the Baltic peoples to start killing one another during the interregnum."

The Colonel then raised the matter of the Marshal's "self-management" policy, *savivaldybe,* its great virtue in western eyes. But the last thing our host Rawlings seemed to want was the whole table to listen rapt while his enviable and subtle brother-in-law held forth at length about so eminent a matter. As it happened, everyone's soup plate was empty and ready to be cleared by Mrs. Tydeman's helper, while she herself brought on the poached salmon with a mayonnaise, the parsley potatoes, the julienned carrots.

Conversation about Tievas lapsed as suddenly as it had

broken out. Lady Templeton began again with the Colonel, newly broaching the whole matter of Haydn's invention of the quartet—"not that we are promised a *quartet* this afternoon, you realize." Down the table her brother declared open season on Michael, saying loudly, "Mr. Brenan, you mentioned just now that what had most to do with your going into English studies at Northfleet with Sir Marcus was your excitement over T.S. Eliot's poems. What do you make of his denouncing English studies as altogether without any proper educational value? In the new edition of *Selected Essays,* I mean."

Poor Michael! Now it was his turn to be the cynosure of neighbouring eyes. He put down his knife and fork and looked around the table sheepishly, his gaze coming to rest on the Colonel, who nodded amiably but almost imperceptibly. Michael was one of those young men who tend always to have an elder and better, whether absent or present, seeing him through. At this point it must have been confusing for him to have his tutor and his new mentor both present, and in opposition, while he was under fire from Rawlings.

It was Sir Marcus who, untypically, took occasion to butt in and sharpen the question for everyone. "My colleague at Northfleet in the Chair of English, Horace Brillingham, likes to preface his reports on the unpreparedness of entering students with an anecdote about you, Mr. Brenan, and your predilection for Eliot. It goes back before my own time at the College. Apparently when, like all new arrivals, you were asked to introduce yourself by writing an appreciation of your preferrred work of English literature, you wrote, not about *The Nun's Priest's Tale,* or *The Faerie Queene,* or *Hamlet,* or *Paradise Lost,* or even *Emma,* but about *The Waste Land*—a first class answer, by all accounts, but not quite what was called for."

Nobody laughed; but Michael said, blushing, "I must've just been reading that long explication by Cleanth Brooks." Then he began speaking to Rawlings' question. "My father wouldn't've minded if, after grammar school, I'd chosen to go into the navy or the army as a regular. In his own way he is as orthodox as Eliot. But my being surprised by poetry at sixteen, especially an exiled American's poetry—I'd started off with Browning—was pretty off-putting. Poetry is an undercover activity. Never not working. It can take up your whole life. It brings in all of tradition. So for the best part of every day you need to have an alibi. By the time I was eighteen I knew that my alibi would be *English Literature*, as Eliot so contemptuously italicizes it. For the next two years, I served my sentence to National Service, confirming, among other things, that it was unquestionably the contemplative life that I was cut out for.

"In that essay of Eliot's, if I remember right, he is busy laying down the best way to train young people in a Christian society. He dismisses the liberal arts—and the sciences—in favour of the Classics, Greek and Latin. I do find it moving when he says it's high time they were rescued from the public schools, from sentimental Toryism, etc., and restored to the cloister and the general curriculum of the laity where they truly belong. When he says this, you can just see his flashing eye and taste the milk of paradise!

"But for a reader, Eliot the poet is a very different kettle of fish from Eliot the essayist—*and* from the now successful West End playwright of the same name." [Here Lady Templeton snickered.] "This essay of his against the liberal arts in their modern form is a period piece from around 1932 when conservative Utopian visions were all the rage for communists and fascists as well as Christians. He even mentions *dictatorship*. I was only an infant at the time and can hardly imagine what being an adult in England then really felt like. Anyway, I am an Arcadian, not a Utopian. A little later, as a boy, I personally wouldn't 've minded if I had been compulsorily schooled by monks or friars in the *Oresteia* or the *Aeneid* in the original Greek and Latin instead of just doing *Treasure Island* and *Macbeth* with Mr. Clark and Miss Hards; nor would I have minded being deprived of Science, Civics, or History as such. The sheep would certainly have been separated from the goats even sooner than they were at Invicta Road Junior (Mixed) and Infant School in Greenwich and at the South East London Emergency Secondary School for Boys in Lewisham where I went when war broke out and I was given a scholarship.

"When in college I opted to do *Eng. Hons.*, none of the theorizing and systematizing that Eliot imputes to English studies meant a damn to me. That was just part of one's alibi as a secret agent of poetry, useful only in moments of crisis, the time of the taking of examinations, and so on. At Northfleet, I notice, those whom the institution really benefits—I mean the faculty—all tend to be secret agents of something; if not poetry, then personal politics, journalism, music."

When he said this, he did not pause to look at Rawlings or Sir Marcus in particular. He did not look at the Colonel. He did not miss a beat. "What matters most to me as a student of English is the wildness of a poem, its system of escape, its anarchy, not the use that can be made of it as doctrine, or for the improvement of society. Poems may be ancient or, like Eliot's own at the time of the Great War, very modern. They can be very mysterious. My favourites, like *The Waste Land*, certainly are mysterious. But you needn't think I came to college expecting someone like Professor Brillingham to *explain* them to me.

"I don't believe that Eliot wrote this piece denouncing English as an academic subject with the readership of his early poems in mind at all. Poetry precedes doctrine no less than existence does essence. He probably still can't conceive that his or anyone's poetry should be *explained*, as French schoolmasters think, or "understood," as the best American professors like to say. A poem does not mean but is; words go far beyond what they say . . . .

"Incidentally, as one of those English-speaking students of English Literature whom Eliot jeers at, I have wondered why he made such a point of the superior *difficulty* of mastering an ancient language like Greek or Latin. He must not have noticed what was going on in English studies along the lines of German philology when he was in college. What did he study at Harvard? Philosophy. That was before the present English curriculum had quite been made up at Oxford or Cambridge. Those who made it up, the academics Eliot is always so careful not to agree with, actually included two difficult ancient languages for students to master, Anglo-Saxon and Middle English. I think I may say, on the strength of two years at Northfleet, that Old English is not much easier to learn than Latin, even if Middle English is easier than Greek. The difference comes, of course, in what a reader can do with a knowledge of classical languages as opposed to archaic English. But if Eliot's reason for restoring the Classics really is that they are the languages of the historical Christian faith, then logically he ought to include *Beowulf* and *Ancrene Riwle* and all the rest of the early English anthology in his argument, oughtn't he?"

Around the table no one failed to take this question as rhetorical.

"My mother left her Suffolk village school at fourteen, in the year when Eliot was doing his thesis on Bradley at Oxford and working on *Prufrock*. But she would be in complete agreement with him that what is most worth studying, if you're going to study anything at all, is the language of the New Testament. Ironical? Certainly, her rule of discipline isn't much different from Eliot's in this instance: 'Don't do what I do; do what I tell you.'"

He looked at Rawlings. "Of course, at Cambridge this question hardly arises since you've hived off from English any so-called dead language." He looked down at his cooling salmon, picked up his knife and fork, and began eating.

So far as Valija knew, Michael had never before put together so many sentences, *viva voce*, at one time, on any topic. It was one of those rare occasions when everyone, including herself, had been ready to let him go on uninterrupted. She was impressed; but not enough to clap her hands even once, as the beaming Lady Templeton did when he fell silent. The Colonel and Sir Marcus simply went on with luncheon, looking justified.

Rawlings said, "Sir Marcus tells me that you have taken up being a Roman Catholic. Why not an Anglican if Eliot is your master?"

With his mouth full, Michael said, "Before Eliot's poems, it was the novels of Graham Greene that got to me, *The Power and the Glory*, *The Ministry of Fear*. My father was a cradle Roman before he lapsed."

"How do you like *The End of the Affair*, Mr. Brenan?" It was Lady Templeton calling down the table to him, under the influence, perhaps, of the Folle Branche . . . . And so the talk drew inconclusively on.

During the pudding, which was apricot tart and cream, a cheerful chaos broke in. The three musicians, Drake, Spalding, and Mather, finally arrived from Aldeburgh and had to be made much of, as well as wined and fed. Mrs. Tydeman came into her own again. She had put her helper to work in the kitchen washing up. Eventually the host proclaimed at the top of his voice that everyone would leave Theobalds for the castle, in the car in which he or she arrived, at a quarter to three sharp. Valija took this opportunity to slip away at once to her room and be alone with her thoughts, not so much of Michael or Garas or the Templetons or Rawlings and his fiddlers three as of Jurgis.

Chapter Ten

Deadlines Missed

i

Nat wote I wel wher that I flot or sink.
~Chaucer

While the Skagerrak was still well in the offing, the two torpedo boats flying the white ensign veered away to the southwest with their sirens whooping and made for Harwich and home. Today everyone was getting away with something. From the sheltered starboard companion-way outside his stateroom, where it was the Marshal's custom to walk and take the air, Dr. Jurgis Didelis lifted a gloved hand graciously in salute. He wondered if, through the flying spray, he were in the least visible to these departing English escorts.

Not to worry; either Ingraham or Frazier, whichever had the watch, was even now sounding from the bridge a sonorous farewell. The *Dolphynas* and all who sailed in her—all thirteen, not to put too fine a point on it—were soon solitary on this final troubled stretch of grey North Sea. Out of the west a rising wind slowly swept the late morning mist away. A curtain of cloud closed down the sky. According to reports, however, the big squall was still far behind.

Anyway, hadn't he his sea legs already? He knew he had. Long since. Watching one surging wave pour upon another, he knew that despite the Marshal's demise, things for him, from today onwards, would go on mending. They could have turned out catastrophic but they hadn't. Contrary to expectation, here he was dressed once again in marshal's uniform, with sea boots and tarp, afloat, strolling the spumy deck, exchanging a jovial word with those of the crew who happened to pass. He knew most of them by name now. *Water and the word.* She was a happy ship, a shipshape little sea fort. On course for Gdainys.

"You can do anything in the world, if you set your mind to it," his mother had used to say, a serious, devout, studious woman from Pomerania, more of a godmother to him than a mother.

It was unbelievable how right for him things felt, how auspicious. Who would have thought Tievas had so little time left? No longer "the Survivor" that people liked to call him. No longer the Baltic deputy. Here at sea and there on shore, already the few who knew he was dead were asking, "Does everyone need to know? Why can't the show go on as it is?" For at least a while.

Why not indeed? The proven stand-in for a famous leading man has been offered the part in a further run. It was not as if he had not studied it, in depth and from every angle, in Gdainys as well as London, with the help of English Intelligence and one or two Baltic generals of long acquaintance, Blaivas and Marcinkus. In times like this, it is always the army that counts.

Who in Gdainys *was* now close enough to the late Marshal to care much or know better when he arrived home a little . . . disoriented after his ill-judged *Englandreise?* Certainly no one who, with a nudge from Whitehall or Washington if need be, could not be managed. The Kremlin had always chosen to work its will from without rather than from within Baltija. Whereas, . . ."the place will be alive with our people, looking out for you," the Old One had said to him, not two hours before. "This time we will make good the failed initiative of '41." A born maker of the promisory speech.

After the morning's urgent signals from Sir Marcus and the shadow foreign secretary, he had begun to wonder whether some deep thinker in the English opposition had not, from the very first, entertained a hope of catastrophe—followed, of course, by this redemptive sequel: Tievas recast. Policy having been served, to the hilt, the prince reforms *in alia persona*, redeeming the time.

It was a fashion of thinking very much after his own—rough hewn, any shaping of ends being left to be provided later. England's international interest was served, obviously, but so was Baltija's, as a nation dependent on brutally strong personal government. Someone had to go on playing the President more persuasively than ever, someone less infirm of will, less complaisant than the aging Marshal, someone Whitehall and Washington knew they could trust *without* his joining NATO and enraging Josef Stalin, someone who could countermand his own syndicalists.

As to the dream of a bloodless *tentative* against Tievas, he did not feel it had been betrayed—certainly not by his English sponsors. In retrospect he could see that he and his little Department had been sucked in by Rawlings to a Tory plot fending off Tievas, embarrassing Labour, and facilitating some long term Washington plan for Jugo-Slavia. He and they, stewing in their own hatred of the Tievas regime, had been ripe for such use. Unlike Rawlings and Templeton, though, they had lacked on their side of the pond any means of exploiting the *coup*. In Gdainys there was no equivalent of a party led by Churchill and braced to take power. There were only, he figured, the disgruntled, factious, frightened remnants of Tievas' once-efficient monopoly of power. But now, with the presidency secretly vacant and a shadow president almost in place, Baltija was suddenly as well-served by the plot as England, if not better.

Had he his Department to thank for the turn things had taken? Sir Marcus seemed to think so. Was it accidental? Drauga was a deep one, capable of rigging any election. The four had taken a severe hit, according to Sir Marcus. Which of them all could he stand to lose? Let's say Drauga and Baltrus . . . ? Time would have to tell. He would know soon enough. For himself, he had never felt more . . . justified. The future beckoned. A landfall.

In a sense, his whole life had been a story of the sea, the North and Baltic. *Only in England, where men and the sea interpenetrate,* would a secret soldier, a landsman following his fortune, find it . . . even after putting to sea in flight. *Life will flow over a man's troubles; it will close upon a sorrow like the sea upon a dead body.* The stages of his faring rose and fell before him.

His father had been a colonel of hussars, a distinguished man to look at, milorded by innkeepers and country tradesmen on the strength of his appearance—killed quite early, unexpectedly, well before the war, while he, Jurgis, was first in Germany on his way to England. Thereafter, when trouble caught up with him, he rose to it, both abroad and at sea, as now.

It was the Reds, not the Nazis, who rooted out his sister Meilutė's family in Vilnius and Medentiltas, her Polish husband and their sons gone to the war, her daughters fugitive overnight. In anglophile Tartu, where he had first discovered English as a discipline, nothing of the Anglo-Baltic culture he loved was spared. Nothing. Escaping by coaster, he heard by chance of his sister's death and her daughter Valija's flight with poor Aldona to Berlin.

In Germany he, too, bided his time, serving more than one master, till the Reds surged back and, in a new Baltija, Tievas emerged. Then it was that he found his niche in the dock city of Gdainys, with Valija to care for, the university, the theatre to work in, and England to visit. Across the sea and up the river to London. Always by water. Phoenician. Byronic pirate. He smiled at himself.

He had never married, having been treated abominably by a woman he thought the world of, the impossible Irene. Little Valija then, own daughter of a sweet, clever sister, became like a daughter to him in Gdainys and London. "A good boy spoiled," the family used to say of her when she was twelve. He loved her to sing for him the folksongs of their homeland.

Whatever would befall him in this new venture, she at least was well provided for, ready to take a place in the university and, if need be, support herself. He had no cause to be troubled on her account. It was a pity he had not been ready to confide in her about his Tievas business. A woman's part in a political situation determined by men can never be enviable. At the Hospital and the College, her part had been *not* to know what was going on, to embody innocence. Would she have been any happier these last two weeks if she had known? Probably not. Sir Marcus said that she had been seeing a student of his who— incredible as it sounds—actually glimpsed Tievas captive in Greenwich! And the worst for her was yet to be, since there was no way to spare her the somewhat premature report of his own sad demise. A great pity. But, when the time came, they would sit together over tea or schnapps and talk, as so often, and he would explain and she understand. She understood so much without many words having to be spoken. What a joy to have seen her at the appearance in Northfleet last night, dancing as in the old days, rising easily to the baffling occasion. By her very way of being in the world, Valija *reassured* him.

This was not something he could say of the rest of her generation—"cold warriors," Ingraham called them, fellow travelers who had come along since the war. It was a conundrum, what they thought it meant to be a man or a woman and belong to a nation, let alone Christendom. The world had been transformed at least twice since he came into it half a century ago. Age sat lightly enough on him but his formative experiences already meant nothing to most of the younger generation. His achievements, such as they were, remained unnoted, largely ignored. He had no fame; and now this opening of a lifetime lay at his feet. Were he to plunge in, and survive, he could still hardly expect to be credited with success in his own person. The man who became someone else . . . .

Would he ever be risking this imposture in Gdainys if it were not for the backing of James Ingraham and Ian Frazier? These two had turned out to be the colleagues, the comrades, one dreamt of: frank, amiable, resourceful, imaginative, unselfengrossed. It was perhaps his greatest single good fortune, in a long life of ups and downs, to have fallen in with them aboard the *Dolphynas*, of all places. He supposed he had Sir Marcus—that cold fish—to thank for throwing the three of them together, him and these two, who hardly knew who Ben Jonson was. "One of Shakespeare's imitators, after the Restoration?" Ingraham had asked, when the name came up.

In their different ways, the forthright iron gray giant of a man and the reserved slender grizzled redhead, they had earned his respect, his gratitude, his liking—as far as liking can go in secret service—*and he theirs,* he felt sure. Once out of Northfleet and at sea, there had been no call for him to suspect them, *finger their packet and in fine withdraw,* as Hamlet rather improbably says. "Ian has called up Control and confirmed the wash out," Ingraham said. "We switch to Plan Zed and press on. Right?" He knew they liked the way his glance fell on them, candid and swift, the way *he* spoke. They had both responded to the peculiar something in his person, the *virtù,* which struck everyone who came in contact with him. "It's as though you were certain of having plenty of time for everything," Frazier had said to him during one of their several vivid unguarded sessions at the stateroom table; and Ingraham had grunted his agreement. "You will be an improvement." There was nothing they seemed to envy him, or begrudge, not even their service of a foreigner—which put them in no less danger than he was in. They were expert, each the good soldier, but without ambition or greed. A touch of the envy that is in all of us, perhaps. Whatever became of him, they would, if they survived, be well rewarded. Yet they were doing their damnedest in his behalf.

To be at sea with others in a good ship tended to simplify things. Ingraham, stern, testy at times, always fair or sensible in judgement, and Frazier, mild, wry, humorous, shrewd, knew how to work together. Ingraham captained her and commanded the Baltic crew irreproachably, while Frazier took care of signals and intelligence, as well as first officer's duties. Tievas had been foresighted enough to have the presidential yacht fitted with dual systems of communication, one for the ship and one for himself. Frazier had been his personal "Sparks." Such a precaution had proved most useful, especially during the last twelve hours when two exclusive conversations had had to be carried on simultaneously, one with the authorities in Gdainys, the other with his English sponsors. Both Ingraham and Frazier had scrupulously kept him in the picture, enabling him to make his risky decision to carry on as Tievas. He could never have come so far without them.

True, they had betrayed Tievas. But they had been put in place purposely to do so, and they knew why. *Thieves of mercy.* Since Tievas had been quite confidential with them, they made excellent coaches for the training of a stand-in. Once back in Baltija, they would accompany him ashore as body guard, with half their crew whose discipline could be counted on, and see him safely through his difficult initiation—or else face disaster with him. *My sad captains.*

The entry into Gdainys in the person of the Marshal was to be made at dusk with as little flourish as possible. The great man would materialize as suddenly as he had departed. By all accounts the city had been quieted, though it and the country were on edge. Suspense reigned. Instead of sailing into the old port where crowds would gather and demonstration be feasible, the *Dolphynas* would anchor at the outermost roadstead, remain there, and make ready for any emergency. Under cover of darkness, in a trio of Mercedes, the presidential party would sweep into the capital and enter his palace. In the aftermath of Tuesday's disturbances, the police and the army patrolled the streets. Restaurants, theatres, cinemas, shops were all open, even if more people than usual were staying at home with an ear to the radio, which told them little they did not know. The ministries, the inner party, functionaries were mostly in place, waiting and seeing—as had been the order of things for many years now under the Marshal's leadership, waiting for the other shoe to drop.

He was to make a broadcast speech to the people on Sunday morning, telling them what he had been doing for them abroad, making promises, conciliating as many different factions as he could, being his old heroic self. Then, on Monday, to a plenary session of the presidium in the state house, he would deliver a blunt but impressive—he thought, brilliantly turned—ultimatum, brief, fresh, and unignorable. By Tuesday the game would be afoot with a vengeance, and he would be either winning or losing, finding something of himself he had never before tapped or else collapsing into incapacity.

Ought he to have been warned by the fate of Jurgis Tievas and the failure of this *coup* in its original form? Was he in a parlous fix now that his escape from the role of President had been foiled? Was he being blind to what must occur? No recoupment but his own unmasking, interrogation, and death by slow punishment. He simply could not believe so. He felt— the men of the *Dolphynas*, they seemed to feel—that he had put on the old man's authority. Progress, the best of what Tievas had only promised, could be made, could be realized. Why should he be afraid? *For we see that the wise die also. Our indiscretion sometimes serves us well.*

Little Valija, Antsoras, Čiabuvis, and all, would come to understand eventually. Why not? After Gdainys, the other cities would listen to him. For how long? To what end? *Let us have conviction of things not seen.* On one of the presidential estates, up the coast beyond Palanga, the Marschallin, Birute, was still summering at her favourite resort, consoling herself, no doubt, with one or other of her several Cherubinos. She would not expect to see him there, arriving from the capital, until emergencies of state permitted. She would know how to possess herself in patience. He would know how to take advantage of her resentment in order to deceive her. Impudence would pay. If not, he always had under his jacket the Beretta carried ever since this jaunt began. And, if all else failed, the cyanide pill taped behind his scrotum and another in his navel.

At breakfast, Frazier had told a memorable tale about the power of mere impudence in a public official, a Machiavellian parable about a recent *coup* in one of the Balkan Cominform republics.

A strongly pro-Soviet Minister of the Interior and leader of the People's Party succeeded, merely by means of misinformation and masquerade, in disposing permanently of both of his political rivals and in discrediting the opposition party of Agrarian Socialists. The first of his victims was none other than the poisonous Minister of Propaganda; and the entire trick turned upon misrepresentation of persons and mistaken identity.

Taking advantage of a crypto-fascist plot against his own life, uncovered and infiltrated by his agents, the ingenious Minister of the Interior mounted a false charge of treason against his other victim, a much-respected, scrupulous old socialist. This proved feasible because one of the five plotters was the old socialist's disaffected only son who bore the same name as he, a name which cropped up on all the incriminating documents in the case. While a spectacular state trial of the innocent father was under way, the Minister brought off a perfect finesse.

He allowed a few of the plotters, including the old socialist's son, to elude arrest and to continue their attempt to assassinate him. However, he made sure that the Spandau which the old socialist's son would be aiming at him had a faulty firing-pin; whereas the other assassin, his infiltrator, would be firing, not at him, but at his enemy the Minister of Propaganda standing near him on the dais in the public square on Celebration Day. All went accordingly. The old socialist was convicted and hanged for his part in the Propaganda Minister's murder. The son and the infiltrator were both killed resisting arrest.

"Enough confidence in yourself," Frazier had said, "enough impudence, and you will get everywhere with the people."

Days like this aboard the *Dolphynas* gave him whatever confidence he might have lacked. In a few minutes eight bells would sound and Ingraham and Frazier come to the stateroom to join him once again around the polished mahogany table reflecting the bottle ensconced at its centre. One of the crew, young Petraitis from Kaunas, would serve them lunch. There was nothing he liked better than a brisk meeting of minds, with equals, at table. *Primus inter pares.*

This one would probably bring to light very little that he was not already aware of concerning the mission, the latest word about his arrival from radio news, what—if anything— the world's newspapers happened to be saying about Baltija today. For himself, he would rehearse with his shipmates every step they were prepared to take with him on shore. But this one, this stateroom meeting, would be more of a routine ritual than an agenda to be gone through, more of a confirmation.

The west wind had risen. He could hear it now singing wildly in the rigging. The vitality of such a ship as this in motion, breasting wave after wave, shuddering with effort and anticipation, the strong beat of the motor, the chorus of thumps, and creaks, and strains, and swishing from everywhere aboard—for him it did not, could not, consort with any fear of failure and death, any end of the tether, only with faring onwards, always forward, whatever lay in wait. To the east the coast of Jutland, beyond the opening shroud of mist, was not as yet even a visible smudge of darkness.

He thrust open the bulkhead in the companion hatchway and stepped into his stateroom, letting the bulkhead slam behind him and leaving wind and spray all outside.

ii

Littus ama, altum alii teneant
Hug the shore. Let others launch into the deep.

~Virgil

— Vaughan here, sir, calling from Holt again. I thought I'd
let you know how things stand at the castle this morning.
— Well, Vaughan, good morning. You know I am always
ready to listen, even to your afterthoughts. What have
you to add to your very . . . finite report of last night?
Was it not good news that the great man made his
getaway on time? You had your part in seeing him safely
on his way, I know.
— *So it was going to be another of those days. For one who had just
lost his son-in-law in the line of duty, Gus was unexpectedly
chipper.* Sir, Morgan and I shut up shop in Northfleet
early today and are headed south. I wanted to take one
more look round the castle once the Removers had been
and gone and before this afternoon's little get-together
there. Professor Didelis—I've still to catch up with
him—and his niece, who has been highly visible these
last few days, are both on the guest list.
— You left the castle yesterday morning, Vaughan, without
making a thorough search.
— On your orders, sir, I went straight back to Northfleet
to look out for the Marshal. But this morning here I
have turned up something nobody seems to have
noticed. On a pallet in one of the rooms around the
basement, in a dark corner—I'm not surprised the
Removers didn't get to it—a twenty-four-hours-dead
man in his sixties. Died of an overdose and organic failure
by the look of him, very ugly. It could be a lot of people.
But my bet would be that it's the Marshal. *With Gus, a
long pause usually means that you have scored a hit. But you can
never be sure.*

— Well done, Vaughan. You're definitely in the running. But this time again you're not going to get the prize. You can take my word for it, the dead man is Dr. Jurgis Didelis of the Baltic embassy, whom you've so been looking forward to meeting. How much of a beard does he have? What clothes is he wearing?

— By the look of him he could be any old tramp, run out of steam between two spikes. Nondescript trousers and shirt, battered piece of army blanket, not *much* beard, as far as one can tell, no personal effects at all—picked clean. I don't have to tell you by whom . . . . *Someone higher up has obviously got to Gus already today.*

— Vaughan, it goes without saying, we don't want the press to get wind of this until the last conceivable minute. You said two out of the four got away from you and Lloyd in the van. I'm expecting to have them picked up today, in Sunderland, where they are booked to skip the country. But you and Morgan I want to stay where you are and, after the concert, bring two of the guests back to town, Valija Didelis and (*he hesitated, as if checking a memo*) Michael Brenan. Put them up at the usual place. I want to see them here in my office tomorrow morning at nine.

— Right you are, sir. I think that can be arranged. Miss Didelis is an alien and a Balt. But what do we have against the Brenan boy?

— One of your Blackheath neighbours, eh, Vaughan? Nothing actionable. He knows too much, and I want to put the fear of God into him. But there's one thing more you must do this afternoon before you leave there. I have an MD arriving at the castle, together with an orderly and an undertaker. Your job is to get a signature on the death certificate from Miss Didelis as next of kin. Then the body can be removed and cremated *toute de suite* with her approval. Everything will be San Fairy Anne.

— Very good, sir. You'll hear from me this evening as usual.
— Click. Dial tone, very faint.

iii

Arcades ambo, id est, blackguards both
~Byron

Between Foulness on the Essex coast and the shorelands north of Ostend in Belgium (not the Ostend in Essex just north of the river Crouch) there used to be a very modest air ferry for tourists who had their own vehicle and were bound for a motoring holiday on the Continent . . . beginning perhaps in Bruges with the Van Eycks and the out-of-context Michelangelo, going on to new-gated Ypres and points south along the Old Front Line as far as Peronne, and then hopping over to Verdun and the Ardennes . . . . Two small landing strips left over from the second war, plus a decommissioned airborne vehicle transport, made driving over to the other side quite an option for the odd holiday maker who knew whom to contact, where to be, and when.

The ferry was little more than a one man operation, most informal—as, on this cloudy, windy Thursday in October, Baltrus and Drauga were much relieved to find. They had camped overnight in the Austin outside Chelmsford. Then, after abandoning some of their unneeded and more incriminating clobber, and making themselves look as presentable as they could, they drove to the airstrip while day was yet coming to be. A solitary, reserved, incurious Englishman saw their little van into the gaping nose of his aircraft with a minimum of formalities. Swinging up into his seat at the controls and coaxing the twin engines into life, he shouted, "Seats for you both up in the rear." He pointed to a side door. "No hostess this time, I'm sorry to say." Along the weathered fuselage the name Bertha was dimly but still legibly inscribed. As soon as his passengers had scrambled aboard and shut the door, he started off, bumping down the overgrown runway, and duly lifted her up into the mist as if he were just one more cross-Channel bus driver.

"God damned flying garage," Drauga muttered against the roar and clatter of the climb. Here he was, yet once more side by side with the egregious, careless Baltrus, belted into a spartan metal seat of more than military rigour, facing at absurdly close range a blank, grubby, shuddering partition. Nothing of sky, land, or sea was to be seen through the opaque porthole to the left behind his head. No other seat was fitted to the floor of the cramped compartment they were in; instead it was stacked almost solid with unlabeled, creaking wooden crates. Feeling the last of his hardheld composure ebb as airsickness began to threaten, he closed his eyes and exhaled shakily.

"Don't knock it," said Baltrus. "If Jurgis hadn't given us this alternative, where would we be right now? In bloody Sunderland, on the dock, walking the plank. The boys who got Ants and Šiauli are on to our Plan A by this time, you can be sure." He reached over casually with his right hand and jerked the Webley out of its holster under Drauga's jacket. He dropped it into a shallow tray fixed to the partition in front of them. A knife, made for throwing as well as stabbing with, appeared in his left hand, only to be placed beside the Webley. He now had Drauga's undivided if bilious attention. "We won't be needing these for the next half hour or so. Let's talk sensibly about ways and means."

On their dash out of Merewell the morning before, horrified at the sudden gunning down of their comrades, they had said next to nothing to one another. Scrambling out of the back of the van into the passenger seat as Drauga accelerated down the yellowing lanes, Baltrus had snarled, "You know where to head for," and Drauga had snapped back, "Essex." That was all; thereafter each had kept his thoughts to himself, brooding angrily over their defeats, watching and being watched like an enemy.

Drauga now scowled nervously at Baltrus. "Neither of us would care much to survive the other, I fancy, not for the time being at least." Looking about them, he sighed, the blackness of his eyes deeper than the fishpools of Hebron. "What price Plan Zed, then? *So the All-Giver were the All-Loving, too.* And Ants and Šiauli hadn't had to die."

"Jurgis? You blame *him*? Why, he didn't even want Tievas to die! Nobody dies in Jurgis' book. Even as we speak, he's on his way to the unthankful city of Gdainys— to do what? To provide, in the person of the Marshal, for you, for me, for everyone who will trust him."

In their flight through Chelmsford they had paused at the railway station to pick up the morning's newspapers. Not a word had they found in them, even in the stop press, about Tievas or his visit. His departure from Northfleet, as foretold, was evidently no longer news. The face of battle in Korea, where a contingent of the British army was deployed, loomed instead of his.

"We have no idea just where the *Dolphynas* may be headed. All we can presume, if you wish, is that officially she's still on course."

"Get real, Drauga! You and Ants let Tievas die in a damp cellar of over-sedation, yet you don't know what a prince like Jurgis is bound to do about it? Keep on playing his part, of course, right to the end."

Drauga sullenly reflected. "Tievas was nowhere near as fit as he looked when we picked him up in Greenwich. On Monday night he went into a coma without even being dosed; and he never came out of it. So, yes, Ants and I let him die, if you like—while you and Šiauli were on your jaunt, killing a witness whose death meant nothing to the mission. Let me tell you, the Special Branch or some such was at Merewell hours before you and Šiauli showed up from Northfleet. You didn't bring them back with you. They were on to us already."

"You'll be telling me next it wasn't Šiauli who forgot to bolt the stairwell cover."

"Those British sponsors of ours, Rawlings, Templeton, are not their own masters. They work against the powers that be, but they also have to be compliant. Don't think they aren't answerable to MI5 or the Special Branch or whomever, as well as to their own lot, the Tory shadow FO. You and I, Baltrus, like Ants and Šiauli, are expendable now—and probably have been from the beginning."

"*Happy are they*, Drauga, *who have not walked in the counsel of the wicked*. This is why, at this very moment, we are high-tailing it to Gdainys to make ourselves once again of service to Jurgis. In his new run as Tievas, he will be more than ever in need of men he can depend on. That snake Rawlings knows all our names and faces, but he may not know for quite a while, if ever, just which of us got away. He was trying to tell me the night before last at Theobalds that I had shot the wrong man and brought the SB back to the castle after me. Bastard! He makes it all up as he goes along."

"So you're trying to tell me now, Baltrus, that all we need to do to ensure a ripe old age is report back to Jurgis, our beloved patron, in Gdainys?"

"Who else? We want the British to believe we are the ones who died—which is why I gave our friendly pilot here the names of Ants and Šiauli. He said he thought there'd be four of us . . . One of the few things he did say . . . . We can leave their trail all the way from Belgium through Germany. That was another of Jurgis' brainwaves, to make our identity papers more or less interchangeable. Once across the border into Baltija, Ants and Šiauli can disappear without trace; and in Gdainys, at Jurgis' discretion, you and I can assume whatever identities seem fit."

Drauga said grudgingly, "You have a point. If there is anywhere that we know how to get to while staying out of sight, it is Gdainys. Instead of looking for safety half way round the world, why not find it at home under an alias?—in a nation small enough for Jurgis' British sponsors to have disposed of before breakfast today." He smiled sourly. "Why, you may even become reunited with the lovely Valija there in his service."

"Trust me, Drauga, this is the way for you to go too. Leave your losses behind. Find again whatever you didn't want to lose. I tell you, tonight we'll drink schnapps somewhere in Germany, and tomorrow night *starka* in Gdainys."

Their clumsy aircraft never climbed out of the cloudbank it was in. At times a swirling wind caused it to lurch sickeningly. Yet onward it lumbered, all the way across the viewless drink.

iv

Ask me no more, the moon may draw the sea
~Tennyson

Michael Brenan at Theobalds sat idly in the death seat of the Hillman, waiting for Garas to be done gossiping with Lady Templeton in the front portico and for the excursion to the castle to start out. Of the trio of cars parked around the drive the Riley, in the back seat of which Valija already sat, stood first in line and the musicians' black pre-war Daimler last. Rawlings had announced that he would bring up the rear in this, "among the other instruments of pleasure." He had added, meaningly, "You, Marcus, must lead us; you know the way." Neither he, nor the musicians, nor the VC had yet come out of the house.

It was two-forty, give or take a minute or two. The afternoon drizzled, confining one to some sheltered or interior space. Brenan lay back, sighing and seeking to relax. Not for the first time he adjusted the holster which was heavy upon his right shin. He reached within the blazer he wore and, hearing something crinkle, suddenly recalled that before leaving Somersby he had picked up a letter from his pigeon hole, a well-stuffed white envelope addressed in his mother's impatient hand.

The stamp was postmarked Tuesday. To slit the topmost fold neatly he used the first tooth of a little metal comb he carried. He extracted and read an enclosing sheet of inky, familiar, careworn scribble:

My dear boy,

Just a line to go along with this important-looking letter from your friend in America, which I expect you have been looking for in the mail. It seemed to me best not just to readdress the same envelope. I don't know why, I'm sure. I certainly shouldn't be wasting my ha'pence. But I want to be sure nothing goes astray—and to give you some word of us here at home as well.

Your father and I are managing well enough. We had a nice long letter from Patrick yesterday—all's well with him. He hopes to be home for Christmas. But, as you probably have heard from John by now, poor Mrs. Offord is back in hospital, very seriously ill, down at St. Alphege's on the lower road. You must give him our best wishes and sympathy next time you see him.

I hope you are keeping well and getting along with your studies. Try not to tax your brain too much. It seems such a long while till December when you will be back with us. I suppose you will work at the P.O. again this Christmas. The weather has broken at last. Overcast and rainy, it makes me want to stay indoors by the fire. Yesterday evening on the Home Service I heard a new serial begin, a proper thriller. You would have loved it. Can't think of the title (what has become of my memory?). One of those quotations, you know, from a well-known work. The usual thing.

Well, I must get along to the stores now and do my day's shopping, after I post this. Your father joins me in sending you our fondest love. Don't forget it's his birthday on the 17th, whatever you do. I shall be sending you a parcel of treats before long, as soon as I have got down to baking.

Your loving Mother.

Brenan could just see her in the old front room, by an as yet unlighted fire, plopped into her armchair with a notepad on her aproned lap, the open ink bottle upon her tea trolley, and a twopenny wooden pen with tin nib clenched in her pale right fist. Among her several counsels she would have liked to include "Read your Bible," but at twenty-two he was too far gone from her.

He took out the other letter enclosed with hers and saw by the writing on the envelope that—to his astonishment and delight—it was from Miss Hollis in far off Alabama. Again with care—why with care?—he found himself breaking the seal:

Sylacauga Friday 10/1/51

My dearest Michael,

It is months since you heard from me, or I from you, but not a day goes by that you are not in my thoughts and prayers. The moment has come for me to try to tell you what my feelings really are about you and me. I dearly hope that you still want to know and, when you have had time to reflect, that you will write and tell me all about your feelings.

What a joy just to be putting on paper again words which you will read—as I trust you will—with loving kindness. I miss very much our being together as we once were over there not six months ago. Please let me know as soon as you can all about your doings and thoughts day by day lately.

As you see, I am now living in Sylacauga, a city of about 25,000 people fifty miles from home. I am teaching Latin to the upper four grades of high school and rooming with a very nice widow, Mrs. Christian, who teaches piano. Sylacauga is prosperous, thanks to the big Avondale cotton mills, which are booming. I earn almost two hundred dollars a month, enough to live on and keep up the secondhand Plymouth which Daddy has financed for me. I hope to put away a little each month towards the cost of graduate study in English at the University of Alabama at Tuscaloosa next summer. Ah, Beowulf! *the* Metaphysicals! Joseph Conrad!

Each working day here I awake to the sound of my landlady's piano, a Chickering grand, being played by one or another of her aspiring young pupils. I fix my own breakfast, and I make it to the high school by eight. I do love teaching my classes: two in eighth grade English, one in seventh grade social studies, one in business math (frightening, isn't it?) and the one I mentioned in Latin, my favorite because it's a bit more of a challenge. Our textbook, Latin for Americans, *is excellent; it tries to make the world of the Romans live as well as show how important the roots of Latin words are for building English vocabulary. In the evening I eat dinner at a nearby boarding house run by two sisters, one—yes, really, the one who actually brings the plates to us at family style tables—by the name of Maggie Belle. (More in my next about the relevance to Southern living of Balzac's human comedy, especially Mme. Vautrin.)*

The high school staff meets in groups after school once a week to discuss teaching methods. You will be pleased to hear that the one I am responsible for discussing is your old love, the moving picture—though not in terms of montage *and* mise en scène! *I wonder sadly which masterpiece you are now seeing and loving all over again with someone else.* Night Mail? The 39 Steps? Orphée? The Third Man?

When you last heard from me, I was still in Montgomery, settling back into life at home after that marvelous year in England. My re-entry turned out to be very stressful. My parents, whom I was so delighted to be with once again, became most difficult to talk to about you and me and my hopes of our being together one day—as you and I have dreamed of being. Mother was not very explicit in her objections. She just withdrew and was more severe in manner about everything than she used to be. But Daddy, whenever I brought up the subject of you and me, would say terrible things such as, if I ever married a Roman Catholic, he could never again hold up his head in the Baptist Church. He is a deacon! You can imagine how desperate this sort of disagreement made me.

However, in the last week of August, when I was in the depths of despondency, and neither hearing from nor writing to you, my sister-in-law Peg rescued me. She invited me to go and stay with her and my brother Jim in New Orleans. He is finishing his medical residency at the V.A. hospital as the final part of his service in the U.S. Navy because the government paid for his education under the V-12 Program. You remember my telling you about his active service in Korea and Japan during the year Peg and I were seniors at Judson—alas not allowed to be roommates any longer "because she was a married woman." How terrified we were when he went in with the Inchon landing and Peg waited day after day for letters telling us he was safe. Only now do I have full sympathy for her fear that she might have lost him.

The first night in New Orleans, a Saturday, they took me out to dinner in the Garden District, the beautiful old residential section of New Orleans, to a place called Commander's Palace. It was, as you would say, "very posh"— air-conditioned even—and the food heavenly: first we had shrimp remoulade (shrimp on a bed of lettuce with a rather tart mayonnaise sauce), then turtle soup, steak, green salad, and potatoes you would have loved, browned but as if air has been blown into them. For dessert, all we could manage was sherbert with our coffee. You would have been on cloud nine—even without apple pie and "nary a sign" of custard on anything. Best of all, Peg and Jim and I all wished you could have been there with us. "Maybe next year," Jim said.

After dinner we drove out by Lake Ponchartrain where the air was a bit cooler. Surprisingly, we could ride with the windows down because the mosquitos weren't as bad as usual. I felt so happy thinking of you and how we might one day be together in New Orleans. Before I went to bed, Jim talked to me for the longest while, very kindly, about you and me and friends of his who are Roman Catholics,

*about interfaith marriages, and also about how English studies
are flourishing in the universities here since the war.*

*Peg and Jim make such a perfect pair of married lovers
in their sparsely furnished "nest" in Metairie. It is in a section
of similar white frame houses that look very much like the mill
village of Sylacauga. Actually, I suspect it reminds Jim more
of an army barracks. Peg is expecting a baby in December
and looks strangely different from my college roommate of the
same name, although she is still the same generous spirit. I just
could not help myself, realizing all over again that in spite of
differences you and I are made in that same image of human
happiness as Jim and Peg, and should not allow it to be lost,
whatever my parents or yours may say—even if you are London
Irish, Roman Catholic, a penniless student and I a respectable
Southern Baptist, gainfully employed. Mother and Daddy
had no occasion to disapprove of Peg and Jim, of course, who
could be brother and sister as compared to you and me, my
dear "Mr. Jackson."*

*When I arrived home from New Orleans on Thursday
last, Mother and Daddy seemed to have become more agreeable.
I tried not to confront them with "us," realizing I had not
been considerate enough of their feelings when I first arrived
from England. Perhaps it was that lovely snowstorm of your
letters in July, and my eagerness to answer every one, that
shocked and upset them. Anyway, before I left Montgomery,
things had grown quieter and more kindly between the two of
them and me. Unhappily, through August, you and I also
dwindled into silence and nothingness, as you know.*

*So my darling, the point of this overdue, overlong letter
is—I love you, more than I can say; I believe you love me; we
should make every effort to stay in touch and be together again
as soon as we can. Why don't you do what we once spoke of
your doing: apply for a fellowship that will bring you here to
the South for graduate study next year. Make your case for
the importance of studying the fiction of William Faulkner,
now that he is a Nobel laureate and all that. England needs*

telling. Tell England. (Another of your beloved old movie
titles?) Such ventures have been carried off a thousand times
before. Didn't your brilliant Vice Chancellor spend a year at
Princeton before the war? You are brilliant enough to bring off
something on the same scale in the Deep South. If only Mother
and Daddy could get to know you as I do, they couldn't help
coming to see you as a desirable son-in-law, especially since you
mean so much to me.

I should probably address this letter to you at Somersby,
but since it may be delivered to your home before you leave for
college, I will address it there and hope it flies fast. Have a
wonderful final year at Northfleet, my love,

Marianne

While he read and began rereading Marianne's letter, the
drizzle outside and his breath within blinded the windows of
the Hillman around him. His thoughts withdrew entirely from
the world of Theobalds and of Northfleet. If this letter had
been delivered to him at Heathdene on Friday morning, he
probably would not have gone out to the Chapel that afternoon,
but stayed at home and written Marianne an endless, joyful
answer.

How long he might have sat there in a brown study he
never knew.

He was startled when the offside door was snatched open
and Garas dropped himself, wet, into the driver's seat. In
mackintosh and tweed hat he made one think of a fisherman
out of Buchan or Hare. "Michael, my boy, there you are!
Reading your programme, waiting for the curtain to go up on
the final act. Put it away. Let me give you my preview of Act
Five, Scene two . . . ."

Chapter Eleven

L'Après-midi d'un Cadavre

i

Even from the tomb the voice of Nature cries
~Gray

Valija sits, still and contemplative, at Michael's side on the south end of the front row in the Merewell pantheon, now all abustle with late arrivals, waiting for Stephen Rawlings to begin his would-be *fête champêtre*. For the moment he is being fussily affectionate with his trio of players, duly perched on a temporary dais, especially the violin, handsome Thom Drake, looking alarmingly like, of all people, Michael, only Michael when at his most composed, most debonair. (Now he lolls on a creaky folding chair, right ankle cocked in left hand across left knee, gaze fallen negligently upon the nearest of the four stairwell covers which square the centre of this circular floor underneath the dome: "These hints of stair rail make one curious to follow them on down." But to Valija the remark seems not to call for response.) Spalding, the viola, a lanky young man bold of forehead with stringy black hair, and the cello, Mather, plump, pink, and grossly featured, are both festinately readying their instruments and one another for the plunge into harmony. Expectation reigns.

What really to expect of such a wet Thursday afternoon in rural Norfolk Valija has not the least idea. Can there be anything else left to go wrong? Her mind is blank—a bottomless black pool. She has on her dark blue taffeta frock, identical in all but colour to the one she wore last night at Blechynden. It always makes her feel as if the worst were yet to be. Here on her left, looking very mild and collected in fawn and brown, sits Lady Templeton, the charming Elizabeth, *tête à tête* with an old school friend, Ella Nathaniel, shockingly beautiful in gray and rather grand to be a mere rector's wife, even the rector of Stiffkey's. Her apolline husband, superbly in voice, can be heard somewhere in the little knots of guests not yet seated. Beside her sits Colonel Garas, in spate as so often, though brilliantly, and beside him Sir Marcus, moodily listening, missing nothing; under those sallow lids the eyes are hooded like a hawk's. Beside him sits no one, the front row at this point being interrupted by a meandering central aisle, but across this an empty chair awaits Rawlings—till he shall be ready to seat himself and listen. Tuning up is taking its accustomed toll of time and almost everybody's patience.

Beyond, behind, all round the Theobalds party are the balance of some two dozen chairs, widely, even haphazardly spaced about the dampish, dingy, tesselated floor, most of these already taken, if only by token of some retrievable item. A few await the latest of the guests to come in, arrive dripping, shed umbrella and mackintosh, greet and be greeted, and settle down serenely to hear whatever it might be that our gracious host will think of to say by way of collective welcome. There is, over the whole busy scene, a curious air of peacetime emergency.

The Friends of Merewell Castle number fewer than a dozen, not counting wives and companions. One or two must be very wealthy indeed, as well as influential, to have been able to mortgage a folly such as this of Lord Burlington's to the postwar British state. They come from all around the county, so says Lady Templeton, from hither and yon. Michael claims to have caught glimpses of their coming—a caravan of fast old cars funneling into the narrow lanes that give onto the castle, forming at the last a *cortège* . . . one that reminded him (he did not fail to say) of that long shot towards the end of *Citizen Kane* which immortalizes a South Californian corniche, crawling with closed cars. Invisible from within the pantheon, vintage models now invest the whole west front below its terrace, indifferently parked along the drowning meadow, drivers and others all gone urgently upstairs and within.

To Valija, only one of the arriving Friends has thus far looked familiar—but he alarmingly so—a Mr. Nick Boyer, formerly manciple at the Merchant Hospital in Greenwich, a very shrewd character indeed; and rather an unlikely one, she would have thought, for Sir Harry Stromgren, Chairman of the Friends, to bring along with him. When brisk, peremptory, apoplectic Sir Harry and his companion were brusquely introduced to her by Rawlings in his role of "Mr. Secretary," she was given no sign of Boyer's remembering her from his time in a former employ, however recent. The thought comes to her, obscurely, of Jurgis in one of his sardonic moments, saying somewhere—was it in a West End theatre foyer?— "Some men, my dear, *prefer* their women dumb." A few of the Friends have come with their wives, good sports like Lady Templeton, underdressed for the occasion but still making a statement. Half the men have come unaccompanied, dressed to suit themselves in careless tweed, or melton and flannel, and all the happier for being so.

She would have to admit that, for her, Rawlings' *concertante* does not feel propitious. Climbing the elbow staircase to the west terrace in the rain, under the same big fawn umbrella as the Templetons, she has thought she heard Colonel Garas, behind and below with Michael, say confidentially, "It's a sort of *alibi*, do you see, earnest of another use for the place than as a dungeon?" And Michael murmur in reply, "Or tomb." Their aside, almost lost in the rain and hurry, yet serves to increase her uneasiness. Then Rawlings himself, ushering them indoors with his habitual *facetiae*, has said brightly to no one in particular, "Our castle you know is haunted," a tease he was not taken up on. Not long afterwards, she has overheard him taunting Sir Marcus, seemingly about the Colonel, "But I protest I love to hear him lie." There is about the master of Theobalds, her host, she decides, scrutinizing him silently from her seat in the front row, something quite . . . poisonous, yes, poisonous is not too strong a word. In all his vividness and readiness to rear up, who is it that he reminds her of? Why Šiauli, of course, Šiauliu Čiabuvis from Riga, true favourite of Jurgis among the departmental Dwarves. *What is it about this mausoleum that makes me think of them? Where on earth could they be at this very moment in the unravelling of things?*

Lady Templeton comes to a pleasant stopping place in her talk with Ella N and decides to enjoy herself in quiet reflection for a while. She has never cared nearly so much for this dilapidated place as Stephen does. To her it has always been the saddest little ruined pavilion, better forgotten, as by most people it is, left to moulder in its overgrown meadow, than refurbished at enormous public expense. Whatever next? The district hospital has wanted modernizing for thirty years. Perhaps something beautiful and useful could come of Merewell—Stephen seems to be sure it will. But when is Stephen ever *not* sure of why he should have whatever it is he fancies?

She does wish he would be in a hurry now, this minute,

and have the beautiful old music begin. . . . *And here's all the good it brings.* The setting up of the buffet for intermission has been accomplished long since—not that it amounts to much in the way of a *smorgasbord* . . . . Later in the proceedings she will overhear him say to one of the wives, "I am sure Mrs. T will be only too happy to run you up a cucumber sandwich, Chloe, with your cup of tea." She is more than willing to be a bidden guest at Stephen's pantomime this afternoon, or any afternoon, but play hostess to him here as well as at Theobalds she will not. Once arrived, she has made sure neither to oversee nor intervene.

The less than military precision with which chairs have been set out irks her but Stephen, when she has mentioned it, has said, "*Sprezzatura*, my dear Elizabeth, *sprezzare*, child of scorn." And that, of course, was that. Over in the north windows, dim with rain and the soil of time, the buffet table, white clothed, stands overlaid with cups, saucers, plates, cutlery, and glasses. Mrs. T and her helpers have brought things to eat, draped for now with muslin—which, when the moment comes, will have to be whisked away very carefully so as not to topple every good thing. There will be tea to drink or wine, at call. It is quaint how on occasion Mrs. T can press into service the most presentable of her several followers as major domo, butler, or whatever. Today he is "the Captain," a bluff, empty fellow who rose in the Pioneers during the war and now likes to haunt gatherings of the gentry in which he can be serviceable without having much to say. No doubt he knows how to draw a pint of ale with just the right head on it, as Mrs. T must be aware. But can he be relied on to pour one of Stephen's bottles of dreggy old Burgundy with proper care?

Here in the front row, little Valija is smiling distantly; now she stands up and moves slowly round the stairwell cover in the floor, taking a turn behind the dais as if to stretch her legs. Lady Templeton finds herself gazing across an empty chair right into the dark lazy eyes of young Mr. Brenan. He, too, smiles distantly at her. Now here is a young egg it is no easy trick to guess the price of. She finds herself saying, conversantly, "*End of the Affair*, you never did say at lunch whether you care for it or not."

The boy screws up his features in a needless grimace. "I'm not the one to ask if it's Criticism you want. Greene has gone into a phase where I personally am more at home with his work than ever: *Fallen Idol*, which takes off from "The Basement Room," *Third Man*—unforgettably good—these are films, of course, brought off with the help of Carol Reed. But *End of the Affair*, it just has to be a masterpiece among *novelle* I would say—so simple, so deep."

"Strange that you should feel close to the work of a cruel and seedy author whose background is quite different from yours. Of course, there's the suburban London scene he does so well, and the wartime mood, I can see that."

"Well, there's also the technical interest, a nice turn on James and Conrad as storytellers—and then there's the religious angle. First person writing takes on a whole other dimension—for me, at least—when the antagonist is God, the McGuffin a woman's salvation, and our hero an angry unbeliever."

"Yes, the man telling the story, so painful a story, could hardly deny God without acknowledging His existence—a fearful predicament, I see that. Are you a Roman Catholic, Mr. Brenan? I suppose you would be."

"I try."

"So you grew up in South London?"

"South East. Not quite Clapham Common. Blackheath, actually. But it has its moments. Last week Miss Didelis and I even managed to run into one another there, on a sort of college occasion. You know her uncle, Dr. Didelis, I gather."

"Not personally, not yet. So your parents live in Blackheath? Will you be slipping home to see them this weekend, since you are so far south already? A Sunday in London?"

"No, I think not—much as I should like to. Virginia Woolf

says somewhere that she is dead against people on Sunday sitting together in one room until a certain hour. But I couldn't agree less. Family Sunday in London is a treat to be savoured, if you have the right family."

"Oh, Virginia Woolf, she can be very trying. A little of that degree of sensibility goes a long way." She looks away from him and up around the pantheon. For all its windows on every side, it is beginning to fill with hints of dusk. There is no electricity, no gas supply. No one has thought of providing candlelight for so early a *soirée*. Yet the cloud and drizzle outdoors think otherwise.

She looks along the front row past Ella, who has the Colonel enthralled by some tale of parish life in Stiffkey. Mark has his eye on Stephen and his ear on this very thorough tuning up by the Sons of Boudrys. The hint of a smile plays with his expression. He is still the fine Florentine head, fit to be portrayed by a court painter, that he was fifteen years before when she first saw him at that Balliol garden party. She catches his eye, and he rises to move into the chair between her and Mr. Brenan which Valija has just vacated. The elegant proportions of him have always pleased her, the way his sleek, dark hair grows close to his head. For some mysterious reason, he is almost in camouflage again this afternoon, wearing *pince nez* and looking very off duty Civil Service in gray flannels.

"Any moment now, Elizabeth, do you suppose? Nothing comes easily without your help." He takes no notice of Mr. Brenan seated nonchalantly to his right watching Valija move slowly about the floor behind the dais.

"You know *Stephen*, darling. Believes in taking his time. It goes to show how well he has everything under control. And you know how much it is your approval he wants."

"And here comes your Mrs. T, intent on making a fuss of Mr. Spalding again, if only he will allow her to."

"I have no idea what she sees in him. It can't be the viola, can it? Such a blunt, nay-saying young man."

Mark smiles his rare, secret smile. "My dear, you're just

not so . . . prodigal of grace as she—as I'm more than glad to say." They strain to hear what Mrs. Tydeman, a woman in a white apron and black stockings for the nonce, is saying to Mr. Spalding as she passes him by. Strangely, it sounds like "To think the North Sea is but a furlong or two from here."

The chairs immediately behind the Templetons are becoming occupied. Someone says soothingly, "I think of Evelyn as my father used to think of Lord Curzon, don't y'know?" "Ah, Evelyn," says a bristling, resonant baritone voice in reply. "Yes, a *most superior perzon.*" It is Sir Harry, no longer exclusively in the company of Nick Boyer.

Valija returns to her seat next to Mr. Brenan, prompting Mark graciously to resume his own beside Colonel Garas. Valija says something about chamber music, and Mr. Brenan says, "My best musical thing is really opera. Symphony I've listened to quite a bit of. But chamber music, I'm afraid I'm pretty much of a dunce about. It's neither solo nor orchestra, is it? All in the give and take."

When the tuning up at last comes to an end, Stephen presents himself at the front of the dais with hands spread and that angelic expression of his. How long and seamy his young face looks, even in this half light. All movement and sound eventually fall away. At the very node of the pantheon the master of Theobalds is in his element as compere of this musicale he has put on for his chosen few. *Ah, Stephen.*

Ladies and gentlemen, friends of Merewell, (there is a patter of applause) *the next time any of us forgather here, whatever the occasion, all fissures in this artful little duomo will have been sealed.* (He leads his listeners in looking up and around at where the rain on the glass splatters and seeps.) *Every* ἀπορία *will have been made good— at public expense—thanks to nobody but . . . Ourselves!* (There are more plaudits and a few responses of "Hear, hear." Sir Harry says in his grating baritone, "Let's hope the Ministry remembers to furnish us with a loo or two, while they're about it." At this there is audible amusement.) *Ah, yes, the loo, Sir Harry, I do regret the inconvenient remove at which a Waterloo of either gender is to be met with, especially today. Al fresco, I'm sorry to say, and under the west staircase here, where we came in, Damen to the left, Herren to the right.* (He pauses, as if to allow Sir Harry to make his exit, but it is Colonel Garas, not Sir Harry, who takes the occasion to exit *solus*. No one, not Sir Marcus, not Nick Boyer, follows suit.) *Of course, the glory of this Palladian design is that any quarter of the compass will do. But here in the west, you'll find, is handiest—a poor thing but our own.* (There is a little more audible amusement.)

Let me say to those who are Friends, "Well met!" Today we have guests: my sister Elizabeth and her husband, Mark Templeton, and three visitors from University College, Northfleet, who are staying with them at Theobalds, Colonel Vytautus Garas, Miss Valija Didelis, and Mr. Michael Brenan. (He indicates the left front row, where the Colonel has yet to return to his seat and the last-named shifts uneasily in his.) *We also have guests who are going to serenade us this afternoon with some of the early trio music of Haydn: Messrs. Thom Drake, Phil Spalding, Ted Mather, whose playing I know you are acquainted with, at Aldeburgh and in London.* (He lifts his hands to right and left and there is a polite burst of applause for the musicians.)

We hoped for good weather, yet more good weather, in which case they would have entertained us out of doors, as if in old Salzburg or Vienna. But even so, within doors, they invite you to move freely about while they play, not to be confined to your seats and to silence, rather to take your pleasure and, as the poet says, "make up fresh adventures for the morrow." These are divertimenti, after all . . . There is the buffet, a groaning board, thanks to Mrs. Tydeman and her retinue, who will be pleased to serve you. (Everyone duly looks away at our humble hostess, but she and the Captain have already begun moving among those seated, handing out a pretty booklet.)

As to the music, here is the programme—a keepsake designed and printed by none other than our own Dr. Nathaniel. Not every rector has a print shop at the bottom of his garden but, as you know, this one in Stiffkey does, and much to our benefit, thanks to his generosity. (There is a general flutter of turning leaves and sending of glances of approval the rector's way, especially from the ladies. Stephen opens his own copy of the keepsake.) *You see we begin with a D major Divertimento and go on with a G major before the interval. Yes, there will be one, if only for the ease of the musicians, after about forty minutes of baroque obstreperousness on the strings, without benefit of chordal instrumentality.* (He turns and beams at his protégés but it is evident that he has yet to conclude their introduction.)

Now here is where I have a serious admission to make concerning our composer, the truth of which is not to be found reflected in the words of our charming keepsake. When we come upon the name of Haydn here in England—that is in the realm of chamber music—it is likely to make us think either of his historic contributions to the emergent form of the string quartet or else, perhaps, of his brilliant late trios for piano, violin, and cello which belong to the 1790s. But that is not the Haydn we are going to hear this afternoon. We are going to hear three of the trio sonatas for, as they used to say in the contemporary editions, "deux violons et basse," composed a full two hundred years ago in the 1750s. (Here he modulates, perhaps without quite noticing, into his professional mode of college explainer.)

Not "chamber" music proper at all, which would be played indoors, of course, and would call for a harpsichord, clavichord, or piano to provide continuo, these festive, freely organized, promiscuous little pieces are really garden or street music, written for whichever strings and players may have been to hand. The one inevitable absentee from any outdoor, itinerant ensemble would be the harpsichord. Thus it was that the young Haydn began early to master the art of diffusing harmony among several instruments instead of relying for continuo on what Rosemary Harris nicely terms a "perpetual wash of harpsichord tone." Indeed, the critical test of a Haydn divertimento would seem to be how much richer it sounds for the strings' being, not accompanied, but artfully combined with one another. The five short movements which as a rule it falls into comprise, as we see, an allegro opening and close, minuet and trio, and an early adagio where the lead violin can shine out solo—nothing sombre; all very cheerful, very moving, very gay.

Now what will you say, ladies and gentlemen, if I tell you that, where you see here in print the illustrious name of Franz Josef, it may in actuality be, not "Papa" Haydn of Salzburg, mentor of Mozart and Beethoven, but his not-so-illustrious younger brother, Johann Michael of Vienna,to whom we are obliged for these particular divertimenti? Our virtuosi, Thom, Phil, and Ted, assure me that such may very well be the case, the provenience of all things, happy or unhappy, being as uncertain as it is.

The brothers Haydn, two boys from a village family of twelve children, a lustrum apart in age, were both in Vienna in the early 1750s, seeking to make their ways in the world as musicians. Josef had yet to be discovered by Count Fürnberg as a promising composer of pieces for four strings; and young Michael, although already recognized as a gifted violinist, was still in transition between the choir of St. Stephens Cathedral and the court music of the Bishop of Grosswardein, far in the east of Austria Hungary. They were still at a stage in their lives when, for the price of a good meal, either was happy to provide any patron with a serenade or some other musical galanterie. Their reputations—especially Michael's—as providers of serious or sacred music, the Miltonics of the choir, were then far in the future. Lightheartedness, mirth, one good thing after another, was their mood in these years. Of the two, young Josef is the one reputed to have been the practical joker; and, in the case of these divertimenti having come down to us as his, the joke does seem to be on Michael, whose brilliance with the strings has proved, in the fullness of time, to be too much like his elder brother's for his own good.

Now, if our virtuosi *have the right of it, and what we are about to hear really is the work of Michael, you and I are in a fair way to try the verdict for ourselves by listening for some deeper strain of melancholy than Josef's in all this ingenious mirth. For myself, I was never in old Vienna, certainly not in time to catch the light music of Haydn as the latest thing. But when Thom and Phil and Ted bring these fine old pieces back to life, it's as if one saw it all. The melancholy, the sense of loss one feels, is for that certain quality of life in the eighteenth century which latecomers will never know or enjoy at first hand, as it really was before the revolutions—except perhaps through the ministry of music.*

He steps off the dais and takes his front row seat on the aisle, setting a poor example of a perambulating audience that he has called for. Behind their respective stands and scores, violin, viola, and cello break into swelling, tremulous song:

ii

Strings in the earth and air
Make music sweet

~Joyce

Colonel Garas cocked an ear at the *allegro* opening the recital as it sounded faintly through the limestone cellars of Merewell. Perched with some difficulty on the top bar of a rotting hurdle wedged upright against the basement wall under the south terrace, he peered down through a rusty grating into one of the cavelike perimeter rooms. This was lighted bleakly from within by a fluttering sodium flare stuck rakishly into an iron sconce. The scene below him was one that he had gone searching for under terrace after terrace, fearing the worst, once he had been give a chance to slip out of the pantheon alone. It was the death bed, sordid and anonymous, of the Marshal, Marshal Tievas himself, his Marshal.

In the middle of a dank, cobbled floor, an ambulance stretcher, set up between trestles, hung like a crude hammock in some sunken undersea fo'c's'le. In it, supine, shabbily clothed, discoloured, bloated, disgusting, lay the body of his old leader. Staring down, blind with tears, at this obscenity, he knew without a scruple of doubt that it was no play actor come at last to grief. This was the old man himself, Uncle Jurgis, "dead and done with," gone to meet his maker.

What a way to go! The vulgarism itself shamed him into realizing that, as always, it was self reference that was prevailing:

It is I! . . . No, it is not I. I shall not be like that. It was himself he wept for, teetering at this climax of a long life spent as soldier and spy—at this moment, all in vain. *Whom man despiseth . . . the nation abhorreth . . . a servant of rulers.* There was no wording more fit for it—*bergžd̃žiai,* all in vain, *bergžd̃žiai darbas.* Hemingway was wrong. *Listen, O coastlands, to me.*

He tried to think continuously of the Marshal as an "astonished condition of soul, unwillingly released," which had gone out not long since from this Christian-named ruin into the weeping autumn air . . . . He tried and, of course, he failed.

Now it was anger coursing through him, bringing with it the springtime warmth of return, repayment, vengeance due, whatever cruelty ought to be done to undo the enemy's advantage—though to what avail, he could not for the time being imagine, the case having been so incontrovertibly altered by Didelis' damnable imposture. The best strategy for himself, as a survivor who knew too much, was to go to ground at once, lie low and wait and see. As a first resort, there was his complaisant ex-wife, her safe flat in Peterborough. However, no need to duck out at this very minute; no one was going to be killed at Rawlings' Haydn recital. Time to warn the young trooper upstairs—as if he needed warning—take him back to his base, and then do the disappearing trick tonight. To think that boy actually saw the Marshal here being taken prisoner last Friday.

Then, with the arrival, in his very limited field of vision, of three ordinary-looking male figures, talking among themselves as if they had just been given instructions, the anger in him evaporated like a cloudburst in summer. They moved in through the open cell door from the shadowy central court of the basement where, audibly, things invisible to him from his tenuous perch had been taking place: movements being made, voices raised and lowered, car or van doors quietly shut. The three men gathered round the corpse with the one or two things they carried and he could soon tell which was the orderly, which the doctor, and which the undertaker. They all looked up when two more men came into view at the doorway and stood watching. One of these Garas thought he recognized as the Special Branch man, Vaughan, who figured so persistently in young Brenan's account of what had been going on. The second man in the doorway, almost Vaughan's double in brown trilby and mac, made a point of curiously inspecting the four smoky walls of the cellar. "What price the inscriptions?" he said jocularly, indicating the faint scratchings here and there of penitential phrases into the soft stone by former denizens.

There was evidently one such inscription near Garas' rusty spyhole, for everyone glanced up in his direction. Fearing he would be seen, he froze shakily, all but toppling from his perch—but needlessly, since he remained unremarked, if precarious. Vaughan's colleague was only trying to be companionable, here in the grim reaper's aftermath, having himself no personal concern either for the deceased or those serving him.

"And what does it say, Dai?" said Vaughan drily, returning his attention to the corpse and the other three, who seemed to be doing little more than stand by it.

"You know, Gil. The usual wisdom, *bach*." Vaughan's partner squinted at the nearest wall. "'O fools . . . to believe all that the prophets have spoken.' Sounds like the physician Luke again, don't it?" This Dai had a loose, unctuous, fleering way to him. Vaughan moved away out into the central court, saying nothing, and all the others followed him.

It was high time, Garas reminded himself, that he make his own reappearance in the pantheon upstairs, while the *allegro* was still in progress. When he looked away from his grille, something in the recesses of his head seemed to shift, sickeningly, like a lock tumbling, and he had to lean against the rough wall and exhale, waiting for his balance to come back. He let himself painstakingly down from a height which, once safe on the wet earth under the terrace, he could tell had been pitifully low, contemptibly so. Too much Folle Branche at lunch.

Back towards the chamber music he made his miserable old man's way.

In the central court of the basement, not far from the open east door where ambulance and Wolseley both waited, Vaughan settled himself as comfortably as he could on the third step of the iron stair that spiraled up to a closed cover in the pantheon floor. Through it, the sound of strings could clearly be heard. The four others of his party stood expectantly about him on the empty flagstoned floor.

"We're here a bit ahead of ourselves," he said. "It will be about half an hour before I have everything we've come for, so make yourselves as easy as you can."

They all knew why they were there and whose call it was, so there was no friction. The doctor strolled back into the cellar where the corpse was. The orderly and the undertaker went over to staircases like the one Vaughan occupied and sat down. Dai Morgan stayed standing in front of Vaughan, one hand resting on the curved end of a stair rail. Business as usual. *Why are we waiting?* Between these two this afternoon there was the edginess of policemen, one of whose number had died here yesterday. The very staircase on which David Lloyd had been killed was the last of the four, the one on which no one now chose to sit.

"What a place this is," Morgan said confidentially. "Makes me think of the pageant they put on in the parish church for the Festival last spring. Proper nightmare it turned out to be. Full of bits of the Bible like Abraham and Isaac. Something about prisoners of war in a chancel struggling to escape—*A Shype of Captives.* No, that wasn't it. Enough to put you to sleep anyway. One of those poetic pieces you don't understand a word of, that tell you nothing you don't already know."

Vaughan, preoccupied, threw him only the crumbs of his thinking about things. "Connie doesn't have much time for religious drama," he said vaguely. "We see some of the West

End shows, the new films, and that's about all." He would have liked Morgan to lose himself for a while, go and sit quietly where the two Baltic hoodlums had bought it, and let him digest his own thoughts quietly. He wondered if the Didelis girl knew that two of her four fellow students from Gdainys had gone down here and the other two gone missing. If Rawlings knew, would he have told her? If she did know, maybe she could be finessed into naming which ones were which. Gus seemed not yet to be sure.

"Well, then, this wouldn't have been your cup of tea at all, would it, Gil? Though it'd've fit right into this place. One of the players kept saying things like, 'They say I'm in a prison,' and 'Who's got the key of the crypt?' I don't know when Dilly and I last saw a West End play. *An Inspector Calls* by Priestley, I suppose. How long ago would that be?"

Vaughan looked at him neutrally, saying nothing.

"You know something that has always puzzled me, Gil, about *tuum et meum*. Here we are, two plain clothes men from the same place in Glamorgan, with good Welsh two-syllable surnames. But one of us pronounces both syllables and the other only one. Why is this? Why isn't my name pronounced 'Morn' or yours 'Vorgan'?"

Vaughan stayed out of the ditch. He said, "I haven't a clue, Dai. But I can see what decided you to become a detective." He said it pleasantly but he made it evident by the set of his head that he was trying also to give an ear to the far off music from upstairs.

"Nice, isn't it?" said Morgan. "The minuet. Nothing like a little early Mozart on a wet afternoon."

Vaughan glanced at his wristwatch. "Not so easy to know just where one is in the order of things with all these variations. We should have picked up a programme on the way in."

"This is the return to the minuet," said Morgan knowledgeably. "There will be a quick wrap up, and then they'll begin again in a different key. I'd say twenty minutes at the outside."

Garas reenters the dusky pantheon as the opening *allegro* gives way to *andante*. There are several people on their feet moving about, conversing quietly, drinking. No one looks at him twice. He makes his way round to the buffet and has the Captain pour him a glass of burgundy. Mrs. Tydeman's comely village helper is standing to at the tea urn in the company of a prognathous village admirer, but the housekeeper herself seems to have a chair of her own among the gentry, somewhere behind Lady Templeton. One of the Friends and one of the wives are enjoying a discreet exchange near where Garas pauses, tasting the wine rather than returning to his front row seat between Templeton and Mrs. Nathaniel. He can just hear what this couple, to whom he had not been introduced, have to say to each other.

The woman is saying, "Stephen always likes to compare this design to that of the Rotunda at Vicenza, but it's actually more like the dovecote, the *columbaía*, at the Villa Capra at Santa Maria di Camisano in the Vicentino, isn't it?"

"Yes. Merewell is really a cross between the Rotunda and the *columbara* at Camisano. It's a question of scale, wouldn't you say? Merewell certainly lacks the *conspicuo insieme di Capra*, but this is rather more than a dovecote, surely."

"Neither of those has an elbow stair, of course. The only one I can remember seeing is at the Villa Piovene in Lonedo."

"How right you are, my dear. This means there's yet a third strain in the mix."

"When Stephen says 'Villa Capra,' does it mean either the Rotunda or the one with the dovecote? Both are named for the same architect who came after Palladio and finished off what he started . . . .Why are you smirking, Richard?"

"Makes me think of the woman Shakespeare and Burbage both knew, in whose history William the First came before Richard the Second."

"Do try to keep your mind on the architecture, my dear, or at least on the music."

"It is enchanting, isn't it, this slow movement. The violin is outdoing himself."

They both look away together and notice Garas near them. He smiles and they smile back. "Homonyms," he says dreamily. "Aren't they the very devil? If one says 'trio'—that it does have its *moment*, as it most certainly will—is one referring either to the three musicians or to the lovely passage after the minuet that we are all waiting for now?" Taking his leave of them, he bows his grizzled head amiably.

"Who is that?" she asks when Garas has gone.

"I have no idea, darling. Some foreigner. Thinks he's Sir Percy Blakeney."

As Garas moves on among the listeners and talkers, those sitting and those standing, he is gladdened to have young Brenan get up and come to his side. "Michael," he says softly, "the Marshal is dead and in his hammock down below. This is a very sad day for me—and for you, too, since we both know more than it's safe to know about who's really dead and who isn't. The consequences could be much worse even than we imagine. I am going to do the Indian rope trick tonight. When I drop you off at Somersby, you would be well-advised to phone your father's friend in the Special Branch and convince him that you believe it is Didelis who is dead—"

He breaks off because Valija, of all people, has left her front row seat and is joining them across the room. "*Panelè Didelyte*," he says by way of acknowledging her presence, "for two people who have as much in common as you and I, we have had as yet precious little to say to one another. To what do we owe this courtesy? It must be owing to the music. I was just asking Michael if the letter I saw him reading earlier today was from his old friend the ocean sailor whom he tells me you met in Greenwich. Gordon McGill, the name is. A great listener to classical music."

She smiles her unforgettable smile from the eyes and looks at Brenan. "Yes, Michael did introduce me to him one evening at the Merchant Hospital. He had his car radio tuned in to the

Brahms' Double Concerto in D for violin and viola, if I remember right. But I can't tell you if the letter you saw Michael reading is from him or not. If it is, he no doubt has something more to say about the four Bs." She looks at Garas and then back at Brenan with an eyebrow raised.

Brenan, embarrassed, says nothing. He sees Mackie again at the Fox Under The Hill, as if in an old snapshot, looking up and smiling, about to say something. But Garas intervenes. "The *four* Bs? I know who the three Bs are. But who is the fourth?"

Valija and Brenan both say "Bruckner" at once, playing Snap, as it were, or Twenty Questions.

"Ah, yes. Bruckner," Garas says heavily. It is as if the shadow of a cloud passes over his face. "Bruckner, of course. Excuse me if I leave you two to go and hear the rest of this sonata at the side of Mrs. Nathaniel." And he goes.

Valija watches him thread his way back to his seat. "When the minuet starts, do you think he will ask her to dance?" she says mischievously. "And how are you finding this chamber music, Michael?"

"With difficulty, delightful as it is. My complaint against live performance as brilliant as this is that one can never cry 'That strain again!' and hear it repeated and repeated and repeated."

"Ah, Michael, you and your old gramophone!"

All during the lilt and crescent of the third and fourth movements, Valija and Brenan look at one another but have nothing to say. They drift through the standing or sitting company, taking the longest way round to their own seats beside Lady Templeton at the end of the front row. On the dais, the musicians go into a brief frenzy bringing the fifth movement to a close. There is an irrepressible burst of applause, but they merely change their scores deftly and plunge into yet one more *allegro,* this a little more elegiac in the key of G.

Valija at last says to Brenan, "Who is your letter from then?" And he answers easily, "My mother."

"Is anything wrong at home?"

"No, I don't think so. They like to keep in touch, Mother and Father. But John Offord's mother is not long for this world. He went home to be at her bedside in hospital yesterday. Did I tell you?"

"Oh, poor John. His mother, the one in all the world he is closest to." She looks sad and feels sad, but for the present the music gives no occasion for sustained mourning.

They sit silently until he says, "I was thinking at that intense finale of the piece before this one, if you don't actually read the music as you listen to it, how much of the pleasure comes from being able to say in Italian something, at least, of what it is you are hearing. How many people here do you suppose were listening delightedly with their bodies but whispering in their minds, as I was, *molto allegro, presto, lieto assai?*"

"You say this, Michael, because you are not a musician. But there is something to what you say. In that finale I did find myself saying *stretto,* and thinking of Mozart's way of achieving excitement, intensity through stricture in the fugue. But there is so much more to our pleasure in music than mere *tempo,* as I'm sure you know."

"I am thinking of Mill in the *Autobiography* when, after praising music for bringing our feelings to an unforgettable pitch of excitement, he confesses—hilariously, I must say— that the thought of Mozart's having exhausted, mathematically, all the possible combinations of tones was a terrible torment to him." Brenan chuckles, but Valija does not.

After the *andante,* Stephen Rawlings rises from his chair, comes along the front row, takes his sister's hand. "What say you to all this labour of love, Elizabeth? This ingenuity! No *toccata,* no *cantata,* just the jolly old strings doing it all. Our rector says we're missing something, deep and more continuous, *basso—contrabbàsso.* But there's more here, as you know, than meets the clerical ear, sadly addicted to diapason, as I tell him."

His sister has been left, as usual, with nothing to add. She reaches up silently to touch his cheek, hoping that what he has said is not audible on the other side of the Colonel where Ella N is still seated.

Stephen slithers back to his own place.

Before long another minuet is deliriously unfolding and folding its lovely wings and there, standing right in front of her, she has her husband Mark. Giving him her hand, she whispers, "We have taken shelter here, surprised by a late summer storm, only just within doors and out of reach of the raindrops. Music comes from the earth and air and consoles us, willing us to be comforted."

He regards her gently for more than a moment, smiling their secret smile, and then moves on past Valija to the end of the row, where he can stand at the side of young Michael Brenan—who looks up at him almost apprehensively. "If this is a pantheon, Mr. Brenan," he says in his wry manner "—and it is—which gods would you say ought to be looking down in effigy from these glassy walls?"

Michael takes his time about answering. He looks around at the four covered stairwells and then up into the clouded dome. No pillars, no niches are to be seen. The music pauses infinitesimally at the turn of minuet into trio. "North, south, east, west," he says, "Minerva, Venus, Apollo, Bacchus. And at the pinnacle 'all-judging Jove.'

"But it could be any of the lesser gods or goddesses, since in poetic theology they are all mutually entailed. So Thalia, Cynthia, Proteus, Pan would do as well.

"It is a great pity this Palladian temple has no statuary, either in here or out among the grasses. Stone figures are the soul of an ensemble such as this."

"Yes, a sundial by moonlight, what? I see that the baroque has had a good deal more to do with your feeling for things than my colleague Brillingham seems to think. How are you liking the music?"

"Very much, thank you, Sir Marcus. Very much. It is a nice change from the usual 'thought-tormented' *Konzertstück*."

"Good. Good. By the bye, your Tievas business of Monday

last seems to have worked itself out, doesn't it? You saw the Marshal taking his leave of us last night."

Michael looks up searchingly. "But not for my friend from Armagh Arthur Bresnahan—ail's not quite well for him—who was shot dead in Somersby on Monday evening."

"Yes, I am very sorry for your loss. So unnecessary. I understand he died by his own hand."

"No, he didn't, not according to Dr. Lacy, at least. He was murdered—by persons as yet unknown to the constabulary."

"Is that so? A terrible waste." The VC sounds truly regretful; indeed, he probably is, given the degree of blunder involved. "It is always worst when youth is taken and the kissing, too, has to stop." He returns to his seat, pensively.

Then, quite suddenly, the music dies completely away, having come to its longest interval yet: listeners break into applause; instruments are set aside; musicians rise and join in a general move towards refreshments. The host is the first to hail his *virtuosi* but, having done so, he for some reason seats himself beside the Colonel and Sir Marcus in Ella N's empty chair, she having gone to be with the rector. He, Stephen, now has Elizabeth at his right hand. Intermittence reigns.

For these opening moments of interval, the whole Theobalds party thus finds itself seated together again. Even Mrs. Tydeman, having seen the muslin safely removed from the buffet and everything to rights with her helpers there, has come back to take a seat immediately behind Lady Templeton. It is as if they all expect something more to materialize.

iii

A time methinks too short
To make a world-without-end bargain in.
~Shakespeare

Both stairwells flanking the dais now open, and a man in brown trilby and mac emerges from either. The one nearer the

Theobalds party, Inspector Vaughan, is not known personally to Lady Templeton, her husband, or her brother, but Mrs. Tydeman and Valija, as well as Brenan, recognize him at once. He takes a step or two forward and speaks directly to Valija.

"Miss Didelis, you know who I am. We met in Northfleet at the Dolphin on Monday. I must ask you to come downstairs with me and see if you can identify someone. We have reason to believe he is your uncle, Dr. Jurgis Didelis of the Baltic Embassy in London."

As always, Valija expresses very little surprise or need to have questions answered. She looks troubled perhaps but she says only, "Very well, Inspector Vaughan. Show me the way." What else is she to say? She thinks she knows what she thinks she knows.

He takes her arm and guides her into the spiral stair. "Mind your step. Take care you don't slip. These old rungs are very steep. Hold on tight to the handrail as you go down."

When Valija moves out of her chair, Brenan stands up and takes an involuntary step forward. Vaughan looks him full in the face and says, "Young Brenan again, eh? All right, you come too." But he does not wait for him to go into the stairwell after Valija; he follows her himself immediately.

When Vaughan and Brenan are both on their way down, Lady Templeton and Mrs. Tydeman come to their feet without a word and follow them like sleepwalkers. However, when Colonel Garas goes to move forward out of his chair, both Sir Marcus and Rawlings restrain him gently between them. "No, old man, let it go," Sir Marcus says reasonably. "Let it go. It's a formality. There's nothing to be done for him now, is there?"

Gentleman that he is, and true wit, the Colonel accedes. His body relaxes and he looks at the floor. "*The sweet war man,*" he sighs, "what did he do to deserve such an end?"

"The dead do not await our judgement, Colonel," says Sir Marcus.

Over at the opposite stairwell, Inspector Morgan watches and waits. He closes his well cover on cue and walks around the dais to the near one. Taking a last look around, he sinks out of sight, closing the cover behind him. This time Sir Marcus, Garas, and Rawlings hear the iron bolts on the underside being shot. But in the busy, festive company behind them, no one seems to be much concerned with what has happened in this empty southeast quarter of the pantheon—somewhere between Venus and Apollo in Brenan's topology. Like the musicians, the rest of the Friends and their guests have descended on the buffet table, where the Captain is busy uncorking bottles and the girl and boy serving tea and tiny sandwiches.

Down in the base court, Vaughan quietly acknowledges the presence of the two women who have accompanied Valija, "Lady Templeton, Mrs. Tydeman: Inspector Vaughan, Special Branch, New Scotland Yard. This is Inspector Morgan.—Dai, don't forget to see that other cover bolted, will you?"

At the open door to one of the grotto-like cellars, the only one lighted, the undertaker stands impassively and, within, the doctor and the orderly wait at the bedhead. "Before going in," Vaughan says to Valija, "let me tell you how very sorry we are for this intrusion into your afternoon—whether it should prove to be of great consequence to you personally, or not. We are in the difficult position of suspecting but not being able to be sure of your uncle's demise. His Majesty's Government has no explanation to offer, as yet, of how it came about. We should be grateful for any help you can give us in the way of evidence. We have been in touch with your Embassy, of course.

"Dr. Didelis appears to be the victim, first, of an overdose of barbiturates, which brought on kidney and liver failure; second, of an assault and robbery which cost him all he was carrying: identification papers, clothes, books, everything but a handmedown shirt and trousers. This is really all we can say for the present. The rest is conjecture. You will appreciate why, reluctantly, we must impose on you for any help that you can give us with identifying the deceased."

"But, Inspector, what makes you suspect it *is* my uncle in the first place? What on earth would he be doing dying here?" She can see Jurgis alive and kicking, in Marshal's gear on the bridge of the *Dolphynas* with binoculars, searching the Pomeranian coast.

"Well, Miss, that is the question. The most I can say is that the body was found here this morning. I found it myself." Vaughan seems to be indulging Valija more than an ordinary police questioner would, letting her find her feet, raise queries. He says gently, "I was, as you know, looking for your uncle in another connection—"

"Juozas Draugiski, you seemed to say on Monday." Valija, despite being taken by surprise and suddenly having too many things to think about all at once, is keeping her head and beginning to see what must be said and done. She has that slight frown on her face which promises nothing.

"Yes. You told me your uncle would be coming to Holt today. I came myself in the hope of contacting him. Unfortunately, there was a shooting incident here in the castle basement yesterday. Two Baltic students from the University of Gdainys and one British police officer were killed."

Valija gasps. Now she begins to show signs of agitation but she still says nothing. Lady Templeton, Mrs. Tydeman, Brenan himself, are agog with interest. *Death Comes To Merewell.*

Vaughan continues patiently, "When the place was being looked over afterwards, we came across this fourth body, also recently deceased, but not from being shot. You will appreciate why, in the circumstances, we thought of your uncle—though why he and his students would be here at the castle remains quite unclear."

"You mean that my uncle and two of his students were here in this place yesterday and now are dead? Which two?"

"Miss Didelis, we are hoping you can help us to understand what happened—why two of his students fired on the police and two more fled the scene. We don't yet know which they were. The two casualties were poorly dressed and carried no identification. We have a list of possible names supplied by your Embassy. We hope you will be able to help us with that later. But for the present we would just like you to tell us if this is indeed the body of Dr. Didelis in the next room."

He leads the way in to the makeshift bedside. "With respect, Miss, let me forewarn you that what you are about to look at is not a pretty sight."

Brenan, following on, finds himself impressed—if chilled—by Vaughan's Machiavellian handling of Valija. Now there can be nothing she would rather do than reassure herself that the dead man is not her uncle. But she knows that, in having done so, she will be well-advised to assure Vaughan of what he wants to hear, which is that the dead man *is* her uncle.

When, later that night, in bed back at Blechynden, Lady Templeton tells her husband what happened in the castle basement, she says nothing of Vaughan's overture. All that haunts her is the mortuary glamour of the whole scene. "You have no idea, darling," she says, "how it felt to go down that impossible twisting stair and over those slippery flagstones into that cave of a room. It was as if, all the way, some huge stone were being rolled away in front of me. And there one was, face to face with the most gruesome cadaver one could imagine. I had no idea that the human form could so quickly become hideous. Heaven knows what poor Valija must have been feeling. She broke down, of course, crying 'O,O,O, I wish I had never seen him, not like this.' Mrs. T and I embraced her and comforted her as best we could. It was appalling. There were scratchings from the Bible on the bare walls—apocalyptic things, such as 'You will be hated by all because of my name' and 'Not one stone will be left upon another.' The basement beyond the room was full of shadows and the only daylight was blocked by an ambulance and a police car in tandem." She shivers. Her husband merely listens kindly, letting her talk herself to sleep. All the way home from Theobalds in the Riley she had sat like a statue, silent.

Valija, however, even in the grotesquerie of things below ground at Merewell, manages as usual to carry on doing what has to be done. She joins the doctor in signing the certificate which Vaughan produces. She agrees with the undertaker that cremation, as soon as possible after any further necessary *post mortem* at the morgue, would be preferable to burial anywhere in England. And she accepts Vaughan's invitation to return with him to London as the guest of the Deputy Assistant Commissioner of New Scotland Yard, Sir Humphrey Gilbert: "You and Mr. Brenan both—the DAC would like to have a word with you tomorrow morning. The cremation could be tomorrow afternoon at Wormwood Scrubs." Brenan is willing.

Vaughan, it is clear, has thought of everything. As they move out into the base court and the orderly and the undertaker load the stretcher and its burden into the back of the ambulance, the trill of the third Haydn *divertimento* on the programme comes faintly from above. "Lady Templeton," says Vaughan, "Don't let us keep you from the recital any longer. Inspector Morgan has an umbrella. He will see you back to the west door. It is hardly raining at all." When she shows agreement, he adds, "Miss Didelis will need her overnight bag. With your permission, Mrs. Tydeman could ride with us as far as Theobalds and from there see her on her way with it." At this point in the proceedings, everybody has accepted that what Vaughan in his quiet way says is what goes.

Lady Templeton nods to Mrs. T and embraces Valija. "If this is how it has to be, my dear," she says dubiously. "When you get back to college, please give me a ring. *Iki greito pasimatymo.*" Morgan unfurls an umbrella for her and she steps out into the slight drizzle with him as if in thrall. They climb the stairs to the terrace.

Vaughan settles Valija, Mrs. Tydeman, and Brenan into the back seat of the Wolseley, has a word with the orderly who will be driving the ambulance, with the doctor seated up front, and with the undertaker in the back beside the body. Then he pulls out of the east door and round to the west front to wait for Morgan. For an instant, a roar of dual combustions has filled the basement. The orderly moves the ambulance outside, gets down and closes the east door behind him, and drives away, past the waiting Wolseley, out of the castle grounds and on to London.

While Morgan is squiring Lady Templeton along the terrace to the pantheon, Brenan looks out of the car window for Garas' Hillman. It stands where it did, under the west terrace. To his great relief, Garas is sitting slumped behind the wheel, watching developments. Brenan says, "Excuse me for a moment. I must say goodbye to the Colonel," and slips out before Vaughan can respond.

The Colonel opens his nearside door. "Ah, Michael," he says, "changing horses in midstream is never easy."

Brenan has his right foot up on the running board; he unstraps the .32 from his shin and lays it away in the glove compartment. "Thank you for the loan, Colonel, and for everything. I'm sorry we failed."

Garas gives him his ruined smile. "You should have been a Balt. Then we could talk about failure." He holds out his hand. "*Laimingai!* If you can't beat 'em, my boy, join 'em."

The horn of the Wolseley sounds discreetly. Morgan is settling into the front seat beside Vaughan. Brenan hurries back to his seat behind Morgan and next to Valija. Nothing is said. The long drive *via* Theobalds to London begins. As the car turns out of the castle meadow into the waterlogged lane, Morgan raises one of his niggling questions. "You would suppose, wouldn't you, that at a place called Merewell there would be a well of some sort, but what sign of one is there?"

Mrs. Tydeman, sunk in anxious silence after being charged with the care of Valija, keeps her peace. She has not yet come to terms with Vaughan's turning out to be a detective. She pats Valija's taffeta-clad knee nervously, like a mother with a daughter in trouble. Valija catches her eye and smiles graciously. Brenan hardly notices. He is cogitating on his own unmended fences—with Huby, who will note with a vengeance any

unexcused absence from Somersby and from lectures—with
the VC perhaps—and now, it seems, with the head of the
Special Branch at New Scotland Yard. He feels as if it is he
who must be the suspect, the conspirator, the betrayer, not
Valija, after all.

Vaughan accelerates impatiently up the empty leafy foggy
lane towards Holt. "True, Dai," he murmurs, "true. And a St.
Mary Well may not be the only thing yet to be uncovered,
would you say, boy?"

Chapter Twelve

On Not Knowing

i

Tuque
Rectius Iliacum carmen deducis in actus,
Quam si proferres ignota indictaque primus.
You will more readily make a tragedy out of the Iliad
Than any subject not previously written about.

~Horace

Some mornings, after waking and settling down to write, I decide that this tale ought to be entitled, not *Neighbouring Eyes*, but *The Need To Know*. Other mornings I do not, since there is more than a little to it that I know very well and from my own eye witness. Unfortunately, there are things that I shall never really be sure of: for instance, whether the man who returned from England to Baltija on October 14, 1951, was Marshal Tievas or not—and, if he was not, how much this mattered. It mattered a great deal to certain individuals, of course, such as the old retainer Garas and the beloved niece Valija. But what did it mean collectively, as part of the political history of Europe in the early 1950s, about which I have to say I profess to know something?

When first regaled by Michael Brenan with his version of the Tievas visit, I somehow accepted that he did not know or much care whether, since the previous October, the President of Baltija had been Jurgis Tievas or Jurgis Didelis. The tale was his parting gift to me at the close of a suburban boyhood spent, in some measure, enjoying mutual tale telling. He had been the keeper of my youth; and once he had confided in me—why *did* he confide in me?—I kept after him, present or absent, first in talk then in imagination, to help me make it my own. But there were certain truths which neither he, the would-be poet, nor I, the would-be historian, could grasp. Most people,he and I included, used to think that the actual identity of the president of a European nation was the sort of knowledge one either had or could handily acquire if one wanted. One knew who Antonas Smetona was because newspapers—and postage stamps—concurred. History was different from poetry and fiction, no? However, after a working life spent here and there in the field, I am still not sure what or whom, from 1951 to 1956, the name of Tievas signified. Indeed, any sequel to *Neighbouring Eyes*, carrying the tale on into its Baltic consequences, would need to be written—if at all—by someone other than me. Preferably, I suppose, by Valija Didelis, if she yet lives.

Whoever it was who ended as President, he hardly figured in Brenan's own purview of the case, such as this was. True, there were times in his—thanks to me—serial account of things when the topic was ostensibly Current Affairs. "What price Tievas as Tory puppet, John?" I remember his saying. "As Ruritanian double, what?" Here he mimicked the VC, still very much a presence in his life. Presumably the VC was then under contribution for one of those dry but effective letters of recommendation, this time seeing Brenan safely into an overseas graduate programme. And we always had poor Arthur

Bresnahan's accidental death clearly in view although, six months and more after the event, it probably moved Brenan less than it did me, learning all the circumstances for the first time. But Brenan's chief concern was obviously to let me know why he left college under a cloud and went off to America to start his life over. Again, the question raised had more than one answer. Did he not go to be together with Marianne Hollis?

He was twenty-three, I twenty-two. We saw ourselves and our situations with none of the clarity or perspective that age can bring. I, living in the present, concentrated on my work for the degree, gave no thought to how much the strictly political aspect of his anecdote might one day mean to me—how much, that is, I might come to wish I had kept a close eye on developments in Baltija while the name of Tievas was one to conjure with. As so often during a new crisis, everyone had jumped to his own conclusion and found no reason afterwards to question it. For Labour, the Tievas visit was a diplomatic embarrassment, and for the Tories a coup that could not be boasted about. Even if I had maturely resolved to supplement Brenan's version of the truth with interviews or research into records, where would I have begun? Aneurin Bevan or Hector McNeil was no more likely to be forthcoming to me than Stephen Rawlings or Sir Marcus. Case closed, I suppose I thought, if I thought at all.

In retrospect, the salient aspect of it proved to be that— the Official Secrets Act withstanding or not—no relevant government papers at all seem to have survived. A senior colleague of mine in History once made a remark which I have never forgotten about this period at the turn of the mid-century. He called it "a curious no man's land of time,"

> . . . too close [then] to be reached effectively by the heavy artillery of history . . . too far for the snipers of contemporary politics and journalism . . . one of those accidentally preserved châteaux between the lines which crop up in plays about the First World War . . . . Much

of the British Empire seemed [still] to survive; Europe
had not [yet] recovered . . . .

Nowadays, it feels as if Brenan no sooner confided in me
and took himself off to the Deep South than I was hearing
and reading about the occupation of Baltija by the Red Army
and the disappearance of President Tievas. In fact, that did
not happen until the summer of 1956, when the Russianizing
of Hungary also took place, while the rest of the world stood
amazed at the last fling of the old empires, England and
France—though not the new one, the United States—in Egypt
over the Suez Canal. There were at least four years prior to
that during which I could have invited myself to visit Valija,
returned home by then, and found out who was who and what
was what in Gdainys. But, by the time I had taken my degree
and finished my graduate work in France, the moment for
answering the Tievas question had passed.

If his visit to England had led immediately to any
observable *Realpolitik* between West and East, then it would
probably have held my youthful curiosity for longer than it
did. At least it would have left a paper trail which anyone
interested could have picked up later. But instead it was at
once overtaken by events which, though related, proved wholly
obtrusive. This, perhaps, is as good a way of putting it as any:
whoever he was, the man who returned to power in Gdainys
in 1951 simply became unobtrusive compared with his
contemporaries. With Churchill back at Number Ten again and
his heir Anthony Eden as Foreign Minister, it was President
Tito of Jugo-Slavia, not Tievas of Baltija, who was called into
the English limelight. When Stalin died in March, 1953, and a
putative end to Stalinism dawned—falsely, as it turned out—
Tito, not Tievas, was at once invited to visit England—and
did so to great acclaim. The worst that could transpire in the
Kremlin would be a take-over by the military, with or without
Malenkov to mask it. There is in the diary of one of Tito's
lieutenants, Vladimir Dedijer, a subtle but telltale reference to

the superior viability of being a Serb rather than a Balt in those years:

> *Look* [magazine] asked me to write an article about Stalin's death, a thousand words for three thousand dollars. I refused. We are not Riga, living by anti-Soviet propaganda and offering analyses to the Americans.

Suddenly no one had time for the Tievas question, myself included. "We are not Riga."

If I had made time for it, things might have felt different later on, much later, when I found myself reverting, sleeplessly, at two in the morning, to my old school friend Brenan's little anecdote. While still a junior member of the History faculty at Northfleet, I managed to live the good life to the full without ever taking a vacation in the Baltic, or even keeping up with any of the news from that picturesque backwater. From Paris, from London, from Cambridge, even from *ultima* Lindsey, Gdainys has always been a bridge too far. Only now, at this very latest stage of my dream life, does what I *failed* for forty years to do or find out feel more urgent than anything I have done or think I know.

In this respect, life has come to seem to me rather like having been at a party. So much goes on, is said and done at a good party that must always go unnoticed, unexperienced, unappreciated by any one partygoer. This one, looking back, will say ruefully, "I missed opportunities for sexual congress but . . . I was always squeamish." Or that one will say coldly, "My acquaintance with my contemporaries has been from first to last very limited." Myself, I have been tempted to think sometimes that the way not to miss anything good is simply not to go at all, but to stay in one's study and read and write one's own party. Even so, one finds too late that something will be missing, will have been left out, lost, unwritten. The collective remains unknowable, reluctant as any historian ought to be to acknowledge as much.

What I have done in this case, accordingly, is not to try to answer the Tievas question but, at best, merely to ask it. My subject, after all, has never been the Baltic deputy himself.

It was at our last meeting, in the early June of 1952, that Brenan filled in for me the details of his overnight visit to London with Valija as guests of Inspector Vaughan. We met in the Dragon over pints of Whitbread brown, having drifted along the Stonham road from Somersby in the dusk. In those days at that hour there was nothing to hear in the pauses of the wind but linnets; no traffic, no other passers by, troubled the highway dust. If I had been then, as I am now, a faculty resident of Louth Hall, I should lack this ninth floor vista of the road to Stonham from my writing desk. When I did see it, on my own two feet or perhaps a bicycle, it would never be as it is now, blackened with transport, crawling with lights. But at this hour of the morning, busy at my desk, I would be anticipating the entry of a serving maid, one like Huby's winsome Mary, with a breakfast tray. Life was different then.

In the Dragon that night I remember both Constable Eccles and Long Will joining the regulars, some loud, some tacit, along the bar and around the dart board until closing time came. But they took no notice of Brenan and me. There were usually a few customers not from the village. We sat by ourselves at a corner table and talked our talk easefully. He told me that Vaughan had fixed him and Valija up for the night in Hackney, at what was evidently a safe address maintained by the police.

"It's at the end of a *cul de sac*," he said, "on the right hand side of a narrow street of mostly grey brick terrace houses. At the end, bottoming the sack, stands the German Hospital, double gated, forbidding; and between it and the redbrick Lutheran church (1872, would you believe?) this pair of mean, two-storey, single-fronted houses like all the rest only detached from them by hospital and church. Home away from home, I don't think.

"Vaughan handed us over to the plainclothes housekeepers

and took off with Morgan, saying he would pick us up at nine in the morning. He asked me, on the side, if I would like a lift home to Blackheath for the night, but I said no. I didn't want Mother and Father worrying that I was mixed up with the police. Vaughan then said that Valija and I were free to go out after dinner, to the pictures or wherever, so long as we were back by eleven.

"Valija was lodged in the women's annexe, a similar semi-detached pair of terrace houses in the next street, back to back with the ones I was in and linked by an arched gate between the close walled gardens of brushed dirt. From my window I could see her being shown into her room by the woman in charge. When Valija came to the window to lower the blind, with the light on behind her, I waved, but either she didn't see me or she didn't want to be seen. 'However deep you might embower the nest, some boy would spy it.' *The Princess*, you know.

"After dinner, which was very ordinary, we agreed to go and find a film to see at one of the cinemas along the Kingsland Road. Our hosts didn't seem to mind what we did. As we walked past the church next door on our way to the bus stop, we could hear the organ being played and a choir singing—practice, I suppose—"

"And you, my dear Holmes, of course can tell me precisely which hymn it was."

"As a matter of fact, Watson, I can. It was a favourite of my late aunt Maggie's. You might think a Lutheran choir would be singing 'Rock of ages, cleft for me.' But it wasn't. Of all things, it was 'My song is love unknown.' Are you satisfied?"

"Yes. Hymns have an eerie way of sounding true even when sung out of context, don't they? One of my Hereford aunts, on my father's side, used to like to tell of the funeral of some drunken profligate or other whose pious sister demanded that the hymn sung be 'Glorious things of Thee are spoken.' The choir, who knew the dear departed all too well, could hardly oblige for laughing."

"'Glorious things,' that's the one that rhymes 'Zion' and 'rely on.'"

"Well, which film did you and Valija end up seeing?"

"From where the bus put us down along the high street we had a choice of two, *Strangers On A Train* or *A Place In The Sun*. Not bad, eh? Valija said, 'Oh dear, Alfred Hitchcock again.' So we saw the George Stevens instead—velvety black and white, beautiful sad Montgomery Clift, beautiful sad Elizabeth Taylor."

"What did Valija make of it?"

"I don't know. Nothing very definite. I forget. At one point she said, 'An American version of Zola'—as if originality were everything in art. I said she was lucky we hadn't looked further and found a western. I wanted very much to see *Red River* at that point, having missed it in '48.

"One thing I remember about the night we spent in Hackney: on the bus back to our lodgings, crowded with passengers out of the pubs as well as the pictures, a closing time crowd, there was a Cockney couple, young to middleaged, married, I presumed, seated right behind us on the lower deck. And all the way to our stop we couldn't but overhear whatever passed between them.

"It was chiefly a monologue by the woman, loud, plump, flushed, well-dressed in what Mother would call 'a nice costume.' The man, in a cloth cap and serge suit, said next to nothing; there was nothing for him to say. The woman vented without interval, the more audibly because she had been drinking.

"She was so indignant, so angry that she couldn't care who heard what she felt. And what *were* her feelings? It was impossible to be sure—something to do with desire and a couple they had been drinking with. Nothing definite.

"This was true Eloquence on her part, emphatic speech flow, all animus, resentment, and naked self, more like the uttering of some magic spell than an actual story or argument. It made you want to shut your ears. Yet you felt you couldn't afford to miss a word.

"I've often wished I could quote *verbatim*. It was a sort of 'found' poem. But I got only the overflow, swung about as I was by the hurrying bus, sitting next to Valija, trying not to catch anybody's eye. The one sentence I can always hear, when I want to, is this: 'And you know bloody well, don't you, he's going to have his way with her when he gets her home?' Just what Valija and I needed to hear at that point."

I asked Brenan if he had found a moment in which he and Valija could confide in one another about what had been going on around them. Had they never been able to open their hearts on the matter of Tievas, either during that first week of adventure, or later, before she transferred to Bedford College, or even lately, since they were still in touch? His answer was not encouraging.

"Think about it, John. Neither of us could very well start speculating openly about her uncle as someone who had brought off a political assassination—however inadvertently—over here and then assumed power back in Baltija—not when she was newly committed to his having died mysteriously at Merewell. What she knew in her own mind was not for anyone else to know."

"But Michael, how about the question you said she asked Vaughan: what on earth would her uncle be doing dying at the castle? Suppose, instead of understanding it rhetorically, one entertains it literally. Isn't it quite possible that the man who died *was* Didelis?"

Although I had jumped to my own conclusion by then— the one I have since had to fall back on in order to get this tale told—I could already see that Valija's question might have an answer other than the one she secretly gave it while letting Vaughan have his way with her at Merewell. After all, *prima facie*, if both Tweedledum and Tweedledee agree to have a battle, then either one is as likely to end up dead as the other.

Brenan tended to give me, willy nilly, the Didelis view of things—Didelis lives. But, Garas or no Garas, how many battalions might Tievas actually have had, invisibly in his service? Enough to see him safely out of England, might one postulate? Why should Garas be the only Baltic counter intelligence man on the scene? What was so peculiar about being found dead at the castle that Didelis himself could not aspire to it?

Brenan, also, had an *arrière pensée* all his own: "Yes, what did I really know except the obvious—a man in uniform kidnapped from the Chapel, a student found shot in the Somersby phone box. Everything else circumstance and hearsay, even all that Garas had given me to understand. And Valija, what chance had she, after the first Friday, to confirm anything with her uncle? I had no idea how much she might or might not know for sure. Nor she I. Neither of us had a clue where to begin a mutual confession."

"What about later? Here at Northfleet, in November, during your secret life together? Weren't there moments when you confided in her and she in you about her uncle and the Marshal? After all, *one* of them was the real victim, wasn't he? He, and Arthur?"

"Yes, he was. They both were. But Valija doesn't seem to be the kind of person who has moments of intimacy during which she's able to confide—not in me, anyway. And, from the first, I must have seemed to her to be involved with the police or some other faction, and so not to be trusted, not implicitly at least—which I suppose I was not. There were as many unmentionables in my situation as there were in hers. You might think that she would have eventually heard from her uncle in Gdainys—if he were not dead, that is. But if she did, she has never told me as much. Anyway, it was next to impossible to know where best to begin telling the whole truth, so we never did."

I was interested, of course, in their interviews the following morning with the head of Special Branch at New Scotland Yard. Brenan talked as if these were the climax, the top of the ladder for him, and as if all there was to do afterwards was come down to earth. He knew nothing except what Valija told him of whatever passed between her and the DAC *in camera*, while he was kept waiting by Vaughan in his less imposing office nearby. Valija went first. If you ever saw her plain, you were surprised at how slight she was in stature, how small boned. So sturdy a spirit ought to have had as strong a frame to inform, but hers did not. Together with that nordic freshness of face and blueness of eye, her slightness will have put the DAC, in all his saturnian cragginess, at some disadvantage as an interrogator. It is tempting to think of a scene in which the head of inquisition tries everything short of torture—so very unEnglish—to unlock the young woman's guilty secret. But, no. She simply would not allow herself to be drawn into questions about her fellow students from Gdainys. There was nothing in the least subversive about her; indeed, she had that fluency, that perfect if not quite native command of English idiom, which would reassure even a desk sergeant. If only her personal situation had not proved so impossibly difficult, she could well have gone on to become some nice Englishman's nice English wife—as near as makes no odds.

The DAC, in deciding to see her by himself, had more than one purpose, no doubt. Besides affirming His Majesty's Government's very proper concern for her, and their condolence in her trouble, he meant to impress her with a need for discretion of every sort. No sympathetic interest in the whys and wherefores of her uncle's sad case could possibly be served by publicity or gossip while the investigation was proceeding. On the other hand, he would be glad to hear anything she could tell him that might help explain her uncle's mysterious demise, especially something as yet unknown to Inspector Vaughan—though this latter *desideratum* was, of course, not imparted to Valija. The DAC also meant to confirm what he supposed was her very real sense, as a foreign national enjoying academic privileges here in England, of being dependent on official approval, vulnerable to censure, and subject to deportation for misconduct. He said he noticed that she still carried, in addition to a current visa, one of those handsome Lithuanian passports issued by the embassy in Holland Park before the world fell apart—or should he say "before things came together"? Truth was all in the point of view, wasn't it? Post-Versailles, President Smetona's Lithuania, this would have been the golden age, he supposed.

Yes, there will have been a very considerable *complexity*, as Dr. Leavis would say, to the tone the DAC took with Valija during their *tête à tête* in his imposing riverside office. She afterwards told Brenan that the old man's aura was more that of a pastoral bishop than the head of Special Branch. When she said this, she did not yet know that the policeman killed at Merewell two days before had been his daughter's husband. Brenan only learned as much from Vaughan while she was with the DAC, and told it her later. With the DAC, Valija would do almost none of the talking. But she still left him reassured of her innocence of any conspiracy against the state—much more so than might be expected. Not that he ever felt that a great deal *more* needed to be known, not at this late stage of an investigation.

One thing he did induce Valija to confide in him was her genuine fearfulness at what had been going on around her in recent days. She told him that there had been times when she was frozen with it. He invited her to say just what it was that she felt so fearful of. Being shown the bloated corpse of a man, she told him, and realizing that it had to be the remains of her beloved uncle, her last living relative—and having not the least idea how he came to be in such a condition.

Here the DAC went into homiletic mode, comforting her with the thought that fear, like faith, creates what it imagines, giving us new confidence in what we believe to be so. "You will find, Miss Didelis, that your horror at your uncle's being found dead in such circumstances will help you to get a grip on things as they really are. Think of the Philippian gaoler, frightened by an earthquake into becoming a believer. From the spirit of fear comes the birth of faith. You can go on with your studies in England, confident that the law serves only to confirm the best that can be known." On the 7:35 from King's Cross that evening, this time in second class courtesy of the CID, Valija wondered aloud to Brenan if the DAC could have been resorting to reading Kierkegaard or Nietzsche for comfort. But Brenan was more inclined to think the text was good old Yankee wisdom—no atheists in foxholes; least said, soonest mended, etc. Valija ended the matter by remarking that she would have thought Brenan's source of choice in this case would be the Old Testament, "Fear of the Lord is the beginning of wisdom" and so on. "Mottoes on sun-dials," she said sadly, to remind him of the inscription he had shown her on his favourite drinking fountain in Blackheath the Saturday before. Had his presentiments already become wholly American, she asked.

When it was his turn to face the music and listen in the spacious, casemented office, Brenan received a rather different impression from Valija's of the DAC: fundamentally benign, perhaps with now and again a hint of badinage, but all business.

"Inspector Vaughan assures me that you did your very best to keep us informed of what you knew, or thought you knew, about what has been going on, Mr. Brenan. You are to be commended for showing a certain initiative, the right initiative. But now that the crisis is past, we want everyone to forgive and forget; and, in your case, we want you especially to be forgiven and forgotten by those less content than we are with your part in things. Who do you suppose they are?"

For the immediate future, Brenan told him, back at college in Northfleet, the one least happy with him would be Dr. Lacy, Warden of Somersby—an answer which brought a faint smile to the DAC's stern countenance. There was also the Vice Chancellor, Brenan said, though he wasn't at all sure what to think about him now.

"No need for you to worry about Sir Marcus—I can vouch for him—so long as you keep your head in your books and say nothing. As for the Warden, and your absence without leave, let me have a word with him on the phone today, and you can expect him to be a little more understanding about it all when you get back. I doubt if he will want to put you up for a prize, but you won't have too much to worry about. Just finish your studies at Northfleet and be done with it—gone."

Brenan then mentioned the worthies who had tried to kill him and had succeeded in killing Arthur Bresnahan instead. The DAC evidently took them seriously, too.

"Yes, the four just men. You will need to keep as much distance between yourself and them as you reasonably can. We don't know as much about them as we would like to. I asked Miss Didelis but, unfortunately, she couldn't tell me anything that I didn't already know, which isn't much. Two of them died resisting arrest. But the other two are still at large. We are tracking them. I don't think they will have any reason to come after you for the time being. However, they, and the Baltic constituency at large, are reasons why we think travel abroad, transatlantic travel, might be the best thing for you, as soon as you're done at Northfleet.

"Inspector Vaughan tells me that you are in *literary* studies and that you would be interested in going to a university in the U.S. Is this so?" He sounded as if the matter were already settled, though he still had his own doubts. When told that Brenan would indeed be interested in going to America, he continued dubiously, "Then, that's settled. I'll see to it that they know your name at Harkness House. Tell me, *is* there an American literature that can be *studied*, Mr. Brenan? Which authors would you concentrate on?"

After Brenan had said a few words about the works of William Faulkner, the DAC sighed. "Ah, so. Can't say I've come across this one. Hemingway, yes. You know, Galsworthy and Maugham are more my cup of tea. William Faulkner was given the Nobel Prize a year or two back, I seem to remember. How would you characterize his *oeuvre*?" When Brenan answered that it was a sort of American cross between Balzac, *La Comédie*

Humaine, and Thomas Hardy, the Wessex novels, the interview came mercifully to its end.

The DAC stood up and moved to one of his huge windows overlooking the Festival site. It was a grey London morning all up and down the stealing Thames. "America it is, then. The wide Missouri. Or Mississippi. Or whatever. You win a prize after all, Mr. Brenan," he said drily, "though you will have to wait for it a while. Don't forget to send for all the forms and fill them in, Grosvenor Square as well as Harkness House.

"And in the meantime, not a word to a soul about any aspect of this Didelis business. Do you understand? Not a word. The Official Secrets Act definitely obtains—and, if you fall foul of it, will be no laughing matter." Brenan's brush with Authority was over. "Goodbye. Good luck."

Vaughan now took Valija and Brenan from the Yard out to Wormwood Scrubs in the Wolseley and saw them through the minimal formality of her uncle's cremation. No one else was present for the occasion except Pruett, the official undertaker who had been at Merewell the afternoon before. Vaughan told Valija in Brenan's hearing that no further information about the cause of death had been uncovered by autopsy. The cause, as originally thought, was renal and hepatic failure owing to an overdose of barbiturates. Once again, she should be assured of His Majesty's Government's sympathy in her loss.

The simple coffin waited for them on a metal trolley in the bare bricked room. Did Valija wish to have the coffin opened? She did not. Did she wish to have a minister present? She did not. Did she wish to say anything or have anything said? She did not. While Vaughan and she and Brenan stood silent, Pruett moved the coffin over to twin doors set at waist height in the back wall. These were huge in their thickness, like the doors of a vault, and evidently fireproof. He opened them deftly and pushed the coffin off the trolley on to rollers which carried it forward into shadowy depths. No glimpse was given of the furnace within, only darkness. Pruett closed his massive cupboard and, with the blandest of glances at Vaughan, left the room by a door to the side.

Valija did not weep or moan or show any sign of grief other than pallour and a shocked silence. Vaughan led her and Brenan out into the hallway where there were chairs, and they could sit and wait. After a while, Pruett brought a small tin box containing the ashes and presented it to Valija. She thanked him.

She and Brenan were then taken by Vaughan out into the yard where his car was parked. From this time forward, he told them, they were free to go wherever they chose. "Just don't do anything I wouldn't do," he said, without smiling. He gave them each a voucher for the return rail fare to Northfleet. Was there anywhere in particular that they would now like to be taken, before he left them to their own devices?

Valija said nothing and looked at Brenan, who made a request he had been harbouring ever since he realized how close Wormwood Scrubs was to Kensal Rise. Would she mind if, while they were nearby, they went up to St. Mary's cemetery in the Harrow Road and looked for the grave of Frederic Manning? He had never visited it. And out among the grasses and stones, while the rain held off, it might be pleasant to take a walk together—even if she did not yet know Manning's work or care about him. Then they could make their way back to the West End by bus and have lunch there.

She agreed, and so Vaughan drove them by busy thoroughfares around to the chapel and the cemetery. In the car he asked carpingly who was this famous Catholic writer he had never heard of. When told, he said, "Oh, Private 19022 of the Shropshires, author of *Her Privates We*. Why didn't you say so? One of the few books I do have my own copy of." He drove off, after the briefest of goodbyes, leaving them outside the cemetery office, Valija holding the tin of ashes and Brenan her overnight bag.

They acquired, at the price of eighteen pence, a sketch map from the attendant in the office, who marked the site of

Manning's grave for them—939 NE—but advised making straight for the tall black monument in front of the mausoleum and then retracing ten rows in order to locate it. "Not an easy find," he said warningly.

Once they were alone together, out among the thickly planted stones of all shapes, tracing narrow paths through overgrown grass under a lowering cloudscape, the metropolis seemed to recede around them and the cemetery to extend in all directions. St. Mary's, where they had come in, made only one of a congeries of burial grounds, each different in nationality as well as religious denomination. Here were Belgians of 1914-18 and there were Canadians of the same war. Here the West London Crematorium encroached on the cemetery of All Souls. Everything unfolded before them in a gentle slope down towards Scrubs Lane where factories and houses arose again. It was a sleeping tract of the great city which neither Valija nor Brenan had ever before seen or imagined, a stratum of the century.

Brenan wondered aloud how anyone could *not* think death had undone so many. And when Valija did not respond, he went on, "You know, this might be the spot to scatter those ashes you are carrying, whoseever they are."

Valija said firmly that she had a different place in mind for her uncle's remains—the Thames at Westminster and Baltic Wharf—if it could be found. Brenan said he thought it could, just this side of Tower Bridge on the South Bank, near Hay's Dock. She would enjoy seeing the Cubitt warehouses along there, he told her, and the fantastic modern design of the Hay's office building. He suddenly thought of his father at work at a counter in Rotherhithe and his mother out shopping somewhere in Greenwich.

Manning's grave did take a while to find. Marked only by a single black sill or lintel of basalt, half obscured by growing leaves of grass, bearing no inscription but the family name, not even date of birth or death, it hardly solicited the passer by. One either knew already or went by without knowing that here lay the author of things so fine as *Scenes And Portraits* or the poem "Kore."

Brenan told Valija that, when notice passed Manning by, as it did in Edward Marsh's Georgian poetry anthology, his response was simply to say with a shrug, "Mais je m'en moque." "I doubt very much," said Brenan, "if there will ever be an equivalent of the blue plaque put up here to inform the uninitiated."

"How is it, Michael, that I have never come across your Frederic Manning's name in literary handbooks and the like?"

"Partly because he was born in Australia to emigré Irish parents. His work was written and published over here, and is very much in the French and English traditions, but it never became popular enough with critics or the public to be preempted into Eng. Lit. And it isn't very Strine. He is not for everybody. Eliot, whom he sometimes wrote for in *The Criterion*, gave him a very dry, ungenerous notice when he died; it signaled to the followers that here was 'No adjunct to the Muses' diadem.' Nobody needed to cope, critically speaking.

"I know it is unwise to try to meet artists whose work one loves. But, for me, Manning is one of a kind in all things, including this. I do wish I could have known him—as the Rothenstein family knew him, William and his wife and their two children, John and Edith. It was William who first memorialized Manning for readers in his *Men And Memories*.

"Let's go by Foyles on the way to King's Cross this evening and see if we can find you a copy of his *Poems* or, if not, *Her Privates We*."

They lingered in the cemetery for a while and found, near Manning's, the grave of his friend Eva's husband, Alfred Fowler. Then they took their way by bus to the Strand and lunched at Lyons Corner House. The rest of the afternoon they must have spent along the river on the other side as well as on the Embankment, doing their duty by the, if not unknown, then indiscernible dead. I have always thought it curious that Brenan never told me later, when he was telling me so much else, about this, this rather touching Jonsonian and Didelite turn to their Friday afternoon—ashes in the Thames in two handfuls, which only Valija ever mentioned to me.

Did Valija invite Brenan to be the scatterer for Ben in the shadowy waters of Westminster? And for Jurgis, did she herself do the office, there in darkest Bermondsey? At the moment of scattering, did she revile her uncle for not confiding in her about the plot? Did Brenan try to console her with the thought that it was the turn of events at the Hospital that afternoon which precluded him from doing so? "You and I, Valija, seeing each other as it were for the first time, interrupted everything for him. He probably meant to tell you what had been going on when you were both at Theobalds on Thursday, and the show was over." And, letting the tin urn follow the ash into the turgid waters and float away, did she answer bitterly: "Even had things gone according to plan, he would have waited to see how the situation in Gdainys went before confiding in me—if then"?

What could these two refugees from the war of all on all have to say to one another on such an occasion? I shall never know now. They must have been rather like one of those couples whose marriage has long since been done with, but who can still consort freely.

As coincidence had it, this was the very afternoon when Janet Feversham and I first had tea together at Christy's.

ii

A moving mist
~Vaughan

Our returns to Northfleet that weekend, Valija and Brenan's and mine, reversed the order of those the weekend before. She and he arrived first and went to ground their different ways in Highfield and Somersby late on Friday, while I delayed until Sunday before bringing the sadness at Mother's death

and comfort of having met Janet back to my third floor room
in E block. For some reason, I have yet to describe that
important little room, to distinguish it from Brenan's, or Al
Yates's, or Valija's even. Our rooms were all quite distinct.
Mine was neither quaint and cosy, nor crammed and disheveled,
nor severe and Slavic; it did not belong, as theirs did, on the
very boards of this melodrama. Rather, it was as if one of the
more expensive boxes in a theatre had been reserved for the
Author to keep an eye on the ups and downs of the production
as it wore on.

Across the suburb from Valija's, neighbouring Brenan's,
down the hall from Al's, right across from Arthur's (now
unoccupied—one I was never actually in), that room of mine
in Somersby was no place of recreation, *otium*, escape, or mere
slumber, but a workshop, *"fabrica, fabricae,"* as Brenan liked to
intone pedantically, the workshop of a mind. Stacked with
books, journals, newspapers, notebooks, and pages of script,
on the walls a few framed photos of our school teams and a
trio of Surtees illustrations inherited from Father, it was always
tidy. Mother's contribution, a lonely grace note, was the green
and gold silk eiderdown. That was all, except for college
furnishings. But it shone. Thanks to the vengeful Sally Purvey,
pellex regis quondam, all visible surfaces were burnished within
an inch of their lives.

Like Al Yates's third floor room, mine looked out, not on
to the quad and the refectory, but into the tops of elm trees
above the tiny river. It was the next best thing to a tree house,
though no one played in it. Mill in the *Autobiography* makes
much of snap dragons growing on the walls opposite his college
rooms—"emblem of my perpetual residence even unto
death"—and down in D block next door Brenan could boast
euonymus outside his window; but what I most remember of
my room is the bird noise, especially early in the morning. It
was a place, not of entertainment or companionship, but
business. When Brenan and I got together, it would be either
in his room or else on neutral ground. Mine was not a room for

dropping into. By the way, while I think of it, my hospitable neighbour Al Yates never once in my presence evinced the least sign of that secret agency which Brenan, or Garas, suspected him of. He went in the summer of '52 as he came in the fall of '51, bustling, vocal, amiable, overloaded; there was no knowing about him one way or the other.

Where and when I next saw Valija and Brenan, they were together among the many at Miss Lightbody's better-late-than-never beginning of term garden party that Monday afternoon. Once again they arrived ahead of me. I found them standing over by the empty tennis courts, sampling the unspiked punch, saying very little, and looking about them like a pair of foreign tourists in Ben Jonson's Venice. Brenan said, "Hello, John, long time no see. I've had a letter from home saying your mother was taken to St. Alfege's." From the way he put this, I gathered that he had yet to hear anything further from Huby concerning Mother—or Arthur—and that he had nothing new to tell me. Since our last exchanges at tea in his room on Tuesday, we all three had in fact come into news very well worth telling. How little would now be told me of his and her doings while I had been at home hardly bears thinking about.

I told them as briefly and unshockingly as I could that Mother had died in Greenwich around midnight on Wednesday, and I had been at her bedside with Father and Babs. I ought now to have been wearing one of those jackets on which Babs had sewn a black patch for me, I suppose; but I was not. Brenan, much taken aback at my news, poured out his kind thoughts for me while Valija, her low voice dropping, was duly sympathetic in my loss. Then Brenan said, "Of all the unhappy coincidences! When Valija and I went to Norfolk on Thursday, you know, to see her uncle Jurgis, ..." He turned as if in doubt and waited for her to finish his sentence.

"Yes, John," she said unevenly, "what Michael wants to say is that we found my uncle gone—dead of a sudden internal collapse—liver and kidney trouble. We saw him cremated before we came back on Friday." She gave the impression of bravely containing her grief.

I said how sorry and shocked I was for her trouble. But it is never easy for young people to condole graciously or to receive condolence. Dying distracts them from all the intensive living they have to do, day by day. Dying is for the old; a dead woman, a dead man, how remote; let the dead bury their dead. On this occasion neither Valija nor Brenan (nor I) found a word to say about Tievas or the gang of four or any officer of the Special Branch—persons of no remark to me either, at the time. Tievas? Who he, alive or dead, that the Lord should be mindful of him?

A certain pall now settles over our trio stationed at this corner of two grass courts, willing, wanting, waiting . . ."where a dead man lay," as the story goes. Who can these strange, beautiful, unknowable young people I am resurrecting actually be? So very distinct in every feature from myself, from ourselves—even from our juniors—of today. In the lane, the church clock of St. Michael sounds the half hour of three-thirty. The day is not ideal for partying outdoors but at least it is dry—at most a little damp, not cloudless but neither cold nor windy. The Highfield grounds, like all else in Miss Lightbody's care, are a model to contemplate: abundant lawn, crowded shrubbery, teeming flower beds, coiling walks of well-swept gravel. No marquee. Plenty of chairs.

Wherever one looks there are couples strolling, standing in groups, talking, laughing. The garden party is not a faculty but a wardenly gathering of students, not the VC and Lady T, not the deanery, but Dr. Aitken of Glen Eyre, Mr. Carruthers of Louth, and, of course, Huby, the Reverend Dr. Lacy of Somersby, together with young ladies and gentlemen of the four halls, whose name is legion but not all of whom are invited. Those of Highfield are present *en masse* in every degree of acceptable dress or undress, hatted and not hatted, sweetly or not. Louise Prendergast, everywhere to be seen with Hazel Cartwright in attendance, has made sure that I am invited.

There is nothing personal to the invitation; as President of the JCR she would be expected to see that plenty of suitable young men show up. My "contemptuaries" in History, as Brenan likes to call them—their names do not matter now—are much in evidence. But Iris Jordan, who does not live in any hall of residence, is nowhere to be seen. Kenneth Higginbotham, who also lives in digs, is here; David Pengelly is not. Nor is Mildred Sayre, who would not be caught dead, thank you, at a drippy affair such as this.

Suddenly, out of the *mêlée*, down the garden path towards us, in cloak, bands, buckles and full sail, comes Huby. "Ah, John, John, it is no use my asking Mr. *Brenan*, of course, but could *you* kindly introduce me, at long last, to Miss Valija Didelis of the University of Gdainys?" The tone in which he names it makes Gdainys sound like a rival to Gomorrah. He has hardly begun to communicate his displeasure with whatever it is Brenan has done or not done this time. Not as yet acknowledging, even by a glance, either Valija or Brenan, he raves on exclusively at me. "But, my dear boy, your mother's death! I am not unaware of it. Bursar was good enough to return your sister's telephone call; so by Friday we knew your sad, sad news. You have my deepest sympathy, John. Please remember to give your father and sister my sincerest regrets for their loss."

He looks away from me at last and beams at Valija, who is bedazzled; but he still does not look at Brenan, who is not. "Ah, Miss Didelis, I am Hubert Lacy, Warden of Somersby. How do you do. We meet at last. If it were up to your Mr. Brenan, we might never be introduced. Much too busy, don't you know, being the *secret* agent of poetry. No time at all for old friends and neighbours. Why give them a thought, when it's *new* friends in high places that one has?" Huby is beside himself, but about what exactly concerning Brenan—or is it Arthur?—I have not the least idea.

He does not quite come to a stop either in passing us by or in his harangue. We three are not the only ones who hear what he has to say. His braying accent carries well on the zephyrs of the afternoon. But what on earth is left for anyone—me, poor Valija, the sullen Mr. Michael Brenan—to say in return? Huby glides on in full voice, broadsiding us and the tennis courts with his contempt for the "Christopher Marlowes of this world," whose employment in matters touching the benefit of their country proves so costly in mere charity. He is making for the Omdurman Road gate, where doubtless that rarely seen pristine Austin Twelve of his awaits. Yet one more *bravura* exit from the awful annual Highfield garden party is being duly brought off in the style to which he and all who know him are accustomed. I find myself thinking of Inspector Hornby. Does he yet know who killed Arthur and why? And, if so, do his findings prove acceptable to the Warden of Somersby? Like Hamlet, the Warden is one of those larger than life egos with whom the police have yet to catch up.

It never was comfortable to see Huby formally encounter any young lady who happened to be the guest or the hostess of one of his favourites. But this must be as painful an instance as any on record of his dealing with a twain he did not approve of. He had his limitations, did our Warden.

Shaking my head shamefacedly at Valija, who is taking it all very well, considering, I ask Brenan, "What in God's name is the matter with Huby?" She smiles her calm, neutral smile and keeps her peace. Her causes for chagrin are all her own, not to be gossiped about.

Brenan shrugs. "You tell *me*, John," he says glumly. "Today is St. Luke's, I think."

Not the least of my quandaries when trying to make sense of Brenan's anecdote was never to know how to catch up with Colonel Garas and hear his view of things unmediated. Getting to know him may have been one of Brenan's chief consolations for becoming a fugitive from ordinary life in England. But to me, as fortune would have it, the Colonel remained no more than hearsay—and so, therefore, did most of what he gave

Brenan to understand about Tievas and the visit. Even though I took it into my head once or twice to track Garas down through the Baltic embassy in Holland Park, which persisted for quite a while after the Soviets' takeover of '56, I failed. What impressions he might have left me with concerning Brenan, whom he must have thought well of, up to a point, I can only guess. Something to the effect perhaps that, good as he could be on occasion, Brenan was of the stuff that traitors— Garas the classicist might have said "Orphic initiates"—are sometimes made. "*Ein grosser Sentimentalisch,* could he ever have his whole heart in a common cause, our Michael?" Another Orpheus whose Eurydice was only half regained.

As to Inspector Vaughan, little as I could expect to learn from him about Tievas, or anything else under wraps, interviewing him was one of my more rewarding experiences of the case after Michael emigrated. It came about thanks to Babs, of all people, and her unending quest for the better place to live. After Father moved to Stokesay and died too few years later, she took it into her head to buy one of the new flats going up around Blackheath, this one in Vanbrugh Park, not far from Westcombe Edge. Before long, she had become a bridge playing friend of Connie Vaughan's at St. Mary's. And eventually, having heard me say idly that I would be curious to meet the Inspector, she set me up, through Connie, with an interview. This must have been sometime late in the 1950s.

By then, Vaughan was living in comfortable retirement from police work, a shadow of his former self, and proved willing, one wet winter afternoon, to reminisce with a young neighbour about the forgotten Tievas visit of '51. Though I would have preferred the little roof garden under its awning, we sat in his second floor study at the back of 57A, with its view from the Edge over the rooftops of Greenwich on to the other bank of the Thames at Island Gardens. These were better known to Brenan and me, I told him in hopes of breaking the ice early, as Scrap Iron Park. He was neither amused nor unamused to hear it.

"No doubt," he said drily. "That's what most of the Isle of Dogs locals call it. But it still gives one of the finest views of the river from anywhere. Puts us in the picture, where we sit here, you might say." It was easily reached, we both knew, by a foot tunnel near Greenwich pier.

"Well, and what do you hear from young Brenan," he went on, "across the drink, in the land of opportunity?"

I said that all I knew was what his parents told me, which was a pity, as I rarely saw them nowadays either. Brenan and I had been close at school and college, but since then had not felt the need to correspond, glad as we would always be to run into one another again.

Vaughan said he knew how this could be. You do not have the same call to put your life down on paper for someone else if part of your own job is to keep a record of cases of one sort or another, as they arise. Coals to Newcastle. He was alluding to my recent appointment as a faculty member at Northfleet, and making a promising move towards common ground for our talk. So I answered agreeably that in most people's lives someone close seems bound to be left behind at some point, deliberately or not. I felt I was someone Brenan had just happened to leave behind without meaning to, and he, I. Life was like this.

Vaughan said, "I knew his father well for a while in the army during the first war, in the West Kents—a good man; did not go in for a commission. But since then we have never exchanged so much as a post card—or more than a word or two in passing. These days, when I am driving about, sometimes five miles and more from here, I will catch a glimpse of him walking the pavement, stepping it out—for exercise, I suppose, now that he, too, is retired."

He took a pipe out of the stand on his desk top and proceeded to fill and light it, imbuing the room with that familiar fragrance of shag tobacco. It was a room without character— no pictures, few books; but among these I spotted a jacketed copy of *Her Privates We* from the '30s. "So you're a student of recent European history," he remarked. "What is it about the Tievas visit that gets your attention, of all the recent nonevents there are to choose from?"

"My field is modern France, but I am always on the lookout for a temporary change of topic, something unexpected. Tievas caught my interest when I was still an undergraduate by showing up first here in Greenwich, then in Northfleet where I was in college—and by making a fiasco of his mission, his ostensible mission anyway. Nobody seems to have been clear what he was up to in coming to England—not even he.

"What really *happened* here in October 1951? This is what I'm curious about. Diplomatic nonevents—take the Stockholm Conference of 1917—usually come to nothing because the interested parties have ends that are not to be reconciled: workers' peace, bosses' war, bosses' peace, workers' war; red, blue, blue, red; nobody wants purple. But in this case both sides wanted *rapprochement;* otherwise they would not have agreed to the visit and the conference in the first place. The only interested party not wanting it, Stalin, the Cominform, was not invited—just as the U.S. was not, the other Big Brother, though presumably not against *rapprochement.* But Stalin, like the U.S., had no need to be present. All that Tievas' getting together with the British meant to him was a final excuse for Russianizing Baltija. Fifty-fifty or bust.

"My question is, when Tievas found himself an honoured guest down there in the Painted Hall, what became of *rapprochement?* Everybody concerned wanted it, for one reason or another, yet it was scotched. How come?" I was putting on my best Bright Young Academic manner for Vaughan, hoping to lull him into a complaisant disclosure.

He took his pipe out of his mouth and gestured at me with it. "If I had been a high up at the F.O., I can see you coming to me with a question like this, Mr. Offord. But I wasn't. I was low man at the Yard; all I did about Tievas was keep an eye on security.

"International politics is as much a mystery to me as to

anybody alive. I see no reason to think that most governments either know what they want from some diplomatic venture or go straight for the goal with the ball at their feet. Our own government must have been in more than one mind about Tievas and what he was good for in 1951. Think about it! Not to mention other governments involved, with the right hand not knowing what the left hand was doing, as usual."

I said how right he was, no question about it—except that what interested me was the "how?" rather than the "why?" of the visit. By what means, logistically, did the visitors and their hosts manage access to the Marshal and his availability, when they weren't sure why he was here?

"All right, the logistics—of a *rapprochement* that never came off—though you already know from the press anything I can tell you. But first let me pontificate for a moment. The world thinks—if it thinks of Marshal Tievas at all any more—that he once visited England and made pronouncements in public and in conference which put an end to his diminishing credit with the western powers, especially the U.S., and left him five years later at the mercy of the Red Army. This is what really happened. He blundered.

"I don't see why any revision of this story is called for. Tievas lived and had his chances; Tievas died."

I couldn't resist the temptation to interrupt. "But, Inspector Vaughan, *when* did Tievas die?"

He let the question hang on the air as long as it took him to get his pipe going well again. "Our friend Michael Brenan has been telling tales out of school, I see."

I waited, saying nothing. Outdoors, the afternoon wore on unpromisingly. The river below retreated into a tent of fog. Then I could bear the silence no longer. "Why did nobody ever go to the newspapers, one of the Leftists? If not about Arthur Bresnahan's death, then about the four corpses in Merewell? How did those opposed to Tievas get away with it?"

This broke the silence, though only for a second or two. It came down again, there in the darkling room as fervourless as before. An old man's memory may take its time remembering, especially a grief, but Vaughan began to make me wonder if he had given up the ghost altogether, without knocking his pipe out first. There he kept me, longer than I should have let him, in that uncomfortable chair at the window, leaning forward. Was this all the enlightenment I could expect? Silence? The whole house was silent.

He said at last, "All right, Mr. Offord, what do we know for sure? Nothing. What do I think? Not much. I've just told you what I think about the Marshal. He wasn't pushed; he fell. That was his way: do it oneself. The other casualties were a series of fatal contingencies, more or less irrelevant. The sniping of the man from Eire remains an unsolved crime. Its most likely explanation would be the IRA. His half-sister in Liverpool said that he got in wrong with them, double crossed somebody. That's what they kill them for. Or else his girl friend blew him away with a different gun from her old man's—but this doesn't seem to me likely. Though she was a piece of work, no doubt about that. You say you're curious about the logistics, but the only where-and-how I am curious about is that last emergency meeting of the Didelis gang in Merewell, when they had to decide what to do about the dead body of their leader. He seems to have died under questioning—and at their hands. I should like to have been a fly on the wall when the four of them tried to hash out the mess they were in and how to handle their sponsors, whoever they were.

"Didelis was a cultural attaché over here, you know, Professor of English at Gdainys, bit of an actor, quite the scholar. Same stamp as the Marshal but a few years younger. He had a niece who went everywhere with him, pretty girl, looked like Veronica Lake, but by no means a dumb blonde. During the Tievas visit something made the gang of four, who were his student protégés, turn on him, take him prisoner, and overdose him with pentobarbitol.

"I have never been clear what was at stake. Perhaps Didelis, who could have been on call as a double for the Marshal, made common cause against him with the old Lithuanian Right at Holland Park and planned some dirty trick that the gang decided to nix. Perhaps it was the gang who were at odds with the Marshal and Didelis who broke with them. Anyway, he died on them in captivity at Merewell and, before they could scarper, the Special Branch caught up with them. They were crazed enough to try to shoot it out. Two of them went down, and so did one policeman. Not the sort of news the authorities want the papers to peddle, you know. Not encouraging enough to the ordinary Englishman."

I remember sitting there listening to him in the winter light and having my very first flash of a scene from the novel to be taken from Brenan's anecdote. Over the years until I had written it down I had many such flashes. *This is how it has to have been*, I would tell myself. But that first one—the gang of four having their final department meeting at Merewell early on Wednesday—I later decided not to write up . . . for what I will call narrative reasons. "So Michael Brenan never saw the Marshal taken prisoner, only his double, the good Doctor?" I said. I sounded hollow.

He kept me waiting again till his pipe was drawing well. "Let me tell you, since I retired Connie has been trying to make a novel reader of me. I go to the library once a week and bring home what the well-read couple is enjoying these days. The example of English life set by what we read, especially from the university writers, strikes me as being, above all things, actorly—play acting, you know, mostly bad, of course, but always acting up, acting out, fantasticating. A year or two back, I caught up with a first novel by one of the new kitchen sink school. I forget who. It was about university life and it made me think of young Brenan and his misadventures. I can't remember what it was called—something forgettable—"

"You must mean *Lucky Jim*. A lot of people seem to have liked that one. But I shouldn't have thought Jim Dixon would remind anyone of Michael Brenan. Too much sex, class, and low comedy for our Michael, too facetious—"

"Wait a minute! That's not the one I'm talking about. This one is an Oxford novel, in which the hero has a sort of waking dream of a girl friend he thinks he has only imagined for himself until one day she actually appears to him in a bookshop. He says, 'Haven't we met before?' She says, 'No, I don't think so,' and goes on her way. But he is convinced that she is the one he invented without thinking that she would come to life. He even knows her name. And a few days later she shows up in his college rooms as one of the guests of his roommate. His dream girl has definitely a life of her own.

"The rest is all about his trying and failing to make her see him as her lover—even though she turns out to be only fifteen. Pretty silly, I felt. Connie liked it—*A Girl In Winter* perhaps it's called? Anyway, it made me realize that, student life being such a dream world, young Brenan probably only saw what he wanted to see at the Merchant Hospital that afternoon, in the way of cloak and dagger I mean. That scuffle in the chapel is where everything else—Arthur Bresnahan's death, your four corpses in Merewell, all—*seems* to come from, Michael Brenan's dream life. Who knows what there was to be seen by someone with a head not overloaded with books?"

I never had to answer this question of Vaughan's—at least, not until now, in this piece of plagiary. His study door opened and there was Connie with a loaded tray. She said, "Gil, I was afraid you would forget to offer Babs's brother a real drink, so I've made some tea. It's nearly three. Wouldn't you two fancy a break?"

That day we looked no further into Brenan and his anecdote—nor any day afterwards, not Vaughan and I, or Connie, the three of us. She never took the least notice of it, so far as I remember. However, Brenan turned out to be our go-between, hers and mine. *Galeotto fu'l libro e chi lo scrisse*, more or less. I saw a good deal of both the Vaughans for some years, especially Connie. She and I fell seriously in love at one point, she with me even worse, perhaps, than I with her. But that is another story.

iii

For what is your life? It is even a vapour that
appeareth for a little while and then vanisheth away.

~James

Colleagues of a lifetime when they read this—if ever they do—will probably wonder why my last years of competence were spent in writing about a nonentity, Michael Brenan, instead of somebody historically important who could usefully be studied—a Simone Weil, say, or an André Malraux. And at such maundering length, too! I can but explain.

What contempt any critical intelligence, informed by, say, Samuel Johnson's, would have to feel for the "great promises and small performance" of Michael Brenan! "There is reason to believe," I can hear the great Cham saying, "that he was regarded in his college with no fondness." Or is this Professor Brillingham echoing the great Cham? When the professor's very respectable little book on *Paradise Lost* (its Homeric similes included) came out in the '60s, I thought of Brenan for the first time in years—that he was not always right in his impressions, not those he shared with me. If I were granted a word or two with Brenan now, after having retold his tale, I would have to ask him outright whether or not he really saw a man abducted from the Hospital chapel or only imagined it. In those days, imagining meant too much to both of us. Were we literary prigs? I think not. To be a prig one has to have more altitude than Brenan or I thought we had. One has to have more to lose, more that one thinks other people want.

As I leave my early seventies behind and move on, morning after morning, a survivor now, I am visited, not by authors great and small I have read with such admiration and failed to salute in writing—or by those I have still to read—but by certain ordinary folk I once knew, when I was young in southeast London, and might otherwise have come to think of as . . . forgettable . . . not worth knowing. It is they who return daily, without my calling them, unwished for, uninvited, unwanted—not only Mother and Father, but the Brenans, too, and other presences from my early and late teens, all saying their injudicious things. It is as if I were setting up as one more hieratic praiser of Erasmian folly.

What they want of me—or I, unknowingly, of them—I cannot tell. But I do know that it is they only who have made me more and more curious, concerned, greedy about our common life as it once was. "Curiosity, tenderness, kindness, ecstasy," the blissful Vladimir Nabokov spells them out; these are the best reasons for writing. "What do you do when you do History?" asked the most inscrutable colleague I ever knew—now dead, of course. These days, what I do is no longer History but a dream of the recent past as I knew it personally. And Michael Brenan, a poetic person of no importance—whom I have yet to see or hear a word from since he was twenty-three—is merely the occasion, the pretext, for this *vade mecum* to that far country of our youth.

Getting there proves unforeseeably delightful, more than half the fun, a part of the ever-moving pilgrimage of pleasure. Most things written seem to devolve before very long into a shifting form of autobiography, or else to be the worse for not doing so. Ego rules. I hear Mark Twain in the *Autobiography* rejoicing over his own boyhood, exultant that he can "bring it all back, blessed as it ever was." And saintly Henry James, I can see why he finally confessed that his tale of Maggie Verver and her prince, moral as it is, had for him "endless worth . . . of *delight* in the compositional method itself." (The emphasis here is mine.) His heroine, great as her "intrinsic value," he enjoyed, he says, as—of all things—a "compositional resource." So the excellent Maggie was really made simply for, in the word of the *Psalms,* the *sport* of it? Even "wholeness of effect," the ultimate cause of readerly delight, James is ready to attribute to its "appeal," the pleasures it affords of "variety"and "incalculability." So, the Old Pretender was nothing less than a new pedlar of pleasing mysteries, a "snapper-up of unconsidered trifles," indulging himself, and us, in as much of the incalculable as he could imagine.

One good reason for anyone's writing a mystery has to be to please oneself—ecstatically, if possible. What explains *Neighbouring Eyes* or *The Need To Know* is my having, with Michael Brenan's help, tried to do so—to please myself—about a little matter that once arose in talk between us and has from time to time come back to mind. And if by chance a reader should be left with some shrewd question about it unanswered, then my explanation would be that *that* simply never struck me, in the way of pleasure, as an important part of the truth. Like Brenan—and Valija, too, in this respect—not knowing, I am pleased enough not to have to know. Yet what I do tell here is by no means all untrue.

It is pleasant and useful to wonder what such a shrewd readerly question might be about—even if, in the very nature of the case, any question that strikes *me* as askable cannot be the one in point. One's own ignorance, too, can be yet more fascinating than someone else's. I do not forget my mute wonderment twenty years back when all a scholarly young woman who had read Frederic Manning on my account said to me was "Of course, he's gay." Brenan, like me, once considered himself blessed not to have to know how *other* "The Other" can be, homosexual, woman, Jew, Nazi, Red, Black, Moslem, Hindu, ... I wonder did he ever come to have to know. But, for an example of something I can imagine being asked, let me give this: why, in a tale retold to please myself— a religious sceptic, it would appear—are the words of the Bible in English so often echoed? As I say, this would be a better question if I did not think I know the answer.

It takes a poet to ask the unanswerable question that demands an answer, such as

What shall we ever do?

I find myself answering—if at all—as Bessie Brenan used to do: look always for what—if anything—is good in nature and human beings and, by cleaving to this, know what goodness

is. Coming to terms with goodness, one comes to terms with
God, if not in one's own words, then in someone else's, the
Good Book's, first of all. In that country of the past to which
I have let myself be called back here, the English Bible is no
more to be ignored than the Brenans are, or the modern edition
of Shakespeare, the Anglican liturgy and hymnal, the novels
of Dickens, the London theatre, the B.B.C.—or "the Cinema,"
as we used to call it. Whatever they mean, whatever one makes
of them, they are undeniably a very large part of what I know
and am, if I know anything, . . . since I am someone . . . for the time
being. What should I be echoing here, as I write to please myself,
if not—as Bessie always called it—"Scripture"? The Christian
culture of my native folk must also be mine. One does not
know all whereof one speaks. Not even Bessie, do I need to
add?

"Well, my stars, John. Fancy its being you! Come you in,
boy, come you in." She flutters her chapped hands and smiles
broadly . . . looking, I sadly note, much older now than her
not so many as sixty years. Her front room looks as fine as
ever, winter having come, with a coal fire in the grate and
window curtains drawn early against the ending day. The trees
outside, the sycamore, the chestnuts, are now bare.

Billy stands up from his easy chair to take my hand, saying
"Good to see you, John old chap. How have you been keeping?
Let me light the gas, so that we can get a good look at you."
They have been sitting by firelight. There are tea things on the
trolley beside Bessie's chair.

Today, after seeing what Vaughan might have to say for himself
concerning Tievas, I have walked back towards Babs's by way of
Vanbrugh East and looked in on Mr. and Mrs. Brenan. Not that
they will have the least thing to tell me about the Marshal's fate.
All I want from them is to be reminded happily of mornings and
evenings at Heathdene that are no more—and any recent word
of Michael.

I remember to comment on how well Billy seems to be
recovering from his run in with colon and prostate troubles a

year or two ago; and he replies distantly, "You never know your luck, do you?" He looks as if he might outlive his wife.

Bessie says at once how sorry they were to see in the local paper that my father died. More of Babs's busybodying, I presume silently, the better part of it, though, since the Brenans have never been on her list of who needs to know what and I have failed to notify them by letter. I treasure the memory of Billy's little trick of shaking his head lugubriously and sighing, "Only a young feller, too." But not when something like Father's death is the occasion. Now is not the moment for any of Billy's old barrack room or Post Office facetiousness. I try to find the words in which to say how much and how little the deaths of both my parents have meant to me, though I feel that to him and Bessie, it hardly needs telling, not to them. This is the point of my visit, not news but phatic communion, gossip with those who know whatever it is I know that really matters.

Bessie offers to make me a cup of tea but I say no thank you. I tell her I am on my way home to dinner with Babs— which is true in some sense or other. I remark, apropos of very little, that the top flat of Heathdene, the Fevershams', looks vacant. I ask what has become of them, Janet included.

"Who's she?" says Billy. Bessie tells him. "The family has moved to a place round the corner," she tells me, "along the Edge but on the wrong side of the road for the view. I don't know what's become of Janet, I'm sure."

I say nothing more about Janet and sit quietly at the table, on which the *Daily Express* lies folded. The first time I came to see the Brenans after being told about the Tievas business by Michael, Bessie, I recall, was still full of indignation at the return of the Tories to office at Westminster. "That old devil Churchill," she grumbled, "when will he ever be finished making a commotion in the world." That was seven years ago: she is less feisty by far this afternoon.

Billy says, "You've just missed seeing our Patrick. He drops in to see us once a week on his way home from Avery Hill. He and Magda have a house in Coleraine Road now, you know. We helped them with the mortgage," he explains. Bessie has always longed for a house of her own to live in, but one thing or another has militated against her having one. It was not to be. The years after the war have not been much easier than those before, not for the wage earning poor. Now Billy is paid only a pension; and they both have low paying supplementary jobs, he clerking, she cleaning. As always, they are working themselves dutifully, patiently, disappointedly, into their not-so-early graves.

I say I wish I had been in time to see Patrick. Is he in good form?

Billy says that teaching French to intending teachers at the training college seems to suit him well enough. He and Magda now have two boys, who keep them both very busy. She has given up nursing to take care of them.

"That's his library book he's left on the table," says Bessie. "You boys would forget your heads if they weren't screwed on."

I pick up the book from the brass table top in front of the couch and look at the title page. Nabokov's *Pnin*.

"Something to read on the bus ride home," says Bessie.

"Funny thing," says Billy, "Pat was speaking of you and Mick just before he left. He had been telling us a bit about his work, and I remarked what a coincidence that all three of you had ended up in teaching. He said he'd noticed it, too, and he put it down to the way you all three grew up together. The name of the game, he said, was 'Catching Up With Michael.' You, John, were always trying to be like Michael in everything and he, Pat, was always trying to be like you. The game never came to a finish; only time ran out.

"I didn't like the sound of this, you know. Pat has always been the sensible one of you three, but this sounded silly to me. He was being serious, though. He said it wasn't till he got away into the army that he realized he had no life of his own, only an impersonation of you or Michael. He used to let you, and you used to let Michael, do the living for all three. Catching up with him accounted for both your lives."

Bessie interjects, "You'd have to go a few thousand miles out of your way to catch up with that Michael just now, I'm thinking." She sounds grim. There is a silence in which the clocks tick. Then she says, "You boys mystify me. All that schooling and scribbling; yet, when you're apart, you never see a line from one another for years on end."

Billy says, "I can't say I see what Pat was getting at. Can you, John?"

I say that imitation, mimicry, has been the way of the world, natural as well as human, since the beginning; and it isn't anything to agonize about because no two versions of any thing or any time ever come out quite the same in the end. Difference rather than sameness seems to be the order of things. (A good example of this rule, I think to myself secretly, is frequent love making, even between the same two people, different every time.) But Patrick must have had a more troubled awakening into adulthood than either Michael or I; and I am sorry to find out that we could have taken better care of him than we did when he was a boy. What happened to *All for one and one for all?*

Billy says, "There's not much about a matter like this in the Bible, is there?"

Bessie says, "There's Jacob and Esau, to start with. Then there's the Prodigal Son. The Bible's full of it!"

"Not from the point of view of the one who feels sold short," says Billy, "the Marthas of this world."

"We used to have a way of keeping Michael in bounds," I say. "It was called 'my new frock.' You know the joke: 'That's enough about me. Let's talk about you: what do you think of my new frock?" Neither Billy nor Bessie is amused.

"What do you hear from Michael, then?" I say.

"Not nearly as much as we would like," says Bessie. "Father sends him the *Listener* and the *Picturegoer* every week, and one of us usually writes. But we don't hear from him for weeks sometimes."

Billy says, "He seems to be keeping busy at the university—not in the South now but in the Midwest—the Twin Cities, Minneapolis and St. Paul. He teaches part-time and is working on another degree. One of these days he'll show up on the doorstep, he says."

I ask if there is any sign of his marrying.

Bessie remains silent.

Billy says they have no way of knowing. He makes up the fire with coal from the scuttle. "You know our Mick; he'll be making the most of it all, I expect.

"I was saying to Pat: I think you boys always knew how to have a good time with whatever you had to do, schooling or odd jobs, it didn't matter—how to keep cheerful. That's the secret."

Bessie interjects bitterly, "It's being so cheerful as keeps me going." She is echoing Mrs. Mop of the wartime wireless. But Billy persists.

"It's a thing worth knowing, how to make a game of it all. I always remember, when we would ask you to work in the front garden for us, pulling up weeds, clipping the privet at the top of the steps here, or the laurels by the gate. You would rather have been on the heath with a bat and ball, but the three of you would have some bit of Latin or other to be throwing about for fun while you worked on the garden. What was it? Something about the secateurs needing sharpening."

"Yes," I say, smiling, "it all comes back. *Reseces*. It means 'cut back!' 'Prune your high hopes' *Spem longam reseces*. It's from the poet Horace. Old Mick could get a lot of mileage out of a saying like that on a quiet summer's afternoon."

It is on the tip of my tongue to add that he would also tell of their having young Pat circumsized for reasons of hygiene and of their encouraging him, Mick, to take care of himself. However, I say no more.

Bessie says, "Makes me think of when he started French at Colfe's and would weep pitifully in the evenings over the homework he couldn't get on with. Do you remember, Father?

How he would be beside himself sometimes. *We* couldn't help him, not with irregular verbs in French."

Billy says, "I had a younger brother Horace, you know, John. Perhaps you met him. He was in the Gunners on Gallipoli, a reservist. It's a few years now since he died, of lung trouble."

The clock on the mantel chimes the hour. It is time for me to be moving on. I take my leave of Brenan's father and mother, not for the first time.

When I was listing Scripture just now, I had to leave out the Classics because they are not in English in the same sense as Shakespeare or even the Bible is. But they, too, are very much "what we know," persons like me from 1951 and before, the so-called Age of Austerity. We were taught them in the original languages and, to some small extent, they became known to us, part of us. Small Latin and less Greek. What did we do when we did Latin? As Billy remarked, we had all sorts of uses for what little Latin we learned.

Turning the corner out of Vanbrugh East this same evening, facing the dusky heath yet once more, with its lights coming on and commuter traffic making for home, I am overtaken by the sounds—till now forgotten—of Michael Brenan doing Latin. *Longam spem reseces.* Cut back your high hopes. Clip, clip. Clip your privet. *Don't arsk,* Leuconoë, what ending the Gods have in mind for me and you—to know [too much] is a crime. *Scire nefas.*

As Bessie is the first to point out, he always gets each new craze worse than the rest of us; this term it is *Carmen XI.* He has a whole litany of phrases from the one brief poem which, on occasion, he works to death—*quidquid erit pati,* whatever happens, put up with it, *sapias, vina liques,* be wise, decant your wine, *spatio brevi,* in the short run, *dum loquimus,* while we are holding forth, *fugerit invida aetas,* envious time will have fled, and so on. We groan; we ask him, is this the *only* one of the thirty-eight in the book that he knows how to construe.

This terrace of late nineteenth century villas, the Vartans' Number Twenty among them, is the way I, and later he, and later Patrick have walked to school and back every weekday for ten years and more, on and off, from 1938. Not far enough to be worth biking, our fathers say, thus precluding any illegal roaring up and down the steep gravel paths on the adjacent heath, going or coming. You can get into more mischief off a bike than on one Brenan assures me in 1943; mostly we simply chatter consummately. But in all these years I find myself only once seated with him in the same classroom for a term—his last. I am *catching up*, as Patrick will have it.

It is the spring of '47, four years after the school's return from Ammanford, a few months before Brenan is called up. Few boys are doing even intermediate Latin for college entrance, and Mr. Scoby is taking the first and second year sixths, mine and Brenan's, together for the set book, Horace *Odes*, I, "the *Carmina*," as he prefers us to call it. I can see it now, a tiny blue Victorian edition in decorated boards *duodecimo,* as clearly as the very slight sneer on Mr. Scoby's long narrow, gentle face.

I say I can see it now, meaning the book, because it lies here on my desk next to Templeton's *Eastern Inclinings* with the *Observer* profile of Tievas laid in. Inscribed on the fly leaf with my name and only one other—that of a predecessor unknown to me—this printing of the *Odes I* is older than I am, having been issued in 1928 as one of MacMillan's series of Elementary Classics for schools. The first edition—subsequently much edited and annotated—appeared in 1879 over the name of T.E. Page, M. A. (Cantab.), Litt.D., formerly Assistant Master at Charterhouse. The illustrations were not added until 1901. My copy, which I must have stolen for a souvenir when I at last left school, remains surprisingly unmarked, undilapidated— much less so, may I say, than I do myself.

However, this afternoon we are in the sixth form room, to the south of the school library on the upper corridor, looking west on to the front gate and, across the street, at the high brick wall of Greenwich Park. It is a fine afternoon in April, and Mr. Scoby has brought into the room with him his usual tweedy air of slightly sinister yet somehow eager satisfaction. The most sophisticated teacher in the school, he makes us suspect how unworthy we really are of his care. There are seven of us, confined in these scattered, timeworn desks, none too convenient for healthy seventeen-year olds. "Bresnahan" Brenan, tall as a crane, has already reached eighteen in January. How well he will stand up under Scoby's cynic scrutiny I am always curious to see. He has two of his year with him and I have three of mine, the aristos of the school, however briefly.

Assistant Master-to-be, not much over forty, quiet, distinguished, subtle, Scoby already enjoys the respect of those boys knowledgeable enough to be able to respect an unathletic classicist. He does little else from Monday to Friday but teach Latin at every level. As to the sign of ultimate acceptance, a nickname, one has yet to be found for him and to catch on widely. My best friend in the lower sixth, Jon Beale (of Basingstoke on his mother's side he boasts), wittiest and most detached of us all, has suggested calling him "Whybrow," because of his superciliousness. But this is far too clever to please a majority, *hoi polloi*. The options favoured by those whose Latin has proven most vulnerable to his irony are "Old Snobby" or "Old Snotty." Cf. Mr. Smugg, "Old Smuggy," the notorious Assistant Master of Red Circle School in the boys' weekly *Hotspur. (Sub par The Magnet.)*

To this adolescent choice of sobriquet there is usually some sort of justice, or rightness. And for all his learning, style, and self-possession, Scoby does suffer from a very slight disability or, to be exact, mannerism in his speech. He always enunciates a little too thickly for comfort, almost adenoidally, especially the voiceless velar stop, a hard c. "Bresnahan" Brenan has a very tolerable imitation of him intoning the alphabetical mnemonic for Latin prepositions taking the accusative, "*Ad, adversus,*" etc. It climaxes comically in the preposterous c's, delivered in Brenan's version with a throat clearing, glottal fullness: c*irciter, circum, cis* [with lingering, sibilant s-s-s], *citra,* *contra*. I can never listen to Scoby in class without hearing this unkind echo of him by one of his greater admirers. Does he know or not of this less than honorific notice among his cohort?

He has warned us to revise the first twelve odes of Horace for general critical discussion this afternoon. All term, in class and out, they have been pored over, word by word, line by line, sentence by sentence. Very few boys become sixth formers without making every effort to shine in their few chosen subjects. In our curriculum, confusingly, the only alternative to the Science sixth is not called the Arts but the Modern, a general preference for English, French, German, History, or Fine Arts over Latin or Greek thus making itself felt, but not yet to the total exclusion of Classics from the "Modern" curriculum. We are, in our adolescent ways, still proud to be doing Latin.

"Now, Brenan," says Scoby testily, "let's begin with you. Which of the first twelve carmina *is the one you find most interesting?" Among those in the room who know which all too well, there is a flicker of amusement, even before Brenan can say dutifully, "Number eleven, sir. That's the one I think I would have to choose." Judicious as ever.*

"And why not?" says Scoby in his slightly tired voice. "It may not have everything one looks for in the Horatian ode, but it is the very briefest of the brief—few words of even four syllables, no serious cruxes of grammar, syntax, or rhetoric. A perfect choice from your point of view, I would say. Why don't you read it aloud, and then parse three words for us, quaesieris, pumicibus, *and* spatio?

Brenan plunges in, clumsily, distractedly, as if he would rather be somewhere else, enjoying something different, as if he were being imposed upon. He does all eight lines of the poem in three long breaths. During the second he is reduced to breathlessness by the length and enjambment of the sentence. His third fails to breathe any emphasis or significance into the famous words towards the end, carpe diem, *a failure not lost on his interlocutor.*

In Brenan's reading, the poem sounds inconsequential, lacking in point. He has less trouble with the grammar Scoby asks about—perfect subjunctive of prohibition in "Do not ask," ablative of means for the pumicelike rocks which oppose the Tyrrhenian Sea and for the short race course (spatium) *which abbreviates this our life—all is explained in the editorial notes, which Brenan represents fairly enough.*

Scoby allows a gloomy silence to impend before he says: "Hearing you recite it, Brenan, no one would gather that this is perhaps the subtlest, most admired, least forgettable of all Horace's lyrics. Or that it rises in the end to one of the few phrases that every literate person knows—probably the most plagiarized poetic thought that ever was! Where would English lyric be without carpe diem?

"What is it that you find so unpleasing, so little to your taste about this phrase? The way you read the poem to us makes me ask why in the world you chose it to begin with."

Brenan's classmates, myself among them, may enjoy it when Scoby performs like this from mood, but we can hardly take much satisfaction in the discomfiture of one of ours; any one of us may be the next to be so embarrassed. "You have a genuine gift," Scoby is saying to fill up the silence, "for grasping the wrong end of the stick." At least Brenan did have a favourite Horace lyric. His uneasiness this afternoon is for some reason unusually palpable. I have to admit, with some amusement, that he has always tended to ignore the one phrase in his chosen poem that most who know it would remember it by. He was never one to be able to hide his confusion when finding his hands suddenly too full. "You know what my epitaph is going to be," he will say to me five years in the future when recounting his experiences at the Hospital that Friday afternoon:

> "All he ever wanted was to be allowed
> To do one thing at a time forever."

"Blank verse?" I will respond for want of something better to say. "Trochaics?"

For the time being it is the coming together in Horace's poetry of four learned elements, diction, syntax, metre, and tone, all at once, all demanding their due, that has proven too much for him as a reader aloud—even of a love lyric. He has yet to collect himself.

Scoby persists in prompting him: "Could it have been the presence of the charming but mysterious Leuconoë that first caught your fancy,

Brenan? A girl who reads the horoscopes carefully. What sort of name is Leuconoë?"

While Brenan looks sulkily down at the notes to his text, Scoby raises an eyebrow at the one seated nearest him. It is Keith Pangbourn, school captain, sprinter, Brylcreem boy—and well-prepared to answer: "Sir, some people think she must be Greek, because her name seems to echo λευκον and νοεω, clear and sighted." This is impressive, because Pangbourn did not find it in Page's notes.

Scoby nods approvingly. But he is still not done with our hero. "Brenan, why don't you scan the line in which Leuconoë's name occurs and let us know what you come up with." While Brenan busies himself, Scoby roves on. He used to make me think of Sergeant Cuff.

"There is a wealth of allusion and association to this name involving, as Pangbourn says, whiteness, brilliance, clarity as well as seeing, perceiving, knowing. It might even remind one of Leucothea, the white goddess in Homer's Odyssey. This is no dumb blonde whom Horace has taken it upon himself to chat up about the Epicurean philosophy. Indeed, the poem's own context appears to give an almost comic value to the resemblance between her name and the modern word clairvoyante—as in

> Madame Sosostris, famous clairvoyante,
> Had a bad cold, nevertheless
> Is known to be the wisest woman in Europe, etc.

"You know the rest, I feel sure. Now, Brenan, what about the scansion of line 2?" The hard c's of his speech are thickening by the minute, brought on by the initial excitement of carpe and clairvoyante, not to mention the medial consonant of Leuconoë.

Brenan, having collected himself somewhat, begins his counter attack. "One of the reasons why I chose Carmen XI, sir, is that it looked to me at first glance like prose, each line running out to the margin." Somebody in the room quietly snickers. "It also sounds to me quite . . . colloquial, like one of Hamlet's bits of blank verse philosophy, full of cliché, such as quicquid erit, pati or sapias, vina liques—which only a prize bore would think of repeating anywhere but at the Drones Club." He is *now voicing his velar stops, as in* quicquid *and* liques *as heavily as Scoby at his most phlegmy. Scoby's, I should add, was a very dry phlegm. "However, the piece* is *in metre, sir, entirely in Greater Aselepiads which, according to our editor, have sixteen syllables to the line as a rule, mostly dactylic. But line 2 scans like this: long, long, long, short, short, long (*finem di dederint). *Then, after the first caesura and before the second, comes the name Leuconoë which scans long, short, short, long. I don't see any exceptions;* di *is really* dii, *the gods, and long. But sir—" "Bresnahan" is at last coming into his own, and most of the class has caught on to the game—"could I ask you a quick question or two?" The sound of his velar stops is now excruciating.*

"Of course you can, Brenan. Why not? But first let me ask you why you say quicquid *instead of* quidquid, *which is what the text has?" And so the net which Brenan has laid for him closes about Scoby, causing him to pronounce very carefully for the class far more voiceless velar stops than are good for him or for discipline. Why all this suppressed amusement in the room, he wonders.*

I find myself turning gratefully into the forecourt of Babs's latest choice of a block of flats to live in: its neo-Georgian splendour has only very recently taken the place of the Volunteers drill hall and an adjacent rustic mews. Just around the corner in Maze Hill, not fifty yards away to the west, beyond bare trees, brick walls, and rising ground, stands the school of my youth, and of the friends of my youth, invisible. My every urge is to go and see. But no miracle will happen there this evening, no faces I know look up, no well-remembered voices sound. It is finished, my day.

Silence, as one of the American poets so well says, is a shape that has passed.

Coming Next

Work In Progress

PERFECT WITNESS

BEING A SEQUEL TO A TALE OF 1951 ENTITLED 'NEIGHBOURING EYES.'

Fame is no plant that grows on mortal soil,
Nor in the glistering foil
Set off to th'world, nor in broad rumour lies,
But lives and spreds aloft by those pure eyes,
And perfet witnes of all judging *Jove*,
As he pronounces lastly on each deed,
Of so much fame in Heav'n thy meed.

~Milton

Set in the Baltic capital of Gdainys during the academic year 1953-4, this further episode in the lives of Michael Brenan and Valija Didelis reintroduces several of the survivors of the Tievas affair from *Neighbouring Eyes*. Unlike John Offord's memoir of England in 1951, this sequel takes a 'God knows' or omniscient view of what came next.

About the Author

The author of *Neighbouring Eyes*, Richard Cody, was born in 1929 and grew up in Blackheath, London, England. He attended the Roan School, Greenwich, did National Service in the army and a B.A. and Dip.Ed. at University College, Southampton. From 1953 he lived in the U.S., studying and teaching at Ole Miss (the University of Mississippi) and the University of Minnesota. In 1963, having an MA and PhD, he was appointed Associate Professor of English at Amherst College, Massachusetts, where he remained until retirement in 2002. His book *The Landscape of the Mind* was published by the Clarendon Press, Oxford, in 1969. He now resides in Anniston, Alabama. The theory that the Author (like God) is dead does not entirely convince him, but he is inclined to believe that all written genres tend towards Autobiography—and plagiary.